FEELING THE HEAT

"They found him in a room on the north side a few days later, after he started to stink. He'd burned to death."

I frowned. For a year there had been reports of people burning up without benefit of fire, always in some slum on the north side.

"Garrett, he burned to death without setting fire to the place where he died. Which was about as awful a tenement as you can imagine."

That jibed with stories I'd heard about other burning deaths. "How could that happen? Sorcery?"

"That would be everybody's first guess, wouldn't it?"

"Always is when an explanation isn't obvious. We're conditioned by long, direct, dire exposure to those idiots on the Hill."

Sorcery, great or small, isn't part of daily life. But the threat of sorcery is. Particularly dark sorcery. Because our true rulers are the wizards who infest the mansions on the Hill. . . .

WHISPERING NICKEL IDOLS

A GARRETT, P.I., NOVEL

GLEN COOK

A ROC BOOK

ROC

Published by New American Library, a division of
Penguin Group (USA) Inc., 375 Hudson Street,
New York, New York 10014, USA
Penguin Group (Canada), 10 Alcorn Avenue, Toronto,
Ontario M4V 3B2, Canada (a division of Pearson Penguin Canada Inc.)
Penguin Books Ltd., 80 Strand, London WC2R 0RL, England
Penguin Ireland, 25 St. Stephen's Green, Dublin 2,
Ireland (a division of Penguin Books Ltd.)
Penguin Group (Australia), 250 Camberwell Road, Camberwell, Victoria 3124,
Australia (a division of Pearson Australia Group Pty. Ltd.)
Penguin Books India Pvt. Ltd., 11 Community Centre, Panchsheel Park,
New Delhi - 110 017, India
Penguin Group (NZ), cnr Airborne and Rosedale Roads, Albany,
Auckland 1310, New Zealand (a division of Pearson New Zealand Ltd.)
Penguin Books (South Africa) (Pty.) Ltd., 24 Sturdee Avenue,
Rosebank, Johannesburg 2196, South Africa

Penguin Books Ltd., Registered Offices:
80 Strand, London WC2R 0RL, England

First published by Roc, an imprint of New American Library,
a division of Penguin Group (USA) Inc.

First Printing, May 2005
10 9 8 7 6 5 4 3 2 1

Copyright © Glen Cook, 2005
All rights reserved

Cover art by Alan Pollack

ROC REGISTERED TRADEMARK—MARCA REGISTRADA

Printed in the United States of America

*This one is for my mom,
who was a rock in a
turbulent stream.*

*With thanks to Jim K.
and Ellen W.*

1

There I was, galumphing downstairs, six feet three of the handsomest, ever-loving blue-eyed ex-Marine you'd ever want to meet. Whistling. But it takes me a big, big bucket to carry a tune. And my bucket had a hole in it.

Something was wrong. I needed my head examined. I'd gone to bed early, all by my own self. And hadn't had a dram to drink before I did. Yet this morning I was ready to break into a song and dance routine.

I felt so good that I forgot to be suspicious.

I can't forget, ever, that the gods have chosen me, sweet baby Garrett, to be their special holy fool and point man in their lunatic entertainments.

I froze on the brink of my traditional morning right turn to the kitchen.

There was a boy in the hallway that runs from my front door back to my kitchen. He was raggedy with reddish ginger hair all tangled, a kid who was his own barber. And his barber was half blind and used a dull butcher knife. There were smudges on the boy's cheeks. He stood just over five feet tall. I made him about twelve, or maybe a puny thirteen. His tailor was a walleyed ragpicker. I assumed he had a pungent personal aura, but wasn't close enough to experience it.

Was he deaf? He'd missed the racket I'd made coming down. Of course, he had his nose stuck in the Dead Man's room. That view can be overwhelming, first time. My partner is a quarter ton of dead gray flesh resembling the illegitimate offspring of a human father and pachydermous mother, vaguely. In the nightmare of some opium-bemused, drunken artist.

"Makes you want to jump in his lap and snuggle up, don't he?"

The kid squeaked and backed toward the front door, bent over so he sort of probed his way with his behind.

"And you would be?" I asked, more interested than I could explain just by my finding a stranger marooned in my hallway.

The kitchen door squeaked. "Mr. Garrett. You're up early."

"Yeah. It ain't even the crack of noon. Clue me in, here."

The party exiting the kitchen was Dean, my live-in cook and housekeeper. He's old enough to be my grandfather but acts like my mom. His turning up explained the kid. He was lugging something wrapped in dirty old paper.

Dean collects strays, be they kittens or kids.

"What?"

"You're up to something. Else you wouldn't call me Mr. Garrett."

Dean's wrinkles pruned into a sour face. "The sun always sets when there is fear of saber-tooth tigers."

That means you see what you're afraid to see. My mother said it a lot, in her time.

"This house is safe from tigers." I stared at the boy, intrigued. He had a million freckles. His eyes sparkled with challenge and curiosity and fright. "Who's this? How come he's poking around my house?" I kept on staring. There was something appealing about that kid.

What the hell was wrong with me?

I expected psychic mirth from my deceased associate. I got nothing.

Old Bones was sound asleep.

There's good and bad in everything.

I focused on Dean. I had a scowl on. A ferocious one, not my "just for business" scowl. "I'm not whistling now, Dean. Talk to me." Grease stained the packet the old boy carried. Once again, at second hand, I would be feeding a stray.

"Uh . . . this is Penny Dreadful. He runs messages for people."

Dreadful? What kind of name was that? "There's a message for me, then?" I gave the urchin the benefit of my best scowl. He wasn't impressed. Likely nothing troubled him as long as he stayed out of grabbing range.

I saw nothing suggesting aristocratic antecedents, though Dreadful is the sort of name favored by the sorcerers and spook chasers on the Hill, our not so subtle, secret masters.

"Yes. There is. In the kitchen," Dean blurted. He pushed past. "I'll get it in a minute. Here, Penny. Mr. Garrett will let you out. Won't you, Mr. Garrett?"

"Sure, I will. I'm one of the good guys, aren't I?" I stood against the wall as Dean pushed past again, headed the other way.

The kid clutched the packet and retreated. Odd. My internal reaction wasn't overpowering, but it was of a strength usually reserved for those darlings who make priests regret their career choices.

I opened the door. The ragamuffin slid out and scurried away, hunched like he expected to get hit. He didn't slow down till he reached the intersection of Macunado Street with Wizard's Reach.

He looked back while he was eating, saw me watching. Startled, he zipped around the corner.

Buzz! Buzz! Tinkling, musical laughter. Something tugged my hair. A tiny voice piped, "Garrett's got a girlfriend."

"Hello, Marienne." Marienne was an adolescent pixie of the female variety. A squabbling nest of the wee folk live in the voids inside the exterior walls of my house. Marienne loved to give me a hard time.

"Looked a little young to me," a second voice observed. My hair suffered again. "Too tender for a butcher whose forest is getting a little thin in back."

"Hollybell. You horrid little bug. I knew you'd never let Marienne out of your sight." Hollybell and Marienne are inseparable. Before the leaves finish falling, though, they'll discover boys who aren't all smell and dirt and stupid. Soon the slightest sigh would have universe-shuddering importance.

"Mr. Garrett?"

Dean wanted me. He always horns in when I want to play with little girls.

2

Dean had fetched the message packet. "Go in your office. Figure out what this is. I'll bring tea and biscuits, then get breakfast started. I was thinking those little sausages and soft-boiled eggs."

"A real treat." I gave the old boy the fisheye. "What are you up to?"

"What do you mean?"

"What I said. You're up to something. It might include that kid—who the pixies say is really a girl." The red-blooded Karentine boy inside me had sensed the truth. "If you turn polite and start acting like a real housekeeper, you're up to some villainy. There's no need for a show of wounded dignity, either."

The old-timer needed to polish his act. He was as predictable as me.

I settled behind my desk, in the glamorized janitor's closet I use for an office. I turned sideways, blew a kiss at Eleanor. She's the woman in the painting hanging behind my chair. She's fleeing a brooding mansion on a really stormy night. A light burns in one window only. She's terrified. But she was in a good mood at the moment. She winked.

I opened the message wallet. A sheaf of documents fell out.

They were from Harvester Temisk. A lawyer. The kind who is at home in lawyer jokes. But with a perpetually dumbfounded look on his clock.

Harvester Temisk has just one client. Chodo Contague, erstwhile emperor of TunFaire's multiple kingdoms of crime. The king of kings of the underworld. The head crook.

These days Chodo snoozes along in a coma while his beautiful, criminally insane daughter runs the family business. Belinda pretends she gets instructions from the emperor's own lips.

Dean brought orange tea and sugar cookies. "The sausages are cooking. And there'll be stewed apples instead of eggs. Singe wants stewed apples."

More proof Dean was up to no good, serving specialty tea and sweets. "She'd live on stewed apples if she could." Pular Singe has weaseled herself into an apprenticeship and is angling for junior partner. She's good people and good company. She keeps me from turning into a disgusting old bachelor.

Dean scurried away. Yet more proof. He didn't want to be questioned.

I started reading.

Harvester Temisk reminded me that I'd promised to visit him once I wrapped the case I was working last time we met. I never got back to him. "Dean!"

"I'm cooking as fast as I can."

"I can't find my notes about Chodo's birthday party. When did I say it was supposed to be?"

"It's tonight. At The Palms. Miss Contague reserved the whole club. How could you forget?"

"Maybe I didn't want to remember." You don't want to socialize with the Contagues. Well . . . Belinda . . . when she isn't totally psychotic . . .

Belinda Contague is the perfect beautiful woman without mercy. The grim, unforgiving world of organized crime quickly grew deadlier after her advent. Only a few people know she's the true brains of the Outfit. The fact that her father is comatose is a closely held secret. Maybe five people know. One of those is Chodo.

I worry about being one of the other four. I have no trouble seeing the logic of reducing four to a more manageable three. Or even two.

The Outfit may collapse into civil war when the underbosses find out that their orders come from a woman. Though Belinda has worked hard to restructure the organization, advancing people she finds more congenial.

I didn't want to attend Chodo's party. Too many people connect me with the Contagues already. My being there would only convince the secret police that I'm more significant than I am.

Beyond the accusatory note, the packet contained documents signed by Chodo. Before the incident that resulted in his coma, presumably. Maybe Chodo saw it coming.

Harvester Temisk held the opinion that his employer conspired against the future as a matter of course. He had given Temisk a power of attorney, picked some fool named Garrett to handle his mouthpiece's legwork.

All through his dark career Chodo had guessed right. He'd been in the right place at the right time. The exception—perhaps—having been that one time when it had become possible for his daughter to live a nightmare, keeping the man she hated most where she could torment him daily.

The Contagues aren't your ideal, warm and loving, fuzzy family. They never were. Chodo murdered Belinda's mother when he found out she was cheating on him. Belinda is still working on forgiving him. She hasn't had much luck.

Dean arrived with breakfast.

Temisk didn't say what he wanted me to do. Mostly, he was worried about whether or not I would keep my word.

I thought and ate and couldn't conjure one workable way to weasel out of the obligation.

I owed Chodo. Multiple ways. He'd helped me frequently, without being asked. He'd known me well enough to understand that I'd trudge through life oppressed by the imbalance.

As well as always being in the right place at the

right time, Chodo understood what made people work. Except Belinda. The mad daughter was his blind spot. Otherwise, he wouldn't be in a wheelchair drooling on himself.

Dean brought more tea. "Do we have a new case?" He was up to something for sure.

"No. I'm about to pay the vig on an old debt." He grunted, underwhelmed.

3

Pular Singe wandered in later. She didn't fit well, on account of her tail. She lugged a big, steaming bowl of stewed apples. "Want some?" She was addicted to stewed apples, a food you don't usually associate with rats.

"No, thank you."

TunFaire is infested with rats, including two species of the regular vermin and several kinds of ratpeople. Ratpeople are intelligent, smaller than human critters, with ancestors who came to life in the laboratories of mad sorcerers early last century. As ratpeople go, Singe is a genius. The smartest I've ever met, the bravest, and the best tracker ever.

"What'll you do after you've gobbled this year's whole apple crop?"

She eyed me speculatively, sorting potential meanings. Ratpeople have no natural sense of humor. Singe does have one, but it's learned and can take a bizarre turn.

She knows that when I ask a question with no obvious connection to daily reality, I'm usually teasing. She even manages the occasional comeback.

This wasn't one of those times. "Is there a new case?" She hisses, dealing with her sibilants. Those old-time sorcerers hadn't done much to make it easy for rats to talk.

"Nothing I'm going to get paid for." I told her about Chodo Contague and my old days.

Singe got hold of her tail, wrapped it around her, and hunkered into a squat. We have only one chair that suits the way she's built. That's in the Dead Man's room. Her usual dress is drab, durable work clothing tailored to her odd dimensions.

Though they walk on their hind legs like people, ratfolk have short legs and long bodies. Not to mention funny arms. And tails that drag.

"So you blame yourself for what happened to that man."

Clever rodent.

"Even though it was unavoidable."

Time to change the subject. "Got any idea what Dean is up to?"

Singe still isn't used to how human thought zigs and zags. Her genius is relative. She's a phenom for a rat. As a human she'd be on the slow side of average— though that fades as she gets a better handle on how things work.

"I did not notice anything unusual. Except the bucket of kittens under the stove." Her nose wrinkled. Her whiskers wiggled. No cat smaller than a saber- tooth was likely to trouble her, but she had the in- stincts of her ancestors.

"I knew it. Kittens, eh? He hasn't tried that for a while."

"Don't be angry. His heart is in the right place."

"His heart may be. But he does this stuff at my expense."

"You can afford it."

"I could if I didn't waste wages on a do-nothing housekeeper."

"Do not yell at him."

That would take half the fun out of having Dean around. "I won't yell. I'll just get him a pail of water. Or maybe a gunnysack with a brick in it."

"You are awful." Then she observed, "You have a lot to do if you are going to be ready for the birth- day party."

True. Besides the business of getting cleaned up and dressed up, I needed to visit Harvester Temisk.

"I just had a great idea. I can take those baby cats along tonight and give them away as party favors."

"You are so bad. Go see them before you decide their fates."

"Cute don't work on me."

"Unless it comes in girl form."

"You got me there."

"Come see the kittens. Before Dean finds a better place to hide them." She rose, collected her empty bowl and my tray. We were getting domestic.

"How do you hide a bucket of kittens? They'd be everywhere."

"These are well-behaved kittens."

That sounded like an oxymoron. "I'll just look in on the old bone bag, then be right with you."

4

One weak candle burned in the Dead Man's room. As always. It's not there to provide illumination. It gives off smoke that most bugs find repugnant.

Old Bones has been dead a long time. But his species, the Loghyr, get in no hurry to leave their flesh. When they're awake they do a fair job of discouraging vermin. But my partner has a tendency toward sloth, as well as championship procrastination. He's getting raggedy.

The candles work pretty good on people, too. They don't smell much sweeter than the northernmost extremity of a southbound polecat.

I try to keep the Dead Man's door closed. But kids keep wandering in. They never leave anything the way they find it.

I entered the kitchen saying, "His Nibs is really asleep. I dumped my trick bag. Nothing worked."

Dean looked worried. Singe sort of collapsed in on herself.

"It ain't a big deal. He's taking a nap. We always get through his off-seasons." Dean didn't want to be reminded, though. I never do things the way he wants them done.

I said, "So, Dean, I hear tell a tribe of baby cats has infiltrated my kitchen."

"They aren't ordinary kittens, Mr. Garrett. They're part of an ancient prophecy."

"A modern prophecy has them taking a trip down the river in a gunnysack with a couple broken bricks as companions on the voyage. What're you babbling about?"

"Penny isn't just another street urchin. She's a priestess."

I poured some tea, eyed the bucket of cats. They looked like gray tabby babies. Though there was something strange about them. "A priestess. Right." No surprise in TunFaire, the most god-plagued city that ever was.

"She's the last priestess of A-Lat. From Ymber. She ran off to TunFaire after her mother was murdered by zealots from the cult of A-Laf. Who're in TunFaire now, looking for the kittens."

Somebody had gotten somebody to invest heavily in off-river wetlands. Similar scams are out there every day. People turn blind stupid if you say there's a god involved.

Even Singe looked skeptical. She said, "They are cats, Dean." Coolly.

"Ymber, eh?" I had only vague knowledge of that little city. It's up the river several days' journey. It has problems with thunder lizards. It's supposedly a party town, ruled by a very loose goddess of love, peace, and whatnot. Ymber ships grain, fruit, sheep, cattle, and timber to TunFaire. And lately, thunder lizard hides. It's not known for exporting religious refugees. Or zealots.

One of TunFaire's own main products is flimflam folk. Though I did not, immediately, see how the girl could sting Dean with a bucket of cats.

The religious angle was suggestive, though.

I said, "I'm listening. I haven't heard how the cats tie in."

"They're the Luck of A-Lat."

I tried to get more than that. He clammed. Probably because that's all he knew.

"I'll have to bring the big guy in on it, then."

The whole front of the house shuddered. I growled like a hungry dire wolf. I've had it with people trying to break down my door.

5

My current front door was next best to a castle gate. I had it installed on account of the last one got busted regularly by large, usually hairy, always uncouth, violent fellows. The character I spied through the spy hole, rubbing his shoulder and looking dimly bewildered, fit all those categories. Especially hairy. Except the top of his head. Its peak glistened.

He wore clothes but looked like Bigfoot's country cousin. With worse fashion sense. Definitely a mixed breed. Maybe including some troll, some giant, gorilla, or bear. All his ancestors must've enjoyed the double uglies. He hadn't just gotten whipped with an ugly stick—a whole damned tree fell on him, then took root.

"Wow!" I said. "You guys got to see this. He's wearing green plaid pants."

Nobody answered. Dean was fumbling with a crossbow. Singe had disappeared. Nothing could be felt from the great blob of sagging meat who was supposed to apply ferocious mental powers at times like this.

The door took another mighty hit. Plaster dust shook loose everywhere. I used the peephole again.

Yeti man wasn't alone. Two more just like him, also in baggy green plaid, polluted my steps. Behind them lurked a guy who might've been their trainer. He wore an anxious expression *and* a hideous pair of pants.

A crowd began to gather.

Most of the adult pixies from my colony were out.

Some buzzed around like huge, colorful bumblebees. Some perched in nooks and crannies, poised for action. And, of all people to reveal a hitherto unsuspected talent for timing, I spied my pal Saucerhead Tharpe half a block down the street.

I glimpsed Penny Dreadful, too.

I strolled back to my office, flirted with Eleanor, dug through the clutter, ferreted out my lead-weighted oaken knobknocker. The stick is a useful conversational ploy if I get to chatting with overly excitable gentlemen like the hair ball out front.

Said gentleman continued exercising his shoulder. My door remained stubbornly unmoved by the brute side of the force. "You ready yet, Dean? Just point the business end between his eyes when he stops rolling."

I stepped up to the peephole. Big Hairy was rubbing his other shoulder. He looked down at the man in the street. That guy nodded. One more try.

Saucerhead stood around awaiting events.

Big Hairy charged.

I opened the door. He barked as he plunged inside, somehow tripping on my foot.

My toy made a satisfying *thwock!* on the back of his skull.

The other two hairy boys started to charge, too, but became distracted as their pelts started to crawl with tiny people armed with tiny weapons. Really, really sharp little weapons. All crusty brown with poison.

Singe leaned down from the porch roof, poking around with a rapier. Its tip was all crusty, too. She'd picked up Morley's wicked habit.

Saucerhead grabbed the guy in the street, slapped him till he stopped wiggling, tucked the guy under one arm, then asked, "What're you into now?"

"I don't got a clue," I said. "You didn't break that guy, did you?"

"He's breathing. He'll wake up. Might wish that he didn't, though, when he does. You want to go clubbing tonight?"

"Can't. I've got a command performance. Chodo's birthday party."

"Yeah? Hey! Is that *tonight*? Damn! I forgot. I'm supposed to work security." Tharpe started walking away.

"Hey!"

"Oh. Yeah. What do you want me to do with this guy?"

"Put him down and head on out. Relway's Runners are coming."

An urban police force sounds like a good idea. And it is. If it don't go getting in your way. Which it's likely to do if you spend time tiptoeing around the edge of the law.

Three Watchmen materialized. Two were regular patrolmen. The third was a Relway Runner. Scithe.

He recognized me, too. "You just draw trouble, Garrett." He eyed my house nervously. The Runners are the visible face of the secret police, known by their red flop caps and military weaponry. They have a lot of power but don't like getting inside reading range of mind-peekers like the Dead Man.

I said, "He's asleep."

Nothing lies more convincingly than the truth. My reassuring Scithe assured him only that the Dead Man was pawing through every dark recess of his empty skull.

He stuck to his job, though. "What were these guys up to, Garrett?"

"Trying to kick my door in." He had to ask. I know. I have to ask a lot of dumb stuff, too. Because you have to have the answers to build toward more significant stuff.

"Why?"

"You'll have to ask them. I've never seen them before. I'd remember. Look at those pants." While we chatted, the patrolmen bound the hairy boys' wrists. "There's another one of those inside, guys. My man's got the drop on him." I moved toward the character

that Saucerhead dropped. I wanted to ask questions
before they dragged him off to an Al-Khar cell.

A patrolman called from the house, "This asshole
won't cooperate, Scithe."

"Keep hitting him. His attitude will improve."
Scithe blew his whistle.

Seconds after, whistles answered from all directions.

I stirred the unconscious man with my foot. "These
guys have a foreign look."

Scithe grunted. "I can tell right off you're a trained
detective. You realized no local tailor would ruin his
reputation that way. People! Gather round. What happened here?" He was talking to onlookers who'd
come out to be entertained.

Amazing changes are going on. Astonishing
changes. Several Karentines admitted having witnessed something. *And* they were willing to talk about
it. The more traditional response, after the law caught
and hog-tied a potential witness, would be protesta-
tions of blindness brought on by congenital deafness
having spread to the eyes. In times past actual witnesses often could not speak Karentine despite having
been born in the kingdom.

Relway was having way too much success selling
civic responsibility.

My pixies were old-school, though.

Witnesses agreed that the Ugly Pants Gang just
came up and started trying to break in, ignoring onlookers like they expected to do whatever they
wanted, fearing no comebacks.

I tickled the down character with my toe, near his
groin, in case he was playing possum.

"Garrett." Scithe wagged a finger. "No, no."

"The victim of the crime should be able to get a
vague notion why somebody wants to bust up his
place."

"We'll let you know what you need to know."

"That's comforting." I didn't have to decide for myself. The secret police would take the worry off my

shoulders. They'd figure it all out for me. I just had to lie back and enjoy it.

I didn't argue. The name Garrett is far too high on Relway's curiosity list already.

Stuff happens around me. I don't know why. Maybe because I'm so handsome and Fortune hates a good-looking man.

I told the pixie sentries that I appreciated their nest's help. "Dean's got some baby cats inside. Tell him I said to roast them up for you."

6

Saucerhead fell into step beside me. I said, "I thought you might not get far."

"Smells like a job opportunity."

"I don't really have anything. . . . Wait. There is one thing. A street kid who calls himself Penny Dreadful. Runs errands. Carries messages. You know the type. There's a thousand of him out there. Looks to be about twelve. Might actually be a girl a little older. And might be connected to what just happened."

"Want me to catch her?"

"No. Just find out what you can. Especially where to find her. She's not real high on my list, though. I'm worrying about Chodo's birthday party."

Saucerhead grunted.

Tharpe is huge. For a human being. And he's strong. And he's not real bright. But he's a damned good friend. And I owe him, so a made-up job when I can manage one is never out of line. Especially when he might turn up something actually interesting.

I couldn't conceive of any connection with what had just happened. Nor could I conceive of another explanation. But TunFaire is overrun with people trying to find a new angle.

Still, there's hardly a bad boy around who doesn't know what happens if they get too close to the Dead Man.

That screwball fable about foreign gods had some *oomph*!

"I'm all over it," Saucerhead promised.

I gave him what little I could, including a description so feeble that all Penny Dreadful had to do to disguise himself would be change his shoes. "Promise me you'll stay away from Winger. My life has been nice lately. I'd rather go right on not having her underfoot." Winger is a mutual friend. Sort of. Being mainly a disaster on the hoof.

She's the most amoral person I've ever met, with the social conscience of a rock. And all of a rock's obsession with making the world a better place.

Winger is completely unaware that there are real, hurting people in this world who aren't Winger.

"I don't figure she's likely to be a problem, Garrett."

"She's always a problem."

"She's in a relationship."

"Winger? She's in love? With somebody besides herself?"

"I don't know about love. There's this little winky who's so gaga about her that she don't get much chance to get into mischief. He follows her all around. Everything she does, he writes it down. Creating her epic cycle."

"All right." As long as Winger didn't pop up, trying to profit from whatever was happening. Which is her usual way of doing business.

"Where're you headed, anyway?" Saucerhead wanted to know.

"To see Chodo's mouthpiece. He's been bugging me to come by. Something to do with the old boy's will, I guess."

"See you tonight, then."

"Sure. Just don't let all that neutrality go to your head. Old buddy."

7

I never visited Harvester Temisk before. I'd had little to do with him even when his client was active. Puzzle as I might, I couldn't imagine what he wanted.

He didn't put up much of a front. His little shop was less cushy than the hole-in-the-wall I used before I partnered up with the Dead Man, then scored big enough to buy us a house. I slept, cooked, lived, loved, and worked in that tight little space, back then.

Harvester Temisk didn't look like a lawyer. Not how I thought a lawyer ought to look, anyway, so we know them when we see them. There wasn't an ounce of slime or oil on him. He looked short because he was wide. Once upon a time he might've been more thug than mouthpiece.

Chodo being Chodo, that might've been protective coloration.

The mouthpiece's prosperity had suffered. His haircut wasn't nearly as nice as it used to be. And he still wore the same clothing.

"Thanks for coming." A note of criticism crept into his voice. He noted me cataloging the evidence of his newfound indigence. "You don't work much when your only client is in a coma. He set up a trust that keeps me from starving, but didn't make good investments. Did you review the stuff I sent you?"

"I did. And couldn't make sense of it. Nor did I figure out what you want."

"I needed to see you face-to-face. Has anybody

from the Outfit been interested in me? Or Chodo's condition?"

"I don't think anybody inside, except for Belinda, knows you're still around."

"That should hurt. But I'm glad. I hope they forget me completely."

He was worried. He couldn't keep still. That didn't suit the image projected by a square head, silver hair, square body, and squinty brown eyes.

"So, basically, you want to remind me that I owe Chodo. And you're ready to call the marker."

"Yes."

He didn't want to talk about it. Once he did, he couldn't ever take it back.

"You'd better get to it. Especially if you want to get something done before the party. Belinda won't reschedule."

Belinda. There was a diversion he could snap up.

"I'm worried about what might happen tonight."

It would be a wonderful opportunity to eliminate a lot of people Belinda didn't like if that was the way she wanted to work it.

Only somebody who knew the truth about Chodo's condition would be suspicious. Though a lot who didn't know still thought that it wasn't natural for the Boss to run things through his daughter. Not for so long.

The rats smelled a rat.

A lot of wise guys would turn up just so they could give the Boss a good glim. His health, or the decline thereof, might suggest a potential for personal advancement.

I mused, "What's she going to pull? How's she going to pull it?"

"Can't figure that out, either."

Something didn't add up. It took me a second to figure out what. "Wait a minute. You got in touch before Belinda announced the party. Did you have inside info?"

"I wish. No. I have almost no contacts inside now.

This isn't about the party. It's about . . . I think it's time to rescue him, Garrett. The party just complicates things."

"Mind if I sit?" His best furniture was his client's chair. "Time to rescue Chodo? You mean like round up a couple squadrons of dragoons and go raid the Contague estate? That isn't going to happen."

"Not rescue physically. Mentally. If we shatter the chains imprisoning his mind, the physical side will take care of itself."

"You've lost me completely. I know coma victims have come back. But not very often. Never, if everybody else thinks you being in a coma is so exquisitely useful that it's the next best thing to you being dead."

"You ever know anybody who came out of a long coma?"

"No."

"Ever know anybody who was even in a coma? Besides Chodo?"

"During the war. Usually somebody who got hit in the head."

"Up close, for very long?"

"No. You headed somewhere?"

"Toward the hypothesis that Chodo isn't in a coma, only a poststroke state resembling a coma, induced chemically or by sorcery. I don't think he's unconscious. I think he just can't communicate."

Giant hairy spiders with cold claws crept all over my back. That presented a gaggle of unpleasant possibilities. "Suppose you're right. Chodo had willpower like nobody I ever met. He'd get around it, somehow."

"Absolutely. He would."

"And you're somehow part of that?"

"That would mean he saw it coming. He was clever, Garrett. He read people like nobody else, but he wasn't a seer."

"But?"

"Yes. But. He was an obsessive contingency planner. We spent hours every week brainstorming contingencies."

"Uhm?" I understood that. We'd done a lot of it when I was still a handsome young Marine making sure the wicked Venagetan hordes didn't come suck the life and spirit and soul out of the king's favorite subjects. Most of whom weren't sure who the king was that week.

"He thought well of you."

"And I'm sure I'm not glad to hear that." We were back to my obligation to Chodo Contague because he'd been so good to me. Whether or not I wanted it.

"His contingencies usually ended up with him or me calling you in to restore the balance."

"Restore the balance?"

"His words. Not mine."

"Have you seen him lately?" I hadn't.

"No. And it was an accident, last time I did. I went out to the estate and just walked in. Like I always did. The guards didn't stop me. I'd done it for years and Belinda hadn't said to keep me out. She wasn't happy, but she was polite. And uncooperative. I didn't actually get to see Chodo up close. I got to watch Belinda pretend to ask him if he felt up to talking business. She told me she was sorry I'd wasted the trip. Her daddy felt too sick to work today. Could I come back some other time? Better yet, how about he came to my place next time he was in the city?"

"And he's never showed up."

"You *are* good."

"I'm a trained detective. Where does that leave us?"

"Here's the thing."

Gods, I hate it when people say that. It guarantees that everything to come will be weasel words. "Umh?"

"Belinda is in and out of town all the time. When she does come in she doesn't leave Chodo behind. Somebody might see him without her standing in between. I found out by spying. By lying in wait, hoping to get to him while she was away."

"Dangerous business."

"Yes."

"The woman isn't stupid."

"Crazy, yes. Stupid, no. She brings him in and stashes him."

"That could be handled by having somebody see when she comes in and find out where she drops him."

Temisk chewed his lower lip.

"You've tried that."

"Yes. And lost the man I hired. I'm lucky he didn't know who I was, anymore. I might've lost me, too."

I tried to recollect someone in my racket turning up dead or missing recently. There aren't many of us. On the other hand, ours isn't a well-known and respected profession like palm reader or potion maker. "Anyone I'd know?"

"No. He was an old soak named Billy Mul Tima who used to run numbers on the north side. I gave him little jobs when I could. He worked hard for Chodo before he got into the sauce too far."

So there I was, snoot to snoot with a crisis, getting a face full of Fortune's bad breath. A cusp. A turning point. An instant when I had to make a moral choice.

I resisted the easy one. And said not one word about a lawyer with a heart, and, more remarkably, a conscience. "Tell me about it."

"There isn't much to tell. I gave Billy Mul what I could and sent him off. I assume he bought all the cheap wine he could carry, then got to work."

"Wino would be a good cover. They're everywhere. And nobody pays attention. Go on."

"They found him in a room on the north side a few days later, after he started to stink. He'd burned to death."

I frowned. For a year there have been reports of people burning up without benefit of a fire, always in some slum on the north side.

"Garrett, he burned to death without setting fire to the place where he died. Which was about as awful a tenement as you can imagine."

I can imagine some pretty awful places. I've visited

a lot of them. Especially back when my clientele wasn't quite so genteel. "Somebody brought him there."

"No. I went up there myself. I talked to people. Even the Watch. He burned right where they found him. Cooked down like a chunk of burned fat. Without getting hot enough to start a bigger fire."

That jibed with stories I'd heard about other burning deaths. "How could that happen? Sorcery?"

"That would be everybody's first guess, wouldn't it?"

"Always is when an explanation isn't obvious. We're conditioned by long, direct, dire exposure to those idiots on the Hill."

Sorcery, great or small, isn't part of daily life. But the threat of sorcery is. The potential for sorcery is. Particularly dark sorcery. Because our true rulers are the wizards who infest the mansions on the Hill.

I said, "You don't think sorcery is the answer."

"Those kind of people don't show up in that part of town."

A self-taught rogue set on becoming a one-man crime wave might, though. But how would he profit from burning winos?

"It's not a part of town where humans show up much, is it? Isn't that Elf Town?"

"No. But right on its edge. It's mainly nonhuman immigrant housing now. Here's the thing, though. The building belonged to Chodo."

I nodded and waited.

"When I went up I thought it looked familiar. I dug into the records when I got back. We bought the place four years ago. I handled the legal stuff."

"Chodo wasn't there."

"Not when the body was found. But he might have been. People remembered a man in a wheelchair."

"Uhm?"

"I didn't take it any further. I didn't want to attract attention."

"Probably the smart thing." It's unhealthy to ask questions near an Outfit operation. You might develop black-and-blue lumps. At the least.

Temisk asked, "Any brilliant theories?"

"Just the obvious one. Billy Mul tried to get to Chodo. Somebody made him dead for his trouble."

"How would they do that?"

"That would be the question, wouldn't it?"

"And why do it that way? Those things are done simple. Unless somebody wants to send a message."

"A burn-up wouldn't be a message anyone could read. They'd just wrinkle their noses and ask, what the hell?"

There wasn't any sense to it. Pieces of the puzzle were missing. Even its general shape wasn't apparent.

Temisk said, "One of the things Chodo paid me to do was bail him out if he got caught up in something weird. This qualifies. And he expected you to help."

"I got that part. I don't like it, but I got it. He knew me better than I know me. What're you thinking about doing?"

"I did it when I got hold of you. You're the expert."

Me. The expert. Cute.

"Then let's set some priorities. What's the most important thing to do?"

"Make sure Chodo is still alive tomorrow morning."

"Back to the birthday party?"

"Back to the party."

8

From Harvester Temisk's digs I ambled over to The Palms, an upscale eatery and club operated by the dark elf Morley Dotes. My number one good buddy. I approached warily. There might be trouble with Belinda's troops if they were setting up already.

"Holy shit! Will ya look at dis? It ain't even been a week an' here it comes agin!"

It's remotely possible that not all of Morley's associates welcome me all the time. "I was passing by. Thought I'd drop in and see how you're all doing. How're you doing, Sarge?"

Sarge is fat and balding and tattooed and nastier than a bushel of scorpions when he's in a good mood. He didn't seem particularly cheerful today.

Another one enough like Sarge to be his ugly big brother, with extra scorpions, shuffled out of the kitchen. "Hey, Puddle. How's it going, man?"

Puddle brandished a commercial-weight rolling pin. This didn't look encouraging.

Morley emerged behind Puddle. Amazing. Dotes seldom has much to do with the daily grind of his place. "What do you want, Garrett?"

"Damn, Morley. Get a sense of humor. I know a guy on the Landing. . . ."

"What do you want, Garrett?"

"Right now I'd like to know why it's hilarious when you stick me with a foul-beaked fowl like the Goddamn Parrot, but it's haul out the meat cleavers when I get you back with a nympho nymph."

Two more staffers materialized. Lugging industrial-grade butcher's equipment. In a vegetarian establishment. "Them new-generation eggplants must be fierce." Everybody seemed intensely interested in managing a wily envelopment of their good buddy Garrett.

Not promising at all.

Dotes made a slight gesture. "One more chance, Garrett."

"I wanted to check on how things are coming, setting up for tonight. And to say hi."

"And why are you interested?"

"Because I have to be here, cabbage breath boy. I can't weasel out. And I don't feel good about the setup."

Morley glared at me. Slim and dark, handsome and always impeccably bedecked in the latest fashion, he radiates a sensuality that sets them swooning even when he strolls through a nun shop.

"You got smudge under your nose." He'd begun sporting a thin little mustache.

Morley didn't grin. "Sit down, Garrett."

I picked a chair. The one closest to the door.

Morley sat across from me. He stared. Eventually, he said, "Word's out that you're on Belinda's payroll now."

"That's a crock. Who said that?"

"Belinda. Last time she was here messing the arrangements around."

"It ain't true. You know me better. I wouldn't work for her even if I needed work. And I don't. I've got me a nice little piece of the hottest manufactory in TunFaire. You're just trolling for an excuse to get your bile up."

"She was convincing." Dotes studied me some more. Something big was bothering him and all his boys. Nobody wanted Mama Garrett's favorite boy for a friend.

"Spit it out, Morley. What's going on?"

"This party is bound to go bad. And here you come, supposedly Belinda's full-time top stud, ambling in ten minutes after your honey sends word the party won't happen here after all. The Palms will just cater. The party will happen in Whitefield Hall. Because my place isn't big enough. Too many people in the life want to pay their respects to the kingpin."

"I don't know anything about any Whitefield Hall. Is that the Veterans' Memorial hall that commemorates the War of Coady Byrne's Broken Tooth?"

Karenta had a lot of little wars over a lot of little provocations in Imperial times. Then we changed up, became a kingdom, and jumped into one big war that lasted over a hundred years. The one I was in. Along with every human male I know, including my brother and father and grandfather, and Grandpa's father and grandfather and all their brothers and cousins and bastard kids.

The killing is over now. So far, the peace has been worse than the war.

"I don't know anything about your wars," Dotes replied. Being half dark elf, he enjoys treaty exemption from some human laws. Like the one establishing conscription. And he doesn't give a feather about history. He doesn't care about last week—unless last week might sneak up and whack him on the back of the head. "But it is some kind of soldiers' memorial."

Morley is shallow. Morley is pretty. Morley is the nightmare that wakes fathers screaming in the night. He's the daydream their daughters take to bed, fantasizing. He's the bad boy the girls all want, thinking they can tame him, before they settle for some dullard who'll just work for a living and treat them like they're people.

I'm so jealous.

"I can't picture it. What's special about it? Why would she move there?"

"I told you. Because she can get more people in. Because it isn't operated by people she doesn't trust."

"Belinda doesn't trust you?"

"Are you that naive? Of course she doesn't. Not to be what she wants me to be."

"What would that be?"

"Her tool, fool."

"Don't start with the vegetarian poetry. It don't make sense on a day when the sun *is* shining."

Dotes shook his pretty head. He didn't want to play. "Belinda wouldn't trust me if I swore ten thousand ironbound oaths. That's part of her insanity. She can't trust anybody. Except you. Probably for the same sick reason Chodo trusted you. From where I sit, that would be because you're too damned dim to be anything but honest."

Morley's morals and ethics are situation dependent. Which doesn't stop him being a nice guy. Most of the time. When it's convenient.

"Your expression of confidence warms the cockles of my heart, Mr. Dotes."

"What does that mean? I've always wondered. What are cockles?"

"Seafood? I don't know. But it sounds good."

"I'm tempted to change my mind again."

Even so, looking sour, Sarge, Puddle, and the rest went back to work.

"This will be the event of the decade for the Outfit."

"Isn't that special?"

"You know Harvester Temisk?"

"Chodo's legal beagle? I'd recognize him if I tripped over him. That's it."

"He's still Chodo's mouthpiece. Know anything about him?"

"He played straight. For a lawyer. He was Chodo's friend since they were kids. Why?"

Sometimes the best way to handle Morley is to tell the truth. Or something approximating truth, truth being so precious you don't just give it away. Something close enough to get him to do what you want, that's the thing. "He came at me when we were putting the three-wheel company together."

"Where they give you extra profit points to stay away. I've heard about what a pain in the ass you are with your moralizing and ethics jabber."

I refused the bait. "I've got a case."

Morley loves to argue. It makes him the center of attention.

"Come tell me all about it when you're done, Garrett."

"You got any idea what she plans to pull tonight?"

"No. But I'll be very careful. Very alert. Very stay in the kitchen. You might do the same. If you really must attend."

"Oh, I must. I must. Maybe I'll wear my iron underwear. You ever hear of Chodo doing anything with sorcery?"

"No. He didn't like it. Though he'd hire a hedge wizard sometimes. That's all. He resented wizards for having more direct power than he did."

"I mean himself. Personally."

"His gifts ran to murder, mayhem, and management. As a wizard he had all the talent of a tombstone."

"That's what I thought." Admitting what I was thinking. Twice. Being right up-front with my pal.

"What have you got going?"

"Temisk says strange things keep happening since Chodo's accident. I want to get a handle."

"That your case?"

"That's not what it's about. It's just something I need to understand."

"Is Temisk working you by claiming you owe Chodo?"

"Some. I need to work that out, too."

"Walk away. Stop being you. Save yourself the pain and grief."

"You know anything about these people who've been catching on fire?"

"No. That part of your case, too?"

"I don't think so. I just wondered. Never hurts to ask you something. You're full up on weird and wonderful. And sometimes, you tell me what you know."

"Weird and wonderful, he says. And he's the one shacking up with a dead thing and a talking rat."

"And Dean. And a bucket of baby cats. I think I'll bring those with me tonight. Give them away."

"There's an original idea. Giving away kittens at a mob summit. The one guy who takes one will feed it to his pet anaconda."

"An idea whose time has come. Feed all the cats to the snakes. Singe would go along."

"Then what do you do with the snakes? They like rats more than cats."

"Know anything about a street kid, calls himself Penny Dreadful?"

"I know he needs to find another name if he doesn't like being smacked around. Otherwise, no. Why?"

"He's really a girl pretending to be a boy. And Dean's source for the bucket of kittens. He has a majorly strange story about the kid."

"Strange stories about people in your life? Fie! Balderdash!"

"Sarcasm doesn't become you, sir. Considering you're one of the main people in my life. And definitely one of the strangest."

"I'm the standard against which everyone else is measured."

"You hang in there. I'll go for help." I eyed the front door, inches away. My chances of making it looked better than they had. "How's your love life?" I cackled evilly, then fled.

Why is another story, already told.

9

"Hey!"

A rock whizzed past my ear. It hit Morley's door so hard it bashed a hole in a panel.

Dotes bounced out beside me, looking ferocious. "What happened?" he asked.

"Somebody took a whack at me with a sling." I assumed. How else throw a rock that hard?

"Primitive."

"But effective if you aren't ready for it."

"Who was it? Where did he go?"

"I'm pretty sure it was that chunky guy over there. Wearing the stupid green pants. The one so busy looking nonchalant." This one looked like the runt of the Ugly Pants litter. He was hard at work pretending to be interested in the gaps between buildings and the shadows under stoops.

"Stay here. He might want you to follow him. I'll round up a crowd. He owes me a door." Dotes went back inside.

I collected the stone that, but for an instant of luck, might have knocked another hole in my noggin. You need a couple extra to get into my racket, but I wasn't prospecting for more.

The stone had a slight egg shape, being an inch and a quarter in one dimension and just under an inch in the other. It was heavy. It was green, like serpentine or low-grade jade. And it was polished. It didn't look like something a guy would pick up strolling down a creek bed.

Morley returned with some of his troops. I said, "This might be a trick to get you away from The Palms."

"I warned Sarge and Puddle. Where did he go?"

"Turned south into Ironstar Lane."

"Let's go spring the trap," Morley said. Very direct, my friend.

"You're too eager. You make me nervous when you're eager."

"I ever mention that you worry too much?"

"Only on those occasions when I'm close enough to hear you talk."

We jogged off with half a dozen guys who pretend to be servers at Morley's place, none the sort who wait tables because they love the work.

Dotes insists that he's out of the life now, yet persists in surrounding himself with men like these.

I worry, what with the dedication shown by the secret police lately. Deal Relway doesn't worry about due process. In his own mind, he *is* the law. Too often, those left behind will agree that you had it coming.

Nevertheless, the underworld goes on. As strong and committed and obsessed as Relway is, he isn't able to do much but nibble at the Outfit's peripheries.

We turned into Ironstar Lane. And came to a many-legged, confused halt.

The character who'd tried to trepan me with a stone wasn't a block ahead. He ambled along, searching shadows, like he had no idea somebody might chase him down.

"What's the game here, Garrett? That moron is toddling along like he doesn't have a care."

"You can't hold me responsible because somebody else is an idiot."

"It's arguable. Sins of the blood and all that stuff." He came close to using bad language.

I asked, "Instead of standing around debating, why don't we take advantage?"

Morley signaled his boys. We moved out.

Traffic was light, but that's normal in Ironstar Lane. There aren't any shops.

We surrounded the squat man before he realized someone was after him. His response was bewilderment. For an instant I thought I'd fingered the wrong guy. Like all of a sudden everybody in TunFaire had taken to wearing hideous green pants, and bad fashion sense wasn't a sure sign of innate villainy.

Then he charged, went right through one of Morley's boys.

"Wow!" I said.

"Yes. Be careful."

The squat man didn't run. He did make it unpleasant to get too close. At intimate range he was quicker than Morley, who, till now, had held the record. In my experience. And he was strong. He flung me thirty feet, easy.

We took turns bopping him from behind. Which was kind of like bull baiting, only this bull never made a sound. He didn't answer questions. He just fought on, emphasizing doing damage to Ma Garrett's only surviving son.

We outnumbered him only eight to one so it was our great good fortune that police whistles began squealing in nearby streets. We broke it up immediately. Nobody wanted to visit the Al-Khar. Not today.

As though there's any good day now.

"That was exhilarating," Morley said as we inventoried limbs, combed cobblestones out of our hair, and figured out who got bragging rights for suffering the biggest bruises. "If I'm alive in the morning, I'm going to give that guy another look. With Doris and Marsha doing the heavy lifting."

Doris and Marsha Roze are relatives of his. Somehow. They're part giant, part troll, part other stuff. They stand twelve feet tall and can bring down small buildings with a single pound. Too bad they weren't along a few minutes ago.

"Why not? There must be another ten thousand streets that could use a good dusting." It's rare as frog fangs to see Morley Dotes all dirty and spiffed up in rags. "I wish I could preserve this vision for posterity."

"I'll put on old clothes next time. Get back to me on this."

He was upset. I wasn't sure why. You can't win them all.

"I'll do that. Good luck tonight."

10

"What happened?" Dean demanded as he let me into the house.

"Somebody tried to kill me."

He grunted, unimpressed.

"You should see the other guy."

He grunted again. He has no respect for my way of life, though it keeps him full of bread and beans.

"Not a scratch on him. Even though I had Morley and six of his guys there lending a hand. We would've turned it around, though, if the Watch hadn't shown up."

That was for Singe's benefit. She'd come to the kitchen to find out what was up. She had a kitten in her paws, petting it. The baby cat didn't mind the incongruity.

I asked, "Think you could pick up a day-old trail using this?" I tossed her the green egg.

"Gak! Underwater. What was it? A bear or an ogre?"

Singe has a talent.

Ratpeople are blessed with an exceptional sense of smell. Some can embarrass a bloodhound. Singe stands out of that crowd.

As noted, she's a genius. For a ratwoman. And has more courage than ten other ratpeople put together. Excluding only her brother.

Even the most daring and wicked ratfolk get scared

around humans. The sorcerers who created them saw no need to take that timidity out.

"He was human. From one of the far fringes of the species."

"What did he do?"

"He tried to kill me. With an old-fashioned sling. Using that egg for ammunition."

"Bathing would not appear to be one of his human vices."

I told Dean, "That tongue gets more wicked every day."

Dean scowled. He can't shed all his prejudices. Singe bounced, though, pleased by the compliment. She has one great character flaw. She tries hard to be human.

She's smart enough to know they'll never let her be.

"Why a day-old trail?"

"I don't have time today. I have Chodo's birthday party to do."

"Who are you taking? Tinnie?"

"Nobody."

"Can I go?"

"No. I'm not taking anybody. It could get ugly fast. I don't want anybody getting hurt." Not to mention that she wouldn't be welcome. Virulent prejudice can be ignored only at great peril. Particularly by persons of goodwill.

Singe knows that on the practical and emotional levels. She doesn't let on when she gets her feelings hurt. She thinks that by revealing her feelings, she'd belittle my effort to save her some pain.

I know. But it works for us.

I asked, "Anything stirring on the undead front?"

If the Dead Man hates any one thing enough to almost let it get his blood pumping, it's being lumped with the undead. Vampires, zombies, and whatnot are all predators. He insists that he isn't.

"Not a sign," Dean said. "Looks like he's down for a while this time."

That wasn't good news. I could use some advice.

Like maybe the top ten ways of surviving Chodo's shindig, barring the obvious: Don't show up.

When you have no choice about hiking the valley of the shadow, you need to brainstorm ways to cover your ass. I got busy.

I had options. I had connections. Some might even be useful.

Singe's brother, for example.

I recalled a conversation with Morley about the truth of what I mean to Belinda Contague. Not the business meaning. Not the former-lover meaning, nor the outright-fear meaning. The symbolic or fetishist meaning to the secret, frightened little girl hidden way down deep inside Miss Belinda. The little girl who, Morley believed, wanted me for the daddy she hadn't had when she was coming up because her real daddy was Chodo Contague, hardly a paragon as a parent.

I've rescued the woman, one way or another, from the deepest shit several times. Morley says she's chosen me as the bellwether of her personal fortunes because of that. That she'll never let me be hurt because the little girl needs Daddy Garrett out there in case another terror closes in.

"Singe. I've got an idea. Maybe a dumb one. Come in the office and help me brainstorm."

"What's up?" she asked, hissing like a sack of rattlers as she forced the contraction.

"You think your brother might help us with something? If we offer him an appropriate fee? I know! I know! But you had the same mother. Humans figure that makes him your brother."

John Stretch—real name, Pound Humility—is the boss of the ratpeople in my part of TunFaire. He's top rat partly thanks to me. He's Singe's half brother from an earlier litter. They have a stronger relationship than most related ratfolk. He tried to rescue her from my clutches one time. She spanked him verbally and told him to go the hell away—she was happy right where she was.

"I do not know. He suspects that you took advantage of him last time."

"I understand a pride problem. You know better than me if we can do business."

"What do you want him to do?"

"This party tonight. He could help me with it. If he really talks to regular rats."

Singe considered. We both knew John Stretch could get inside the minds of regular rats and use them as spies. He had admitted it in front of us.

"You want him to go over to the place where Chodo Contague's birthday party is going to happen."

"Yes." But now my idea was growing up. "If we could hide him close by, he could stay on the job right through the party and warn me so there wouldn't be any ugly surprises."

"You might not be able to meet his price."

"I'm not hurting for cash."

"He will not ask for cash."

I groaned. "A favor for a favor."

"What use can you be to a ratman gangster?"

A human agent could be very useful to a rat king who knew what he wanted.

"You want me to find him? You do not have a lot of time."

In fact, it was too late. Almost certainly. Nevertheless, "See what you can do."

Singe was ready to go in minutes. I told her, "Leave the kitten. It won't be welcome where you're headed."

She returned the critter to the bucket. "They grow on you."

"So do lice. Don't get too attached. They aren't staying."

I let Singe out right into a major pixie squabble. Those bugs are worse than sparrows. But they're so constant about it that I don't much notice anymore.

I told them, "I want to talk to Shakespear and Melondie Kadare, please." Polite helps a little. Sometimes. Unpredictably. About as often as it does with big people.

If I couldn't get ratpeople help, I might enlist some

pixies. Which would be cheaper, anyway, since helping me is how they're supposed to pay their rent.

Melondie Kadare came out, a gorgeous specimen of pixie womanhood. Sadly, pixies live fast. Melondie will hit middle age in about six months. She was a typically obnoxious adolescent when I met her, a month ago. Now she was a woman of standing in her nest.

She piped, "Shakespear isn't here anymore, Garrett. He married a Daletripses. He decided to join her nest."

Pixie clusters are strongly matrilineal. Most times the boys follow the girls.

"Congratulations. I guess. That's an important connection." My pixies are newcomers to TunFaire. Refugees. The Daletripses cluster is an old line, as local pixie tribes go. A marital alliance would serve my tenants well. "Though I thought that you and he . . ."

"Let's not talk about that. I have a husband of my own now. And he don't like hearing about the good old days."

"I'm sorry. If that's the appropriate sentiment."

"Not to worry. He's a little stupid, a lot lazy, and way too jealous, but I'll whip him into shape."

Marriage doesn't take the same form with pixies. Passion is unimportant. Forging alliances and preserving estates are. Passion gets indulged on the side. In some clusters a girl isn't marriage material unless she's demonstrated her fertility with several merrybegots.

"I want to know if I can get some help with a case."

"Hey! We've got to pay the rent, don't we?"

"It might be dangerous."

"Talk to me, Garrett."

I told my story.

"So you have a history with the Contagues."

"More than one."

"Better tell me about that, then. It could have an impact on how decisions are made at the head table."

Belinda wouldn't let sentiment hamstring business decisions. She was harder than her father. And Chodo seldom let emotion get in the way.

"This hall, Garrett. Where this will happen. Is it far out of our territory?"

"You know where the Bledsoe is? The charity hospital? That whole area was all government buildings in olden times. When the Empire was in charge. The hall is over there. It was something else before they turned it into a war memorial. They were more frugal in the old days."

"Are there any pixies around there? Or anybody else who might think we're trespassing?"

TunFaire is a hundred cities piled onto the same hapless patch of dirt, a different one for every race. Some peoples are so different, their TunFaires scarcely intersect. More often, they do, and only us big, numerous types don't need to invest in getting along. We can be as awful as we want to be. And usually are.

"I don't know. I only just found out that the shindig is moving there from Morley's place. I haven't been in that part of town since somebody got me committed to the crazy ward at the Bledsoe."

"That must've been an adventure. How'd you lie your way out? Convince them you were sane?"

"I convinced them I was so crazy they didn't want me there."

"There isn't much time. You'll have to take us with you when you go. Keeping us out of sight."

That wouldn't work. I couldn't walk for miles lugging a carpetbag full of squabbling pixies.

Melondie read my mind. So to speak. "Don't be such a cheap-ass, Garrett. Hire a coach. We can get there unseen. And you can show up without looking like a refugee yourself."

Everybody nags me about the way I dress.

Nobody believes me if I poor-mouth. They all think I'm rich. Just because I have those points in the three-wheel factory.

Melondie's idea was sound. "Can somebody fly a note to Playmate's stable?" My friend Playmate doesn't have a coach of his own, but he can come up with one at a moment's notice, usually. And I like to give my business to friends. Plus, as a bonus, Playmate is about nine feet tall and handy to have around when a debate turns physical.

"I suppose." She wasn't enthusiastic. Long-distance flights are risky for pixies. Too many things out there think they look like food.

"Excellent. I'll write one up and we can get the circus moving."

I spied Singe returning. A couple human kids were giving her a hard time. I didn't go chase them. She wouldn't like that. She wants to fight her own battles.

Melondie had none of my problems. She whistled into the gap her tribe uses to get in and out of my walls. A half dozen adolescent bugs zipped out and hummed down the street. They got behind the human kids' heads and started tormenting them.

Singe arrived. "John Stretch says he will be thrilled to help the great Garrett with a case. He insists that he bring his own rats instead of relying on those that will be in place already, though."

"Fine. I'm sending a note to Playmate to bring a coach."

"You changed your mind!"

"Don't go getting all excited. You'll stay inside it. You'll help John Stretch run his game."

11

Playmate brought a huge mahogany coach. It had to belong to somebody from way up the food chain. "This isn't going to be missed, is it?"

"Not unless we don't let it get back before the end of the week." Playmate jumped down to help load. "I'm more worried about getting blood all over it. Or leaving a corpse inside."

"That wasn't my fault. You need to take a more positive attitude."

"Familiarity with the Garrett experience suggests that guarded pessimism is the safer approach."

Playmate is a huge black man who looms even huger than he is.

He's bigger than me, stronger than me, and almost as handsome. His big shortcoming is that he's a wannabe preacher who isn't as mean as he looks. Who isn't *really* nine feet tall. But seven feet wouldn't be out of the question.

"You're sure?" I could see where a crest had been removed from the coach door. "I don't want some stormwarden stomping me because his coach isn't there when he decides to go for a ride."

"Want me to take it back?"

"That's all right. I was just checking. What's this?"

A goat cart stopped behind the coach. No goat was employed in its locomotion, though. A ratman had put himself into the traces.

Singe's brother. With a load of wooden cages filled with large, brown, unhappy rats. "Am here," John Stretch said. His Karentine wasn't as polished as his sister's.

"Let's get those critters into the coach, then."

"Where is Singe?"

"Taking her good sweet time getting ready. You sure you can manage this?"

"Will have Singe to help. And them. Yes?" Pixies swarmed into the coach like Melondie meant to bring all her friends and relations.

Playmate remarked, "You're looking pretty good there, Garrett. Did you hire a consultant to dress you up?"

I spread my arms to the sky. "You see the torments I suffer? Take me home now."

Singe came fluttering out of the house, a young woman running late. Though how you get behind when your wardrobe is as limited as hers, I don't know. But what I know about women, even limiting the sample to my own tribe, would fit in a thimble with room left over for a brigade of dancing angels.

Singe brought the kittens with her. She piled into the coach.

"We're ready," I told Playmate. I glanced at the goat cart. "John Stretch, you'll lose your cart if you just leave it there."

"No problem. Is not my cart."

Great. So now the Watch would find a stolen goat cart in front of my house. Because, with my luck, the damned thing would sit there undisturbed for six months if it took that long to embarrass me.

I clambered aboard the coach.

Total silence reigned inside.

The pixies warily split their attention between the baby cats and the rat cages. The baby cats peeked out of their bucket, intrigued by the bug people and the rats. The rats glared at everybody.

What should have become chaos on the hoof declined into inexplicable relaxation.

"Well," I said, relaxed myself, despite what lay ahead. "How about that?"

The pixies found perches. They gossiped. They didn't squabble and they didn't bother the rats. Normally, given half a chance, they would've swarmed any rodent. A plump rat could provide the main course for a huge feast.

Singe couldn't control the kittens, though. Several got away and began investigating everything. Without bothering the rats or bugs. They were remarkably well-mannered, for cats.

As we turned into Wizard's Reach I glimpsed a familiar face outside. It belonged to the man Morley and I had had the misfortune to catch earlier. He was watching my house. From a bruised visage.

His presence made me nervous. If he got obnoxious and kicked my door in, the Dead Man would be no help at all.

I couldn't turn back. I'd have to trust the process. A notion I find dubious in the best of times.

My neighbor Mrs. Cardonlos is a police spy. And, possibly, a friend of Mr. Deal Relway, director of what, this week, is called something like the Unpublished Committee for Royal Security. Mrs. Cardonlos' great pleasure in life is spying on me and imagining my life being more exciting than it is. Relway pays her a small stipend.

She'd keep an eye out while I was gone. The most interesting stuff happens at my place when I'm not home. That's when the stupid shines. That's when the unprepared find out that they should've done more research.

The Dead Man has fun with stupid thugs.

My partner can be as cruel as a cat with an unbreakable mouse.

But, oh, woe! He was on a sleeping holiday today.

"What kind of kittens are those?" I wondered out loud. They looked like basic gray stripy alley lurkers, but not quite. They were odd. However, all I know about cats is that I like them better than dogs, except maybe beagle and sausage dog puppies.

Oh, wondrous day! Singe and John Stretch both actually understood that I didn't expect an answer. Both looked like they expected praise for being that clever.

I nodded and smiled my approval.

Speaking of pixies, which I wasn't, "Melondie. Did you guys get into some poison, or something? I've never heard you all so quiet."

Miss Kadare fluttered over a tad drunkenly. She assumed a widespread stance on my left palm, hands on hips, wobbling, not in time to the coach's rocking.

"You been drinking?" Pixies love alcohol.

"Not a drop." She staggered, plopped down on her tiny but gorgeous behind.

"You *are* drunk!" I accused.

"No way!" she snapped. Then she giggled. "I don't know what's happened. I was fine when we flew in here."

The other pixies were drunk, too. Most more so than Melondie Kadare.

I nudged a curious kitten away from a male pixie who had fallen to the coach floor and lay there on his back, buzzing occasionally, like a downed locust.

It was weird. But I had trouble giving a rat's ass. I was mellow, at peace. Without personal ambition whatsoever.

Some acquaintances would insist that was nothing new.

Singe and John Stretch seemed vaguely puzzled and sleepy.

Ditto, the rats.

I never heard of a drunk spell, but that didn't mean one couldn't exist. It only meant that I'd never been hit by one before.

The pixies passed out. I started suffering urges to sing the Marine Corps hymn or something similarly patriotic. Which don't hit me when I get snockered the hard way. Not often.

The coach suddenly bucked, jolted to a halt. What the hell? Traffic couldn't be that bad. Could it?

I was two heartbeats away from falling asleep when Playmate yanked the door open. "We're here. Huh? What's the matter with you all?"

I extended a hand. He helped me descend as elegantly as a duchess. Good man he, he did the same with John Stretch and Pular Singe while deftly keeping the kittens from getting away.

He closed the door on the pixies and baby cats. "What I'm going to do now is, I'm going to stay right here. I'll come in and pull you out if something bad happens."

That said a ton about Playmate.

"That's white of you, Play. I'll be more relaxed in there, knowing you'll rescue me if I need it."

Playmate had nothing more to say. His eyes had begun to wobble. Meantime, I was recovering. Fast.

I was way early in arriving. Even so, several coaches were lined up beside the hall already, each cared for by somebody big and dumb and covered with scars. And with tattoo collections for seasoning. They stared at my companions and their cages filled with rats.

"Round up those kittens, Singe." The drunk was gone. Just that fast.

"You want to take them inside?"

"Oh, hell yeah. They're going to be all over in there."

These kittens did not behave like cats. They weren't contrary. They let themselves be caught and tucked into their bucket, with the cloth folded over them, theoretically to keep them in. Only a couple had to be caught and tucked a second time.

"How many of these monsters are there?" I asked Singe. I couldn't get a hard count. Hasty estimates during the day had ranged from four to nine. Since even a dead cat can create havoc in two places at once, I suspected the true number was closer to four.

Singe said, "Five or six. It's hard to tell because their markings are so alike."

It didn't matter. As long as I had the majority with me when I went in.

As I approached the goons checking invitations, I tried to work out why I thought I should go armed with baby cats.

I guess because I hoped nobody would stay belligerent with a gang of them underfoot.

One of the goons asked, "The hell you luggin' a pail a pussy for, slick?"

"Somebody might want a kitten. I got some to adopt out." I saluted him with my pussy pail and strolled on into Whitefield Hall.

12

Belinda had a second goon squad set up behind an inverted L of tables inside the front entrance. Clever girl, she'd made sure these guys weren't beholden to her. They were freelancers. Saucerhead Tharpe was one. I recognized two of his three companions, Orion Comstock and June Nicolist. Both had reputations much like Tharpe's. Absolutely neutral.

"Garrett."

"Mr. Tharpe." I've known him for years, but his real first name escaped me. No matter. He prefers Saucerhead.

"Anything to declare?"

"Eh?"

"Weapons. Of any sort. You got 'em, you got to declare 'em. You don't got to surrender 'em, though we'd rather you did. You do, June gives you one of them beautiful scarves. You collect your tools when you leave." June held up a bright green kerchief. He had a pile handy, and a grin that betrayed teeth of the same shade. Saucerhead said, "That'll mark you safe."

"All right. Give me a hankie. This's all I've got. One bucket of cats." One bucket of remarkable cats. There was something wrong with them. Any other litter would have staged several jailbreaks by now.

Saucerhead eyed the kittens. He looked at me. "You're serious."

"As a dose of typhoid." I needed to move on. I had

to fix up some way for Melondie Kadare to sneak inside.

Tharpe asked, "You didn't even bring your knob-knocker?"

"Nope. Nothing but my own bare hands."

Saucerhead sighed. "You may be sorry."

"I'm a trained Royal Marine."

"You used to be. Here." He handed me a yellow kerchief instead of letting June give me a green one.

"Yellow, huh?"

"It don't mean nothing. Green and yellow was what was the cheapest."

"What keeps a guy from just stuffing the hankie in his pocket?"

"Nothing. Except that you should be wearing it."

He waved me past. I proceeded to hunt for a window to crack. Behind me, Saucerhead's pals expressed doubts about me being the famous Garrett.

I was still looking for a window when I spied a plump brown rat. The critter took time out to stop and wink.

Once I jiggered a window, Melondie and her swarm wobbled inside and fluttered around, finding places to hide. Nobody noticed. Everybody focused on a screeching knock-down-drag-out about table setups. I shut the window, grabbed my bucket, went looking for the hostess and guest of honor.

I heard scurryings in the walls and floors and the hum of little wings overhead.

I glanced back. Somebody I didn't know was suffering through Saucerhead's checkpoint.

Maybe Tharpe did do me a favor. He never patted me down like that. Though if I wanted to sneak something in, I would've hidden it under a stack of docile baby cats.

Whitefield Hall had been slapped together with nothing but function in mind. It was mainly an open floor where you could dance, hold a banquet, have a grand meeting, put on a play, do anything you wanted to do without having to endure a lot of weather. Nowadays plays were the big thing.

Plays are a big thing around town, period. Drama is the latest fad.

The memorial commission also rented the hall for private functions. Like wedding receptions. Or birthday parties for underclass personalities who loom large in city life.

The floor had enjoyed loving care forever but remembered generations of feet shod in working-class shoes. The ceiling was twenty feet high. There were tilt windows up there so you could let the heat out in summer—or whenever there were too many bodies jammed into the hall. There was a stage at the end opposite the main entrance, facing it from a hundred feet away, three feet higher than the floor. Bickering workmen dragged tables in through a door to the left of the stage.

The two directing setup might have been chosen for their devotion to stereotype. Their wrists were limper than a dead octopus's arms. They bullied one another like a pair of harebrained girls. Still, there's hardly an adult male human today who isn't tough. Anybody over twenty-four had what it took to get through five years of wartime service with his ass still attached. Including this squawking brace of fancies.

The guys doing the actual work were the sort you don't offend gratuitously. They didn't have half a neck between them. If their shirts got ripped off by a freak wind, they'd show more body hair than cave bears. They probably had trouble recognizing their own names in print even if you gave them two weeks' head start.

Our hostess made her appearance through the doorway to the right of the stage, from the kitchen area. She wasn't dressed for the occasion. Yet.

"Garrett. You sweet man. You came early."

Strange. My eyes didn't roll up inside my head. I didn't drool. No gush of nonsense syllables erupted from my mouth. I didn't forget she was deadly and dangerous. Maybe I was immune. Finally.

Belinda Contague is a tall, slim woman in her mid-twenties, as beautiful as you can imagine a woman to be. Her hair, as ever, was absolute black, with sheen. Her skin she'd whitened whiter than ivory, I hoped with makeup rather than arsenic. Her eyes were so blue I suspected cosmetic sorcery. Her lips were the color of arterial blood. She has serious emotional problems.

And all this before she put herself together for the evening.

"I had to be early. I heard there'll be some unsavory characters showing up. Have you lost weight?"

"You noticed. You are a good man. Yes. A few pounds."

Too many pounds, I thought. She was gaunt. Another indication of internal problems?

She was in a positive mood. That's always good.

She said, "I need to get Keron and Arnot focused on their work. They shouldn't bring personal problems with them." She gave me a peck on the cheek. It was one of her specials. It told me she'd gladly put it somewhere else. "Then I'll have the technical staff try to turn me into something presentable."

"You're a step or two beyond that already."

"Hardly. Wait till you see. You won't be able to resist."

"Go. Do what you need to do. And don't blame yourself if you find out that I've turned into an old man."

"Why do you have a pail of kittens? Are they dead? I guess not. One just winked at me."

"You know Dean. He took in a litter. I brought them because I had this crazy notion somebody might want one." A mad idea, indeed. Most people looking for free cats are furriers, violin makers, or those guys who turn up at the edge of crowds, selling pigs in a blanket and other theoretically meat-based products of mysterious provenance.

Belinda shrugged, then set sail toward the two men trying to set up according to two different plans.

The squabbling ceased instantly, and was heard no more. The two clowns turned almost as pale as Belinda herself.

You could look her in the eye and know, absolutely, that you were nose to nose with swift, remorseless death. There would be no appeals, no continuances, no stays, no reprieves, no commutations, no mercy. This death no more cared for your soul or emotions than it did for those of a roach.

Chodo had had that knack, too. But he'd indulged in random acts of commutation. All of which had worked out in the long run.

Where *was* the old man?

Melondie Kadare dropped onto my shoulder. "You're a real bright candle, aren't you?"

"What did I do now?"

"You shut the window after you let us in. We need to come and go. Unless you're figuring on getting reports from the rat king through divine inspiration."

"Oh. Yeah." I hadn't thought that part through. But I'm not used to deploying a special-needs entourage. "I'll fix it. Have you seen an old man in a fancy wheelchair, looks like he might be dead?"

"No. The rats might have. They're all over. Ask John Stretch."

"I can take a hint."

"Really? Amaze me."

Is that a female thing? A youth thing? Or am I just a lightning rod for cynicism and sarcasm?

I cracked the same window a few inches, then roamed around trying to spot villainy before it happened. And looked for Chodo. I wanted to see what Belinda planned to roll out.

Melondie Kadare buzzed up behind my right ear. "When are you going to open that window, ace?"

"I just did, bug. You were there. You saw me."

"Oh. Yeah. I did, didn't I? Well, it ain't open no more, stud. And Aliki Nadkarni wants in."

She was right. Some moron had closed the window.
I opened it, then headed for the kitchen.

I didn't get there. Melondie brought her henchwom-
an's report about what John Stretch had heard from
his rats. Wouldn't it be grand to leave out the middle-
pixies and middleratfolk? Where could I get a fast
lesson in conversational rat?

The information was good, considering. It gave me
a fair idea of the layout, including more than I wanted
to know about odors in the basements and under the
building where there were no basements.

I learned where Chodo was stashed. A dark pie
pantry, halfway underground. Like an idiot cousin
who had to be kept out of sight so he wouldn't embarrass the family.

Nobody paid attention to anyone who was inside
already. You must be all right. You'd been checked
out. I could go anywhere I wanted.

Melondie Kadare caught up as I headed for Chodo's
hiding place. "That window is closed again, Big Boy.
You want to do something about that? Like jamming
it in its frame?"

I set my pail of cats down. "You guys wait here."
Like I thought they'd stay put. Just because their behavior had been exemplary. From the human point
of view.

Hello, Garrett. The relationship between cats and
people has just one dimension: the value to the cat, at
a given moment, of a handy set of opposable thumbs.

I opened the window, stood back, waited. Pixies
zipped in and out. Rats slunk along the base of the
wall. Or rattled around inside it. No one else noticed.

One of the setup queens came by, spotted the window. "Darn it! Who keeps opening this thing?"

"I do. And I'm not in a charitable mood. Next time
I find it closed I'll throw somebody through it. You
get the picture?"

The young man looked willing to fight. Briefly. "It's
too darned cold. . . ." His belligerence faded. I'd been
about to recommend a place he could go if he wanted

to warm up. But the window suddenly wasn't worth a fight.

A kitten mewed and started climbing my pants.

Even when they're little their claws are sharp. "What're you doing? Hell. I guess the honeymoon is over."

My bucket had sprung a leak. Baby cats were everywhere. Thirty or forty of them, it looked like. I steeled myself for a blowup.

It didn't come. Nobody seemed upset. They *were* weird cats. They never made anybody jump or stumble.

The skinny gink with the window fetish went back to his tables. Still without feuding with his partner.

13

I went back to hunting the man whose birthday was the excuse for the gathering.

I stole a candle, lit it, slipped into the pie pantry. There he was, slumped in a wheelchair, looking two decades older. "These aren't the best circumstances," I told him. There was barely room for all of us and the wheelchair. "But I promised Harvester Temisk that I'd do what I could. That guy is your best friend." Near as I could tell. A few years in my racket will leave a saint cynical about the motives of nuns. Too many people don't have a pimple of conscience to slow them down.

Chodo did not move, twitch, or demonstrate any awareness of my presence.

A kitten did meow nearby. I took that to be a good omen. But there was a scurry as a rat took an opposing view.

"I wish there was a way to tell if your mind is alive in there. But I can't get you away someplace where we could work on it."

Speaking of out, there my candle went.

I headed over where there was enough light to see while I relit the candle. Somebody hustled past, duck waddling with a huge pot.

"Smells good," I told him.

He clomped onward, dead silent. I don't think he agreed.

There was a lot of new racket as the catering crew arrived. I wouldn't have much more time with Chodo.

I ducked back into the pie pantry. "You didn't sneak away when you had the chance." Chodo hadn't done anything but breathe. Which was good. Real good. Because, all of a sudden, I had an awful spooky feeling.

Something wasn't right. And I didn't know how to make sense of it. Or figure out what it was.

I dropped to my knees so I could look Chodo in the eyes. They were open. They blinked. But they weren't seeing anything. They weren't blinking out messages. I told him to blink once for yes and twice for no, then asked questions. He blinked yes at random.

Was his brain alive at all? Temisk thought so, but I saw no evidence here. If I had him stashed somewhere safe, I could study and experiment on him. Or I could take him home and put him in with the Dead Man. Old Bones would wake up someday.

Yelling broke out not far off. Time to get back on the job. One last experiment, though. To see if he felt anything. "Nothing personal here, Chief." I touched the candle flame to the outside of his left wrist.

The pie pantry filled up with burned-hair smell.

Chodo did nothing. I could've roasted him whole if I wanted.

Voices were almost close enough to be understood.

The candle went out. *Snap!* That sudden, without a breath of air in motion.

A shriek came from the kitchen.

"Got to go, Boss."

Burned-hair and burned-meat smells hit me. In the scullery I found people standing around a smoldering rat. But the screaming came from the kitchen proper. Voices yelled the sort of things people do in an emergency where nobody knows what should be done, but everybody wants somebody to do something.

The burned-flesh smell was stronger there. I heard a crackle like bacon frying.

Water flew through the air. A slim tide washed my toes, then receded. The crackle of bacon lost its zeal.

People made unhappy noises. I recognized some as part-time kitchen help of Morley's. "Out of the way!" I barked. "If you're not doing something useful, change your luck by getting the hell out of the way."

I got through. Somebody calmer than most had rolled a heavy woman in wet tablecloths. A couple guys kept dousing her with water. She kept screaming. She was on fire under those wraps, somehow. The bacon sizzle was all her. Buckets of water rapidly slowed that down.

Morley appeared. "What's happening?"

I shook my head and shrugged, then nudged a couple men who were supposed to be setting tables. "Hoist her into the tub where the beer kegs are cooling. After the kegs are out."

That bacon crackle was coming back.

The woman never stopped screaming.

She went into the ice bath as Belinda Contague arrived. The woman went silent as the fire finally died. She would hurt for a long time, though, if she was burned as badly as I suspected.

Belinda eased close. "What happened?"

"I don't know. It started before I got here. Looks like she caught on fire somehow." I raised my voice. "Anybody see how this started?"

"People don't catch on fire, Garrett." She didn't sound convinced, though.

"Check her out. Tell me I'm wrong." They lifted the woman out of the ice bath. She was unconscious. The crackling didn't start up again.

A short man in an apron, with nervous hands, told us, "I was here first. Because she started yelling. She was beating on herself. I thought she'd caught her clothes on fire. I wrapped the wet tablecloths around her."

Naturally. No witnesses to how it started. The stoves? It was a kitchen setting up to serve a banquet.

"Belinda, you got a healer laid on? She'll need a shit-load of help."

The Contagues' underworld reign is characterized by care for its foot soldiers. Those who keep faith find the Boss looking out for them in the crunch. Chodo understood two-way loyalty instinctively. He took care of his people and they took care of him. Belinda stuck to the precedent.

She told me, "I'll have her cared for. What was that?"

"What was what?"

"I thought I saw a rat."

"You're in the city now. They haven't caused any trouble."

Belinda kept toward the pie pantry. She wanted to check on her father, but she didn't want to be seen doing it.

She eased away. I paid no attention. The burned woman was being stripped. A challenge. Bits of clothing had become embedded in her flesh. The burned fabric seemed to have acted as wicks for burning off body fat.

Weird. Creepy. Yet the physical evidence couldn't be denied.

A couple kittens seemed extremely interested in the burned woman. They kept darting out to sniff her and touch her with their paws.

Belinda was back. "What do you want to happen here?" I asked. She looked mad enough to chew rocks.

"Get her over to the Bledsoe? Find out her family situation? I don't know. Why do I have to worry about this stuff?"

"Because it's your party. Because you're in charge. Because you're the one who's going to get blamed."

Belinda indulged in a bout of creative linguistics, then demanded, "Why doesn't somebody do something about the rats?"

14

I went back to the main hall. Progress had been made. A couple dozen thugs had accumulated on the safe side of Saucerhead Tharpe. The little fellows had them help set tables.

My window remained cracked. I went to it. In moments I had a pixie woman ornamenting my shoulder. "What news, Melondie?"

"There's something going on, for sure. Your vampire woman may not be the worst schemer."

"Oh?"

"That's from Singe. She heard it from John Stretch. Who got it from his rats. That's a long chain full of feeble links."

"You're getting contemplative."

"I'm getting worried. Everybody thinks some people might not survive the celebration."

"Really?"

"Would I make this stuff up?"

"When Belinda's father took charge he held a do so the differences between neighborhood bosses could be settled. They were. He got rid of underbosses who might cause trouble later. By bashing their heads in with a centaur tribal mace."

A minor numbers man called Squint Vrolet approached me. "Who you talking to, Garrett?" He wore the perpetually suspicious expression of a man too dim to grasp the whole picture—though he did manage the numbers on his patch honestly and well.

He had the territory from his cousin Green Bean Rac-tic. Green Bean killed two birds with one rockhead. He found a relative a job and he put the patch in the hands of a guy who didn't have imagination enough to skim.

Squint Vrolet didn't even have imagination enough to take advantage of the fact that he was a known gangster.

"I talk to myself, Squint. Because I know somebody who cares is listening."

Squint squinted. It was his signature move. "That's right. You don't got that frickin' parrot no more? Them elves done conned you out of him."

"Somebody ran a con on somebody, Squint. So what's your take on tonight? Is it true, Chodo's gonna retire and leave everything to his kid?"

Squint gawked. "I never heard that. Hey! Great to see you, G. But I got to go see a man about a dog." He headed straight for his cousin Green Bean instead of the garderobes, though.

Melondie Kadare told me, "That was mean, Garrett."

"When he comes to double-check if he heard right, I'll twist it around."

"Why torment him?"

"I'm not. I'm messing with Green Bean. He'll be sure Squint heard something important but got it twisted between his ears and his mouth."

"That's still cruel."

"Don't you do that to me?"

"No."

"You sure?"

"Sure, I'm sure. I can think of more amusing ways to mess with you. One of your sweeties drops by. Say, Tinnie Tate. I slide in and whisper some other honey's name in the redhead's ear at just the right time. . . ."

"That don't sound like fun."

"Not for you. I'd laugh till I puked and my wings fell off. Tinnie's too good for you, anyway. . . . Whoa!

Peace! Just teasing. You'd better mingle. So that something unexpected doesn't happen."

"You might think about getting in the psychic racket."

Belinda turned. She'd changed clothes again, to something more businesslike. "I sent that woman to the Bledsoe. Under my name. Would you check on her tomorrow? Make sure they're really treating her?"

"Sure." So she expected me to have a tomorrow. Good to know.

"What do you think happened?" she asked.

"I don't. I've never seen anything like it."

"You think there's something strange going on?"

"Is that a trick question?"

"Garrett, don't do that. I'm not in the mood. I feel this getting out of hand before it even starts."

"All right, yes. There's something strange going on. I just figured you were behind it."

"There're rats everywhere. There weren't any when I looked at the place. And there's your kittens. Cute and friendly buggers, but still cats. You shouldn't have brought them. And, I swear, I even saw pixies from the corner of my eye. Only they weren't there when I looked."

That was the essence of pixie. Delivering more annoyance than a gaggle of mosquitoes.

"Watch my back, Garrett."

"I always do."

"Why?"

"Because it's a lovely back."

"You're full of shit. But I like it. I think."

Moments later, Melondie Kadare sneered, "It's such a lovely back? Could you be any more lame?"

"I wasn't at my best. I was distracted. I had a big-ass bug buzzing in my ear. And a lovely back to contemplate."

Miss Kadare bit me on the aforementioned ear. "You're lucky I'm not your size."

15

The celebration got started. It rolled along just fine. Night fell. Morley's waitstaff fired the floating wicks of globular little oil lamps at each place at table. They poured wine, TunFaire Gold, the best rotted grape juice in the world. The bad guys settled themselves and sucked it down. They got happier by the minute. The majority seemed amazed to find themselves having a good time. But whenever somebody cracked a dirty punch line the astonishment went away for a minute.

I was surprised by the number of guests. Not only the underbosses and their lieutenants had shown, but so had Squint Vrolet, Spider Webb, and dozens of other foot soldiers of little consequence.

No matter. Everyone seemed pleased to honor their empress. The fun grew more exuberant without growing rowdier. Louder without getting physical. Food came. More wine flowed. And a whole orchestra of alarm horns hooted and tooted in the paranoid cellars of my mind.

Of the gathering I was alone in not swilling wine. I have no taste for spoiled grape. I'm a beer, ale, mead, and stout man. Though the stout brewers tend to shovel in too much mud.

A baffled Morley Dotes observed from the door of the passage to the kitchen. More drink than food was coming out now.

Would tonight turn out like evenings in the old-time valhalls, where the thane's men drank themselves unconscious and collapsed on the straw-strewn floors? In their own puke. Among the household livestock and table waste.

No straw here. Darn.

Up front, Saucerhead and his crew had scorned the demon grape, too.

My rat and pixie friends did not immediately fall under the influence, either, though not for lack of trying. I heard Melondie Kadare bitching because the biggies were tracking every ounce of TunFaire Gold. The cheap-ass bastards.

I left my table and drifted over to Morley. "What do you think, old buddy?"

Dotes murmured, "If you know anything, you're two legs up on me. It's like one of those temples where they smoke and drink to get closer to God."

"Yeah. They'll bring out the accordions any minute. Meantime, what the hell is happening?"

"All I know is, I had to send out for more wine. Look at them. They're completely messed up."

"So the bloodshed we imagined don't look like it's going to happen. How are we fixed for Relway alerts?"

This gathering would be a wet dream come true for Relway's crowd. So how come they weren't all over outside?

"Don't worry about them," Morley said. "Worry about what Belinda still has in her trick sack. All this happy might be part of her scheme."

Our hostess was being kittenishly cheerful with the top goombahs—with a kitten in her lap. But . . . "She hasn't been drinking." I nudged a cat away from my foot. "That's a new shoe, hair ball." Then, "Think she put something in the wine?"

"No. I bought it. From vendors she wouldn't know. It isn't the wine. If it was that, they'd be cutting each other's throats."

Right. No one was immune, drinking or not. "It's in the air. The wine just makes it worse."

"Picture the possibilities if dancing girls came in."

"Put the old emperors to shame. Look. Even Belinda isn't immune."

Miss Contague loosed a blast of cackling laughter. She slapped Rory Sculdyte on the back. Rory bellowed his own hilarity.

Rory Sculdyte was the man most likely to treat Belinda to a dip in the river wearing iron swimwear. Rory knew in his secret heart that he had been cheated of his birthright when Chodo took over.

I told Morley, "You better get back to work.'Cause here she comes." Morley did. And Belinda did. I told her, "You need to laugh more, woman. You're more attractive when you laugh."

"And when I don't?"

"You're still attractive, he admitted reluctantly because it blunted his point."

"Tell me something, old friend. Why am I having fun?"

"If I knew, I'd get my business partners to come bottle it."

"Seriously, Garrett."

"Seriously, Contague. Maybe somebody put wormwood in the wine casks. You saying it's not your fault? Not part of your evil master plan?"

"I'll take credit. But I didn't plan it. No. You know I expected tonight to turn darker. But I can't go through with it now."

"Then get on with the business with your father. Save the bad-girl stuff for when I'm on the other side of town. Work some magic here so you don't have to do the bad-girl stuff."

"What have you been smoking?"

"I don't do that. I can dream, can't I?"

"Not now. Now I need you wide-awake and alert. I'm going to bring Dad out."

Melondie Kadare p
rial navigation was
Gold, Bug?"

"Just a little. They're
this was supposed to turn

"Everybody did. What's t

"There's a situation shaping up outside. Those ugly
men who tried to break into our house are prowling
around, looking for trouble."

"They're here?" Too many puzzles for one night.

"Yup."

"Why would they want to get into it with this
bunch?"

"Garrett, none of them look smart enough to put
on a hat when it rains. They don't know what's going
on here. They don't care. They might not care if they
did know." Then she confided, "I think they're after
that girlie boy. That Penny. She was skulking around
out there, too. Maybe they followed her."

"Did they?"

"We maybe haven't been paying enough attention.
Blair and Russ figured out how to get some wine."

"The rats aren't drinking, too, are they?"

"I don't know about the little ones. The big ones
got a taste or two."

I wanted to bark and howl and go spank Singe.
Instead, I said, "Melondie, slide back out there and
keep an eye out. I'll send help if I can."

p the window well

ere now enjoying their
ie party. I went to visit.

ere you come in one of your

ie guys in green pants outside, looking
The drivers might not be able to handle
es."

lank-shank sack a camel snot . . ."

eft too soon to appreciate Tharpe's full list of my
rrible shortcomings. I know what they are, anyway.
Tinnie keeps me posted.

I got back to my table just as the guest of honor
came out.

Belinda had gotten Chodo looking presentable. He
appeared to be asleep in his chair, not incapacitated.

That impression lasted only briefly.

Silence filled Whitefield Hall. Although there had
been rumors, they'd been disregarded because the
Outfit retained its Contague edge. But here was proof
that Chodo Contague wasn't the Boss anymore.
Clearly, he hadn't been in charge for a long time.

A neatly arranged blanket covered his lap and legs.
His bony talons lay in his lap, right on left. His bare
forearms were purplish. His chin rested on his chest.
He drooled.

Hard men there were appalled and repelled.

Belinda said, "The guest of honor. My father.
Chodo Contague. Celebrating his sixtieth birthday.
Let's toast the man responsible for our prosperity."

The shock waned under the weight of wine and
good cheer. Some shill burst into song. Others picked
it up. A few wondered what this meant to the overall organization.

I caught snippets. Some saw this as a chance to
improve themselves. But they couldn't concentrate,
even though they kept talking about trying.

I was ten feet away when Chodo came to life, though only just barely. He raised his chin three inches, the effort herculean. His whole body shook. His gaze found me momentarily.

A kitten leaped desperately toward his lap.

The hall slammed into darkness. Then fire exploded as the decorative lamps shattered and spewed burning oil. People pounded their clothing, to kill the flames there. The air began to heat up.

So did panic.

The latter included Belinda, who ran blindly.

This definitely wasn't on her program.

I caught her, gripped her arm with one hand, and spun Chodo's chair with the other, headed them toward the kitchen. Everybody else rushed the front door.

Morley quickly sent his troops to fight the fires. He keeps a cool head however filthy the scat storm gets. When even queens of the underworld are losing control, Morley stands short, proud and calm.

A swarm of cats streamed past. Rats were in motion, too. Pixies zoomed around overhead.

The confusion eased in the kitchen. "You stay here," I told Belinda. "Where are your bodyguards?"

"Good question. I mean to ask."

"I'll find them." It was a puzzle, them vanishing. They should've surrounded Belinda the instant the excitement started.

The baby cats headed back into the big hall.

Belinda seized my arm, for one moment a scared little girl. Which is one way she manipulates me. Then the woman who ran the Outfit reemerged. She snagged a butcher knife. "Be careful."

"Watch out. Don't leave unless you have to. There's some kind of excitement going on outside." I followed my kitties.

Fires still pranced and murmured in a dozen places. Only the little blazes had been slain. The excitement up front had ended. A few bold fellows had turned back to help, though the effort looked hopeless. The remaining fires weren't going to let mere mortals push them around.

I found Belinda's bodyguards. They'd gone down where they were posted. They hadn't bailed on her at all. Two were smoldering and dead. One was just plain dead. Two more were smoldering but alive, unconscious, in desperate need of help.

I discovered several more goombahs in like condition, alive but unconscious. "Morley! Over here! Problems bigger than those fires." The goombahs were burning like that woman had. "How do we get them out?"

Dotes barked, "Theodore! Take Beans up front. See if you can't get some help in here." He bounced over beside me. "This is ugly, Garrett. Really ugly. Smells like sorcery." Thugs crackled and popped.

"I don't know. Grab his legs." We huffed and puffed and dragged a man out to the ice bath. I reminded Morley about my meeting with Harvester Temisk.

"It had something to do with all this?"

"Maybe. But I don't know where he'd fit. Cause or effect? Symptom or disease? On three. One. Two. Three."

Ice water splashed. A kitten protested getting its feet wet. It strutted off indignantly, shaking each paw as it came off the floor.

The cat led us back into the main hall, where it bounded into the pail I'd used to bring the litter aboard. That pail was full of cats already, all with paws on the rim, watching anxiously. I shouted, "Just find somebody who's breathing and get him out of here!"

Morley told me, "Grab your cats and go, Garrett. I'll get these guys out. Hell! This one is gone now. Sharps! Give me a hand with this."

Melondie Kadare appeared, wobbling worse than ever. "Help," she whimpered. "I'm too ripped. . . ."

"What're you doing back inside?"

She squeaked. "I need to get my people out."

"How many are in here? It's going up."

"What was I going to tell you? Shit. It's hard to think straight when you're fucked-up. Oh. Yeah. You need to get away from here. The Watch are coming. Because of the fighting."

"What fighting?"

"Outside . . . it went all to shit. I need to get out of here. But I'm ripped."

"Hang on to me, then."

Morley and his guys got out, carrying the last surviving bodyguard to the ice bath. I warned him, "Get going. Relway is coming."

Where had Relway been? Belinda would've arranged a diversion. Something blatantly political. Deal Relway loves racialists less than gangsters.

Me and my pail roared through the back door. It was every-man-for-himself time. The coaches were gone. The parking area retained nothing but a dusting of large, ugly men who were either unconscious or dead. They had no friends to help them get away.

Morley faded into the night with his men, disappointed because their efforts had been wasted. Both bodyguards had died in the ice bath.

I made like the good shepherd myself, wondering about a batch of baby cats who would get together so their staff could lug them out of danger more easily.

Melondie Kadare started snoring. Brutally. I tucked her into a chest pocket.

17

It didn't take long to realize that somebody was following me. Somebody either very good or blessed with a little magical assistance. I couldn't shake him, nor did I manage to ambush him.

Melondie Kadare kept on snoring.

The kittens didn't like delays. They got antsy when I tried to lie in wait. Then noisy when I fooled around too long.

"You guys getting hungry?"

It was quiet tonight, the weather good despite the season. A big old moon up top silhouetted bats zipping around above the rooftops. There was a nip in the air. Scatters of cottony cloud tumbled across the sky. I didn't think the bats would find many bugs. Winter wasn't far away.

Melondie groaned and whimpered. "It's your own fault, Bug." In the distance, Whitefield Hall cast a cheery glow. The pixie crawled out of my pocket. She tried her wings. I caught her before she crashed, tried to put her away again. She wasn't interested. She clung to my shoulder instead. But when I stopped to listen for footsteps she slithered inside my shirt. When you're small you lose body heat fast.

"Don't bounce around so much, Biggie. And keep them cats away."

The streets remained deserted, which was unusual. TunFaire goes round the clock. But I was content.

It's nice when no sense of dark imminence hangs in the air.

"Hey, Bug. We're almost home. And I've got an idea. How about you help me catch this spook that's dogging us."

"My head!" She groaned. "What you mean, us, Big'un?"

"All right. You. Because who the hell would be after me for a bucket of cats?"

"Smart-ass. All right. I'm listening. But keep your voice down. What's the plan?"

The plan was, I plunked my little friend on a ledge, out of sight, then headed on along. I took a right at the next cross street, took another right and then another, and soldiered on until there I was, plucking my shivering sidekick off her ledge.

"Did you have to stop for a beer?"

"Whiner. I would have, if I'd seen a place. It's past my time to start sipping. So, Bug. What's the evil word? What wicked dark lord off the Hill is dogging me through the alleys of the night?"

"You're so full of shit, Garrett. A blivit. Hell, the world's first hyperblivit. Forty pounds of shit jammed into a ten-pound sack instead of just twenty."

"But I'm so pretty. All the girls want to love me."

"If they're some kind of weird, like sky elves. Or ratgirls. Or troll jiggles so ugly they can't find themselves a guy who's rock hard."

"Unfair." No troll girl ever chased me. "You're upset because you're too teeny to enjoy the special Garrett charm." I wondered how trolls tell the girls from the boys.

"Sure you're not imagining things, Garrett? Because that's not what I hear."

"Ooh! How sharper than a frog's tooth. Come on, Mel. Who am I dragging along behind me? Before I need to scope out how to turn my last two hairs into the perfect comb-over."

"You're no fun anymore. All right. It was that

little girl-boy. Or boy-girl. The one who brought the cats."

"Penny Dreadful? That kid can bang around behind me, keeping up, and I can't catch her? That's hard to believe."

"I can believe that. You being you, with your appreciation of you. Face it. You don't have the mojo this time, Big Guy."

"I'm thinking about showing you some genuine Garrett mojo, Bug. I know some things. I know some people. I could have you bigasized."

"You couldn't handle it. You'd have a stroke or a heart attack."

And so it went. We headed south on Wizard's Reach, turned west on Macunado. And there we were, home again, home again, ziggity-zig. In time to get behind the door ahead of a band of do-gooder city employees who missed seeing us by half a minute.

They pounded on my door. I used the peephole but didn't open up. Melondie Kadare snickered and giggled. She was having a good time.

"Why don't you check on your people? I've got cats to feed."

She couldn't do that from inside. I'd been clever enough to make sure the pixies couldn't bring their special culture into my castle.

My bucket leaked cats fast. They bounded off toward the kitchen. I followed.

Singe and her brother were there, each with a beer in paw. The platter between could serve a party of forty. Singe asked, "Where have you been?"

"I had to work tonight. Then I had to walk home because my ride disappeared. Leaving me lugging a bucket of ungrateful meows while listening to the world's worst bitching pixie complain because she's too small to be my girlfriend."

Even John Stretch looked me askance then. Melondie produced a resounding raspberry and started wobbling around in search of something small enough to use as a beer mug.

Singe shook her head, too damned human. "You hungry?"

"Just like a rat. Everything comes down to food. I could use a sandwich. I didn't get a chance to eat at Chodo's party."

What a dumb failure. Nobody ought to be so focused on business that he forgets to eat free food.

The platter had a dozen fried cakes aboard. Dean delivered four more, still crackling from the hot oil. "The square ones are sweet. The round ones have sausage inside."

"Uhm?"

"An experiment. Looking for something different."

Pigs in a blanket weren't new at my house. But this wasn't a biscuit dough production.

Melondie gave up looking for a mug. She went to work on a square cake half as big as she was. The wee folk eat more than we do. Because of all that flying.

I tried a sausage cake. "Good," I said with my wet mouth full.

Dean scowled, not flattered, as he brought me a cold lager. He put down more food for the cats.

I asked, "Singe, you got any thoughts about tonight?"

"Not unless you want to hear your species belittled."

"Belittle away. If you have any useful observations."

"Useful, how? John Stretch and I went along and tried to help, but we do not understand what you hoped to accomplish. That may be because you were not clear on that yourself."

I need new people around me. My old crew knows me too well. "Dean. Any sign of life from His Nibs?" I could run what I had through the bone bag's multiple minds.

I'm not as dumb as I let on. Hard to be, some might say. There were at least two different things going on. Maybe three. All getting tangled up because of a common denominator named me.

Dean was not encouraging. "The thing remains inert. Sadly, it's still too early to dispose of the remains."

"Way too soon," Melondie Kadare piped. "There're a dozen sparks still burning inside that blubber pile."

"You can tell?" I asked. "You can read that sack of rotting meat?"

"I need a drink. And it better be something more substantial than this off-color lager. Something with a little kick."

"I'll give you a kick, Bug. Answer the question."

"Nope."

"Nope? Nope, what?"

"Nope, I can't read him, Biggie. Not the way you want. All I can do is tell he ain't gone. He might be thinking about going, though."

"Huh?" I dumped another mug down the hatch. Having started late, I had to hurry to catch up.

Another frosty mug settled in front of me. A dream come true. It was hailing beers. Dean earned himself a suspicious glare. There's always reason for caution when Dean caters.

He was up to something, hoping that getting me tanked would distract me from something or make me agreeable to something. Again.

John Stretch shipped an admirable quantity of beer in one big gulp. "It was an interesting evening."

Singe told me, "Find out what he found out right now, Garrett. He does not handle alcohol well."

So I focused on the big rat in the rodent underground and listened to what he had to say. Which didn't make much sense, since, evidently, regular rats mostly understand their surroundings in terms of sounds and odors.

Interesting.

Melondie had little to report. Except that she hadn't gotten much from her cohorts. Yet. She promised, over and over, to deliver the best from the rest after she sobered up.

Dean filled our mugs. He was smug. Things were

going his way. We all were concentrating on getting outside as much beer as possible. The four-legged, furry crew focused on filling feline bellies. Nobody asked him uncomfortable questions.

Full of sausage, bread, and milk, the kittens piled into their bucket and fell asleep in one warm, purring pile.

We talked till we could no longer understand one another. Dean excepted. Killjoy boy hit the sack as soon as he was done cooking.

18

The second morning was nothing like the first. I wakened in a foul temper, head pounding. Dean and I needed to share a word. Cutting costs is all very well, but not by buying cheap brew. Just so he could pocket a few extra coppers that, no doubt, he'd waste on food for cripples and orphans.

I was first downstairs. Except for Dean, of course. But Dean was out shopping. Or something. Because he'd left food on the table, around the suffering remnants of Melondie Kadare.

The John Stretch leftovers would be around the house somewhere, too.

The rain-on-your-parade boys from the city were on the job. They pounded the oak occasionally. It stubbornly refused to open. Eventually, they gave up.

The rules are odd. And Relway sticks to them like a limpet—if he suspects that you might be one of the good guys.

Those associated with the dark side increasingly show an alarming tendency to disappear. Alarming to the bad boys, that is.

People applaud that, saying nobody with a clear conscience needs to worry. Till Relway's troops show up because they've done something that, in their reasoned opinion, wasn't really a crime. Never mind what the law says.

Let's review:

1. Absolute power corrupts absolutely.
2. The road to Hell is paved with good intentions.
3. No good deed goes unpunished.

All applicable where Deal Relway is concerned.

Brother Relway has only the best interest of the people at heart.

I have trouble faulting the man. Sometimes. "He needed killing" is a valid argument before the bench. Director Relway seems able to meet the burden of proof when challenged.

I ate. Biscuits with honey. Biscuits with damson preserves. Leftover sausage from the previous night that the cats hadn't gotten.

The sweet buns with sausage inside aren't good cold.

Finished eating, I scooped Melondie and headed up front to hand her over to her own people.

Through abiding and ancient habit, I used the peephole.

There were people out there. Big, ugly, hairy people. Only one wore green pants. The rest were incognito. Every man jack came equipped with bandages. One had an arm in a sling. Another had a leg in splints. He and a third were getting around on multiple crutches. None of them seemed to have concluded that bothering me was not a good idea.

Penny Dreadful's friends. What had become of her? She'd faded like a wisp of steam once Melondie identified her.

The Ugly Pants Gang had to be in an even bleaker mood than I was. Considering the state they'd been in when last seen, I assumed they would be grumpy.

Trust sweet old Garrett to get stricken paranoid. Why would this crew be on my doorstep?

I shrugged. Not a worry. I had a ton of food laid in. I had a backup keg of beer. Dean had a platoon of homely nieces he could stay with during a siege. If he was smart enough to spot the watchers and stay away.

Meantime, I could do some speculating. Why was I involved in this? And I could figure out some way to waken the Dead Man.

I went back to the kitchen, made tea, took a mug into my office. Eleanor wore a sneer of disdain. "So you're in a mood this morning, too." Which only squeezed more juice out of the lemon.

Somebody pounded on my door. I didn't go see who. I was comfortable with my brooding and Eleanor's dreary mood.

I shunted from puzzle to puzzle, free-associating. The medicine I'd added to the tea quieted the worst pounding inside my head. What really happened at Whitefield Hall?

"Meow."

A cat climbed my leg. A second bounced into the client's chair. Two or three more chased each other around the room, then back into the hall. I scratched and petted the one in my lap, then hoisted him and gave him the full eyeball bath.

He was just a baby cat. Though chunkier than most. Maybe his daddy was a bobcat.

"What's so special about you, little guy? How come the world's ugliest fashion retards are out to get you?" But were they? That deserved reflection, too.

He didn't answer. Flat refused to solve any puzzles for me. The people—and critters—you have to deal with in this racket. Ugh.

"Eleanor. What do you think? Is it all about the cats? Or the bucket they came in?"

Eleanor didn't say. I felt her worrying about me being slow to grasp the obvious.

The drill instructors and senior sergeants figured me out quick in the Corps. They'd already seen every get-around and get-out-of-it scam ever invented a long time before I turned up making like I was dumber than a bushel of rocks. But I can work that on most people here in TunFaire. People in this burg see what they want to see.

I strive to remain underestimated.

Or so I tell myself.

"This feels good," I told Eleanor. "I could just lean back with a lapful of cats and nap the afternoon away." Then I'd go out tonight because I couldn't sleep. Somebody would tell Tinnie Tate, who thinks she has a claim on me. And does. And *vice versa.* But I've got the worst case of Retarded Commitment Capacity Syndrome west of Morley Dotes. Morley being of international-competitor status.

Eleanor's disapproval pattered down like an iron rain. I needed to do three things. See Harvester Temisk. Visit the Bledsoe. And catch Penny Dreadful. While dodging Relway thugs and large men in hideous pants.

It sounded like the sappers had brought up a battering ram. The door remained stubborn.

I might be betting to an inside straight, but I couldn't see Relway not responding if the Ugly Pants Gang stuck around long.

His top men would be out there keeping an eye on my place.

"I'm going to try to get Old Bones to bestir himself. Again."

Eleanor's attitude was suitably discouraging.

"If I have to, I'll fill his room up with cranky old women."

The Dead Man doesn't have much use for the obstinate sex. And he's never been pleased that my attitude is the opposite.

He's been dead for four hundred years. He's forgotten all the good stuff.

Old Bones did exactly what I expected. A whole lot of nothing.

The assault on my front door faded briefly, resumed as a new villain laid on.

My pixies ran out of tolerance. A flurry of anger

heralded a whir of little wings. It sounded like a full
cluster launch.

I sighed, lit a new bug candle, proceeded to commence to begin out there on my front stoop.

Muttering like one of those scramble brains who
bustle through the streets on grave, unimaginable mis-
sions, debating it all with themselves, I went to the
peephole. Outside, chaos celebrated the spontaneous
self-creation of the deities of disorder of the thousand
pantheons that afflict TunFaire.

Pixies, pixies everywhere, pestering biggies without
prejudice.

Relway's Runners and their fellow travelers had arrived but were waiting to see what developed.

I offered no evidence that my place was anything
but deserted. The Watch knew better, but wouldn't
press the issue.

Only the Green Pants Gang were dim enough to
keep on keeping on. They *had* to be clueless about
the Dead Man.

I snickered at the prancing big guys as the pixies
pestered them. Like a dance number in a musical play
about an army field hospital.

I spotted Dean. The old boy did have sense enough
to stand back.

I spied Penny Dreadful, too, across the street, to the
left of and behind Dean. She couldn't be seen by the
big guys unless the one at my door turned and looked
for her. She did well at being just another gawker.

The pixies pricked the big guys enough with their
poisoned blades. They began slowing down. They just
couldn't get a handle on the fact that people might
keep them from doing whatever they wanted. Ymber
must be a strange town.

Whistles shrieked.

The Watch moved in.

They couldn't wait anymore. My neighbors were
getting restless. The Watch couldn't let the situation
deteriorate till witnesses began damaging city property. The property in question being the street itself.

When a TunFairen crowd gets rowdy it rips up cobblestones for ammunition. A grand brawl can strip an entire neighborhood of its pavements.

Relway's boys didn't have much trouble with the groggy bad guys.

The villains seemed less numerous when they were laid out like logs ready to be floated off to the mill. There were just four of them.

Some must have gotten away.

19

The next man to hammer on my door was an old acquaintance. And no surprise. Whenever anything interesting happens in my life, Colonel Westman Block turns up drooling official remarks.

I opened up. "You're half vulture, aren't you?" The door wouldn't swing all the way back. I scowled grimly at its mutilated face.

Block surprised me. "Bring out your dead."

"So what the hell is it now?" I grumbled. "Why'd Relway let those oversize morons go and sic them on me?"

"You're a pip, Garrett," the good colonel assured me. "But you won't be selling me a bucket of your bullshit this time."

"But it's the good stuff. The only kind I've got. If you want a better grade of poo . . ."

"Can it. You've been mostly straight with me. Meaning I still haven't caught you in a bald-faced lie. I will, someday. Meantime, I'll remain confident that you suffer a congenital inability to tell the whole truth."

"You want the truth? You can't—"

"Save your breath. Let's go in your office. I've been on my feet all day. While you're walking, make up a good story about why those thugs were trying to bust into your place."

"I don't know. This stuff just happens. It's like weather to me anymore."

"But have a notion or two, because you're never as dumb as you make out."

"I'm thinking maybe it's time I moved on. To somewhere where everybody don't think they know what's going on inside my head."

"Here's a thought, old friend. Take a barge upriver and set up shop in Ymber."

"I don't get it."

"Sure, you do. Those guys are all from Ymber."

Being the villain he thought I was, I volunteered nothing. "Uhm?"

"There are ten of the big, ugly, stupid creeps in green pants, plus two normal-looking management types who run things. We think. We now have nine thugs and one normal clown in custody. It could take time for Deal's specialists to make them explain themselves, though."

So. Relway hadn't turned anybody loose. He'd staked out my place so he could collect some more ugly pants.

Colonel Block's nondescript face presented an expectant expression.

I saw no reason not to be forthright with the one man able to control Deal Relway. "I'm not real clear on this mess. It's all Dean's fault. He brought home this bunch of kittens and the kid who had the cats. I didn't get a good look at him before he made tracks. Dean has a whole song and dance about priestesses and prophecies. You can squeeze the snot out of him when he turns up, if you want."

Block grunted.

We have that kind of relationship. Half inarticulate noise.

"You really don't have any idea? You've had part of the herd since yesterday."

"They haven't said much. Yet. They're too stupid to connect their silence with the pain they're exposed to."

"You've got one of the managers. Officer types don't usually stand up . . . oops."

Block glowered. Being an officer type.

"Oops again," I said. "I get so comfortable with you I forget you aren't one of my pals from down in the islands."

"Move to the country, Garrett. You could fertilize a whole county."

I shrugged. "It's the times we live in."

He wasn't buying what I was selling, even though I was giving it away.

"I don't get you, Colonel. I've always been straight with you. Ever since Prince Rupert made you the top guy at the Al-Khar. But you never believe me."

"Because you never tell the whole truth, only what you think I'll work out for myself."

"So where do we stand?" I asked. "You aren't half as dumb as you let on, either. You've got something on your mind."

"Of course I do. But it doesn't have much to do with those lunatics."

"I love how you work to make me glad I was born when I was, in this time and place, when life was never better."

"You might fertilize more than one county."

"Even so."

"Even so, I admit to a passing curiosity about what happened at Whitefield Hall last night."

"You and me both, brother. Somebody tried to burn the place down with me inside." I gave him a mildly edited story. Certain he knew the basics already. I left out unimportant details like pixies, rat-people, Chodo's health, and people catching fire. "You can ask all the questions you want. I don't know what it means. I don't know what was supposed to happen. I can't explain what did happen. Despite what you may have heard, I was there only in a professional capacity."

"Save the snow, Garrett. I'm just interested in what you picked up about the kingpin."

Dirty trick. For sure the man wasn't as dumb as he looked.

"I saw him one time, right before the fires started. He was in a wheelchair. He didn't look healthy. I didn't hear him say anything. Then the situation went all to hell. Bam! Lamps exploded. Burning oil flew everywhere. I ran like hell."

Block wasn't happy but had no grounds to challenge me. He would've been all over me if he had anything. "Was the fire an attempt to get Chodo?"

"I never thought of that. Let me think about it. Man, it'd have to be somebody who wouldn't care if he wiped out the whole Combine."

Westman Block will grab any angle to nab an advantage. He never reveals all he knows despite deploring the identical attitude on my part. He won't bore in hard. Giving you the benefit of the doubt. Meaning you can't ever forget that he's always handing you yards and yards of just enough rope.

"No. Chodo wasn't the target. Not even Relway would wholesale it that way. I do think the fires were started by sorcery. Or something."

"There's no obvious evidence. Experts checked." Block glared at Eleanor. "There any way I can buy that off you?"

"Eleanor? No. Why?"

"It's haunted. It gives me the creeps. I know a fireplace I'd like it to meet."

"Sir, you're disparaging my first love." Maybe he didn't know that story.

"Where is Chodo now?"

"I don't know. Wherever Belinda is, I imagine."

"Maybe. And maybe she lost track of him, too."

"What?" That couldn't be. That wouldn't be good. Especially not for Belinda.

But she wouldn't have rolled Chodo out if she hadn't been sure she had everything under control. Would she?

"You know where she might be?"

"At home?"

"She flew there if she is. She didn't leave town through the gates."

My subversive side urged me to keep him talking. He was letting slip facets of the Watch's capabilities, both to collect information and to move it. Meaning that Block and Relway had more manpower than was suspected. Which implied that . . .

Well, every implication suggests something else. This time the indicators pointed to a possible serious outbreak of law and order.

Which would stumble once it inconvenienced our more substantial royal subjects. Privilege means private law.

"You know everything I know, Colonel. Really. I don't have any interest to protect. Other than my poor front door."

"There are rumors about you and Belinda Contague."

"I've heard. She started them. They aren't true." I cocked my head, listening to a voice only I could hear. Like the Dead Man was giving me the razz without including Block. "Yeah. Good point. I've got stuff I need to do. Now that I can get out without being eaten by dragons. Dean! Good. You're home."

The old boy had come to the office door. He looked grumpy.

I said, "You need to get hold of the door guy. Those morons bent the hinges."

Dean scowled at Colonel Block, dragged his haul on toward the kitchen. He doesn't approve of Westman Block. Simply because Block exists in his peculiar professional niche he guarantees that there's mischief afoot. Dean would prefer a world where the law and order were fixed in place before he arrived.

Block said, "You're not going to help me."

"I gave you everything I've got. Including the news that I don't have any reason to hold out on you. What more do you want?"

"I hope that's true." He headed for the front door. I followed. He said, "You're a likable guy, Garrett. I don't want you to get in so deep we can't save your ass when the big changes come."

"Say what?"

"The wild era is about over, Garrett. We've worked hard to do what Prince Rupert wants done. The rule of law is about to dawn."

I had no idea what that was about. It sounded scary.

I'm a law-and-order guy myself. But I don't want the people involved interfering in *my* life.

I did say, "You're too optimistic. How bleak a season would it be if your hard-liner secret backers get everything they want?"

Block beamed. "Wouldn't that be marvelous?"

He didn't get it. And never would. People like him make life inconvenient for the rest of us.

"You'll let me know what you find out from those guys, won't you?"

"You don't make me want to do you a lot of favors."

"My heart is breaking. Here's something I really do want to know. How come those idiots wear those stupid green pants?"

Block chuckled as he slipped outside.

I closed. The door shut easily enough. Fortress Garrett remained sound and inviolate.

20

I checked Dead Man. He wasn't stirring. I told Dean, "I'm going out. I've got stuff to do." I mapped a route in my head. Morley's place, Temisk's office, then the Bledsoe to check on the burned woman.

"You have your stick?"

"What?" His asking startled me.

"Shouldn't you be ready for the worst? Considering recent events?"

I gawked. That was out of character. But he was right. And didn't know the half. A lot of bad guys saw me at Whitefield Hall. Some would believe I was hooked up with Belinda.

I loaded up on self-defense devices, a few enthusiastically disapproved by the city Watch.

The boys at The Palms weren't pleased to see me, but they didn't haul out any cleavers. For a wonder, though, I caught Morley working for the second day in a row.

"What's going on?" I asked Puddle. "What's his problem?"

Puddle's face exploded in a big old ugly, broken-tooth grin. "He's down here getting in da way. He don't got to be upstairs."

I raised an eyebrow.

"One a dem silver-elf womens is here."

I chuckled an evil chuckle. "It took me a long

time. . . . Hey, buddy! I came to see what you think about last night."

Morley pulled up a chair. "Sit. Puddle, tell Skif we want a pot of tea. The real stuff. My friend doesn't like weed leaves."

"You don't really drink herb tea, do you?"

"I serve it. You give the marks what they want. I've heard a rumor, says you've already had some excitement today."

"A double dose. Some Green Pants guys tried to break in. Then Block showed up, wanting to know all about everybody's business."

"And you told him?"

"The truth, the whole truth, and nothing but the truth. I don't know nothing about nothing. He mostly wanted to know what happened to Belinda and Chodo after the party. He didn't care about the fires, the riot, or the dead men."

"Belinda better take care of Chodo. We're picking up storm warnings. Some of the underbosses are getting ambitious."

"Rory Sculdyte?"

"Teacher White, too."

That wasn't good. Though they do tend to kill only each other. Which Relway would encourage wherever he could. "Figures. They got out alive."

"You said the Green Pants Gang hit your place again?"

"Yes." Stupid me, I'd been too excited about being able to get out. I hadn't gotten the promised reports from John Stretch and Melondie Kadare. "Block's gang has them. He claims he has all but two locked up now. One of those two is following me right now."

"We can take care of that."

"You might want to be better prepared than yesterday."

"Same guy?"

"I think so."

"Not to worry. Help is on its way. About last night. What happened?"

"You were there."

"I was kitchen help, Garrett. I didn't see anything."

"You saw as much as I did. Probably more. You had a whole crew in there and none of them were blind."

"I'm sure it was your fault everything turned weird. Weird things happen when you're around."

"Only because of my unfortunate taste in friends."

"You're a misfortune for anyone who gets close to you. What's the thing with Block and Chodo?"

I explained.

He said, "There was a lot of confusion. Somebody might've grabbed Chodo. But you would've heard about that from Belinda. She'd want Daddy Garrett to save her again."

"Maybe."

"Want some advice, Garrett? Stay away from Belinda. No telling how hairy it might get, but she isn't likely to be the winner."

I drank the tea Skif brought. "They'll be that knee-jerk?"

Of course they would. The Outfit includes the most old-fashioned people alive. They don't want a girl running the show.

I mused, "I wonder, though. Last night fell apart on Belinda, but it didn't go the way anybody else expected, either. She's no dummy. And she's got a big head start."

"She remains, still, just a woman."

"I'm telling you, don't underestimate her. Especially if you suddenly notice yourself between her and somebody giving her a hard time."

He nodded. I doubt that he meant it. He asked, "Where are you headed from here?"

"Harvester Temisk's place. Then the Bledsoe."

"You can stand that place?"

"I don't hold any grudges."

"I mean, it's the antechamber of one of your most pedestrian human hells. I get the wet-spine creeps just thinking about it. Let alone getting close enough to smell it."

I held my tongue. TunFaire's poor depend entirely on that nightmare establishment for what little medical attention they receive.

"I know what you're thinking, Garrett. And I don't care. You know perfectly well where the road paved with good intentions leads."

21

I was being followed. As I'd reported. But now I had an entourage. The guy in the green pants was only the closest and most obvious tagalong. And the least skilled or most naive. He seemed to think I wouldn't notice him. He didn't notice the parade behind him. Which, at first, I thought was Morley's crew.

Using a few tricks meant to look like accidents, I decided I was wrong. One was a man who worked for Relway. And Spider Webb, an enforcer for Teacher White, who was a small-time renaissance crook Chodo never liked but who'd always avoided giving offense enough to get his run canceled.

Why would Webb and Teacher be interested in me? White wasn't big enough to try for Chodo's spot.

Were my fans aware of one another?

They all knew about Ugly Pants. Webb didn't seem to notice Relway's people, maybe because half a dozen were taking turns.

I decided to forget Harvester Temisk. I angled off toward the Bledsoe. I took a stroll through a tight neighborhood, turned a few corners quickly, ducked into a church. I scampered up into its bell tower. That gave me a view of the developing confusion.

Morley did have men out, including himself. They laid way back, observing. Morley eyed the belfry as soon as he knew that I'd disappeared.

The Watch had a less relaxed attitude. Their immediate response was to arrest Spider Webb and Ugly

Pants. Spider surrendered meekly. He knew you don't mess with Relway's Runners.

When I left the church there were six people dead or crippled. Ugly Pants had developed a bad case of being the former. I was glad I didn't like green. The secret police was about to make green pants a lethal stylistic faux pas. Meantime, Spider would be back on the street before dark. He'd helped them drop the moron in the ugly trousers.

I'd just hove in sight of the Bledsoe when Morley fell into step beside me. "Any theories?" he asked.

"Other than that Ymber breeds them strong but stupid?"

"That was a dirty trick, back there."

"I learned from a master."

"Conscience not bothering you?"

I looked inward. "You know, it isn't."

"You sound surprised."

"I am."

"You've turned into one of the boss class since you got involved in that manufactory business."

"What're you talking about?"

"Some other time. I have a new venture, too. It'll be a place where crackpots can spout whatever nonsense infests their pointy heads."

"We have a place for that. The Chancellery steps."

"Not anymore. Relway is moving them out. Nobody was making any money off it, apparently."

"Sure, there was. The sausage guys. The rat-on-a-stick guys. The tempura tarantula guy."

"Who bought those?"

"I don't know. Somebody. Or he wouldn't be out there every day. Yuck!"

That wasn't a comment on deep-fried spider. We were close enough to the Bledsoe to hear and smell the place.

It's a hell in brick. Those who deliver themselves to the hospital's mercy are, generally, thoroughly desperate. Meaning parts may be falling off already. The stenches of disease, rotting flesh, and deep despair lie heavy on the whole area. The neighbors pray for foul weather to wash and blow the stink away.

The sound was the choir of madness singing in the insane wards—lair of the Bledsoe's deepest and most abiding horrors.

Those wards do help finance the hospital. For a few coppers you can tour them. For an extra copper you can rent a stick to torment the mad folk. You can even rent the most dramatic loons for home entertainment.

Money. That's why.

Money and the complete indifference of ninety percent of the population. That's why.

The Bledsoe is a charity hospital. Its main support comes from the family that provided emperors to the Empire before the kings of Karenta replaced them. The Empire survives in the imaginations of that one family, so there are still emperors around. But nobody cares. Other than the directors of the Bledsoe, who depend on the imperial family for the donations they steal.

The Bledsoe is the most corrupt institution in Tun-Faire. We'll see truly interesting, entertaining times if Director Relway ever goes after the parasites there.

"What the hell is going on?" I asked, stopping to stare once I got a clear look at the hospital. Its face was covered by scaffolding. Masons, hod carriers, and other workmen bustled around cleaning and restoring the facade. Though there weren't many of them.

"You know, I don't know," Morley said. "This is new to me, too."

Repairs were decades overdue. How come the money for this hadn't gotten stolen? I had no trouble imagining somebody donating enough to renovate the place. But I couldn't believe that its directors would use the money for its intended purpose. "We need to look into this."

"Why?"

"Uh . . ." He had a point. This wasn't a battle that needed Garrett galloping in in rusty, secondhand armor. Garrett was here to look dark and dangerous and make sure a client of Belinda's got the sort of treatment the Bledsoe can provide when its staff wants to bother. "You're right. One thing at a time. I'll do what I came to do. Relway will get to this place someday."

"I'll just stroll along with you. I'm curious about the construction."

He did sound curious. Like a gangster wondering how anybody would be doing something without getting his permission first.

A large man without a hair on his head had a notion not to let us in. I'd never run into guards before. Morley asked, "You're kidding, right? You don't really want to be the next patient here, do you?"

My guess is, the bald guy recognized Morley. He got out of the way.

Next obstacle, an admissions clerk. Who was no challenge at all.

The clerk was a volunteer. Of the female persuasion. Ellie Jacques. Meaning it took Morley about thirty-seven seconds to have her ready to jump her counter and devour him. She gave up the whereabouts of the burned woman immediately. The patient was Buy Claxton. She *was* getting the *best* care the Bledsoe could deliver. With Morley making eyes Ellie admitted Mrs. Claxton was getting the best because the doctors knew the Contague name.

The Contagues and the Relways tend to get results.

I asked the clerk, "What's going on outside?" Which earned me a look of disdain. How dare I intrude on her romantic interlude?

Morley offered a whispered apology. I was good of heart. And the question intrigued him, too.

Homely and middle-aged, Ellie was desperate to please. "A charitable trust came in. They wanted to fix the place up. But they wouldn't hand over the money. I guess they're not stupid, even if they are bumpkins. They insisted on doing the work themselves. The directors resisted till they came up with the notion of going after matching funds."

Morley batted his eyes and made implied promises. Ellie implied a willingness to play any game Morley wanted.

Bumpkins? Yes. A consortium of civic-minded, successful businessmen from Ymber. Yada yada yada. The "give something back" yammer nobody with smarts enough to get in out of the rain ever buys. Give it back? What did you get in the first place? From whom?

Morley suggested, "Why don't you visit Mrs. Claxton?" Reminding me that I had a mission. He swung the charm beam back to the volunteer. Who admitted she was a Mrs., too, but wasn't fanatic about it.

"Right," I said. "Why don't I go check on her while you hang around here?"

"Absolutely perfect, my friend."

Enjoying the therapeutic aroma of the Bledsoe, I climbed two flights of stairs to one of the hospital's celebrity suites. The crooks in charge are clever enough to keep a few available in case somebody with lots of money stumbles in, bleeding. Belinda's father had used one occasionally when he was younger and got into those sorts of situations.

Buy Claxton's physicians had betrayed their normally hidden competence by making her pain go away, then followed up by doing mysterious, wonderful things to reduce the damage caused her by burns. Their respect for the Contague name led them to bring in a wizard with a strong healing talent.

I don't doubt that they found gentle, unobtrusive ways to pad their fees.

Buy was awake. "I remember you. You tried to help."

"Yes, I did. Miss Contague asked me to make sure they're taking care of you. And to see if you need anything."

"They're treating me like a princess. Because they're scared shitless of what'll happen if they don't."

"Are you unhappy about that?"

"Shit, no. I'm thinking maybe I'll just camp out here from now on. I got no fuckin' desire for my ass to be some kind a symbol to them what thinks the ruling class . . ." They must have drugged her as soon as I showed up downstairs. Just in case. She mumbled through most of that, then faded completely.

"Belinda put the fear of God in them," I told Morley as we left. "And how was your day?"

"The things I suffer for friendship."

"Bet you she cooks you a nice two-pound steak. . . . What do you suppose these clowns are really doing?" We'd stopped to watch the men working on the Bledsoe's sad face.

"Looks like they're taking bad bricks out and putting in new ones."

"No. They aren't. I worked as a bricklayer's apprentice for about six months one week, back before I went in the Marines."

"You left an honest career for life as a tick on society's underbelly?"

"I got fired. I couldn't make them understand that the workday shouldn't start before noon."

"All right. You're an authority on bricklaying. What do you see that I don't?"

"They're fixing things that aren't broken. This place is still sound. It just needs the rotten mortar scraped out and new mortar tucked in. But they're making holes in the wall." I could see several places where bricks had been removed to create hollows.

"All right. I see that."

"Didn't your friend say most of the workmen didn't show up today?"

"She said the financing came from Ymber. I recall that."

"Why don't you pop back in and find out if those philanthropists had bad taste in trousers. I'll talk to these guys here."

Dotes looked sour, but he went. He had his own beef with the Ugly Pants Gang.

I strolled over to a hod carrier of fifteen summers who seemed to share my youthful lack of enthusiasm for clambering up ladders lugging mass quantities of bricks or mortar. "I'm trying to figure out what they're doing up there."

I got the right note of naive bewilderment into that. After an instant to decide whether the old guy deserved some attitude, the kid grunted. "They're just tuck-pointing and replacing bad bricks." TunFaire is built almost entirely of brick. Everybody knows something about the upkeep of brick buildings.

"I get that. I did your job when I was your age, a couple hundred years ago. I never saw nobody pull good bricks out."

"Oh. That. They're making these niches. Usually, there's a lot more guys working. They put these metal things inside, then brick them up. Over there you can see where they've already done that about ten times."

"So you're, like, getting in on a slow day, eh?"

He chuckled. "This is the best day I've had since this job started. Aw, crap! I had to open my yap. Now my old man wants me to bring up some mortar."

The boy stirred the mortar in a nearby mixing boat, splatted twenty pounds into a mortar hod, then went up the ladders and scaffolding like a monkey. I wasted ten seconds hating him for being that young, then drifted over to where the boy had pointed out some finished Ymber craftsmanship.

They weren't bricklayers by trade. Not even apprentice bricklayers.

Morley said, "You're psychic," from behind me.

"I've been accused of everything else. Why not that?"

"The philanthropists from Ymber brought a crew of volunteer workmen. Every single one wore filthy green plaid pants."

My new young friend spidered to the ground as Morley made his remarks. He overheard. I asked, "Would those be the guys who didn't show up today?"

"Yeah. And I ain't missing them, neither. I never seen such a bunch of useless assholes."

I tried to find out more, but somebody up top kept hollering nonsense about lollygagging and slacking. I told Morley, "Sounds just like the guy who fired *me* fifteen years ago."

The kid said, "That's my old man. Don't worry about him. He's all hot air." But he got busy working the mortar boat. You don't, the mortar sets up.

22

Morley seemed preoccupied.

I was preoccupied myself. Just what was going on at the Bledsoe?

Here it was, direct as a smack in the chops with an iron fist. The Green Pants Gang was underwriting renovations in order to install metal somethings inside the Bledsoe's outside walls. Dean was sure the gang was in town to catch Penny Dreadful and her kittens.

What would Penny say, if pressed? "We need to catch that kid who dumped the kittens on Dean."

"*We* do? Believe it or not, I do have a life outside my career as your sidekick. Considering Belinda Contague is involved, you might look into doing your own lifting and carrying."

"Ouch!"

"My point being, I don't need to catch something that's looking for you."

"Man. You're a pal, all of a sudden. Like Puddle or Sarge in a bleak mood."

"Could be. Life isn't fair. You going to try Harvester Temisk now?"

"Yes."

"Good luck. I'm headed home. Before one of those idiots burns the place down."

What suddenly made him want to get away fast?

Harvester Temisk hadn't resurfaced. He had, however, begun to interest somebody besides me. A minor, dim thug named Welby Dell was asleep across the street from Temisk's, in a spot well suited for lurking and watching. Dell was another associate of Teacher White's.

Being a thoughtful kind of guy, I toddled on without disturbing Welby's nap.

I picked up a tail. He wasn't anybody I knew. He didn't care if I knew he was there. Meaning he was a Relway Runner.

I changed course, headed for the Al-Khar, where I asked to see Colonel Block. Naturally, the ground level of the bureaucracy made that impossible. So I asked for Director Relway. With identical results.

I trudged on home. Smug. Block couldn't accuse me of evading my civic duty. Dean was in the throes of creating chicken and dumplings. He can be a killer in the kitchen when he wants.

Melondie Kadare was on the table, still hungover, in a foul temper. Singe sulked because I'd taken off without getting John Stretch's report. Her brother had gone and come and gone again in my absence.

Dean was in a good mood. "Mr. Mulclar will be here to fix the door tomorrow."

"Good." I settled down to eat. A kitten climbed my leg and set up shop in my lap. Others prowled the kitchen. Singe held one. It wore the smug look of master instead of pet.

"Dean, talk to me about Penny Dreadful and these cats."

He started to hem and haw.

"Dean, this is serious. People are getting busted up. They're getting dead. The guys who keep trying to break our door down got into fights with Belinda's people, Morley's guys, and Relway's gang. More than once. And when they aren't picking fights they're doing exterior renovations on the Bledsoe. What's the connection there?"

Dean grimly said, "You'd better tell me the whole thing. I may have been too trusting."

"You think so? That's never happened before, has it?"

Singe said, "You do not have to be nasty, Garrett."

I resisted a temptation to insist that I had the right. I related the highlights. "I don't think the Watch has the whole gang. Colonel Block says there were ten guys in green and two more who were in charge. At the Bledsoe, though, I got the impression that there were more than that."

Dean sucked in a gallon of air, set it free. "All I know is, those men serve A-Laf, some kind of masculine devil god. His cult has taken over in Ymber. It's really aggressive and intolerant. The feminine cult of A-Lat was its big competitor. I told you what Penny had to say already."

"And because she big-eye-orphaned you, you swallowed her story whole."

"Admitted. Which doesn't mean she was lying."

"Don't mean she was telling the truth, either. How do we get hold of her?"

Dean shrugged. "That's up to her. I don't think she'll come back here. Not since she saw the Dead Man. That rattled her."

"I'll bet." Hardly anybody wants to be around the Dead Man when he's awake. If they know what he is. I have reservations myself. I continued. "Give me a guess about the connection with the Bledsoe. The Ugly Pants Gang is putting out a ton of money so they can put metal statues in the walls."

Dean looked bewildered. "I don't have any idea. This is the first I've heard."

Singe brought me a cold mug of beer, reminding me that we had business of our own to attend.

She made sure surly little Melondie got a tiny cup to nurse, too. Always thoughtful, my pal Pular Singe.

"So, darling junior junior partner. What do I need to know that nobody's bothered to tell me yet?"

Melondie Kadare piped, "You need to know that your goddamn superior friggin' attitude needs a major adjustment, Biggie."

"Ouch!"

Singe said, "She is giving you attitude because her

tribe was most incompetent at gathering useful information. They were too busy stealing food, wine, beer, and small valuables to accomplish anything."

That started Melondie on a classic rant. She sputtered and raved for eight or ten minutes. Her big problem was Singe's being right. Her tribe had demonstrated a decided lack of discipline.

"Do you have any idea how the fires started?"

"No. I was outside." She produced a fair picture of the encounter between the Ugly Pants crew and Playmate, Saucerhead Tharpe, and the drivers of sundry carriages. The good guys won by weight of numbers. Though Melondie thought the outlanders were sluggish, confused, and weak.

For no clear reason, and to his own astonishment, Dean announced, "It was dark, wasn't it? 'A-Lat' means 'Queen of the Night.' "

"Uh . . ." I mused. "I guess that's handy to know."

Not to be outdone, Singe promised, "John Stretch will have a better report once he gets his rats together."

"That's good," I said. Not believing for an instant. The rats from Whitefield Hall couldn't possibly remember details this long after having their brains scrambled by terror.

"It's been a hard day," I grumbled. "And it's getting dangerous out there. I'd better not go drinking. So here's my strategy. I'll do my drinking and thinking here, after you all go to bed."

Singe filled my mug. She refilled her own. Melondie tapped the rim of hers, an ivory thimble that came down to me from my mom.

23

Dean said, "It's Colonel Block again."

"Uhn?"

"At the door? You just told me to answer it? Remember?"

"Sir, I have no recollection of those events." Making mock of a statement heard frequently in the High Court lately, as the Crown reluctantly prosecutes the most egregious disturbers of the peace involved in recent human rights rioting and minority persecution. The Crown Advocate's usual attitude toward minorities is that they should expect to be treated like minorities. If they don't like it, they shouldn't come here in the first place.

Dean brought the Colonel to my office. I'd already settled in to sweet-talk Eleanor in fluent Drunkenese. I asked, "Don't you ever take time off?"

Block isn't married. He isn't engaged. He isn't the other kind, either. He has just one love. And she's blind.

He romances her continuously, hoping she stays blind.

He'll be sorry someday.

"Uh . . ." It never occurred to him to step away and relax.

"Go fishing."

"I tried that once. I didn't like it. But if you want to come along? . . ."

I flashed a yard of my most charming smile. "Point

taken." To go fishing you need to go out into the country. Where the wild bugs are, and the hungry critters, some of them as big as houses. I don't go there, given a choice.

I did my time with the bloodsuckers and carnivores in the Corps. "You wanted to share something with me?"

"I was more hoping that you'd open up to me."

"Naturally. You're hoping I did Relway's job for him and now, because I'm a civic-minded kind of guy, I'll fill you in on anything that's puzzling you. Like Relway don't have a couple brigades of thugs to do his hoof work for him."

"Good point, Garrett. But Deal isn't on the inside. Deal somehow managed not to have even one friendly eye in the neighborhood when Belinda Contague held her summit at Whitefield Hall."

I flashed another yard of charm. "I was you, I'd think about that. How could she flimflam the whole damned Watch? What did you do, all go roaring off to the far south side after a bunch of human rights nuts? Were there even any nuts down there?"

"An orchard full. They haven't gone away. There was a bureaucratic screwup. The right hand didn't keep the left posted. The people responsible have been reassigned to Bustee patrol."

"And next time I visit the Al-Khar their identical twins will be sitting in their old seats."

Block nodded, shrugged. "What can you do about human nature? We still have Watchmen willing to supplement their salaries by selling inside info or by doing favors." He slumped like a jilted lover.

"That's good. You can face the truth."

"There's a lot of wishful thinking at my shop. You're right. But changes are coming."

"I hope you're right. Your guests in green say anything interesting yet?"

"Yeah. They're gonna save the world from the Queen of Darkness."

"Oh, goody! What's that mean to us who aren't religious wacks?"

"I don't know. We're looking for an expert on Ymberian cults. I want to know what's really going on."

That was why I admired Block. He understands that when people are involved, not much is what it seems at first glimpse. Though you never go wrong by suspecting the worst and working back.

Feeling generous, I talked about my thwarted visit to the Al-Khar.

"They're putting statues in the walls of the Bledsoe?"

"Not anymore. You've got most of them locked up."

"Why would they do that?"

"I hope you're just asking you. Because I have no idea." I doubted the Green Pants guys really felt compelled to do charitable deeds. Old cynic, I.

"I'm fishing. One must when dealing with you."

"Here's a notion. Assuming the Green Pants boys are religious gangsters, maybe the Bledsoe business has to do with their religion."

Captain Block gaped. My leap of intuition stunned him. "I'll be damned, Garrett. I take back everything I ever said about you. I bet you *can* find your toes without the Dead Man and Morley Dotes to show the way. You might even be able to count them without having to borrow an extra hand."

"Oh! How sharper than a serpent's tooth the cruel envy of a civil servant. Dean! We need a pot of tea."

"Don't bother. I'll be going. I found out what I needed to know."

That had a sinister edge. "Uhm?"

He didn't explain. Which left my nerves with split ends. Which was his whole point.

"Here's a thought, Garrett. Or two. Find Harvester Temisk before anyone else does. Then keep him away from the Combine."

"Uhm?" You can count on Detective Garrett to spout argot and attitude and sparkling repartee.

"Deal has friends in low places. There's a new trend in goombah thinking. They're all asking, 'Where's Harvester Temisk?' Even underbosses who aren't sure who Temisk is are looking. They don't want to get left behind. They haven't done much yet because they're all still nursing totally hairy hangovers."

"They did party like it was their last shot before the Trumps of Doom." I levered myself out of my chair, to take up guide duties so Block didn't get lost on his way back to the door. He's been known to do that. "Did you notice anyone watching the place when you got here? Besides Mrs. Cardonlos and the Watch goon squad operating out of her place?"

"Goon squad? You wound me, sir. The Watch employs only the cream of the cream of TunFaire's most civic-minded subjects." Denying nothing. "Tell you the truth, Garrett, I didn't pay attention. That's a luxury we're starting to enjoy more."

"What's that?"

"Not having to give a damn who's watching. Or why. Comes from knowing you're doing such a good job your credit with the people who could fire you is inexhaustible."

"Oh." That was a message.

Somebody somewhere liked what the Watch was doing just fine.

"I'll have the boys poke around under the stoops and in the breezeways."

I gave him a look at my raised eyebrow.

"All part of the service, Garrett. We maintain order and protect the public." Out he went into the chaos of Macunado Street.

What had he come to find out? More disturbingly, what were the people behind him up to now that the war was over?

Soon after Block disappeared a stir passed through the neighborhood like an unexpected gust through a poplar grove. A dozen clean-cut men rousted out another dozen who looked much less obviously official.

24

When I wakened I ambled back into the kitchen in search of fuel.

Dean was darning socks and slow cooking a sauce involving tomatoes, spices, garlic, and shredded onions. He had an admirably large mug of wine in front of him, which was out of character. He splashed some into the sauce. Oh.

Singe had swilled enough beer to get silly. Time to order in a new backup keg. Melondie Kadare was in a state where she wasn't much more than a sack of jelly, venting noises vaguely reminiscent of primitive language.

I said, "We need to lock Mel in a box until she dries out."

Singe snickered. A sight to behold and a unique, gurgly sound to hear. She was feeling less pain than I'd first thought.

There were kittens all over. I couldn't keep track.

Dean said, "Get the front door. I'm too busy."

His ears were sharper than mine. This guy must have mislaid his sledgehammer.

I was the only hind-legger able to navigate, so I snagged my mug and headed south. After a weary trek, o'er dale and under mountain, I positioned myself at my peephole.

One gorgeous, thoroughly frazzled, blue-eyed brunette had taken station on my stoop. I was surprised. I was more surprised to see that it was dark out. And still more surprised that she'd shown up without body-guards or her ugly black coach. She wasn't wearing her usual vampire wannabe look, either. She wasn't stylish at all. She had gone lower-class, raggedy, housewifey instead of whorish.

I opened up. Eyeballing the darkness behind her, I observed, "A lot of work go into the new look?"

"Yes. You want to move so I can get in before somebody figures it out?"

I moved. Belinda got inside.

"You by yourself?" I was used to seeing her motate around with several shadows who resembled woolly mammoths operating on their hind legs.

"All by my lonesome. I don't want anybody guessing I'm me. Not to mention that I lost my whole crew in the fire."

"Uhm?" My vocabulary word of the day.

"You know how many people are watching your place?"

"I have a notion. What I'm not sure of is why. I thought they'd go away after they swept up the last bunch of vandals who tried to wreck my door."

"I have no idea what you're babbling about. From a business point of view it would make sense to look over your shoulder twenty-five hours a day, eight days a week."

"Uhm?" There I went again.

"Shit happens around you, Garrett. Weird shit. *Really* weird shit. You draw it like horse apples draw flies."

"And here you are, buzzing around my hall." A gurgling peal of pixie laughter reminded me. "We're having a party in the kitchen. Come on back."

Belinda scowled.

She'd lost something. Emotionally, she was back where she'd been when I'd met her. Scared, beautiful, crazy, in a shitload of trouble. She wasn't as scattered as she'd been back then, but she wasn't the ferocious Contague crime queen anymore, either.

I said, "Come on. You need to relax."

Not the best strategy, possibly. Belinda wasn't beloved by anyone in my kitchen—though Dean probably thinks her worst flaw is her willingness to be seen with me.

Singe gave me bitter looks Belinda didn't recognize because she doesn't know ratpeople. Melondie Kadare didn't contribute. She was on her way to becoming extinct. The kittens *were* pleased to see Belinda. Fifteen or twenty of them piled on as soon as she sat down.

I scooped Melondie off the tabletop. "I'll take Mel home. Before one of these critters forgets his manners." The pixie buzzed feebly. I got a grip so she wouldn't flutter off and smash her head against a wall or ceiling she couldn't see.

I checked the peephole, saw nothing but bats zipping through the moonlight. I opened up, whistled softly. There would be a sentry. He might need waking up, though. Pixies greatly prefer the daytime.

They found Melondie's husband. He and her family took over. She was snoring like a six-inch-long, horizontal lumberjack. They bound her wings so she wouldn't do anything lethal in her sleep.

I went back inside.

Belinda was at the door to my office. She had a pitcher of beer, a pot of tea, a small oil lamp, and appropriate auxiliaries on a tray.

"What's up?"

"I didn't feel welcome in there. And I don't want them listening."

"Let me get the lamp going. Damn!" I missed stomping a kitten by a cat's whisker. I dumped another cat out of the client's chair. It bounced onto my desktop, where it puffed up and hissed at the stone that had come another whisker short of braining me.

Belinda filled me a mug and poured herself a cup of tea, added cream and a hunk of sugar the size of a flagstone. She stroked the kitten that laid claim to her lap.

I asked, "So what's up?"

She stalled. She wasn't sure she wanted to talk after all. She forced it. "Do you know where my father is?"

What? "No. Last I saw him, you were getting him out of the hall."

"Oh."

"Why? What happened? Did you mislay him?"

"Sort of. I got him out, got him into the coach, started to look for you. The coach took off and hasn't been seen since."

"Wow." I found myself playing with the stone egg— in preference to the unhappy cat in my lap. In a leap of intuition I understood why folks were interested in Temisk. "Any chance one of the district captains grabbed him?"

"No. I'd feel my arm being twisted already. Instead, they're running in circles trying to figure out what's going on."

"Maybe he decided to make a run for it."

"What?"

"Maybe he'd had enough and made a run for it."

"He was in a coma, Garrett."

"You think? You're sure? One hundred percent? He wasn't just paralyzed?"

"You know better than that."

"No, I don't," I lied. "You never let anybody get close enough to tell."

She didn't bother to argue.

I recalled Morley's hypothesis that some guy named Garrett was the moral anchor and emotional touchstone of the spider woman. I didn't want the job. Everybody knows what girl spiders do when boys get too close.

Maybe it was one of those deals where, you save a life, it's your responsibility forever after.

You put the knightly armor on, and sometimes they don't let you take it off.

"What're you thinking?"

"I'm thinking you're a dangerous woman to be around. And I'm around you a lot."

"Tinnie knows you pretty well, then."

"Unfortunately. But my personal life isn't what I meant."

"You're afraid of me?"

"There's that. You've got a temper. But the real problem is, you swim with sharks. I expect jaws to clamp on me any minute."

"With all your guardian angels?"

"Angels? Name two."

"Morley Dotes. Deal Relway. Westman Block. Playmate. Saucerhead Tharpe. Not to mention your business partners. Max Weider is no angel. Neither is Lester Tate. And then there's me."

Made me feel humble. For maybe ten seconds. Then my natural cynicism got its second wind. Someday I should fake my own death and see how things shake out.

"So you lost track of your dad. Let's slink on down to the bottom line. How come you're in a state where you sneak off? . . . You aren't just looking to hide out, are you?"

"No. I walk back out of here in the morning and be who I've been since the first time we met."

"In the morning?"

"I don't have anywhere to go tonight."

I began to fiddle with that slingshot stone a whole lot more seriously.

"It isn't like you don't have other friends stay over."

"You want to know the truth?"

"Maybe not, the way you're looking at me."

"None of those friends are as scary as you."

Belinda went on petting that kitten, scowling because she'd heard something she didn't like. She stared at my hands. "What the hell is that thing? What're you doing?"

I explained. "I left it here before I went to the party. I don't know. It relaxes me when I handle it."

Belinda extended a hand. I let her have the stone. "You're right."

Dean stuck his head in. "You need anything before I go to bed?" He was lugging a brat cat of his own.

"I can't think of anything."

He scowled at Belinda but couldn't get his heart into it. He sighed and went away.

Singe didn't bother to check us out. Which meant she was sulking but didn't have ambition enough to make anybody miserable.

Belinda poured herself a beer once she finished her tea. We played with kittens and let our hair down, talked like teenagers deep into the night, giggling at stupid jokes. I found out that she'd never had any girlfriends when she was younger. Never had the chance. Her role models were all the sort polite folk don't invite to holiday dinners.

We drank a lot of beer.

25

Singe wakened me at some godsforsaken hour, chivied in by Dean, who couldn't face direct evidence confirming or disclaiming the prurient imaginings slithering round the interior of his hard black skull. The fact that his imaginings were exactly that, and only that, meant nothing.

By the time we'd retired neither Belinda nor I was sober enough for anything more energetic than sleep.

Singe's attitude was sour enough.

"What?" I snarled. The morning light at play on my curtains shrieked that it wasn't anywhere near noon. In fact, it had to be closer to dawn, a time when only mad dogs and madmen got after the early worm.

"A messenger brought a letter from Colonel Block."

A kitten crabbed out of the covers, stretched, hopped down, and stalked proudly out of the room. Belinda made "Leave me alone!" growls and burrowed deeper into the covers. "Do I need to sign or something?"

"No. It was just a letter."

Then why was she waking me up now? "Then why are you waking me up now?"

"I thought you'd want to know."

"Sure, you did."

Feelings bruised, Singe left. I didn't care. There is no courtesy and no compassion before noon.

I didn't care, but I couldn't get back to sleep.

When Belinda started snarling about the tossing and turning and threatened me with an amateur sex reassignment, I surrendered to my conscience and dragged on out.

I sipped black tea thick with honey. No help. I kept seeing two of everything. If I hadn't spent five unforgettable years as a Royal Marine, I might've suspected double vision to be nature's revenge on fools who believe rational behavior includes hauling out at sunrise in less than apocalyptic circumstances.

Singe bustled around, doing chores, so Dean could do even less real work to earn his board and bread. She was fanatically perky and cheerful. And her co-conspirator had put the butcher knives out of reach.

"You are awful in the morning," Singe declared.

Exercising maximum restraint, I chirped, "Yep."

"Is that the best you can do?"

"I could say, 'Eat mud and die!' But you'd get your feelings hurt. I have more consideration for you than that. So how about we get together with this critical communiqué?"

Dean and Singe installed me in my office with hot black tea, biscuits, and honey. I got started. More or less. Weighted heavily toward the less.

"What does the note say?" She'd tried to read the message but Colonel Block's clerk had inscribed it in cursive. She can't read that yet.

She's a fast learner, though she'll never teach Karentine literature. Which consists mainly of sagas and epics inhabited by thoroughly despicable people being praised by the poets for their bad behavior. Or passion plays, which are hot today, but which are moronic if you read them instead of watching them.

"It says the priest at the temple of Eis and Igory, in the Dream Quarter, is from Ymber. It says the Watch wouldn't be disappointed in their old pal Garrett if his curiosity caused him to visit this Bittegurn Brittigarn, whose thoughts about guys in green pants might be of mutual interest."

"Meaning they do not think the priest will talk to them and they have no convincing excuse to pull him in."

"Basically."

"Garrett, what would the world be like if everyone was as caring as Dean?"

"It would be knee-deep in hypocrisy, standing on its head."

"Which still makes him better than most everyone else."

"Glory be, girl. Don't *you* go turning into a street preacher."

"The more I become a person, the more I get upset by how people treat each other for being different."

"I don't want to get into a debate."

"Too early in the morning?"

"No. Because I'd have to play devil's advocate and argue that stranger means danger. Which nobody can say is wrong. We've all got those harsh moments somewhere in our lives."

"Very good, Mr. Garrett," Dean said from the office doorway. "Indeed, flawless."

"We can't afford it."

"Sir?"

"Whatever you're buttering me up for. Hey, I don't want either one of you outside today." I heard Belinda beginning to stir upstairs.

Dean and Singe looked puzzled.

"The Dead Man." I told them, "We've had several visitors the last couple days. The kind that pay attention. They've probably picked up on the fact that he isn't doing much singing or dancing right now. Folks tend to get bold when they think he's snoozing."

Dean looked numb. This was his nightmare. He loathes the Dead Man. But we need the Loghyr's protection. People carry grudges.

"It would help if you two took a real shot at waking him up while I'm out there, one lonely man, a flawed white knight holding the fragile barricade between honor and the chaotic abyss."

Belinda appeared behind Dean. "Gorm, Garrett. You couldn't be more full of shit if they pounded it in with a hammer."

Dean headed for the kitchen. He came right back with everything Belinda needed to tame a hangover and get set herself for another glorious day of crime and corruption.

She announced, "Whatever Garrett claims, it's a lie. He was snoring before I got my shoes off."

Dean was pleased. Though he'd heard it before, from me. But that was different. My version didn't signify. He preferred not to believe me if that could be avoided.

I asked, "What am I supposed to do with you? Besides get you out of here before Tinnie hears rumors?"

She hadn't considered that. But really didn't care.

"Take care of it, Dean," I said. "Try to avoid making a millennial-celebration kind of production moving her out."

The old man gave me a look. It said I had the advantage of him, this once. And he didn't like it. "I'll handle it, Mr. Garrett."

I might ought to put on my chain mail underpants.

26

I didn't wander alone. A secret-police tail fell in behind me half a block from the house. He made no effort to be discreet.

Spider Webb was intimidated. But he didn't give up. He just dropped back. He vanished later, when I wasn't looking. So did several others whose fashion sense suggested a connection with the world of untaxed adult entertainment. But my main man just shuffled along with me, so close I had to listen to him hum.

He never stopped. But he had more trouble lugging a tune than my favorite antisinger, me. I never could tell what he was laying down.

The Dream Quarter gets its name because humanity's spiritual imagination runs riot there. And because the war in the Cantard produced generations of veterans so cynical that belief in anything traditionally religious could only be a bad joke that nobody got. In the Cantard nobody prayed for help cleaving to the path of righteousness. It was all, "Dear Lord, won't you please save my scruffy butt?"

Heavenly responses were random and erratic. Some of the sorriest clowns in the Cantard were guys who got what they asked for. Life with an ass but no arms or legs ain't all it's cracked up to be.

The Dream Quarter is one long street that runs from the river's edge deep into one of TunFaire's wealthiest enclaves. Location on the street defines the status of the deities established there. In a complex dance that remains mysterious even after my several encounters, the gods and goddesses of the Dream Quarter move sedately up and down the street, from temple to temple, according to how many worshippers they claim. And, more significantly, according to how rich their congregations are.

One rich, backsliding hypocrite of a parishioner is worth a gaggle of destitute mendicants, however devoted. A god can make the eye of a needle big enough to pass the whole damned herd of camels. And try to find a goddess who doesn't have six or eight hands out for contributions.

Bizarrely, the temples change to accommodate the look expected of their particular gods, goddesses, or pantheons.

I've heard that the gods reflect us instead of the reverse. Well, a smart god would have better sense than to create worshippers in his own image. Given a choice.

My instincts told me to start at the bottom end, down where a couple temples teeter over the chunky russet flood. The first person I asked indicated wreckage two steps short of the worst on the street. I'd visited the place once before, a while back, on another case. New management hadn't made any improvements.

Eis and Igory were doing better than other cults. Which meant the river would have to go a yard over flood instead of a foot to sweep their cathedral away.

Mind like a steel trap, I realized that this Ymber cult was faring better locally than the two visiting the miseries on me. A-Laf and A-Lat had no temples at all.

Even after having lived with me for thirty years I was reluctant to approach the hovel. It boasted one open room capable of holding thirty people—if they were small and didn't mind finding their noses in each other's armpits.

The priest wasn't what I expected. Which should

have been no surprise since religion and I have so little in common. He could've passed as a fat apprentice friar from one of the regular churches at the successful end of the street. He even wore similar black robes. But his had eluded soap and water for so long that, at this late date, congress would be fatal for the cloth.

It was still some unholy hour before noon when I stepped inside. Brother Bittegurn Brittigarn got his tongue tied trying to introduce himself in turn. He'd already had a couple or nine pick-me-ups to start his day. By the time he pulled himself together he'd forgotten my name. "Who the hell are you? What the hell do you want?"

"I hear you're the top expert on the religions of Ymber. I've got problems with people from Ymber. I'm knee-deep in cats and plagued by big guys too stupid to know that you ought to grin and suffer frostbitten buns before you wear plaid green pants."

"Huh?" Brittigarn took a pull of wine. He was my kind of guy. He had his priorities set. He wouldn't fake anything to please anybody.

The Dead Man encourages me to cope with the unexpected by drawing on experience and common sense. Meaning, basically, don't run blindfold sprints in an active cemetery. Experience suggested that Bittegurn Brittigarn was dimmer than a bushel of rocks.

Bittegurn had a round, apple-cheeked face notable for a huge white drooping mustache. The hair had migrated there from the top of his head. He growled, "Well, is it a secret?" He took another swig of wine. I could smell the vinegar from ten feet away. "Smooth." He sneered, wiped his mouth on his sleeve.

I explained again. "I'm Garrett. I find things out. I look for people. I ask questions. I'm here to ask questions about religion in Ymber."

"Ain't no religion in Ymber."

"What?"

"It's all here in TunFaire now. Which one are you doing now?"

"Asking questions so I can figure things out."

He waited. Probably hoping I'd offer a bribe. I waited. He asked, "You going to start?"

"All right. To review. You're from Ymber. Supposed to be an expert on its religions. I'm having trouble with religious people from Ymber. My house is overrun by cats dumped on me by a street urchin who's supposedly a religious princess. Who's disappeared. Now my neighborhood is infested with thugs wearing hideous green pants. They supposedly work for a god named Aleph. When they're not destroying private property they do volunteer maintenance and rehab at the Bledsoe. Where they're putting metal animal statues in the walls."

"A-Laf."

"Huh?"

"The god's name is A-Laf. Not Aleph."

"I stand corrected. Is that important?"

"I doubt it. Damn. That dead soldier was the last of his regiment."

Subtle.

"I'll see if I can't scare up some recruits. As soon as we finish." Part of being a crack investigator is finding a thread to tug. I'd grabbed hold of a rope.

"What's that?"

"What?"

"That thing you're fiddling with."

"A rock. Somebody tried to kill me with it. Tell me about A-Lat."

He didn't correct my pronunciation. "A-Lat is the Queen of the Night. The Mother of Darkness. Love and death wrapped up in one ugly bundle. Her cult used to be big on temple prostitution. It doesn't exist anymore. Can I see the stone? It don't look natural."

"How long ago did you leave Ymber? If the cult is extinct, how come I'm up to my ears in its enemies?"

"I've been here two years. My faith fled when the A-Laf cultists began murdering unbelievers. Especially A-Lat's women. They tortured the last high priestess to death. They sacrificed the goddess's sacred feline avatar to the idiot idol in A-Laf's temple."

Ah. Finally. Actual information.

The Dead Man is right. Patience wins.

Notions fell into place. There was a pattern and rhythm here. TunFaire would be the secondary impact zone. In Ymber there'd be prophecies and rumors of secret heirs to unknown obligations. There'd be brave fighters continuing the struggle even though all hope seemed lost. One-eyed men and left-handed men missing a finger from their right hand. The stuff of high heroic tales. On a farm community scale, of course. Where most of the king's subjects don't give a rat's ass about any of that. They have thunder lizards to skin and crops to get in.

"Let me see that thing."

I handed BB the stone despite an instant of irrational reluctance.

He grunted. He stared. He grew pale as he moved deeper into the light flung off by a phalanx of votive candles. He squeaked, fumbled the stone, regained control, shoved the rock back at me. "Keep that away from fire. Any kind of fire. No matter what else you do."

"Huh?"

"You let a flame touch it, you'll be sorry the rest of your life. Which will last maybe as long as another minute. If you're friggin' beloved of the gods."

I didn't like the sound of that. "What the hell?"

"You don't got no idea what you got there, do you?"

"I have a green rock. Somebody tried to brain me with it. I started carrying it around because I tend to slow down, relax, and think clearer thoughts when I'm fiddling with it."

"Your hands are warm. It likes that. So it makes you feel good."

Warm hands? Tell that to Tinnie. "How about a little hint?"

"It's egg shaped. Right? That's on account of it's an egg."

"Huh?" Old Garrett is quick as a glacier sometimes.

"Friend, you've laid hands on a roc's egg. I don't know why anybody would try to brain you with it, but—"

"Great pun, Slick. Egg-shaped rock. Rock's egg. Where baby boulders come from."

"Roc. Bird of fire. Burn your house down around you in half a minute if the egg touches flame and it hatches, roc."

"Bird of fire? I thought that was a phoenix."

"Same difference. I was you, I'd jump outside and see how far I could fling it out in the river. It'd stay plenty cold down in the mud."

"Rocs are huge. They carry off mammoths."

"An exaggeration. There are four species around Ymber. The biggest might be able to take a lamb or a small dog. People remember them big because they're so busy getting under cover they don't have time to look close. The littlest roc ain't much bigger than a sparrow. Zips around like a hummingbird. That egg you got, that's from what they call the bird of paradise phoenix. Looks kind of like a pheasant in a clown suit."

"Like a parrot?"

"Gaudier. Tenderloin gaudy. On account of which, they've pretty much been hunted out for their feathers."

"How do you hunt a roc down and take his feathers?"

"Like the joke says. Carefully."

I gave him the fisheye. He'd distracted me from comparative-religion research. "My mother used to call things 'rare as roc's eggs.' When she wasn't on about frog fur or hen's teeth."

"More roc's eggs around than frog fur coats. But they ain't common. Especially the big ones. It takes a rare combination of guts and inspired stupidity to raid a phoenix's nest."

"I know some guys who'd fit."

"Indeed. A-Laf's sextons are chock-full of stupid and brave. But the deacons, the dicks who tell them what to do, wouldn't waste them that way. You got a sweet mystery there, my friend. No telling how one a them got hold of an egg. Maybe from when they took A-Lat's temple. She had them all." BB paused to irrigate his pipes by chugging half a pint of wine.

"Thought that dead soldier was the last of his tribe."

"You didn't run out and volunteer to . . . you didn't volunteer to run out and . . . hell. We got a new regiment coming into the line. Aged in the cask since last Sedonaday."

"Which?"

"Sedonaday. Holy day of obligation for Ymnamics. Day before yesterday. Man, I'm telling you, if that was my egg, I'd prance outside and see how far out I could throw it. Get it way out there, down deep in the cold, cold mud."

I ignored BB's chatter, which was one hundred percent pure bull specks. But he had gotten me thinking. "Suppose I wanted to kill somebody by setting them on fire?"

BB's face got redder. "I ain't getting rich here, Slick, but I ain't the kind that—"

"I don't want to kill anybody. I want to figure out why they're dying. It's something else I'm looking at. People catching on fire." I explained a little, naming no names.

"I can see where you might think rocs' eggs, not having heard about them before. But your target would have to cooperate. The big question is, why even try? There're easier ways to kill people. It does sound like a sorcery problem, though. Look for a fire kind of wizard with rabid bats in his belfry. Or some stray pyro talent who hasn't been spotted by the horrors on the Hill yet. A refugee, maybe."

BB's latest bottle, come out of nowhere, seemed particularly potent. He developed difficulties enunciating. Before long he would shift to a language no one but Bittegurn Brittigarn understood.

"Maybe somebody who came to his abilities late and thought he could keep them hidden? Somebody with a deep streak of darkness?"

"There you go, Chief. You keep on keeping on, there you'll be."

This was starting to head for one-hand-clapping country.

"Give me a little help before you get all the way gone, Pastor. I need to know about the A-Lat cult. You say it's dead. But I know a girl who says she's the high priestess of A-Lat."

Bittegurn Brittigarn focused on those skills needed to lift a wine container to his lips with no wastage.

I asked, "How does a roc's egg turn into a projectile meant to brain me?" If that really was an egg, how come it was hard as a rock?

"I don' know, man. Go ask the sexton what flung it."

That was on my list. If Block and Relway would indulge me.

BB was sliding fast. "The A-Laf crowd. Why would they rehab the Bledsoe?"

He wasn't native born. He had to have the charity hospital explained. Then, "For fifty years nobody but the imperial pretenders have put one copper into the Bledsoe." Gross exaggeration. The Bledsoe is *the* big charity for TunFaire's well-to-do. But that didn't matter now. "I really want to know why they're putting those metal animals in the wall."

Bittegurn Brittigarn took him a long, long pull of wine. "For the pain."

"What does that mean?"

The priest's eyes closed. When they opened again they held a strong "You still here?" quality. He didn't say anything. Probably couldn't. But I had some interesting angles to pursue now. "I appreciate you taking time out of your busy day. I have to go. My mom is probably in a panic."

He didn't respond, other than to drool. In half an hour he'd gone from sober, friendly, and evasive to slobbering waste.

He did mutter, "The pain," over and over. "They feed on the pain."

He settled on the floor with his back to a wall. Making sure he had a fresh bottle in hand and several more in easy reach. He began to mutter a song in dialect, either liturgical or that dread tongue known only to those who drink sufficiently deep.

Wham!

The impact flung me against the wall. I turned as I bounced, wobbled toward a wide little woman swinging the business end of a broom in from the other side of town.

Wham!

"Hey! What the—?"

"So you're the bastard who's lured Bitte into the Realm of Sin!" *Wham!* She got all her weight into her swing.

"Lady, I never saw this guy before half an hour ago."

"You maggot! You bottom-feeding pustule of sin! You . . ." There was more unjust defamation. A lot. By dint of longer limbs and skills honed in combat, I maneuvered around the stout little harridan and escaped.

She didn't chase me.

I stood beside the doorway, out of sight, and eavesdropped as she turned her fury on a shiftless, lying, no-good, wine-soaked bastard Bittegurn Brittigarn.

I headed home convinced that I knew why Brittigarn had developed a love affair with the spoiled grape.

27

Armed with marvelous new knowledge, I ambled toward my own part of town. I didn't pay attention. It took me a while to realize my secret-police angel was gone and Spider Webb was back.

Spidey just wanted to know where I went and who I saw. Chuckle, chuckle. I led him to the Al-Khar, then wandered on after being refused access to Block and Relway. Relway's very existence having been denied despite his being publicly proclaimed chief of the Unpublished Committee for Royal Security. I detoured past Harvester Temisk's digs. He wasn't there. I circled The Palms without disturbing Morley Dotes or any cranky henchmen. By then I was running cross-eyed. It don't pay to get up early.

I ran into Saucerhead Tharpe four blocks from home. He wasn't alone. I didn't duck in time.

"Hey, Butthead Boy," Winger bellowed. "I seen you. Don't you be trying to hide." The woman has a tendency toward loud. Tharpe seemed embarrassed to be caught in her company.

Winger is a good-looking woman. Blond, with the right stuff in all the right places, and the gods were generous when they built the best parts. But there are detractions from those natural attractions. Her size and her attitude.

Winger is as tall as me. And argumentative on her best day. Lucky me, I manage to avoid her a lot nowadays.

Saucerhead tried to look apologetic without saying anything that would get him an ass kicking. "I done some checking on that thing you wanted me to find. I know where it's hid."

"Do you? You know where it is now?" Because I could see Penny Dreadful down the block, conspicuously inconspicuous as she lurked and loitered. She was tailing Tharpe and his convoy. No doubt trying to find out who was sneaking around her and why.

A squeak of a voice caught my ear. "Are you really Garrett? *The* Garrett? The man who—?"

"Yeah," Winger said. "That's him. Definitely the man who."

Set beside Winger this guy was almost invisible. He was ten inches shorter, bone skinny, bone pale, twitchy as a whore in church. "Jon Salvation, Mr. Garrett. It's a *huge* honor to meet you. I've heard *so* much about you."

"His name is Pilsuds Vilchik," Winger barked. "I call him the Remora."

Jon Salvation broke out a big, nervous smile.

Saucerhead said, "He's the boy I told you about. Follows Winger around and writes up everything she does."

Jon Salvation smiled again and bobbed his head.

I asked, "How come?"

Winger said, "On account of I'm a heroic figure and I'm so busy being heroic I don't have time to write my own saga down."

"Not to mention that you're illiterate, eh?"

Saucerhead chuckled. "The real story is, she let the boy have a little one time when she was plotzed. He liked it so much she ain't been able to shake him since."

Winger snarled, "That ain't what happened. Not quite."

I glanced at Jon Salvation. Seemed he didn't mind being talked about like he wasn't there. The story of his life, probably. Some people are like that. Naturally invisible. There are years when I envy them.

Salvation produced a little board with sheets of cheap paper fastened to it by rivets at the top. He scribbled furiously using the writing stick we make in the manufactory where I'm a minor shareholder.

Feel sorry for them if you like. Jon Salvations create themselves.

"Pleased to meet you," I said. "Don't write down anything the Watch can use for evidence." I wondered what he'd done in the war. Obviously, he'd survived.

Winger sneered.

I told her, "You're always on the edge, sweetie." That's her nature. The way she wants it. Fine by me. As long as she don't drag me in. "Saucerhead. One more time. Where's the item of interest right now?"

"On the shelf, I reckon. Worried about getting out and about."

"Actually, she's right over there, skulking around in front of Scuttleman's coal yard. Watching you."

Nobody looked. Not even the Remora. Tharpe muttered, "Damn sharp for a kid."

"I don't know." Plenty of kids Penny's age are resourceful enough to survive. Saucerhead was one himself once upon a time. "This one may have more talents and resources than most."

Saucerhead eyed me expectantly.

I told him, "I'm headed home. If somebody turned up at my door with a special prize, I might turn up holding a fat bonus."

"Gotcha."

Winger tried to horn in, hoping she could carve off a slice. I ignored her, which isn't always wise. She's liable to knock you down just to get your attention. "Good job, Saucerhead. Thing you could do next is, find Harvester Temisk."

"The shyster?"

"Him. Don't be obvious. Especially not if you find him. Teacher White wants him, too. And not to give him a birthday present."

"Gotcha."

"Later, then. Winger. How about you stun the gods above and the gods below speechless?"

"What?"

"Stay out of trouble."

"You're a complete horse's ass, Garrett."

"But snuggly warm and lovable."

"Like one a them giant porkypine thunder lizard things."

She *is* a woman. She *will* have the last word. Since they live longer, there was no point me trying to win out of stubborn. I made my getaway.

Jon Salvation wrote it all down.

28

There was a subtle difference about home when I got there. And it wasn't all the loiterers from the Watch and Teacher White's gang. Welby Dell and a sidekick. Welby's partner was a six-foot-five albino so emaciated a little girl once called him Skelington. It stuck. They seemed unaware of the presence of the law. The law, on the other hand, was well aware of them.

There were Relway Runners all over. Mrs. Cardonlos' place was busier than a termite mound.

I knocked. The door man obviously hadn't come round yet. My key would be useless.

Pular Singe let me in. "Did you learn anything?"

"I'm more popular than I thought I could ever be. Fans by the legion are following me around. None getting in my way, though."

Singe hissed. She saw something behind me. I turned, too late. "What?"

"One of those men with the obscene trousers."

"So Relway hasn't caught them all. What's going on?"

"Unh?"

"Something feels funny."

"John Stretch is in the kitchen."

"And he wants something."

"He wants to give you his report. Why don't you come in so I can shut the door?"

Not a bad idea with a Green Pants goon around. He might own a sling and have a pocket full of rocs' eggs.

On cue something whizzed past my right ear. Not a sniper's effort, though. It was Melondie Kadare. She hovered momentarily, then headed for the kitchen, doubtless after hair of the mad dog. Where she got into it with Dean. Dean had no sympathy for her. The man has an attitude problem. He's determined to call a hangover a self-inflicted wound.

Being a trained observer, I observed, "He's in a foul mood."

Singe said, "Things have not gone his way today."

I sensed a story. She didn't give it up.

John Stretch followed his nose from the kitchen to my office. I said, "I never noticed how long his snoot is before."

John Stretch scowled. As much as a ratperson can.

"Just messing with Singe," I said. I helped myself to a seat behind my desk. My lap had a cat on board almost instantly. Melondie Kadare whirred in a moment later. "He didn't use a flyswatter on you. Puts you ahead of the game. So don't go whining to me."

John Stretch started telling me what his rats had seen at Whitefield Hall. I stopped him. "Hang on. I need to write stuff down." He had much more than I'd expected. He had quotes from Belinda's underbosses, some quite revealing of their thinking.

Before he finished I had an idea where every major player stood. I just hoped he wasn't making stuff up because he thought I wanted to hear it.

"You're a gold mine, John Stretch." These nuggets would set Director Relway to singing and dancing. Plainly, Chodo's appearance at Whitefield Hall had changed the underworld dramatically.

Unfortunately, none of it was of any use to me.

"Hang on," I told the lord of the rats, figuring John Stretch so styled himself in his own heart. "Melondie, girl of my fantasies, I see you bubbling. You remembered something you haven't told me already?"

Not really, it turned out.

"So, did anybody figure out how the fires started?"

No. All those eyes hadn't seen a thing I'd missed.

"Was it some kind of sorcery?" Fire just doesn't materialize out of nowhere. Does it?

Neither Melondie nor John Stretch had detected any obvious sorcery.

"Any speculations? The first victim was a rat. Then Buy Claxton. How did they catch fire? Nothing else in that kitchen was harmed."

They had nothing.

It made no sense. Though it did look like Chodo Contague was the common denominator in a lot of incidents.

Damn! I wished I hadn't sent Saucerhead to catch Penny Dreadful. He could go up north to do all the miserable but necessary legwork.

"I'd tell you if I could. If I knew!" Melondie Kadare snapped. "You're special to me."

I glanced over my shoulder. Eleanor seemed amused. Which convinced me immediately that things were about to get worse.

It began as I pulled the notion together.

Dean appeared with refreshments. His clock radiated the kind of smug, wicked look he gets when he knows that I'm inescapably in for a life experience involving a whole hell of a lot of work. Not because we need money but because, in his lame view, it's good for my soul.

Somebody started pounding on the door.

Dean's smirk deserted him.

He couldn't avoid answering. The rest of us were busy. Plus, it's his job.

Muttering, he headed up front. I poured tea. Singe and John Stretch hit the muffins, fattening up for the winter.

Dean returned, his sneer restored. "Mr. Tharpe is here, sir."

Saucerhead filled the office doorway. He looked scared, an eventuality rare as rocs' eggs. "You got a back way out, Garrett?"

"What's up? What did you do?"

"I didn't do nothin' but what you told me. Which you owe me for. It's all your fault."

"Whoa, big guy. Put some blinders on that mule. And back the cart up to where it started."

"You told me to go catch that Penny Dreadful kid. So I did. No sooner do I lay hands on her, though, than she starts yelping rape an' sodomy an' incest an' all that shit." Which didn't bother him nearly as much as the fact that, "An' people *listened*! You hear me talking, Garrett? People *listened*. An' not only that, some a them come an' tried to help her! An' not only *that,* they chased me when I guve it up as a bad job an' decided to go away."

"That what the crowd noise out front is all about?"

"I don't know. They's probably getting all rowdy an' shit because they want you to come out an' teach them to dance the dublarfared. You being a famous dancer."

I shook my head. I took a deep breath, sighed. I shook my head again. What was the world coming to? When did TunFairens start caring what happened to one of the city's countless feral brats?

Saucerhead blubbered, "This is all your fault, Garrett! Ever since you got in this investigation racket you been doing the meek-are-gonna-inherit polka. An' now half the burg is buying into your do-gooder crap."

"It won't last," I promised, despairing of his ever grasping the do-gooder point. "Too much social inertia. Too many people too vested in the old ways. Especially up on the Hill. Just take it easy. They'll get bored and go away. Dean. Did you get Belinda off all right?"

He admitted that he had. And that she hadn't attracted any attention. Meaning the watchers outside figured her for one of my sleepover friends. Meaning, further, that I'd have some explaining to do once Tinnie got word.

She always does.

"Long as you're all here and don't have anything

better to do. Listen to this." I told the tale of my
visit to Brother Bittegurn Brittigarn's temple of Eis
and Igory.

I hadn't gotten BB pinned down about his own religious attitudes. Dean pointed that out. Smugly.

Singe wanted to see the roc's egg.

They all did. I let them pass it around.

John Stretch said, "That priest pulled your leg, Garrett. This rock came out of a creek bed. You can get
a thousand just like it at the arms bazaar."

Singe said, "Our ancestors collected slingers' shot
for the army."

The sling was never an official weapon in any Karentine formation, but both sides employed native auxiliaries in the Cantard, some so backward they considered
the sling a technological marvel of such murderous
capacity that the gods themselves would rail against
its use.

There was universal agreement. My roc's egg was a
rock and BB would still be snickering.

There was a racket at the front door. Saucerhead
jumped. He developed a haunted look. Scowling about
the injustice, Dean headed for the bows of the Garrett barge.

He came right back to announce, "Just neighborhood rabble. Did you want to talk to them?"

"No. If you took in dogs instead of cats, we could
set those on them."

The monster in my lap stirred, but only to wriggle
into a more comfortable position.

John Stretch asked, "Does it look like a long siege?
I need to get back. My people have a knack for
mischief."

Dean shrugged. "I don't know. But Mr. Garrett is
right. Eventually, they'll get bored and go away."

Once my pals in the Watch started rumors that
would make the idiots decide that home-cooked food
was more interesting than hanging around shouting
obscenities about a fake complaint.

Oops. Suppose Relway's Runners snatched the girl?

"Hey, Saucerhead," I said. "What happened to Winger and her pet?"

Tharpe sneered. "Closed chapter, buddy. Winger is all after a fisa . . . fiso . . . something collalogistical of some kind who wants to shove things up our . . ."

I shuddered, absent the remotest notion. If I understood him at all, Winger was right and we needed to hunt down somebody who found that stuff exciting. Whatever it was.

I said, "That's interesting." Like I meant it. "This has been one of the longer days of my life. Thanks to these two villains." I pointed an indicting finger at Singe and Dean. "They started on me before the worms came out looking for the early birds. I'm so tired now that I probably won't go over to the factory tonight."

Singe said, "Tinnie is not finished being mad at you. You should stay away till she's ready to accept your apology."

"And when she hears about Belinda?" Life gets complicated if you get too engaged with it.

Dean sneered.

Saucerhead asked, "How was you figuring on getting out? On account of I still need to get out of here myself."

"Just wait till they get bored."

"There's still plenty of racket out there."

I shrugged. Tired was wearing me down. Also, that hint of the weird closing in that I'd begun to feel as soon as I came home.

Crash! Thunder shook the house. Stuff fell off my desk. Eleanor's portrait wobbled and ended up at a steep tilt. Dean dashed off to the kitchen. My ears rang. I hadn't heard anything fall out there but probably only because I couldn't hear.

Singe's eyes went wide with terror. John Stretch's, too. The primal rat took over. They didn't run only because there was nowhere to go.

Melondie Kadare was out cold.

"That was a close one," I said. My voice sounded

weird to me. I felt rather than heard the thunder rumble off into the distance. "That must have hit down here in the neighborhood."

Saucerhead grunted feebly.

I've never been bothered by thunder and lightning. I find a good lightning show enjoyable. But I'd seldom had the hobnailed boot of a god slam down quite so close. "That ought to break up the mob out front, Saucerhead."

He couldn't hear me, but the idea occurred to him on its own. He got moving toward the front door.

Dean returned, half of his favorite teapot dangling from his right forefinger. There were tears in his eyes.

A second peal of thunder started way off to the east and stumbled toward us, roared overhead, hugely loud, then ambled on westward, diminuendo. Soon afterward a lightning symphony opened to a vast audience.

Then some antic vandal of a boy god knocked open the sluice gates of heaven. The rain came. Torrents hammered the house.

Kittens poked their noses out of hiding places. Well. The world was still here.

Saucerhead came back. "That broke them up. Man, you got to see the hailstones coming down." He was more awed than frightened now.

I went to look.

Tharpe was right. It was an awesome show, the lightning flailing around, thunder's hammers pounding the anvil of the sky, hail coming in a downpour heavier than any I'd ever seen.

People always exaggerate the size of hailstones. That's human nature. So I'll say only that there were tons of them, they were big, and on the ricochet they knocked over carts and wagons. Then daring, enterprising, dim-witted youths hit the street with buckets and baskets, harvesting the ice while it still hammered down.

A flash almost blinded me. Thunder's roar came a heartbeat later, so strong I felt it right through my body. Had gangs of stormwardens decided to rumble? My ex-army pals claim they saw a lot of this sort of thing in the main war theater.

There were material as well as social advantages to being a Marine. Marines on swampy islands in the Gulf didn't have to worry about getting caught between dueling sorcerers. Sorcerers, on both sides, didn't mind cruel and deadly warfare, but they refused to become physically uncomfortable while they were fighting.

Saucerhead pushed past behind me. "I might freeze or drown, but I'm getting while I can get."

I had a couple of kittens underfoot, trying to figure out what hailstones were. They weren't impressed.

I asked, "You want a cat?"

Tharpe gave me a look colder than a bushel of hailstones.

"They're cute."

He left me with a one-finger salute.

29

Once again I got up earlier than was rational. Since I'd gone to bed early, though, I missed no sleep. I just didn't regain what I'd lost the day before.

Everybody else was up before me. Of course. Go figure. And they were all in good moods, despite wet and windy weather. Dean had a warm fire going. I settled in and observed professionally while he continued to deal with the storm damage. "How much do we need to replace?"

"I'm making a list. Not a lot. We had too much to begin with, since we never entertain." He produced tea in a cracked beaker. I drank.

"What's Singe up to?"

"She and her brother are in talking to the thing."

"The thing? Old Jolly woke up? Why didn't you say so?"

"It may be old age confusing me. I thought I just did. The fury of the storm woke him up."

I didn't buy that. Now I knew why I'd felt weird after I got home yesterday. Old Bones was awake and lying back in the weeds.

"Give me a refill, here, and I'll be off."

He muttered something about my not needing any tea to get there.

Singe had half the lamps in the house in the Dead Man's room. He makes her nervous. Though I don't know many people who are comfortable around corpses. Particularly around corpses still inhabited by the original occupants, like a ghost that can't get up and walk.

Asking what kind of mood he was in would waste time. Ill-tempered usually covered it. Instead, I asked, "Where are the cats?"

"Hiding," Singe said. "They are terrified."

"Makes sense. In his time His Nibs was known as Terror of Kittens."

John Stretch eyed me like he wasn't sure I was joking. He was rattled. If he were human, he'd have been a bloodless white.

"You sure he's awake?" I asked. "I've been in here a whole minute and he hasn't contradicted me yet."

There are matters of greater weight to consider, Garrett. A dozen minds in the street outside need examination. Employing a pickpocket's touch inasmuch as they believe that I am no longer viable.

"Ah. Were you ever?"

And still the man wonders why I prefer sleep to suffering his company.

He was employing one of his lesser minds to communicate. He didn't have his heart behind his snaps. He was distracted. Which was a good sign. He'd found this new world exciting enough to engage his intellect.

Here is what you must do. Beginning immediately. Have Mr. Tharpe and Ms. Winger come see me. Employing your considerable talent for fabrication, get each of the following to visit, as well. Colonel Block and Deal Relway. Miss Contague. The child, Penny Dreadful. Any of the men who wear green pants. Or their handlers. The priest you visited. Teacher White or one of his henchmen.

Once I have interviewed a few of them it should become possible to develop strategies. Finding Mr. Contague and Mr. Temisk will be critical. Those two will be able to clarify the developing shakeout in organized crime.

That's the Dead Man. He goes on and on. And on. The bottom line is legwork for me.

Where is the bird? I do not sense the parrot.

"Gone," I said. I tried to sound thrilled, but the truth is, I do miss the foulmouthed chicken. Just a little. In rare, maudlin moments.

Ah. An interesting turn of events. Most of which I am thankful to have missed.

"You didn't miss much."

Do you honestly believe you can mislead me?

"I don't remember who, but somebody said that where there's life, there's hope."

My cousin Duphel said it first.

"What?"

He responded with the mental equivalent of a shrug. He had wasted time enough. *Here is your schedule.*

My partner. Already in there bullying me to collect the bits he needed to make sense of the senseless. He makes connections quicker than I do.

Should you prove able to approach Mr. Dotes in such fashion that his subsequent actions appear to be independent of your visit, ask him to stop by. Then go to the Bledsoe. See what more the outlanders have done.

Didn't seem like they could've gotten much done. Most of them were in jail.

There is a witch you know.

"I know several."

Exclude your stable of floozies.

"Ouch! I was."

Retain one and ask her to come here.

"One who doesn't know about you?"

That would be preferable.

"I'm starting to wonder why I'm always determined to wake you up. Life is simpler when you're asleep."

But it goes nowhere.

"Wrong, Butterbutt. It goes the best places of all."

He started rummaging around inside my head, evidently under the delusion that he'd been invited. In seconds he was appalled in a big way.

Where is the parrot?

"Mr. Big? Pursuing a higher calling." The Goddamn

Parrot belongs to days gone by and other stories. If there's any mercy in heaven, he'll never be more than another dyspeptic memory.

Chuckles tromped around inside my skull like twenty drug-crazed home invaders wearing sensible shoes. Being Himself, he dropped the question of the pestiferous, overdressed chicken like a maggoty dead mouse. He plowed on as though Mr. Big never existed.

"Speaking of critters. Tell me about the cats infesting the house. They don't seem normal."

It is impossible to slip anything past you.

"Answer the question."

They are not normal cats. As you have surmised. They do demonstrate points of character we associate with domestic cats. I am unable, yet, to see into their minds. They are afraid of me.

"Sounds like a healthy attitude. Everybody ought to be."

You might adopt it yourself.

"But I know what a big old cuddle bear you really are."

Be careful when you leave. The kittens may attempt to escape.

I was being dismissed. Told to get on with my chores. Sometimes he forgets who the senior partner is.

I returned to my office, found me a scrap of paper with a little clean on one side, made myself a list.

30

I leaned into the Dead Man's room. "You awake enough to reach somebody a block away?"

Be more specific.

"I just took a look out front. If you can reach a block, you can nab a character called Skelington, who works for Teacher White."

Where?

I described the spot.

It may be that I am not sufficiently awake. If that bird was here, I could send him out and ride along.

"Gotcha." He wanted me to go out there. "Don't be surprised if Skelington runs when he sees me coming, though."

At this point in your career you should be capable of making an unthreatening approach.

No point debating. "I'm on my way." I hitched my pants, patted myself down. I had an adequate low-intensity arsenal on board.

I was ready.

The weather drama was over, but a drizzle continued. Not a day when I'd work if Himself weren't back there with a sharp stick, poking.

Skelington was less thrilled to be out than I. Huddled in misery, he failed to see me coming till it was too late.

I told myself, "That went well," as Skelington entered my house. Maybe drizzly weather wasn't all bad, after all.

                    *   *   *

Nobody was at home at Saucerhead's place. He hadn't been seen since yesterday. So he hadn't gone home from my place. I left a message mentioning the possibility of paid work.

Winger wasn't in her usual haunts. I couldn't run her down at home because I didn't know where she lived. I left word that Garrett had cash for her if she came to my house.

I couldn't think of a scheme to lure Block or Relway.

I strolled past Morley's place. Sarge was out front doing some wet-weather sweeping, pushing litter and horse apples over in front of a neighbor's dump. He showed me a scowl so black I waved and kept rolling. Just passing through. Didn't have no notion to drop in.

At Harvester Temisk's place two no-neck types muttered to one another about the chances of snow. I didn't recognize them. I did spot a familiar Relway Runner keeping an eye on the two brunos.

Not once during my icy-drizzle-down-the-back-of-my-neck wanderings did I spot Penny Dreadful. Which goes to show that even a fourteen-year-old girl has better sense.

Belinda I disregarded. I had no idea where to look for her nor any notion where to leave a message.

I wandered over to Playmate's stable, just to get in out of the miseries.

"Garrett, you look like that thing they talk about the cat dragging in." Playmate was banging hot iron in the smithy of his stable. Building horseshoes. Weather got in because he hadn't repaired all the damage done during some excitement we were involved in not long ago. He grumbled about not having the money.

Money couldn't be the problem. He had points in the same manufactory I did.

"Us honest folk got to work no matter what the weather is like."

Play whopped a hot horseshoe. "You make me regret that I've heard a calling, Garrett. Sometimes I want to cut loose and tell you how full of the stinky you are. This is one of those times."

"How come everybody does me that way, Play?"

"Everybody knows you."

I grumbled but didn't remind him that I was always there when any of them needed something.

"So to what do I owe the honor of your presence? What favor do you want now?"

"Nothing. Except to get in out of the rain. I'm headed somewhere else."

"Why aren't you home resting up for an evening of debauchery?"

"The Dead Man is awake."

"Oh. Thanks."

"You see? You're forewarned. The only guy in this cesspool of a city who is. So don't pass it along."

"I said thank you. Want some tea? There's water." He never lacks for heat in the smithy.

"Sure. Hey. You have any idea what happened to Antik Oder, used to have a storefront down the street?"

"Aha! So now we get to it."

"To what? The Dead Man wants a witch. Elderberry Whine kicked off when I wasn't looking."

Playmate made tea, his grin ivory in a mahogany sea. "Antik is still there. She isn't what you're looking for, though."

"Why not?"

"She's a fraud."

I grunted, sipped tea. "There's something in this."

"I dribbled in a dollop of vanilla rum."

I'm not big on hard liquor, but this was *good*. I rendered myself incapable of competent behavior in minutes.

It seemed like a good idea at the time.

Playmate isn't the kind who lets friendship get in the way of business. Much. "Rain's slowing down, Garrett. Time to move on."

I'd told him most of what was happening, hoping he'd have a suggestion. I'd wasted my breath. He asked, "Where are you headed from here?"

"I don't know. I'm thinking about crawling into the hayloft and grabbing forty winks."

Playmate frowned. He thought I was scamming, but couldn't figure my angle. "I guess it can't hurt. But shouldn't you show more ambition?"

"Ambition? About what?"

"Your job."

"Why? There ain't nobody paying me."

He doesn't stint the critters. The hay in the loft was first-rate. It retained enough sweet clover smell to remind me of idylls in country pastures.

He was wrong. The drizzle hadn't slowed. It had grown into a steady rain. The rattle on the shingles overhead was a powerful soporific. Or maybe that was the rum.

I was gone in half a minute.

31

First I thought it was the change in the patter of the rain. Then I thought it was the cold. But the war taught me to wake up carefully and not to trust first impressions. I lay still, controlled my breathing, listened.

Playmate had company. That company wasn't looking for a place to stash horses.

I moved glacially till I could see.

Teacher White was down there, safely distant from Playmate, not coming across half as fierce as he wanted. He looked more like a pretend bad guy.

Assisting Teacher were two wide-load no-necks who looked like they were from out of town. Plausible, given that Teacher had only a half dozen soldiers of his own, none heftier than Spider Webb or Skelington.

Teacher cautioned the wide bodies, "Careful. There's more to the man than meets the eye." Though I can't imagine anybody underestimating Playmate.

Teacher told him, "There ain't no need for nobody to get hurt, Play. All you—"

"There is, you come in here pushing me around."

I steeled myself to jump in, though I suspected Playmate would be all right. The shoe might be on the other hoof. The bad guys might need help before the straw settled.

Playmate is all religious. He preaches turn the other cheek. But he takes an eye-for-an-eye attitude when it comes to professional scum.

Teacher asked, "Where's Garrett?"

Playmate didn't answer.

The wide loads moved in. Playmate met one with an invisibly fast straight jab to the schnoz that rocked the man's head back like it was about to pop off its stump. He plopped down on his back of beyond with a stunned, goofy look.

The second thug took a punch to the chest. Pure amazement filled his face. This didn't happen when you educated civilians.

Playmate collected a hammer. He showed it to Teacher White. Teacher took note. "Time to move along, boys."

Good thing, too, because I was just about to jump down and make life really harsh for Teacher.

Then I saw what I would've jumped into.

Spider Webb and guys named Original Dick and Vernor Choke showed up to help the wide loads leave. They hadn't made a sound there under the hayloft.

Vernor Choke had been born to his name. I didn't know the story on Original Dick. I wouldn't hang the moniker on anybody, but that didn't mean his mother hadn't.

I climbed down half a minute after Spider Webb exited, the last of the crew to leave.

Playmate observed, "Once again there's proof that just knowing you is a bad idea."

"What was that all about?"

"They're looking for some guy named Garrett. Said they followed him here. They didn't say why. They seemed pretty determined, though."

I put on my best baffled face. Without faking. "I don't get it. They've been following me around long enough to see that I can't tell them what they want to know."

"And what would that be, Garrett?"

"Huh? What would what be?"

"What do they want to know?"

"Well, hell!" I had no real idea. "Maybe just a closer look at my pretty face."

They *did* know that I couldn't find Chodo or Harvester. Didn't they?

"Oh, sure. That's got to be it, Garrett. How did that get past me?"

32

I gave Teacher and his crew fifteen minutes to hurry off to some far place where they could get out of the wet and forget harassing a handsome but ignorant investigator. Playmate supported my tactical view.

"I couldn't figure out what they *really* wanted," he admitted. "They changed stories three times. The bottom line, though, was that they really, really, *really* wanted to lay hands on a guy named Garrett."

"Thanks for not giving me up."

"Gratitude noted in the Book of for Whatever That's Worth."

"I am a handsome young man."

"Duly noted in the Book of Natural Fertilizers. Why don't you get out of here so I can get some work done?"

Some folks are obsessed with being productive.

"I can take a hint." I left messages for Saucerhead and Winger, in case he saw them before they got the word somewhere else.

The rain wasn't heavy, but it was steady. It wasn't one to please the farmers. They want their soakers in the springtime.

A voice husked, "Garrett."

I was a block from Playmate's. I was hunched over, wishing I had a poncho. The ones we'd used in the islands hadn't kept us dry, but they did keep us from being wounded by the larger raindrops.

"Spider." I hit Webb alongside the head with my stick, then spun and got Original Dick in his namesake. I wove easily past a wide-eyed Vernor Choke, smacked Teacher White between the eyes, and slid behind him while he wobbled. My stick lay across his throat. I lifted him a little.

Spider leaned against a wall, trying not to get dragged under by a concussion. Original lay curled up on the cobblestones in a smear of his own puke, fighting for air. Choke put on a show of dancing around looking for an opening. Teacher complained, "You broke my nose! I got blood all over my new jacket!"

They hadn't expected me to explode.

I hadn't brought enough explosives. I whispered, "Teacher, how about you tell me why you guys keep dogging me?" Then the big boys responded to all the whining.

I popped Teacher again, from behind, with immense enthusiasm, then faked right and ran left, headed for Playmate's place.

One of the brunos grabbed Vernor Choke and flung him like a bola. And Choke did the job, what with all those legs and arms trying to latch on to something as he flew by. I took several solid thumps before I got untangled. Seeing double, I had legs too watery to run.

Where was the Watch when a little interference might be useful?

Following Welby Dell, who was disguised as a handsome investigator by a cute illusion you can pick up for next to nothing on the black market.

I was too busy hurting to care. I got in a good whack at a kneecap. The other wide body kicked me in the ribs. Then somebody hit me from behind with that bucket of rocks than which he was dumber.

33

"Hey, Teach, I fink da asshole's comin' round," a voice said. It turned out to be Vernor Choke's.

I was tied into an ancient wooden armchair. The setting was the sort of hideout gang guys run to when there's a war on. There were pallets scattered around. Spider Webb and Original Dick occupied two. Both were in worse shape than me.

Choke got behind me. He lifted my chin, showed me Teacher White slumped in a chair close by, still leaking a little red.

Welby Dell appeared with a bowl of water, some cloth pieces, and a dirty hunk of sponge. He went to work on Teacher's face.

White mumbled something.

Dell relayed. "Where's Chodo?"

I shrugged. "I don't know. At home, I reckon. He don't get out much."

White mumbled. Dell asked, "Where's Harvester Temisk?"

"He don't keep me posted." I tried to turn my head. I wanted a fix on the wide bodies. Choke wouldn't let me. "Aren't you a little low on the food chain for this kind of crap?"

Welby Dell grimaced. Exactly what he thought. All this was going to make life tough later. Teacher was betting their asses on one pass of the dice.

So Teacher hadn't polled the troops before hiring outsiders and dumping everybody in the kettle. Nor had he leveled with them yet. They'd have a grand scramble, saving their butts.

Teacher mumbled, "I believe you, Garrett. I was pretty sure you wouldn't know. But you're a whiz at finding things. So you're going to find Harvester and Chodo for me."

I tried to work my muscles so they'd be loose when I jumped up out of the chair.

Teacher grumbled, "Where the fuck is Skelington? I got Original and Spider down. . . . That asshole was supposed to be . . . he bail on me?" White's eyes narrowed. He'd had a thought. That was so unusual that he took a while to get used to it before he asked, "You know where Skelington is, Garrett?"

I shook my head. That hurt. "Ask Director Relway." Maybe I wouldn't do much flying around. I had cracked ribs to go with my dented head.

Something was nuts. Teacher White wasn't stupid enough to come at me like this. He had to have an angle.

"Fucking Skelington! Fucking moron Skelington! He chickened out! He bailed. We gotta get the fuck outta here. Goddamn Skelington."

White's intelligibility began to fade.

"Brett. Bart. About time, you assholes. You find Kolda? You get the stuff from him? Give it to Garrett. Now. We got to get the fuck out of here."

A ham of a hand grabbed my hair and yanked. Another got hold of my chin and forced my mouth open. Another one packed my mouth with shredded weed that had enjoyed a generation as skunk bedding before it got into the herbal-supplement racket. Yet another hand turned up with a lumpy old unfired mug full of water, most of which ended up on my outside.

The several hands forced my mouth shut, then covered my nose so I couldn't breathe. The ancient trick for making a critter take its medicine.

"Swallow, Garrett," Teacher told me.

I fought, but there was no winning. The lump went down like a clump of raw chaw, blazing all the way.

Teacher told me, "You'll nap for a while, Garrett. You just swallowed a drug that will see to that while Kolda's weeds have time to work." Teacher strained to hold it together long enough to give me all the bad news. "When you wake up you'll notice that it's getting hard to breathe. After a while, if you don't think about it, you'll stop. If you stop, you'll die."

I felt something spreading from my belly already. It wasn't the happy warmth of a Weider Select lager.

"Here's the deal. You stay awake and pay attention, you'll be all right. You fall asleep, you'll die. You can't remember to breathe if you're asleep. Bring me Chodo or Harvester before you croak—I'll give you the antidote. You know my word is solid."

That was Teacher's reputation. Though it did rest exclusively on the testimony of people who were still alive. Those he'd done real dirt to weren't around to bear witness.

"Nighty-night, Garrett. Don't waste no fucking time when you wake back up." White snarled, "The rest of you get this mess cleaned up. We got to get away from here."

The man was an idiot. He'd jumped on what looked like a good idea without thinking it through. His biggest failing was right on the tip of my tongue when the sleepy drug dragged me off into the dark.

The question was, how did I find him when I was ready to hand Chodo over? Assuming I found Chodo.

Overall, Teacher White qualified as a smart crook. The proof? He was still alive. He'd reached middle management. He'd stayed alive by being careful never to show any imagination.

His actions now constituted rock-hard evidence that he didn't have what it took to be a schemer.

He was going to get killed.

There was a damned good chance he'd take me with him.

34

Damn, my head hurt.

That wasn't a hangover. This was real pain caused by real blows to the head. Accompanied by pains everywhere else.

I was in the same chair. I wasn't tied down anymore. It was raining. Still. Moist air gusted in through a door that banged in the wind. It was the middle of the night. The rain was no heavier, but the wind was colder and more fierce. Occasional barks of thunder rattled the walls.

I got up. The change in elevation made my head swirl. My temples throbbed. My ribs screamed in protest. I might have made a sound or two myself.

There was no light. I wasted no time looking for a lamp. I headed for the doorway, landmarked by the lightning. I had to get out. I had to get moving. I couldn't get caught here.

I was at street level but didn't recognize where. I tried to get my thoughts wrapped around memories of Teacher White's territory. That didn't help.

It was cold and wet out. I wasn't dressed for it.

Not only had Teacher's guys disarmed me, but they had taken my jacket. They'd taken my roc's egg and my belt. I was going to be cold and wet and miserable before I got home. Assuming I figured out which way to go.

I clung to the doorframe, feeling too sick to move. Chunks of hardened rain took the occasional nick out of my face. I looked back at what I needed to leave behind, fast.

There were dead bodies in there. Original Dick and Spider Webb. I didn't know why. Or how. I wasn't going to check. Original was still curled up where he'd been all along, clinging to his midnight specials.

I staggered into the weather and hiked. I reached an intersection. It told me nothing. I clung to my assumption that I was inside Teacher's patch. I turned left because that would take me uphill. A higher vantage might reveal a familiar landmark next time the lightning flashed.

I shivered a lot.

I figured out where I was after two more blocks. Headed the wrong direction. Four blocks down that way . . . stumble. Stumble. And there I was, in a lane I knew, that led me to a street everyone knows. Two blocks east I hit a thoroughfare that would take me home.

But my head wasn't clearing up. I had a serious concussion. And huge trouble breathing.

35

Somebody too close to me had breath that should've drawn flies. Then I realized that stinky mouth had kept me breathing with the kiss of life.

Then I was home. Installed in a chair in the Dead Man's room. With no clue how I'd gotten there.

In a chair. Again. Barely rational. Among many chairs, some occupied by people maybe worse off than me.

The Dead Man had them under control. I felt his grip on me, which I resented immensely till I worked out that I was still alive because old Smiley was working my lungs for me.

The Dead Man's company included Skelington, looking more cadaverous than ever, John Stretch in his sister's chair, Saucerhead, Winger, and the Remora. Jon Salvation glowed because he was mind to mind with the famous Dead Man. Oh, and there were three guys who worked for Block or Relway, tossed in a corner.

Relax, Garrett. I have to examine your memories directly.

I was focused on breathing so didn't argue. Ah. Here came hot soup and a toddy. Here came Singe and a baby cat that wanted nothing to do with the Dead Man's room. She set it in my lap. The arch went out of its back. Its fur lay down. It started purring. And I became both calm and optimistic.

Winger and Jon Salvation got up and left, obviously

on a mission. Saucerhead left soon afterward. Then Dean appeared. He said the rain had eased up enough for pixies to fly. If any flying had to be done.

He went away and returned shortly with a toddy for my other hand.

I began to feel more upbeat. My tummy was full, the toddies were warming me, and Singe was tending my dents and dings. "Careful with the ribs." The concussion seemed to have faded.

Old Bones had turned off all my pain. Singe is no light-fingered nightingale. She poked, prodded, dug, gouged. "Nothing broken. This time. I need your shirt off to see how bad you are bruised."

Several of Morley's men were on hand, looking nervous and inclined to be elsewhere. One snickered. Puddle's hulking shape made a sharp gesture. The others kept it to themselves after that.

I focused a thought, wondering what they were doing here.

It will be done as soon as possible. I must install memories in the one named Puddle that will permit him to carry information to Mr. Dotes without his recalling having had contact with me.

"What happened to me?"

My mind filled with outside recollections.

One of Morley's boys had found me on his way to work. He'd been late. A woman was responsible. Married. To somebody who wasn't him. He wouldn't have noticed me if I hadn't been pointed out by some street kid.

He told Morley that his friend Garrett was in the gutter down the street, bleeding in the rain.

So I'd tried to reach The Palms after realizing that I couldn't make it home.

A rescue team went out and scraped me up.

There.

Puddle and the boys departed, zombielike. Dean made sure they all left the premises.

I recalled the terrible bad breath. And decided never to mention the kiss of life.

Puddle has trouble with his breath.

I find myself in a quandary.

"Yeah? That anywhere near Ymber? Dean. How about another toddy?" I'd apologize to Max Weider someday. Rare though they be, in some moments beer isn't the best choice.

Dean looked to the Dead Man momentarily before stating, "You get one more. Then there'll be no more drink."

"The quandary?"

I must see Colonel Block or Deal Relway. I will need them to help me get into the minds of the servants of A-Laf.

"Then you turned Puddle loose too soon. Him and his crew could spread the word about how they brought me home and it don't look like I'll make it and you won't wake up to help. Or send that stack o' Watch in the corner."

The front wall reverberated to a major pixie launch.

I will correct that oversight. Dean. Take a few coins to the front door to express our gratitude to Mr. Dotes' men.

Let Miss Pular put you to bed now, Garrett. You need not worry. As you surmised, Teacher White blundered badly.

"Makes you wonder if *anybody* could be that dumb, don't it?"

Never underestimate the reserves of stupid lying within this city. Nevertheless, an amble through Mr. White's mind might prove interesting.

I wanted to ask what Skelington had revealed, but Singe didn't give me time.

I know where to find you. Dean, see to the door, please.

36

I slept like a baby, thanks to my partner. One of his lesser minds managed my breathing. The samsom weed caused a sleep almost as deep as a coma. I had visitors during the night and was unaware of it. They included the herbalist who named what I'd been given but who knew of no antidote except good luck, time, and lots of water. He was amazed that I was still alive, so the luck did seem to be in.

Skelington knew Teacher White got the sleepy weed from a character named Kolda. Skelington believed there was an antidote and he thought Kolda had it.

Also in were a witch and a healer of the laying-on-of-hands variety. Neither did me any immediate good. Both agreed that I should drink water by the gallon. And Old Bones got to visit with a witch even though I'd been unable to deliver. He never explained why.

Others came in response to rumors of my ill health but waited till sunrise. Except for Tinnie Tate. She found a way to put the contrary aside when life got down to its sharp edges.

I woke up long enough to say, "Sometimes dreams do come true."

Tinnie Tate is one incredible redhead. All the superlatives apply. She's the light of my life—when she's not its despair. In some ways she's the gold standard of women, in some the source of all confusion and frustration. The trouble with Tinnie is, she doesn't know what she wants any better than I do. But she won't admit it.

She was there. And that was enough for now. She looked thoroughly distressed—until she realized that I was awake. Then her demeanor turned severe.

"When you do that, the freckles just stand out."

"You're a bastard even on your deathbed."

"I'm not gonna die, woman. 'Cept maybe from lack of Tate."

"And crude to your last breath."

"Cold. It's so cold. If I just had some way to keep warm . . ."

She was a step ahead.

Only one weak candle provided light. It was enough. For the hundredth time I was stunned and awed that this woman was part of my life.

How can I rail against the gods when once in a while they back off and let wonders like this happen?

Nothing happened. The Dead Man was right there in my head, disdaining discretion.

37

It don't matter who spends the night, snuggled up or otherwise. Pular Singe will drop in before the birds start chirping. And blame it on Dean. Or the Dead Man. Which was the case this time.

"You are needed downstairs."

I doubted it. His Nibs could have summoned me without troubling Singe. I grumbled, growled, muttered, disparaged some folks' ancestry. But by the time I arrived in what Old Bones had turned into an operations center, I knew all he wanted was my managing my own breathing so he could free up the secondary mind, keeping me huffing and puffing.

There was a vast, ugly conspiracy afoot, designed to get me to the house. So I wouldn't get involved in anything strenuous, like, say, discouraging somebody who wanted to twist little bits off of me.

I sat. I watched folks come and go. I breathed. Smiley didn't fill me in. This was how he worked. He gathered information. He looked for unexpected connections. Usually, though, I'm the main data capture device.

Dean brought food and tea. I ate. And sat some more while people came and went. I wondered who was paying them. Being a natural-born, ever-loving blue-eyed investigator, I intuited the answer. And felt the wealth sucking right out of me. My associates have no concept of money management.

I wondered who all my guests were. Some were complete strangers. Not Relway Runners, Combine players, Green Pants thugs, nor even part of the Morley Dotes menagerie.

"What are we doing?"

The Dead Man didn't answer me. *You believe Teacher White's men took your roc's egg?*

"I had it before I turned unconscious. I didn't have it when I woke up."

Exactly.

"Excuse me?"

I sent Mr. Tharpe to the place where you were held, immediately after I determined where it was. His examination of the site and the corpses suggests third-party involvement.

"Huh?"

When drugged you were supposed to remain able to do Teacher White's dirty work. The you who staggered away from there may not have been intended to wake up at all. You have contusions and abrasions unaccounted for in your memories. There are indications that someone attempted to strangle you.

"How do you figure all that?"

Circumstantial evidence. Your condition. The fact that Spider Webb was strangled with your belt. It was still around his neck when Mr. Tharpe arrived. The other man was strangled, too. There are bruises on his throat. Similar bruises are on your throat.

More suggestive is the fact that the bodies and other evidence were gone when Miss Winger went up there this morning.

"Teacher is in deep gravy and don't even know it? Who?"

That would be the question.

"A question, certainly."

We may be able to ask Mr. White himself soon. His associate Mr. Brix has told us where to find him.

"Who's Mr. Brix?"

The man you know as Skelington. His name is Emmaus P. Brix. With the middle initial standing for nothing. Ah. Mr. Tharpe has achieved another success.

Two minutes later Saucerhead's associates from

Whitefield Hall, Orion Comstock and June Nicolist, stumbled in, struggling with a wooden box obviously heavy for its size. Dean appeared immediately, armed with a specialized pry tool. Another product of my manufactory.

Singe paid Nicolist and Comtock, painstakingly recording the transaction. Neither seemed troubled by the Dead Man. They thought he was still hibernating. Despite the crowd, all of whom seemed part of the Dead Man's club.

These gentlemen have not been here before. They may not come here again.

"Oh."

Orion Comstock took the pry bar from Dean.

Nails shrieked as they came loose.

Kittens screamed all over the house. I heard them run, in confusion, upstairs, then back down into the kitchen.

Ah. As I suspected.

"What?"

To whom do you suppose they will think you are speaking?

I covered by heading for the hallway. Dean said, "I'll go. You need to be here." He sounded upset.

Singe, too, seemed troubled. Her exposed fur had risen. That doesn't happen often.

There was even an undercurrent of revulsion in my connection with the Dead Man. Then I started to hear new voices. Inside my head.

I edged nearer Comstock and Nicolist.

The wooden box was lined with sheets of lead. Inside sat a matched pair of shiny metal sitting dogs, each nine inches tall.

Jackals, Old Bones opined. *Almost certainly carrion eaters.*

"You guys get these from the Bledsoe?"

Comstock eyed me suspiciously. "That was the contract, wasn't it, slick? You saying—"

"Just startled. Saucerhead trusts you—I trust you. The ones I saw weren't sitting."

Comstock shrugged. "We seen some that was standing and some that was lying down. One was suckling pups. But Saucerhead said you wanted ones that was sealed up already. These are them."

"That's true. You did fine." I started to shove my mitts into the box.

Stop! Disappointed whispers echoed afterward.

"Careful there, slick. You don't want to touch them things with your bare skin."

I stopped. Cold rolled off the statues.

Nicolist showed me the outside edge of his left little finger. "That was just an accidental swipe."

A piece of skin was missing, a quarter inch wide and three quarters long. Cruel bruising surrounded the wound.

"Aches a bit," I supposed aloud.

"A bit. We need to get out of here, Orion. Runners are bound to turn up."

A concern that hadn't occurred to me, though it was inherent in the situation. "I'll let you out. And thanks, guys. You really helped out. We'll come to you first next time we have a tough job."

Orion and June exchanged looks, shrugs, and headshakes.

I used the peephole. I didn't see anything remarkable. Except that my door-fixer-upping technician, Junker Mulclar, had pulled his cart up behind one that must have brought the metal dogs. I told Comstock and Nicolist, "Nobody there but the people who always are. Move out cool and nobody will notice."

They went to the street. Mr. Mulclar hoisted his toolbox to his shoulder. He was wide, short, dark, craggy, an ugly man who counted a dwarf among his ancestors somewhere. He owned one of those faces that need shaving three times a day just to look dirty.

Junker is overly fond of cabbage, in both kraut and unpickled form. Whenever he stays in one place long that becomes overwhelmingly evident.

"Good morning, Mr. Mulclar. It seems to be the hinges this time."

"Call me Junk, Mr. Garrett. Everybody does. What happened?" He rumbled enthusiastically at the nether end. He didn't apologize. All part of the natural cycle.

"Same as always. These bad guys were bigger than usual, though."

"No! That can't be." He punctuated with a minor poot. "That door I put in last time ought to stand up to—"

"It isn't the door, Mr. Mulclar. It's the hinges. And if you saw those guys, you'd preen like a peacock for ten years because your work stood up so well."

Mulclar indulged in a rumbling chuckle, proud. Then rumbled in the opposite direction. The air was getting thick. Junk didn't notice. "You got some spare room in your basement? Space you ain't using? On account of I'm over here a whole lot anyway and my wife is throwing me out. . . ." He cut a competition class ripper. "Not sure why. Maybe she found a new heartthrob. Anyways, then I'd be right here whenever it was time to service my mainest account."

"That don't sound like such a bad idea, Junk." Hard to converse when you don't want to inhale. "But I already have more people living here than I can manage. And, nothing personal, but I owe them all more than I owe you."

"So it goes. I'll stay with my cousin Sepp. Or my sister." *Rip!* "It'll all work out. Though I'm going to have to diversify. With all this law and order going on they ain't so many doors getting broke down."

Junker Mulclar is a genius with hands and tools. There aren't enough like him in the Brave New Tun-Faire of postwar Karenta.

I gulped in some fresh air as a whiff breezed past. "Junk, I'm going to do you a favor. If you swear on your mother's grave you'll fix my doors forever."

Rumble! "Sure, Mr. Garrett. I thought we had that deal already."

"You know where the three-wheel manufactory is in Stepcross Pool?"

"Sure."

"You go find the green door, tell the man there I said you should see Mr. Dale Pickle. Take your tools. They'll give you all the work you can handle, and then some. And a place to stay, if that's what you need."

My business associates, all of whom possess percentages bigger than mine, agree that we should take care of our workers. Max Weider built his brewing empire by valuing and rewarding the people who made it happen for him.

Weider brewing employees are happy and ferociously loyal.

The manufactory could use a man of Mr. Mulclar's skills. And if he lived in, he'd soon become less aromatic. They wouldn't let him do his own cooking.

Mulclar did me an immense favor. "If you'll move out of the way, I can get those hinges fixed. It'll take maybe an hour."

Good luck with that, I thought.

I noted that Comstock and Nicolist hadn't taken their cart. If stolen carts kept turning up out front, there were bound to be questions.

I went in to warn everybody that we wouldn't have a door for a while.

38

It was quiet in the Dead Man's room. Singe and Dean had grown scarce to the point of invisibility. Several guests remained fixed in place. So did the metal statues in their lead-lined coffin.

"Those two had a point, Chuckles. It can't be long before we have a visit from the Watch." I heard whispers again. Saying evil things.

Excellent.

"You want them to?"

I hope Colonel Block comes himself.

"There's a chance. If he thinks you're snoozing. We'll never see Relway again, though. He's too clever and too paranoid to take a chance."

No doubt.

"You seem distracted."

I am trying to locate the creature Penny Dreadful. I feel her close by, but she is extremely elusive. Even the pixies could not pinpoint her when I sent them out last night. If the parrot were available . . .

"He's gone to a better place, far, far away. Tell me about these statues." I could make out no words, but the whispers continued.

In a moment. I want to examine an idea I found cowering in the back of your mind.

It must have been skulking around *way* back there. I couldn't recall having any that didn't involve heading back upstairs to Tinnie.

Yes. I do have sufficient capacity. Think about your

breathing. You will have to manage for yourself for a while.

"Huh?"

I felt a distinct difference when he let go. I thought he had already.

Minutes later one of our guests got up and sleep-walked out of the house. Focusing on my work, I breathed steadily as I watched him ease past Mr. Mulclar. He didn't notice the miasma, which had taken over the hallway. He didn't hear the voices. He was operating on another plane.

Old Bones retained control all the way down to Wizard's Reach, well away from Mrs. Cardonlos' place.

So. Now I knew what had been plucked from my brain. A wisp about filling empty heads with conflicting false memories so we could get these people out from underfoot. So we didn't have to feed them and take them potty and otherwise be weighted down with them.

A second man rose and went away. I didn't see him off. I didn't need another exposure to Mr. Mulclar. "Is this premature? Letting them go before we get somebody in to ask about the metal dogs?"

Jackals.

"Whatever. You see my point? Them being missing for a while, then turning up all confused and not knowing anything?"

I see your point. However, you fail to credit me with sufficient ability to confuse the issue.

"I'd never do that."

Do you recall past instances of dereliction by members of the Watch?

"Sure. There's probably a lot, but less than before Block and Relway took over."

The rest of our guests, excepting Skelington, left us eventually.

"So. About these dogs—all right! I know. Jackals. We've got them. What about them? What are they? Why have them stolen?" Getting rid of them would suit me fine. Especially if doing so would get rid of the voices in my head.

I have not heard of this cult of A-Laf, but there are suggestive similarities with others, particularly in the matter of the metal animals. If they are nickel, or some alloy that is mainly nickel, their function will be much like that of the nickel figurines that graced the altars of Taintai the Gift some centuries ago.

I'd never heard of Taintai the Gift. But there must be brigades of gods, goddesses, and their supporting casts who haven't sailed across my bows. Deities come and go. Their cycles are just longer than human ones.

"Interesting stuff, Chuckles. It'd be even more interesting if you'd drop a hint or two about what's going on."

I felt his amusement as he sent, *That will have to wait. We are about to have official company. Deal with it in your office instead of here.*

Vaguely, I caught the edge of a thought directed at Melondie Kadare. My pixie tribe were paying their rent now.

I scooted across to my office. I couldn't hear the incessant dark whispering over there.

Dean passed me in the hallway, headed for the front doorway. Where, after an hour, Mr. Mulclar did not yet have the bent hinges repaired or replaced.

I wondered if he heard the dark mutterings.

39

There was some racket in the hallway. Dean making offended noises. Somebody had gotten past Mr. Mulclar. More clever than I thought he could be, Dean fought a valiant retrograde action that lured the invader past the Dead Man's room to the open door of my office.

The man who burst into my office looked like he had been slapped together from parts taken from other people. On the south end he had spindly little legs and almost no butt. On top he had the chest and shoulders of a Saucerhead or Playmate. Then a head that went with his antipodes. All wrapped up in a badly fitted blue uniform.

He came in with mouth a-running. "What do you think you're doing, stealing religious relics?" Followed by fulminations that grew louder when I failed to acknowledge his presence.

Gently, calmly, conversationally, I asked, "Are you right-handed?"

"Huh? What the hell?"

"Which hand do you use to abuse yourself? That's the arm I'll break first." I ignored his associates. One wore a blue uniform jacket but not the matching trousers. His were brown. Maybe he couldn't afford the full outfit.

The fact that I remained more interested in paperwork than a raving home invader took the blusterer aback. Clearly, I rated him barely a nuisance.

I pretended to sign something, then looked up. "You didn't answer me. Nor have you introduced yourself. Are you married?"

"Married?"

"You keep on being an asshole, I'll need to know where to send the pieces."

I was playing a dumb, macho game. I could afford to. I had the Dead Man behind me.

Said sidekick let me know, *This nimrod is named Ramey List. He is a political appointee assigned to the Watch over the objections of Prince Rupert, who seems to have had little choice. His rank is captain. He is, nominally, a staff officer. The motive for putting him into the Watch seems to have been both political and to position him where he can get himself killed.*

"So that's what the new staff uniforms look like."

Captain Ramey List gaped.

His sort aren't uncommon. He was an incompetent aristocrat who suspected his own shortcomings and compensated by being obnoxious to social inferiors.

"Now that we're civil, what can I do for you, Captain List?" The Dead Man hadn't explained what he'd sent me. I assumed he'd raided the heads of List's companions for perspective. "Have a seat."

Captain List sat. Chuckles would be sedating him some.

List's companions remained at the doorway. The one with a uniform jacket offered a slight nod of approval.

"What can I do for my friends in the Watch?"

Captain List was confused. "Uh . . . Colonel Block wants to know why you defaced the Bledsoe and stole certain metal ornaments."

"I didn't. If that happened, I had nothing to do with it." Which was true.

List believed me, a remarkable eventuation for an officer of the law.

Dean brought refreshments, identical little trays for List and his companions.

In minutes List relaxed and, puzzled, was trying to

swap jokes. He butchered every attempt. A born dip-
lomat, I tossed in the occasional charitable chuckle. I
said, "It's still early, but if anybody wants a beer? . . ."

Something stirred behind List's eyes. Bingo! I knew
his vice without Old Bones clueing me in. A problem
with drink combined with a vile personality is a recipe
for unpleasant excitement.

Captain List won that fall with his demon. It was
early in the day. The devil wasn't wide-awake and
thirsty yet.

Then Dean appeared with a tray of frosty mugs.
Nobody shunned the opportunity.

Dean said, "I'll need to go out today, Mr. Garrett.
Unless you choose to stop entertaining. We're down
to the bottom of the backup keg."

"Ouch."

"There's wine in the cellar. But it's probably gone
off."

"We'll arrange something. Later."

*One beer should leave the man marked by aroma
enough to make him suspect.*

"I suppose."

Captain List frowned. "You suppose?"

"I suppose it's time to get back to work. Dean, do
you have your shopping list? Where did he go?"

The Watchman in the blue jacket told me, "He went
back to your kitchen."

I got up. List did the same. We shook hands, me
thanking him for coming by.

Keep him moving. Do not give him time to think.

Which I did. And during his flustered exit he did
what might be the only socially useful deed he'd ever
perform. "Dagon's balls, man!" he snarled at Mr. Mulclar. "Did a skunk crawl up your ass and die? Do
something! You could gag a maggot."

The Watchman not in uniform hung back. "I don't
know what you just did, buddy, but if you figure out
how to bottle it, I want some. I've got to babysit that
asshole six days a week."

"Some time when there's just you and him in a bad

part of town, get behind him with a board and whack him in the back of the head."

The man grinned. "I like the way you think. Shit. There he goes, starting to whine."

I turned to head back inside to visit the Dead Man. Mr. Mulclar asked, "Do I have a problem, Mr. Garrett?"

"Sir?"

"That fellow that just left said . . ."

"Yes, Junk, you're eating too much kraut. That's something you can change, though. He'll never stop being a dickhead." I hurried on into the Dead Man's room. "Was there a point to any of that?"

That man is, in effect, Colonel Block's second-in-command. He is convinced that he will replace the Colonel before the end of the year. He has been assured that that will be the case.

"There's a plot to get rid of Block?" I was surprised but not amazed. "Is List more competent than he lets on?"

Less. Under his supervision the Watch will collapse back to its corrupt old days. At best. At worst he will become a puppet of conspirators no more competent than he. They discount Deal Relway because he is not of their social stratum.

"Then they're in for a nasty surprise."

Indeed. The nastiest. There is no practical brake on Mr. Relway but Westman Block. Who removes the Colonel sows the whirlwind.

"Did we find out anything else useful?"

If you are interested in making a chain-of-command chart for the Watch, we now have all the names. Or if you're interested in the identities of informants and undercover operatives who work for Colonel Block, we have that. The list includes one Sofgienec Cardonlos. Never legally married.

"Aha! I was sure she belonged to Relway."

That is not impossible.

Of course. "Anything about the Green Pants Gang?"

He is not allowed near them. But he hears rumors.

We went back and forth until I knew what he wanted me to know. I asked, "So how about we get back to the dog statues?"

Jackals! Are you stupid?

"No. Why is the distinction a big deal?"

Words are important, Garrett. Especially when they are names. The same is true of symbols. Religious symbols in particular. The jackal is important in many religions. None more so than those with a dark view of earthly existence. The cult of A-Laf appears to hold one of the darkest.

He'd clue me in about the jackals in his own sweet time. If he had any real notion. He isn't above claiming knowledge he doesn't actually have. He doesn't just have multiple minds—he has multiple egos.

"You reached that conclusion based on what?"

Their behavior. The all-round implication that the cult is blacker than its feminine counterpart, which seems grim itself. Combined with recollections of historical precedents.

"You mentioned past cults before. Without explaining."

Past cults, yes. None quite like this. These people are not creating the pain and despair they harvest on behalf of their god. They collect it where . . . oh.

"What?"

We are about to have company. Again. Get them inside as quickly as you can.

"You keeping an eye on Mulclar? He's seeing a lot of coming and going."

He is oblivious. His entire being is focused on his work and his unfortunate flatulence. The possibility that his gassy nature is responsible for his outcast status never occurred to him before. Get those people inside.

So he wasn't going to explain the jackals now, either.

Did he have any real idea?

40

"Those people" arrived aboard a big black coach driven by Morley's man Sarge. The guy I knew only as Theodore rode beside Sarge. They were alert.

The coach door facing the house opened. Puddle popped out. He cursed when he banged into the cart abandoned by Comstock and Nicolist, looked around like he expected to see Venageti skirmishers. I saw no weapons but suspected an arsenal was available.

Puddle beckoned. A man descended from the coach, pushed. He had his hands bound behind him. He was blindfolded. Welby Dell. Ah. Interesting. Puddle made him run.

Theodore jumped down and helped Puddle extract a reluctant Teacher White. Teacher had no idea where he was headed, but he meant to fight all the way. It took Puddle and Theodore both to get him in the house.

There were two more passengers. A Combine third-stringer named Trash Blaser and my very good pal Mr. Morley Dotes. I wasn't entirely surprised to see him. Nor was I stunned when neither of Teacher's imported thugs tumbled out of the coach. Which headed on up the street as soon as Sarge saw his boss slide past Mr. Mulclar.

There was a roar that could only be the tradesman losing control of something he'd been holding far too long. Morley gasped, "Oh, gods of the Rime!"

I delayed a half minute, hoping the breeze would

disperse the miasma. While waiting, I noted that my pixies were as busy as bees, to sling an old chestnut.

My wait was pointless. Mr. Mulclar repeated himself with a true cathedral clearer just as I got there.

"I'm sorry, Mr. Garrett. I can't help it."

"I know that, Junk. None of us can. But we can watch what we eat. How much longer are you going to be?"

"It shouldn't be long. What the problem is, the screws—"

"I'm not concerned. It's your craft. One thing you can do for me, though, is keep an eye out for anybody who looks like they're interested in my place. The kind who try to break doors down might try to get in while this one is off its hinges."

"Oh. Yeah." *Rumble!* "I never even thought about that. I'll keep a eye out for sure."

"Excellent. You're a good man, Junk." I beat a hasty retreat. Teacher might have done me a favor, fixing it so I didn't have to breathe.

The new arrivals gathered in the Dead Man's room. None of them were happy. Morley less than most, probably. He sensed the truth immediately. The Dead Man wasn't napping anymore.

I confirmed his suspicion. "You and your guys want to get on out of here, go. If you'd be more comfortable."

They would. The whole bunch tramped back out, Morley leaving me with a dark look and an invitation. "Come by the club when you get a chance."

"Sure."

He followed his guys.

The ghost of a chuckle filled the psychic atmosphere.

"They didn't get out fast enough, did they?"

No. More psychic mirth. *They never do.*

He was having a good time, glad, now, that he'd wakened.

Singe came in, halfway slinking. She still isn't comfortable with the Dead Man, either.

His Nibs gave us our instructions.

Singe removed Teacher's blindfold and gag, but left his hands tied behind him. He found me seated facing him.

"So. Teacher. Things change. You got anything to say?"

Teacher wasn't happy. Not even a little. But he couldn't see the Dead Man from where he sat. He didn't yet know true despair.

He didn't respond. He wasn't a complete mental lightweight. He wanted to scope out his situation before he did anything.

"Here's how it is. Your poison didn't take. Not completely. So I'm not going to hold a grudge." I raised an eyebrow, then winked. He wasn't naturally as pale as Skelington, but he came close. He couldn't see the Dead Man. Skelington was in plain sight.

His mind is well shielded. I am making headway. While moving carefully enough not to make him suspicious. Distract him.

"Teacher, didn't you do your homework? Why didn't you know that you couldn't pull something like you tried and get away with it?"

Teacher had nothing to say.

"Seemed like a good idea at the time, though, eh?" I gave him a few seconds. "Somebody put you up to it? Dean, I'm getting dry. Can you bring me some water?"

The supporting staff know little of any value. Although, between them, they have developed an extended list of places that Mr. Contague and Mr. Temisk cannot be.

"And might there be a pattern? A hole somewhere?"

Your continued queries have alerted Mr. White to the possibility that I may not be fully expired.

I didn't need Chuckles to tell me when Teacher grasped the truth. He turned paler than he had been already.

I asked, "What did you do with my stuff you took?

In your wallet? Good. So. Who killed Spider and Original? No? You can't tell me? You didn't know? You left them there with me."

"They was supposed to look out for you. To make sure you didn't croak or nothing before you woke up."

He believes that to be true.

"What happened to Brett and Bart?"

"I didn't need them no more. I paid them off. Cut them loose."

Dean arrived with water. And a shopping list. Which looked all right. And made clear just how expensive all the entertaining was getting. "We're completely out of tea?"

"We are."

Grumble. "What's Singe up to? She get the kittens settled down?"

"They aren't happy. They're all huddled in their bucket. But they're not in a panic anymore."

The voice in my head told me, *The gentlemen from out of town were subcontracted through one Squint Vrolet.*

A ladder of wickedness popped into mind. Squint worked for Green Bean Ractic. Neither ran a patch where they'd have need of Bretts and Barts. But Green Bean reported to Tizzy Baggs. Tizzy's sister was married to Merry Sculdyte, Rory Sculdyte's stupid but enthusiastically homicidal brother.

Rory's psychotic little sibling managed a stable of violence specialists.

"Teacher, any chance you've been doing legwork for somebody without knowing? Merry S., maybe?"

He thinks so now.

Teacher had nothing to say, though.

Our reluctant guest is extremely angry, Garrett.

"I would be, too. Teacher. What about my antidote?"

White looked at me like he wondered if I was hopelessly naive. He asked, "Am I going to get out of here?"

"You got a good chance. What shape you'll be in

remains to be determined. Think we could get Squint and Green Bean in for a sit-down?"

He understood me perfectly. "There *is* an antidote."

"I know that. But I don't trust you enough to send you after it. Not until we fix you up with an unpleasant situation of your own."

Easily done.

"Huh?"

This man has a strong natural wall around his thoughts. But he cannot protect them consciously.

"Where are you going?"

He has friends inside the Watch. Inside the Al-Khar. Properly pushed, he might help us lay hands on one of those Green Pants fellows.

"Interesting. But why waste the knowledge? Block himself might bring them over."

You could be right, he admitted. Reluctantly.

"Here's your situation," I told Teacher. "My friend just planted a Loghyr mindworm in your brain. It'll make you go crazy. Slowly. Like those guys you see walking around arguing with themselves. Only it'll keep getting worse. Until a Loghyr pulls it back out. And there's only one Loghyr around these days."

I didn't highlight any ironies. I didn't say anything about who did what to whom. At the Dead Man's urging, I told White, "Get any of these people over for a chat—your life will get a whole lot easier."

The Dead Man sent him a roster that included the heaviest heavyweights of TunFairen crime. Teacher promised to get someone into the Dead Man's clutches somehow, but it might not happen fast enough to suit us.

It will, the Dead Man predicted, including Teacher in his sending. *Or it will not happen at all.* Moments later, White was loose. The Dead Man surrounded him with confusion so he could get a head start.

41

"Was that mindworm business for real?"

He will think so. That will be sufficient.

"I hope. Those people don't like to be bullied."

They tolerate it from one another. Did you recover the egg?

"I've got it right here." He doesn't miss much.

Bring it here.

I did so. That put me in position to see the doorway. Several kittens were watching from the hall. Singe slid past them. "Mr. Mulclar has finished." She made an entry in the ledger, took money to pay Mulclar. Finally.

The miasma had reached the Dead Man's room.

I asked, "Are Saucerhead or Winger likely to be around soon?"

I do not expect them.

"I was hoping one of them could go shopping with Dean. We need groceries. And he's a little old to be out there alone in times like these."

I see. Are you certain this is the egg that was thrown at you?

I looked closer. "The light ain't so good, but . . . it looks a little different."

This is a stone. And nothing but a stone. Either Bittegurn Brittigarn spun you a tall tale or you no longer have the original.

"I'll take it out into a better light."

I went to the front door, intending to go out into the daylight. I peeked past Singe, saw Mr. Mulclar just getting his cart moving. And . . . a couple of pedestrian women stared at Mr. Mulclar in awe. Then began gasping and waving their hands in a vain attempt to make it go away. "Hey, Chuckles. That Penny Dreadful is right across the street."

Where?

"In front of Elmer Stick's apartment building."

I sense nothing. Be as precise as possible.

"On the steps. Second step up, left side, leaning against the railing." I eased on outside, to get a better view.

Ah!

Penny Dreadful leaped like somebody had just branded her bottom. She ran, bumping off pedestrians who flung curses after her. She had trouble controlling her limbs, but she never fell down.

The farther she ran, the more control she gained.

I studied my rock in the better light.

It wasn't the same stone. There were tiny red veins in its surface. It wasn't as smooth. And it didn't produce that warm, relaxed feel when I fiddled with it.

I stepped back inside. "She too slippery for you?"

Exactly. She presents an incredibly small target. And an elusive one. One that senses my interest the instant it touches her.

"This isn't the same rock."

I did not think so. It is time we examined your memories concerning that rock.

"Why?"

It must be important. Certainly, important enough to be switched.

"Teacher White—"

Do not get ahead of yourself. Things do happen without the connivance or awareness of Mr. White. Sit down. Relax. Consider how useful it would be to have that parrot available for situations like the one with the Dreadful urchin.

"I do wish you wouldn't keep harping on that."

A good partner nags. To The Palms. To your first encounter with the stone.

I felt his mental tentacles slide into my brain, down deep into my memories of those brief moments.

I'm used to this—though I don't like it—so I focus on something else while he relives my life, rooting out details I failed to note consciously. I concentrated on breathing.

Done.

"And?"

You made some incorrect assumptions.

"That would be a first. Bring them on."

It starts when you walked out the door of The Palms. You did not, in fact, see the Green Pants Gang member sling the stone at you. The stone whizzed past you; you ducked; then you spotted the Green Pants thug. You put three and three together and came up with five. Green Pants did not do the dirty deed. His presence may have been happenstance.

"He ran away."

Did he?

"That's the way I remember it."

He did not. You do recall that he was amazed when you and Mr. Dotes set upon him.

"Yeah." Green Pants *had* acted like he was completely boggled. "I get a feeling we'll never find out the whole truth there because that guy got himself dead.

"If he didn't do it, who did? And why?"

Excellent questions, both. You did not see anything, even at the unconscious level, at the time, that sheds any light. And, with wicked glee, he nailed me. *So you may have been right in the first place, but for all the wrong reasons.*

"What the hell are you blathering about?"

The Green Pants goon may have slung the stone at you after all.

"Is this where I jump up and run in circles, shrieking and yanking out my hair?"

The point is, you may have come to the truth back then, but if you did, you did not do so based on the evidence. You harkened to your own prejudice and the fact that you saw no one else in the street.

"I'm thinking about setting fire to this place and walking away. So I don't have to suffer these convolutions again."

I am exposing you to the sort of thought processes that unravel. . . .

What could've turned into a fun squabble over not much went on hiatus when a frazzled Tinnie slipped in and demanded, "Why didn't you wake me up?"

"I tried. You said you'd chop my ears off if I didn't leave you the hell alone. That you were up all night and you needed some sleep." Tinnie hasn't been much of a morning person lately. Either.

The other thing we have in common, from a red-headed point of view, is that I'm always wrong. "Guess I should've been a little more firm, eh?"

She used to snap up that kind of straight line. Maybe we've gotten too comfortable. Her language wasn't ladylike. "I was supposed to be in the office four hours ago."

"Sorry I disappointed you by surviving, love. I'll time it more conveniently for you next time."

She glared but kept quiet.

I said, "Since you're late, and since everybody in your family will assume that a woman your age who was out all night in a situation involving somebody named Garrett was up to no good . . ."

Usually that sort of stuff winds Tinnie up. This time she was in no mood. She just kept scowling.

"Since you're going to be late anyway, how about you take Dean to the market?" Tinnie is a recognizable personality. People would stand back, not because she's my girl but because she's Willard Tate's niece. Willard Tate is one of those New Wave industrialists whose genius has begun to make him a huge power in postwar TunFaire.

Tinnie's expression was priceless. Too bad there's

no way to record all those freckles in motion. "You want *me* to bodyguard Dean? Why? So you can lay around with your beer and any bimbo who drops in?"

Her eyes glazed over. For half a minute she was the perfect girlfriend. Drop-dead gorgeous. And quiet.

The Dead Man was talking to her.

Tinnie clicked back. "I'm sorry," she said, moving in and bringing the heat. "I forgot what that villain did with his drugs."

I suffered her consolations for as long as it took Old Bones to become impatient.

"All right!" she snapped, pulling away.

I'd reconsidered. "You just go on home, sweets. You don't have the skills to protect Dean from the kind of people who're bothering us."

Tinnie is the contrariest person I know. Excepting my partner. I expected a big ration. Being contrary, she fooled me for the thousandth time. She didn't argue at all.

Maybe she was learning to listen.

It could happen. Even with a redhead. Sometimes the dice do come up snake eyes.

I suffered an inspiration as I walked Tinnie to the door, where a peek revealed nothing untoward. As we exchanged sweet sorrows, I suggested, "Go over to the Cardonlos place. There'll be police types all over. See if you can't get a couple of them to walk you home."

Right. A wiggle, a jiggle, and a giggle and the herd would take off carrying her on their shoulders.

"That might be a good idea. While I'm at it, why don't I borrow a couple to babysit Dean?"

Truth be told, I'd thought of that before I thought of looking out for her. But a certain minimal cunning has infected me lately. "Why didn't I think of that? I guess you distracted me."

"I'll distract you permanently if I find out you've got something going with Belinda Contague that isn't just business."

How do you spank a rat? The tail gets in the way.

Not Miss Pular's fault, Garrett. All mine, I am afraid.

Ah. Just as well, probably. Tinnie wouldn't listen to anybody else. Especially not some clown named Garrett.

After a final bout of nuzzling, the professional redhead moved out. And could she move. She passed through the crowd oblivious to the drooling, staring, and stumbling.

She's never been conscious of how strikingly attractive she is. If I say anything, she figures that's just me being me.

I watched her sail boldly into the Cardonlos harbor, where she disconcerted the crowd. And was on her way again in five minutes with a big, brave, alert policeman on either hand. While another headed my way.

"Scithe."

"Garrett."

"What can I do for you?"

"Miss Tate suggested that you might be able to get my wife's name bumped up the waiting list for three-wheelers."

"She did, did she? But she put it on me when she has a bigger piece of the pie than I do?"

"She said to remind you that she isn't the one who needs the favor."

"She would, too. All right. I can get her moved, but not all the way to the top. I don't have that much juice."

This stuff started the minute our three-wheels became the hot novelty everybody had to have, demand dramatically exceeding supply. The waiting list is two thousand names long. My ethically challenged associates pad corporate income by taking bribes to move names up the list. They'll harvest every loose copper in the kingdom if they can.

"Here's what I'm thinking," I told Scithe. And wove an elaborate scheme that used Dean for bad-guy bait. "All I'm interested in is having my man get his shopping done safely. If somebody messes with him, the credit, the collar, and any info bonus is all yours. Unless it has to do with me. Then I'm majorly interested, of course."

"Of course."

We exchanged a few more pleasantries, then I went inside and told Dean he could go marketing now. "And be sure not to forget the new keg."

Then back into the Dead Man's room. "How long before I get enough poison out of me so I can go outside?"

You have just begun detoxification. And you are not taking your fluids.

Sullenly, I reported, "Penny Dreadful is watching us again."

Let her. It means nothing. Except that she is worried about her kittens. We need to get Bittegurn Brittigarn in here. By whatever means necessary. He was the one who took your roc's egg. While spinning a tale meant to get you to fling the substitute into the river. Which would eliminate any suspicion.

"You really think he's a villain?"

He may be. Given the chance to interview him, I could deliver a definitive answer. He may just be weak.

"And what I get for my troubles is sarcasm."

42

Saucerhead dropped in. "They done forgot me already out there, Garrett. Nobody yelled nothing about there goes the guy what tried to rape the little boy the other night. Speaking of which, that nasty little critter is sitting on Elmer Stick's steps, bold as brass, eyeballing your place. Was I a betting kind of guy, I'd put money on she's trying to figure out how to bust in here, then make a getaway. The big guy still awake?"

"Once he wakes up he tends not to go down again till he drives the rest of us buggers. Unless him going to sleep will inconvenience somebody in some really huge way."

"I need to see him. See if Dean's got—"

"Dean's out shopping. On account of we're out of everything, especially tea and beer."

"Damn! I need something liquid."

The Dead Man let an implied sneer ride along on my shoulder as I headed for the kitchen. *Drink some water. Water is your only reliable antidote.* There wasn't an ounce of beer in the house.

I grumbled and mumbled but did as I was told. He was right.

I handed Saucerhead his water. Muttering about Bittegurn Brittigarn.

Excellent. Though you have to grant the priest his due. His sleight of hand was so fine I cannot pinpoint the instant when he made the exchange.

The more I reflected, the more I wanted to spank

BB till he gave up something useful. The roc's-egg story was a bushel of salamander dust. But the stone must have some bizarre, rare quality. And value.

He must be lured here somehow. Although unlikely to be part of the puzzle, he may hold the key.

I considered Saucerhead. Tharpe was babbling a report that was a waste of breath. The Dead Man was sucking info straight from his head.

Old Bones was impatient.

Saucerhead had been out getting the skinny on human combustions, the when, where, and who. The latter being the most difficult because the victims hadn't been anybody anyone missed. Too bad we don't have connections on the Hill anymore. One of the heavyweights up there might be able to save me tons of work.

Good work, as always, Mr. Tharpe. Miss Pular will pay you. If you wish further employment, there is a man in the Dream Quarter I want to see. Chances are, however, that he will not come here voluntarily. Explain, Garrett.

I told Tharpe about Bittegurn Brittigarn.

"Drinks a bit, eh?"

"Like a school of fish."

"Then he won't be that hard. He passes out down there. He wakes up here."

"He does have a guardian harpy," I explained.

"Maybe you could get Morley to go with me."

"I doubt that we'll see Morley for a while. Too much excitement in the underworld. He'll want to stay out of the way."

"Best thing, till it settles. I reckon. Guess I'll have to sweet-talk her myself."

I said nothing. That wasn't easy. For Saucerhead sweet talk means hitting things with a smaller hammer.

Singe paid Tharpe and recorded the outlay. Saucerhead cooled his bunions for a while, grumbling about his love life. It was the usual story. He had him a woman who treated him bad.

"Pity there's nobody in our circle who's musical.

We could set your life to music and create us a tragical passion play."

"It ain't funny, Garrett."

"So you keep telling me. Then you go pick the same kind of woman and make the same dumb mistake all over again."

"Yeah. Only I never see it out until it's too late. I'm on my way. Do I got any expense latitude?"

Just bring the man here.

"Hey!" I protested. "That's my money you're throwing away."

Cost it out in your Keep On Breathing account.

"This puzzle really grabs you, eh?"

Your cases always wander the tombs of chaos. This time more than most. Good luck, Mr. Tharpe. Help us create order out of incoherence.

I said, "It only looks chaotic because there's a bunch of different things going on at the same time."

True. But those things keep banging into and tripping over one another because they have you in common.

A couple of kittens grew bold enough to enter the Dead Man's room. Tentatively, though. "That's kind of scary."

It is, indeed.

43

I snoozed. My partner kept me breathing. Next thing I knew, Singe was shaking me. "Dean needs help bringing stuff in."

I grumbled but dragged the loose parts together and headed for the front door. This was TunFaire. Somebody had to watch the goods while somebody else lugged stuff inside.

Dean probably planned to deploy his skills as watcher, yielding to me as a journeyman lugger.

He fooled me. "You stand by the cart and look ferocious. Mr. Sanderin and I will get the kegs installed. Singe, will you help? Or are you just going to stand there looking pretty?"

Singe scooted down and loaded up.

I spied Scithe and a pal across the street, headed for the Cardonlos place. Scithe waved.

Dean had conned a beer delivery guy into going out of his way. A Weider brewery guy. They're hard to distract, normally. But this Mr. Sanderin had let Dean pile on a bit of everything we needed around the house, including a sack of potatoes and a bushel of apples, which wouldn't last long once Singe got to stewing.

Sanderin had a case of nerves, probably because I'm the guy who checks up on Weider brewery employees. "Relax, Sanderin. I didn't even see you today."

When Dean came back after moving the first keg

inside, I said, "Your pal Penny is hanging out across the street again."

"She's worried about her kittens. But she's afraid to come across and find out how they are."

"So you told her, eh?"

"I told her they were all right. They're getting enough to eat. Nobody is hurting them."

"Which would be why she suckered you into taking them aboard in the first place. Right?"

"She wanted to take advantage of the Dead Man's reputation. Without having to deal with Himself. But he woke up."

"Pity."

"No need to be sarcastic, Mr. Garrett."

"Maybe not. But it sure feels good. She's welcome any time. We don't bite. Well, I might. But I promise not to leave scars."

"You need to see the situation from her viewpoint."

"Dean, don't bullshit me. You don't *get* to bullshit me. That's no child. She's not twelve years old."

Dean sighed. "You're right. She's just small for her age. And she's been on her own since she was twelve. She's sharp as a knife about some things and stone naive about others. And I want it to stay that way."

I got the message. "I should feel hurt by your underlying assumptions. How about you tote a barge or two? Lift a bale? Singe is on her third load."

Dean got Mr. Sanderin to help him. Once they couldn't see, I blew Penny Dreadful a kiss.

Relway's boys noticed. Maybe they'd give the kid a hard time and she'd come looking for shelter.

Singe caught me. "You are a black-hearted villain, Garrett."

I grinned. "Ain't life fun?"

She just said, "Looks like more rain."

Yes. It did, actually.

44

The rain started in the afternoon. It began gently, but cold. After a round of thunder, it turned to freezing rain. Lucky me, I didn't have to hazard streets gone foul and treacherous.

I was in with the Dead Man, halfway napping, feeling restless. Like I never would have if I'd been free to go out. The Dead Man was having fun needling me about my sudden surge of ambition.

Somebody came to the door.

Dean clumped on up there. He was tired of playing with kittens and trying to manage an intelligent conversation with Singe. He can't ignore what she is for long.

Voices rattled but got lost in the clatter of the rain. Which fell with great enthusiasm, coating everything with ice. Morley came in looking as bedraggled as ever I've seen. He had ice on his head and shoulders. I said, "I'm speechless."

"If only that were true."

"What's a dog like you doing out on a night like this?"

"It wasn't bad when I started. I was two-thirds of the way here when it turned awful. I huddled in a doorway with refugees until it was obvious it wasn't just weather god whimsy. Here was closer than home, so I came ahead. I fell several times. I may have sprained my wrist."

I chuckled, picturing him huddled up with a bunch of street folk. "I suppose I ought to sit on my mirth until you tell us what you're up to."

Morley told the Dead Man, "Your little boy is finally beginning to develop social skills."

Enough contusions and abrasions eventually wear the corners off even the roughest blockheads, given time.

"I can't argue with that," I confessed. I started to lever myself out of my chair.

Never mind. Dean and Singe are coming. They are eager for something to do that does not require them to be good company to one another.

Dean arrived carrying a chair. Singe was equipped to dry Morley out and wrap him in a comforter. Dean said, "We'll get something warm inside you as soon as can be."

"I'll be fine," Morley said. "I just hope those idiots at The Palms don't burn it down while I'm gone."

Morley is a micromanager. He isn't comfortable giving his people an assignment and letting them run. I said, "You went off to the Cantard with me one time and it was still there when we got back."

"That was in the old days. You couldn't hurt the place when it was the Joy House."

He went on, but I listened with only half an ear. I was marveling at the Dead Man. He'd dropped "Miss Pular" in favor of the informal "Singe." He had accepted her into the family.

Such as it is. Strange as it is.

Maybe I ought to recruit a dwarf now.

I asked, "What's become of all the dwarfs?"

Which question garnered bewildered looks.

I said, "It just hit me. I don't see dwarfs anymore. Come to think, there aren't many trolls around anymore, either. Even elves aren't as common as they used to be."

"Members of the Other Races are leaving Tun-Faire," Morley said.

I gulped me some water. I couldn't tell if it was all in my head, but I seemed thirstier all the time. "You saying all that human rights racialist stuff is working?"

"It is. Though not quite the way you're thinking."

"Eh?"

"You don't really think a bunch of drunken yahoos with ax handles would intimidate a troll, do you?"

I had to admit it. That didn't seem likely. "We're getting old."

"Speak for yourself. What brought that on?"

"We're sitting around a fire talking instead of being out in the weather having adventures."

"And I'm just as happy. If I'm careful, I'll last for centuries."

"Then how come you're out when even the mad dogs have crawled under the porch?"

"I didn't plan it."

"I got that much. Thanks, Singe. Pull up a chair. Listen to the master tell tall tales."

"I wish," Dotes said. "What did you do to Teacher White?"

"Nothing. Just chatted him up. What you'd expect. Why?"

"He's gone insane. He hit Merry Sculdyte. You don't mess with Merry—unless you catch him with his pants down. Which is what Teacher must have done. Rory will have smoke coming out his ears."

"So Teacher did something stupid. Is that a major departure? You got any more details?"

"No."

I noted the Dead Man's absence from the conversation.

"What got into Teacher?" I mused rhetorically. "He was pissed off because two heavies he borrowed from Merry croaked Spider Webb and Original Dick on him. But he didn't seem suicidal when he left."

The Dead Man said nothing. I'm sure he wasn't feeling guilty, though.

I admitted, "We did ask him to get a couple people to come by. I didn't think he'd go start a war."

Dotes mistook me. "Your name isn't in it. Yet."

"Not entirely reassuring. But good to know."

Dean seldom takes an interest. But he had no work and it was too early for bed. He brought a chair in and nurtured the fire while he listened. He kept quiet.

I told Morley, "Interesting stuff, but why come out in this?"

"I was concerned that Rory might think you had something to do with his brother's misfortune." Friendship and the showmanship involved in being a manly man lead us through dumb contortions, sometimes.

"What do you think, Old Bones?"

Nothing.

"Come on. I know you're not asleep."

Indeed not. I am monitoring the approach of the grand villain Teacher White and his merry men. Including a man named Merry, whose appellation seems singularly inappropriate.

"Headed here?"

Five minutes. Teacher White knows the truth, but Merry Sculdyte will come in blind.

I felt him get busy telling everybody else what to do. He's a take-charge kind of guy.

45

Though Morley was bedraggled, he was his old svelte self compared to Teacher White, his crew, and their prisoners. That whole gaggle was on the far marches of the drowned-rat category. Though Singe would have bristled at the cliché.

Teacher told me, "Here you go, asshole. Green Bean, Squint, Brett Batt, and Merry Sculdyte. This'll probably get me killed. And here's what Kolda told me was your friggin' antidote when I bought the samsom weed. Now have your monster get this nightmare outta my head."

I stood around gaping like a yokel while Teacher's henchmen piled bodies in the hallway, and halfway wished my monster would get the whispering nightmares out of mine. The black murmurs just wouldn't go away. Dean sputtered about the water being tracked in. The captives were bound. They were all bloody. Some were still leaking. That did nothing to make Dean happy, either. I couldn't imagine what White's bunch must have done to pull this off. I had more difficulty imagining what the Dead Man could've done to Teacher to get him so motivated.

Excellent. Most excellent. You have performed prodigies, Mr. White. I am sure that, at this point, you would like to disappear for a while.

"No shit."

Go quickly, then. The watchers are paying no attention because of the weather. Go quietly.

"What about the mindworm thing?"

I have removed it already.

"That fast?"

That fast. That easily. You will begin to feel much better soon. Go. Watch your footing. Move that coach away from here, even if it is stolen.

Just what we needed. Another stolen vehicle abandoned in front of the house.

The White crew went away, fast.

"Did you get anything new from them before they left?"

Nothing useful. Though Mr. White certainly had himself an adventure. It will become an underworld saga if he survives.

"Interesting." I checked the pile of twitching, battered bodies delivered by my once and future enemy. "What about this lot?"

Where to start?

I gave Brett Batt a huge kick in the ribs. "Right here. Put in two of those mindworms."

Garrett.

"All right. I'll be civilized."

Morley opined, "I was beginning to wonder."

"Meaning?"

"I was beginning to wonder if you hadn't developed sense enough to bust a moose like that up when the chance was there instead of waiting till it's fair."

Move Mr. Vrolet out into the weather. Leave him under someone's stoop. He knows nothing.

There was an edge to his thought that left me mildly suspicious. "It's freezing out there."

The chill will wake him up.

"Everything's covered with ice."

Then you will have to make sure of your footing. No one will see you. Those tasked with watching us have chosen to do so in warm, dry places.

I muttered and grumbled. The crowd of Dean and Morley eyed me like they thought I was being a big baby. And I was. It was nasty out there. But I latched on to Squint. Dean worked the door. I hauled the villain off into the night. The front steps didn't improve his complexion.

"How many times did you fall down?" Morley asked when I stumbled back into the Dead Man's room.

"I lost count. Dean. Can you make hot cocoa?"

It arrived immediately. A cup all around, except for the bad guys. Maybe smelling it cooking was why I asked.

Mr. Ractic can be removed now, Garrett. Once you finish your cocoa.

"Is that the way it's going to be with all of these goons?"

You have a better plan?

"Any plan that doesn't take me out into the weather."

That would result in our guests' waking up here in the house. And, possibly, remembering it later. An insalubrious eventuation.

"Easy for you to say." I considered kicking Brett another time or two. "How am I supposed to move this ox?"

I am confident that something will occur to you. Deeply amused.

He was having fun with me. And I didn't know what it was all about.

I sighed and got to work dragging Green Bean. I didn't damage him much getting down the front steps. I planned to dump him somewhere on Wizard's Reach, but when I got to the stoop where I'd left Squint, Vrolet was gone. I replaced him with Green Bean.

The rain continued to fall. Most of it found a way to get under my collar in back. I needed a hood or a big hat.

Gloves wouldn't hurt, either.

Garrett!

I jumped, startled. "What?" I was still ten yards from my stoop, clinging to an abandoned, stolen goat cart, halfway unconscious, trying to keep from sliding back downhill.

Remember to breathe. You are lucky to be close enough to be assisted.

Yeah? I had a feeling that I'd just been manipulated somehow, so I'd learn a lesson.

I went in and attacked some more cocoa. Then hot tea, then cold water. I crowded the fire. I asked, "Are we learning anything? Has any of this been worth my trouble?"

You will be pleased to learn that Mr. Rory Sculdyte considers you one of the most dangerous men in Tun-Faire. Worth murdering preemptively.

"Oh, my. I'm a made man now. Are we headed for another anticlimax, with these guys all being marginal?"

Not quite. You were a target of opportunity for the Batt brothers, not the point of the exercise. Merry Sculdyte had instructions to put you to sleep if the opportunity arose. Perhaps the stone egg was slung at you by an opportunist Sculdyte soldier. You are on the list not only because you are a general nuisance but because you might find Chodo before the Sculdyte crew. You have an astonishing reputation among these thugs. Clearly, they do not know you at all well.

"What're my chances of digging them out?"

Getting better by the minute. Every thug able to get up on his hind legs has been looking. We know a very great deal about where Mr. Contague is not.

"Is he with Belinda? Or does Harvester Temisk have him?"

The consensus is that Miss Contague is hunting her father with more vigor than anyone else. And your idea did occur to me. I have asked John Stretch to put word out in the ratman community, offering a substantial reward.

Clever. Ratfolk go everywhere. Nobody pays attention, except to yell. I glanced at Singe. She seemed quite pleased. And tired.

It was getting late. I realized, with some surprise, that we hadn't yet tapped the new keg.

How long could that last?

This Brett Batt is ready to go. You cannot imagine what a banal personality the man has. Though knowledgeable. Certainly knowledgeable.

"You got something useful?"

A few points of interest did lurk in the corners of his mind.

"Such as?"

I will see that you know what you need to know if a situation should arise where you need to know it.

All right. We were going to play games. More games. He'd fished something tasty out of Brett's head. He didn't want me to know. Or maybe to obsess about it.

More or less. It has little to do with anything we are investigating now. Take him out of here.

Grumbling, I laid a two-hand grip on Brett's collar and started hauling. The only help I got was Singe's volunteering to work the front door.

Brett was one lucky bruno. His good buddy Garrett had hold of him at the head end instead of by the feet. Because of this his good buddy Garrett one-manned him down the ice-rimed front steps without banging his skull on even one.

"What'cha doin'?" Saucerhead Tharpe asked. He had collected coagulated precipitation till he looked like the abominable iceman. He wasn't alone. A wobbling companion, clinging to his arm, also looked like a perambulating ice creature.

"I'm dragging this butthead over to that cart." I'd suffered the inspiration of a fanatic slacker. If I could just get Brett aboard that thing . . .

Tharpe and his pal grabbed hold and helped me hoist Brett into the cart. Then Tharpe said, "Me an' Bitte are gonna get on in outta the weather. All right?"

"Go ahead on. There's hot cocoa. And we got a new keg in. I'll be there in a minute." I eased in between the double trees, got a good hold on those poles. When I broke their ends loose from the ice, the cart began to roll.

It worked like a rickshaw in reverse. Me behind. Trying to keep up.

Macunado Street slopes gently down for a third of a mile. Long before that I turned loose. The cart rolled. It went on. I flailed around, slipping and sliding, never quite falling down. I couldn't keep up and didn't try.

Brett's ride managed not to smash into anything for longer than it took me to lose sight of it in the dark. I heard it glance off something, continue on, ricochet off something else, then participate in a huge crash. I imagined Brett flying through the night, then spinning on up the glassy street on his prodigious pecs.

His problem. I headed on home wondering why I hadn't broken some of his bones before I let him roll.

I found Singe waiting to let me in. She was amused. "How many times did you fall this time?"

"Not even once."

She was disappointed.

Saucerhead and his drinking buddy wandered on into the Dead Man's room, where Old Bones continued to entertain Merry Sculdyte. *Garrett, I need you to transcribe what I am recovering from this villain. It is not my custom to meddle in civil affairs. However, my rudimentary sense of social obligation compels me to provide this information to Colonel Block and Director Relway. This man is intimate with the darkest and most secret machinery of the underworld. Much more so than Mr. Dotes. Or even Miss Contague. This man knows where the bodies are buried because he buried most of them. He knows which officials are corrupt. He has a good notion which people on his own side could be suborned by Director Relway. In a mundane manner of describing it, Mr. Merry Sculdyte is the pot at the end of the information rainbow.*

"Excellent. We're in the money. Have you noticed Saucerhead's guest?"

Brother Brittigarn wasn't so wasted that he failed to notice that I wasn't talking to Morley. He wasn't so wasted that he failed to recognize me in the light. "Oh, shit. Man.'Head, you jobbed me."

I am aware. I will start on him once you begin writing.

Brittigarn decided to make a break for it. He managed a step and a half before he froze. Then he turned and walked to my usual chair. Mechanically. He sat, rested his palms on his thighs, stared at infinity. And dripped.

Dean peeked in. "Is there anything more you need from me? It's past my bedtime."

"Some rags for this clown to drip on. Where'd Singe get to?"

"She's in the kitchen trying to tap the new keg."

"That should be amusing."

I went over to my office, where I could be comfortable while I wrote.

It was around sixteen o'clock. My hand was an aching claw. I couldn't go on.

Get some sleep. We will continue later.

"How much more is there?"

The man is a bottomless well of wicked memoirs.

What I'd already recorded would be invaluable to Colonel Block and Belinda both. And any number of Combine second-stringers like Teacher White scheduled for involuntary retirement after Rory Sculdyte helped himself to his patrimony.

"How're you doing with BB?"

The man has an intriguing mind. Get some sleep.

I pried myself out of my office chair, joints creaking and popping. I need more exercise. My body is beginning to show wear and tear.

I stuck my head into the Dead Man's room. People were all over, sleeping. Singe was nowhere to be seen.

46

This time the old slug thug himself dragged me out at a criminal hour. He was eager to go on. Excited, even. He borrowed a colloquialism when I protested the absurdity of the hour. *Paybacks are a bitch.*

I didn't get it until I was halfway through my second mug of black tea. When he started nagging me about dragging my feet.

He was getting even for all the times I'd dragged him out of his little naps, just so he could earn his keep.

"Life's a bitch."

How is your breathing?

I hadn't paid attention. It was working. What did I care?

He withdrew. It wasn't me making it work. I wasn't back on automatic yet.

"I still have to think about it. Maybe the stuff Teacher brought isn't the real antidote."

Possibly not. He was not deeply concerned about an antidote when he purchased the samsom weed.

"Typical of the breed."

I let Dean serve me breakfast. Singe came in. She'd been outside. I felt the cold roll off her fur. She said, "You need to take a look out there before it all goes away."

I finished my mug, went and looked.

The world was glass. Or crystal. Actually, all coated with ice. So much ice that the weight had broken limbs

off trees and pulled gutters off buildings. A kitten
thought about going out with me but changed up as
soon as he laid paws on ice. He jumped back, shook
each paw in turn, indignant. "Don't blame me. You're
the one who wanted out."

I surveyed my neighborhood. Nothing moved but a
family of mountain dwarfs trudging up Macunado like
this was just a brisk morning in the hills back home.
It had been an age since I'd seen TunFaire this quiet.

I retreated from the cold. "You're right, Singe. It's
fairy-tale beautiful. And now it's starting to snow."
Which would make the ice even more treacherous by
masking its wicked face.

Dean met me at the door to the Dead Man's room.
He'd brought more tea. "You'll need this."

I accepted and went inside.

The faces in the crowd remained the same. Saucerhead was sprawled on his back, taking up a vast
amount of floor space, snoring. Brittigarn and Merry
Sculdyte were in chairs, limp, under mental sedation.
Morley was awake. But he's the sort of pervert who
doesn't mind being in that state when the sun comes
up.

"You still here?"

"You brought a blast of cold air in with you. Meaning you just looked outside."

"It's pretty out there."

"Pretty isn't a problem for you. You're already
home."

I raised an eyebrow.

"I'm nimble. But not nimble enough to make it to
The Palms without breaking something."

"I saw a family of dwarfs out front. They were
managing."

"This is skinny-dipping weather where they come
from. And you said there aren't any dwarfs around
anymore."

"I said you don't see many. I just caught the not
many on the move."

"You may have to give up beer."

"That's a zig when I expected you to zag. What brought that on?"

"Singe."

"Oh." It would be a problem if she became too dedicated to barley soup. "You don't suppose all that smoke out there is because Sarge and Puddle burned your place down?"

"I have an abiding suspicion that people are firing up their fireplaces."

"It isn't winter yet." The sharp, softly bitter smell of woodsmoke is a sure sign of winter. More than snow is. People fire up their fireplaces only when they're sure that the cold has arrived for real.

Fuel is dear. Most of it is barged in from way upriver.

I noted the presence of several kittens. One had homesteaded Saucerhead's chest. Another had set up housekeeping in Merry Sculdyte's lap.

The Dead Man didn't intimidate them anymore.

They avoided BB, though. Despite his snoring.

Morley observed, "It won't be Sarge and Puddle who do me in. Neither one of them is smart enough to start a fire. The ones who worry me are the ones who *think* they're smart enough."

The Dead Man didn't acknowledge my arrival until then. *How is your hand this morning? Are you ready to resume?*

I noted that I was favoring my left. "It's stiff. I won't be able to do much."

Find a trustworthy professional letter writer.

"Have you paid any attention to me and Morley?"

I try not to indulge in frivolity.

"The weather situation isn't frivolous."

Oh, my.

He did seem surprised.

The season sneaked up on me.

I felt him recalculating how long he'd been asleep. "It's unseasonable. But severe."

It is snowing heavily now. Once several inches accumulate, the footing will become less of a problem.

"Hell, there's an old pair of skates down in the basement somewhere. I could dig them out. I could fix them up, sharpen them up, refurbish them up, put them on Morley. . . ."

Morley said, "Morley don't skate."

"Oh?"

"I tried it once. See this scar? In my eyebrow? That's what hit the ice first. Split me right open. Why are you grinning?"

"Nothing, really." I was just delighted to discover that I could do something he couldn't, well and with style.

We will make do until the footing improves.

I noted a twinkle from under BB's brows. He was awake but pretending not to be.

Old Bones noticed, too. *Our friend from Ymber is producing some interesting information.*

"So give me all the gory details. Unless all that needs to be written down, too."

Some will have to be, eventually. The man is a charlatan. A successful charlatan, to be sure, but a charlatan nonetheless. He was not born in Ymber. He migrated there before the religious squabbles turned bloody. One of his recent ancestors was not human. He has a touch of what he sells as psychic power. His religion he cobbled together himself. It went over well in Ymber because many people were tired of the feud between A-Lat and A-Laf.

"I thought open warfare was something recent."

Yes. It would be instructive to compare Penny Dreadful's recollections with those of Mr. Brittigarn. His are entirely self-serving.

Old Bones fed me the tale of a con man whose scam had worked well until it caught the attention of A-Laf's deacons and sextons after a fundamentalist, activist faction seized control of A-Laf's cult. They sharpened their teeth on BB's followers. The survivors fled to TunFaire, where they failed to support their pastor in the style to which he wanted to be accustomed. The sin pots of the big city picked them off.

Now that the battle between A-Lat and A-Laf had immigrated, it didn't seem likely that Brother Brittigarn would enjoy the Dream Quarter much longer.

"How about my roc's egg?"

He did not bring that with him. Mr. Tharpe received no instructions concerning it. So the stone is still in the temple of Eis and Igory.

"But he did switch it out and then not fling it in the river?"

The stone is much too precious to be thrown away.

"No!"

Sarcasm does not become you.

"No. But I do tend to get sarcastic when you say something that obvious."

He is reconsidering making a run for it.

"Then stop him. How hard is that to figure?"

It may not be that simple if he realizes what natural tools he possesses.

"Use your standard tactic. Baffle him with bullshit. Why does he want the stone?"

Proof that Old Bones hadn't lavished much attention on BB then surfaced. He didn't yet know why. He had to go pearl diving in a mind naturally indisposed to surrender its treasures.

This will take a while. He appears to have been of several minds concerning the stone. Though each of those focused on wringing the biggest profit possible from the windfall.

Classic crook-think. Calling a theft a windfall. "Why?"

I felt a little prickle in my mind. He was checking to see what I meant. Instead of asking.

"You're awfully impatient this time, Old Bones."

There is so much going on. And I am so excited.

"You've become sarcasm incarnate. How is the egg important? Why is it valuable?"

Because he may have told the truth about how dangerous the rock is. Even though it might not have been stolen from the nest of a fabulous bird. He wants to auction the egg on the Hill for enough to get out of the priest racket. The stone does rate description as "rare as rocs' eggs."

"I'm confused."

I am surprised that you would notice.

He has a bite like a saber-toothed toad.

"Have Singe do your transcription. She needs the practice. And it'll keep her out of the beer."

He offered the mental equivalent of a harrumph.

"So. About the stone?"

It can be used to start fires.

"Is that so?" I sensed that he didn't know anything else, in any concrete way, but was chock-full of speculation.

I have Miss Winger working an angle that may tell us something useful.

Which he wouldn't share right now, of course, because he doesn't like to speculate or brainstorm—except among his own minds. He doesn't like being wrong. But I could guess what he was thinking. I'd considered it myself and decided the idea was too far-fetched. *You should have mentioned the stone to Mr. Tharpe.*

Saucerhead groaned. He sat up, clapped his hands to his temples, swore, and lied, "I'll never do that again."

"What is that?"

He realized he hadn't taken on his career as a cat mattress by indulging in too many adult beverages. "What happened?"

Morley told him, "It was too nasty for you to go home last night."

"What time is it? Oh, gods! I shoulda been over to . . . she's gonna kill me!" He tugged at his clothes, retied his shoes, hoisted himself to his feet, and headed for the front door. I tagged along so his misery would have company once he looked outside.

Saucerhead took his look. "Holy shit! What did you do?"

"Man, you can't blame the weather on me."

"Sure, I can. No law says I got to be logical." He

showed me his biggest shit-eating grin. He stuck his head back outside, retreated again. "I blame it on the peace."

"What? You blame what on the peace?"

"The weather, man. When we had us a war going we never had no weather like this. Not this early."

"What the hell are you babbling about?"

He grinned again. "Just yanking your chain, brother. I keep hearing that kind of crap out there in the taverns."

"Oh."

"You don't get out there no more. You don't know the latest lunatic theories."

Saucerhead Tharpe lecturing me about lunacy. It's a strange old world. "You going to jump on out there or not?"

"I think I'll hang out here. That's just plain too ugly."

It was a good thing Dean got a chance to lay in supplies.

I did what I could to loosen my writing hand, went back to work transcribing Merry Sculdyte's memoirs. Singe and Morley spelled me. There wasn't much else to do but try to play chess.

I found one more area where I could feel superior to my favorite pretty-boy dark-elf breed buddy. Though he insisted I was getting secret help from my sidekick.

And his handwriting is barely legible.

47

One by one my guests slipped away.

Morley left first, after waiting almost all day. An hour later Saucerhead plunged into the snowfall, which had passed its peak. It now consisted of glistening little flakes that looked artificial. There was a foot on the ground. And not much wind, which helped ease the misery.

With Tharpe gone, I asked, "What do we do with these other two? BB has a wife."

The woman at the temple is his sister. He lets her believe she is the brains behind his confidence games.

Singe was writing, tongue hanging out the left side of her mouth. She concentrated ferociously, head tilted way over. She wasn't quite ready for illuminated manuscripts.

"Singe. You think other ratfolk could learn to copy stuff?"

"What?"

"Do they have a high tolerance for boredom and repetition? If they could learn how, we could start a copy business."

I turned back to the Dead Man and BB. "Is she? The mind behind?"

He does not believe it. He may be incorrect. You will have to feed him. Soon.

"Have to? Can't I just cut him loose, chock-full of confusion?"

There is more to be had from him. Something he does not know he knows. Something that has his unrealized talent fully wrapped around it, protecting it.

"Is it critical?"

I will not know till I chip it out. It could be the final clue to the meaning of life. Or his mother's recipe for buttered parsnips.

Taking into account my standing as fool to the gods, a quick calculation suggested that Brother B. would be partial to parsnips.

The Dead Man suggested I take over for Singe. He was impatient with her striving for perfection. I refused.

"We aren't going anywhere in any hurry. How about Merry? Is he mined out?"

There is nothing left to be learned from Mr. Sculdyte. But his release into the wild must be handled carefully—after long delay.

His absence will leave his brother indecisive. It will cause competing underworld factions to act with restraint. They will all be nervous and his disappearance from the criminal scene will work to Miss Contague's advantage. Merry Sculdyte is the one enemy who was able to penetrate the Contague household.

"What?" This was news to me.

Perhaps he was exaggerating to make himself look better. Read the manuscript and find out.

"But—"

Read the manuscript. That will keep you out of trouble.

Dean brought supper for everyone. After supper Singe and I moved over to the office to read each other's transcripts.

When I went up to bed I was aswirl with emotions. Once the Unpublished Committee for Royal Security reviewed Merry Sculdyte's memoirs, organized crime would suffer hugely.

The nagging question, as I fell asleep, remained, where were Chodo and Harvester? Were they together? Was all this something they planned way back when? Had Temisk pulled a dramatic rescue? Or was he working some huge scam?

I shivered down under my winter comforter. It seemed my bed would never warm up. I checked my breathing.

Despite having downed a well full of water and most of Teacher White's antidote, I still needed help.

I kept on shivering.

48

Dean made soft-boiled eggs for breakfast, an expensive treat this time of year.

The whole crew was determined to spend me into the poorhouse.

"Stop whining," Singe told me. "You are not poor."

"I'm going to be, though. I'm working for nothing. You're all eating like princes and throwing money down . . . the storm sewers." I'd been about to mention rat holes.

Dean grumbled about quails' eggs and giving me something to bitch about if I really wanted to bitch.

Singe said, "He is this way because it is morning."

She had a point. It was way early. And I couldn't blame my situation on anybody but me. Nobody dragged me out this time. I did it to myself.

I shivered. I hadn't shaken that yet. And I heard the whispering of the damned, in relaxed moments, from far, far off in my mind.

After I ate I checked the weather.

There wasn't a cloud in the sky. It was blinding bright out. Pedestrians slogged through half a foot of slush, carefully. The ice hadn't gone away. Scavengers were gathering fallen branches for firewood.

I retreated to the Dead Man's room. The contrast in light levels left me blind.

How is your breathing?

Startled, I realized I was breathing on my own.

Be cautious. You are but a third of the way recov-

ered. *You have no wind. It will be days yet before you dare strain your self.*

"No running or fighting?" Maybe the samsom weed was why I couldn't stop shivering.

Nor anything else you indulge in that causes an increased heart rate.

"Oh."

Psychic snicker.

"Then you'd better scare the redhead off if she comes around. Because I don't have a surplus of self-discipline where she's concerned. Hey! Where's my pal Bittegurn?"

I sent him back to his temple to recover the firestone.

That didn't sound like the smartest move. "Think he'll bother to come back?"

He will return. He is convinced that he has found a way to make the big score that has been the secret goal of his life.

"I feel you wanting to crow. What did you do? Crack that last shell inside his head?"

Exactly.

"So how much stroking will I need to do to get you to tell me about it?" I shuddered, the worst fit of shivering yet. "Did you do that?"

Did I do what?

"I've been shivering since last night. But this was worse. A completely creepy feeling for a second. That feeling people get when they say somebody walked over their grave. It wasn't the first time, either. And I hear things. Whispers. That are just a hair too far off to make out. So. What did you get from BB?"

The connection. No. A connection.

"With what?"

Between the excitement in the underworld and the Ymberian question.

"Huh? No. There isn't any connection. There can't be."

Historically, there is. However, you are correct in thinking that there is not one now. Not directly. None of those ambitious felons out there, eager to take pos-

*session of Chodo Contague, are aware that while he
was establishing himself, he rented muscle from the cult
of A-Laf. They did great violence that could not be
traced back to him. For his part, he later provided similar services to the aggressive faction now controlling
the cult. You will remember Mr. Crask and Mr. Sadler.*

"You got all that out of Brother Brittigarn?" I shivered, just remembering Crask and Sadler. Being glad
that those two were among the angels now. Because,
in their time, they'd been much worse than Merry
Sculdyte. Much more in my face, far more often.

*I did. That is, he knew the secret history of the A-
Laf cult well enough to let me fill the gaps. He did not
know the name of the TunFairen criminal captain
whose blood money financed the growth of the cult.
But what he knew made it obvious that Chodo Contague must be that hidden ally. I expect Mr. Contague
would be considerably nonplussed to discover what his
assistance has made possible.*

"No shit."

Excellent thinking.

"What?"

*You were thinking that it might be useful to see Mrs.
Claxton again and interview her from a new
perspective.*

"Yeah? Yeah! I'm so clever." I shuddered again,
again stricken by that totally creepy feeling that made
the chills worse than ever. The whispers were almost
intelligible. I had a notion that it would not be good
to really understand.

Got that this time. Ugh. I should have seen it.

"You going to fade into one of your mystery moods
while I figure it out for myself?"

*Not this time. It would be too dangerous to wait that
long. The mood you feel, the whispers you hear, are
caused by the nickel jackal idols. They came here fully
charged with pain and misery and madness. All that
has begun to boil off. Someone did not reseal the box
properly.*

"Begun? This has been going on since they dragged

those things in here. I just didn't make the connection." I began to have trouble breathing. But none whatsoever shivering.

No need to get upset.

You can't breathe, maybe you do need to fuss.

I stared at that damned box. The lid was closed. But it hadn't been nailed down tight.

A baby cat trotted in, headed my way, bounced, landed in my lap. It made itself at home. But it stared at that box, too. With an intensity suggesting that it saw things invisible to me.

Much better.

"What?"

You are calmer now. Once you are comfortable with it, nail that box shut.

"Sure. I'm a rock." But he was right. The panic was gone. The whispers had receded. My hands weren't trembling. "How much longer is this going to last?"

That cannot be predicted. It may become necessary to catch this Kolda and make him tell us about samsom weed. I do not want to deal with flashbacks and seizures indefinitely.

"Yeah? Consider my point of view."

Ah.

"Ah? Ah, what?"

The rumor of your imminent demise may be about to pay dividends.

"I am on my way," Singe said, heading for the front door. A moment later I heard Scithe talking, though I couldn't make out individual words. Singe came back to report. "That was a Watchman. He wanted to know if it was true about you. I said yes. On inspiration, I told him you had been forced to take a poison Teacher White got from somebody named Kolda."

I did not cue her, Chuckles informed me. *She thought of that herself.*

"Good going, Singe. They'll round them all up."

Singe puffed up with pride.

No time for patting one another on the back. Garrett, you need to be in bed, dying.

"Block is at the Cardonlos place, eh?"

It seems logical. I believe he is. Mr. Scithe suspects he is, though he has not seen the Colonel. He was sent here because of his ignorance. But he is brighter than they suspect. He believed his real task was to find out if I am awake. He will report that he found nothing suspicious.

Block being Block, *that* would be suspicious.

"They'll think you messed with his head, then."

Not amusing. Go be sick.

49

The being sick part didn't require much acting. I still had aches in my pains and bruises on my bruises and those were turning colorful. I hadn't gotten near a razor in modern times. I kept hoping Tinnie would come back and give me a sponge bath. I shivered and shook.

I fell asleep. Which I needed to do. I'd wasted altogether too much time not sleeping.

Tinnie woke me up.

"Oh, hell!"

"Thank you so very much. I'll just go back home."

"I wasn't being . . . you're here because you heard I was dying. Somebody from the Watch told you, right?"

"Yes. How did you know?"

They knew she'd been here before. They'd walked her home. They'd visited her before doing anything else.

"And you told them I'd be all right because the Dead Man keeps me breathing."

"Oh-oh. I goofed."

"Yep. We wanted to fish Block into coming over here. The Colonel was too clever for us this time." Did Block know something he was eager to keep to himself? Probably not. He just had a dislike for having his secret mind exposed.

My breathing seemed almost natural. But thinking

about Tinnie and sponge baths alerted me that I wouldn't be living the fantasy anytime soon. "Life is a raging bitch."

"Dean said you'd be in a bad mood. You haven't been drinking as much as you should. Water, I mean."

My, my. She could be right. I was thirsty right then. I climbed out of bed, rocked dizzily. "Oh."

"You all right?"

"Dizzy."

"You're shaking, too. Is the Dead Man starting to rub off?"

"He's been contagious lately." I sat back down. She was right about the shakes. My dizziness didn't improve. "Maybe you'd better get Dean or Singe to bring some water."

The dizziness not only did not relent. It got worse. Likewise, the shakes. I felt the Dead Man touch me, concerned. Dean brought water. I sucked a pint down without taking a breath.

You are not supposed to become genuinely sick.

"I guarantee you, it wasn't in my master plan."

Tinnie said, "You're running a fever."

I collapsed back onto the bed. "This may need to run its course."

Dean invited himself in. He seemed disappointed not to have caught us in midfrolic. "I brought a pitcher of beer. A rapid pass-through might do some good."

I gave him the most potent fisheye I could muster while teetering at the brink of unconsciousness.

I drank all the barley soup I could hold. It was prescribed. I did pass out then, shivering, outraged because this had happened to *me, now*.

Vaguely, I heard Dean opine that I must've caught it that night I was out in the weather. Less vaguely, I tried to get the Dead Man's attention because it might be those damned metal dogs again.

Jackals.

I wakened with a mild headache and a solid, coughing cold well started in my left lung. Tinnie materialized before I got all the way upright. I grumbled, "Aren't we getting domestic?"

She had thoughts on the matter. She didn't share. "Drink this." She'd brought a steaming hot mug of something more fetid than aged swamp water.

"Are there wiggly things in here?"

"Dean forgot to add them. I'll go get some. Start on this in the meantime."

I took the mug, held my breath, downed a long draft. Fighting a cough as I did. I don't get sick often. If I do, Dean usually conjures some effective remedy.

Tinnie didn't leave. She made like a stern mother forcing her recalcitrant scion to polish off his ruta-baga pie.

"Guess the poison and the exposure did me in."

Tinnie smirked. "Once you're strong enough, go downstairs. Dean has a steam thing set up."

A steam thing. I hadn't been steamed and herb-alized since I was a kid. Somebody thought I was on the brink of pneumonia.

"What the hell? This morning I was—"

Miss Tate silenced me with a scowl. "This morning was a different world. You got sick. Fast. In a big way."

I didn't collapse when I got up. But my world whirled on its axis. I was in trouble.

The kind of trouble you're in when a gorgeous red-head gets under your arm and up against you, pre-tending she's helping you when she's actually torturing you with no shred of shame.

I didn't have much trouble breathing while Tinnie was helping me. Just the opposite.

It looks like the worst may have passed. Which means you will be back to your usual uncouth self before the rest of us adjust.

"I'm hoping, Old Bones. Before this one gets away."

That earned me an elbow in the ribs. The sore ribs.

"Easy, woman. What've you got against compli-ments?"

"Their artificiality? Their lack of sincerity?"

"I'm a little lame in the brain right now. How does that saying go about sharper than a frog's fang?"

"Serpent's tooth. Which you know. Because you haul it out every time somebody disagrees with you."

"Who could possibly disagree with me? I'm so cute." I had to sit back down, then lie back down. I'd used me all up.

"Drink some water."

"You're awful cranky."

"I haven't been getting enough sleep."

Sense was setting in. I thought before I spoke. "How long have you been here?"

"Fifteen hours."

Wow! That explained some things. "I must've been a long way gone."

"You're lucky the Dead Man is awake. And not just because of the breathing."

"Huh?"

"You made me so mad I almost killed you last night. You tried to die on me."

"Uh . . . all right." This sounded like one of those times when anything I said would be the wrong thing. Even silence wouldn't cut it. But silence would bring on the fewest lumps and bruises.

"You probably shouldn't get up. But we need to get you bathed and get your bed changed."

"Sickness is a bitch. Has to happen right in the middle of everything." We'd lost what, two days already?

Nothing has been lost by your suffering. Nothing has happened.

Tinnie got that, too. She told me, "It's snowing again. It's weird. We've had half a winter's worth and it really shouldn't have started yet."

More water arrived. Dean didn't carp about anything. That meant I'd definitely had a close call. I drank some, then said, "I'm starving. But I feel nothing better than chicken soup coming on."

"And be thankful for that."

"Old Bones. Was it the samsom weed? Or something else?"

You have Mr. White to thank for your situation. If not the person called Kolda. The supposed antidote appears to be another poison.

Teacher. The kind of guy who went to the trouble he'd gone to to get even for Spider Webb and Original Dick might've wanted to get even with me.

"Hey! Why didn't you warn me? Wouldn't you have seen it in Teacher's head if he was trying to poison me?"

White appeared to have no conscious villainy in progress.

Dean brought the anticipated chicken soup. Only it was nothing but broth. All the good stuff had been strained out.

It was warm and thick and I was starving. I sucked it down till I couldn't hold any more.

Minutes later I declared, "I'm starting to feel human." Pause. "Well? Somebody going to jump on the straight line?"

"Nobody's in the mood, Garrett. The last fifteen hours were misery curdled. Ready downstairs, Dean?"

"Steamer's going. Water's hot. The tub is out. I'll get something to dry him off and we'll be set."

Tinnie snapped, "Off your butt, big boy. It's bath time."

I stood. With help. The world hadn't gone stable, but it didn't have that awful wobble where I tripped and stumbled into a nightmare dreamland.

I felt stronger by the time we hit the kitchen. Where the air was thick with steam, the herb stench watered my eyes, and the heat was overpowering.

Dean had dragged the big copper laundry tub up from the cellar. Two smaller tubs were heating on the stove. I said, "This ought to cook a few demons out of me."

"If only," Tinnie and Dean sneered at the same instant.

If only. You should be beyond crisis, Garrett. But we must make sure. You are doing most of your own breathing. Secondarily, Dean and Miss Tate wish to render your personal aroma somewhat less piquant.

I didn't have energy enough to get my feelings bruised.

Tinnie grumbled, "Arms over your head. Off with those filthy duds."

In the steam and heat I caught whiffs of what everybody else had been suffering all along.

No wonder Singe and her miracle nose were elsewhere.

That weed sweat was pretty awful.

50

They steamed me for the rest of the century. They were generous with water and beer, but still I sweated a good ten pungent pounds. And was too weak afterward to make it back to bed on my own.

My bedding had been changed. Somebody had opened the window briefly, despite the weather. A charcoal burner was warming the room now. Herbs had been added, meant to mask bad smells.

I collapsed. My last recollection was Tinnie cursing like a Marine as she levered loose extremities into bed.

I regained consciousness with a furious hangover—again—and a worse attitude. How many times would I go round this circle of misery? Hell. Maybe I could get my karma all polished up in one lifetime.

I had no strength. I was a big glob of pancake goo, just splattered there. If I'd been able to feel sorry for anybody else, I would've reflected on how awful life must be for Chodo. But from the surface of the griddle the horizon is close. Only a strong caution from the Dead Man and a residual dollop of survival instinct kept me from taking it out on Tinnie.

It is not her fault. It is not her fault. He is handy, sometimes.

"The Dead Man says you're cured." Damn her eyes, she was chipper. Perky, even. Which made it harder to hold back. "There's some work you can do today. Notice, you're breathing on your own now." Tinnie fed me watery porridge and honeyed tea. "You more inclined to concentrate on the manufactory full-time now?"

Here came some potholes in the high road to romance.

"I thought you all wanted me to stay away." On account of I mutter and sputter and carry on like the group conscience. Particularly when they're trying to expand the corporate profit margin.

"You could keep your mouth shut. You can contribute without making everybody want to smack you with a shaping mallet. Security is getting to be a challenge. We've had parts go missing. We think somebody is trying to build a three-wheel at home."

Singe arrived with a tray. But no food. "This tea has willow bark in it. Dean thought you might have a hangover."

I did, but I was getting better. "Thanks. How come nothing else?"

Singe eyed Tinnie's tray. "Your gut can't handle anything heavier."

I was ready to tie into a mammoth steak. "Not even soup?"

"Soup for lunch. Maybe. Maybe something solid for supper. If you keep the soup down."

I was cranky enough to chew rocks. But some damnable shred of decency wouldn't let me snarl and bitch when people were babying me. Probably supplemented by a suspicion that the babying would stop.

I drank tea. I drank water. By the time I finished dressing and got downstairs I was thirsty again.

Dean gave me apple juice. The flavor hit my mouth like an unexpected explosion. After an almost painful moment I understood that I had my sense of taste back, never having realized that it was gone.

How is your writing hand? Recovered, I trust?

I muttered. I grumbled. I made noises like I might

not only go to work at the manufactory full-time. I might move there with all my treasures and none of my burdens.

I got a big mental sneer in reply. And a confession that, *The transcription is complete. Merry Sculdyte has departed, in a state of vast confusion. He has memories he knows are not his own. But he cannot sort those out from others that are. He is afflicted with suspicions of his brother and benevolent feelings toward Teacher White. Who, he vaguely recollects, saved his life and nursed him back to health after somebody tried to assassinate him.*

"You seem to have lost some scruples."

They are not lost. They are in abeyance.

I was so amazed I forgot to feel sorry for Ma Garrett's baby boy for nearly a minute. "Oh? Explain a little more."

The Sculdyte family has a plan. An extreme plan. Not advantageous for TunFaire. Much better if Miss Contague continues to wrangle the underworld. Her victims are her own kind. And deserving.

I understood once I skimmed notes from those Merry memories not recorded in my own fair hand.

Rory did have a plan. It involved destroying the Watch. He expected backing from the Hill once the killing started. But Merry had known no names. It sounded more like raw wish fulfillment than solid scheme, but Sculdyte was convinced that a reckoning with the Watch was imminent. Upon removal of Chodo and his wicked daughter.

The Contague name still had conjure power.

51

I napped while Colonel Block read. The trudge over to the Cardonlos place had worn me out. Even with Tinnie along to pick me up if I got lost in a snowdrift.

My honey shook me when it was time. The poor girl was ragged.

Block was done. And hot enough to boil water. He glared at me. "How dare they? How *dare* they?" Then, less rhetorically, "Did you really have a close call?"

"You're going to worry about me? That makes me nervous." But I sketched my age of suffering.

"I don't need to hear about every twitch and burp, Garrett." Then, "That doesn't allay my natural cynicism. I can't help wondering, if you're willing to turn this over, how much more interesting is the stuff you're holding back?"

"It's hard, going through life misunderstood."

"I doubt that anyone misunderstands you even a little, Garrett. Eh, Miss Tate? Nevertheless, we're in your debt."

"Really? We could use a visit from some Green Pants guys."

"That might serve our purposes." Without hesitation or argument.

"Send a clerk, too. Somebody without imagination enough to be scared of the Dead Man. I can't write anymore." I showed him a hand shriveled into a claw.

"It isn't that I don't believe you're literate, Garrett.

I've witnessed incidents. What I can't envision is you doing that much work."

I shrugged. I'd surprised him before.

His heart wasn't in his banter. It was broken. Somebody out there was so indisposed to the rule of law that he meant to make war on it. "Where is Merry now?"

I shrugged again. I was getting a heavy workout. "I was asleep. They put him out in the snow. In a state of confusion, apparently."

"Assuming your story has a nodding acquaintance with the truth, then, Rory may guess that his baby brother ran into the only Loghyr left in TunFaire."

Not all of TunFaire's crooks are terminally stupid. Only most of them.

I asked, "Any idea where Belinda Contague is?"

"No. She's as elusive as her father. Why?"

"Curiosity."

Block grunted. He was antsy. He wanted me to go away so he could go talk this over with his unsocial sidekick. His claw within the shadows.

Sighing, Tinnie hoisted me to my feet. I groaned. It would be a long, cold trek home. I told Block, "We wouldn't mind seeing one of the foreman type Ymberians, in addition to the standard wide load with the bad fashion sense."

The good Colonel nodded, distracted. He wasn't exactly caught up in the moment.

52

The wind was no longer as wicked. It was behind us now. And I was too wiped out to be distracted by externals. I couldn't focus on much but hunger and wanting to get back to bed.

Nevertheless, that old Marine training persisted. "See the waif beside the steps down there?"

"Yes. That the kitten girl with the mighty name?"

"The very one."

"She don't look like a princess."

"How do I convince her she doesn't have to be afraid?"

"Get the eunuch operation?"

"Come on, Tinnie."

"I love you, buddy. But love doesn't have to be blind. She's female. She's old enough to stand on her own hind legs. Which means she'd better not get close enough for you to do your helpless little-boy routine."

Story of my life. They want to mother me instead of let me treat them badly, Morley Dotes style.

"You're too young and beautiful to be so cynical."

"You might wonder who made me that way."

"I will. When I find out who she is, I'll give her a piece of my mind."

"Sure you can spare it?"

We were home. She whacked on the castle gate. I puffed and panted. The long climb up left me without wind to argue.

I swear, there were still echoing whiffs of Mulclar swirling round the stoop.

Singe opened up. Tinnie handed me over. "Give him lots of water, some broth, and let him nap. I'll be back." She returned to the street. Singe didn't give me time to thank her.

The Dead Man demanded, *Do you have something to report?*

"Save time. Do it the easy way." I settled into my chair, halfheartedly trying to remember when we'd shed all our guests.

I felt him stir the sludge inside my head. I went to sleep. After what didn't seem like thirty winks, I woke up to a meal set up on a small table beside me. Singe ambled in from up front, where she had admitted a snow-encrusted redhead.

I said, "I thought you went home."

Tinnie frowned. Then, "No. I went to talk to the princess." She didn't sound like she was awash in sympathy for Penny. "She's as stubborn as a rock. She won't come over and get warm."

I asked, "She sat still? She talked to you?"

"She didn't feel threatened."

"What's her problem?"

"She's the last one standing, Garrett. She's still a kid. But she saw her mother, her aunts, and her grandmother murdered. By men."

"Men in green pants, not harmless little fuzz balls like me."

"Men. That's the point. The A-Laf cult. Which, the way she tells it, is a lot nastier than we imagined. They think women are evil. That they're fit only to be breeding slaves."

I sensed faint but constrained mirth. "Careful, Old Bones. She's wound up. And your attitude is pretty bad."

"It isn't his attitude I had in mind, big boy."

Time for a change of subject. "Dean! Where are you? Bring something for Miss Tate. Singe, how about you help her with those wet things?"

Tinnie glared. I was being thoughtful.

The air of amusement grew. *As I have observed previously, when you get hit hard enough for long enough, you do begin to learn.*

Tinnie glowered.

Your visit with the girl was more productive than you think, Miss Tate.

He left it at that. Until Tinnie had eaten and warmed up and grown less cranky. Then he told us that Tinnie had distracted Penny enough for him to slip a couple of suggestions into her divine head. *I could not browse. The girl has been trained to recognize and resist a probe. Therefore, I fed what was there. Fear. Despair. Loneliness. And physical misery.*

He didn't share the latter with Tinnie, who was likely to turn all outraged.

She was still eating. And listening to Singe talk about chances for a bath followed by a long nap. Singe suddenly shut up, stood upright, and stared at the Dead Man with glazed eyes. Then she headed for the front door.

This should be interesting. He didn't explain. Back to Penny Dreadful. *The impulses insinuated should heighten the child's entire range of emotion. We can expect her to look for emotional support.*

It would behoove you to make sure that Dean does not leave the house before she cracks.

53

Butterbutt sent Dean to the door. Dean did try to sneak out. Chuckles didn't let him. The old boy got all foamy-mouthed about supposed shortages in our stores.

The rest of us got excited about the three bipeds delivered by Scithe and several Relway Runners. Scithe told me, "Ask and ye shall receive. Sign this receipt, Garrett."

I signed, checked his catch. "The bruno seems a bit dull."

"That would be his natural state. Though they did drug him up. It was the only way to keep him docile. This other one, you smack him some and he gets cooperative."

"The long, skinny one the clerk?"

The third man was tall and vague. He slouched with hands in pockets. Defeated. The part in his hair was four inches wide and ran back to his crown.

"Yeah. He's a twofer. A bonus baby. He'll do your transcription. Call it public service, to work off bad behavior. The Director gets a kick out of that kind of thing."

"What'd he do?"

"He poisoned one of our more exotic Karentine subjects."

I didn't get it. I was in slow mode.

"Kolda, Garrett. Your herbalist. They ran him down this morning."

"Relway has a twisted sense of humor."

"We enjoy it. Got to go. Always more bad boys to catch."

Dean saw the strongarms of the law to the door. He attempted another escape. Old Bones shut him down. Singe took him back to the kitchen.

I stared at Kolda. Stared and stared. The man almost killed me. Though not deliberately. Teacher White asked for a tool. Kolda delivered. He would've sold the same drug to me if I'd asked, with silver in hand.

He does not know who you are.

"Too bad. Suppose we put him to work." I'd get even later.

Before he started on the Green Pants crew, the Dead Man rifled Kolda's head. He didn't find much. *You have brought women home who have more between the ears.*

"Hey! Tinnie resents that!" Knowing he wouldn't have included her in his last.

He is a power within his own field, however. He could write a major grimoire on medicinal herbs. He is not a social creature. Though he does have a wife and three children.

"Marvelous. Good for him. I can barely keep my eyes open. Before I fall asleep I'd like to know if you mined any nuggets out of these fools."

Kolda and the Ymberian foreman became suspicious. Kolda turned scared. The Dead Man calmed him down, set him up to record what he dug out of the other two.

Ah. Here is an interesting tidbit. Our once-upon-a-time friends Mr. Crask and Mr. Sadler began their careers as sextons in the A-Laf cult. Chodo Contague suborned them. Not that they were especially devout. Being sextons allowed them to indulge their needs to hurt people.

That sounded like those boys. And my old pal Chodo.

The Dead Man made the equivalent of a girlish squeal of dismay.

"What?" I couldn't keep my eyes open.

Tinnie had gone up to bed already. But she'd had a hard few days.

The smaller one has hidden defenses. Nasty ones. He is pulling them together now. He has only just realized the truth of his situation.

"A little slow, is he?" Not surprising, though. A lot of line boss types amble around with their heads stuck in dark and smelly places.

Our friends in the Unpublished Committee treated him with a preparatory drug, too. Therefore, he is slower than he might be.

Ouch!

"What?"

There are mousetraps in there. I got a finger nipped. This will be challenging. He was excited. *And dangerous. He has some minor training in the use of sorcery.*

Oh, hell. What did I get myself into now?

I'd worry about it after another nap. If Butterbutt didn't provoke the Ymberian into imploding the house.

54

Three hours was time enough to restore me to a functional level.

There'd been changes. Saucerhead had turned up. He nursed a mug of something warm. John Stretch was in Singe's personal chair, hard at work on a big bowl of stewed apples. My mouth watered. Melondie Kadare was absent. I hadn't seen her for a while. The weather must have caught up with her tribe.

Singe brought me a bowl. Summoned by Chuckles, no doubt. It was gruel.

"I see the place is still standing." Both the Ugly Pants foot soldier and Ugly Pants manager appeared to be sleeping.

The most powerful wizard who ever lived cannot work his wickedness if he cannot focus. The key to sorcery is will and concentration.

What might the Dead Man be doing inside the deacon's skull? He had me confused and boggled without even trying.

"Good to know. To what do we owe the honor of foul-weather visits from Saucerhead Tharpe and John Stretch?"

Ask them. I am occupied. As you proceed, however, go through the pockets of the sexton.

Singe brought John Stretch another bowl of apples and a mug of beer. Saucerhead had a beer himself. Singe is a generous girl when it isn't her purse that's being drained.

Saucerhead seemed less likely to be distracted. "So what's the word?"

"I got your rock back. Bitte put up a fight, but . . . actually, I brung that back when you was still sick. It's on your curio shelf."

We have a set of shelves where we keep memorabilia. Some are good for a chuckle. Now that the pain has gone away.

"Thanks. And?"

"I been going on tracking down all those times where somebody caught on fire and died."

That must've been exciting. Maybe the gods did me a big favor, letting me get poisoned. "So?"

"So I started with forty-one cases where human combustion was supposed to be involved. That was bullshit, mostly."

Huh? "All right. Go on."

"Well, right away I found six times when what it was, it was kitchen accidents. Grease fires. And with the other cases, almost every time they was a ordinary explanation. What're you doing to that guy?"

"Rolling him. Chuckles thinks he has something in his pocket."

Singe, pandering to our freeloaders, asked, "How is the new girlfriend?"

Color appeared in Tharpe's cheeks.

I said, "Huh?"

Far be it from me to discourage a man, however hopeless. I did not pursue it now, though I did wonder how Saucerhead had found time to get involved with another woman. "So most of the supposed . . . what did you call them? Human combustions?"

"Yeah. Spontaneous human combustion. It's sorcerer talk."

Really? We'd look at that later. "So most weren't what rumors make them out to be."

"Nope. They was some that there wasn't no explanation for, though. I got the feeling some more could be explained if somebody can work themselves up to admit that they done something really stupid. But, even so, some has got to be them spontaneous human combustions."

"Including Buy Claxton?"

"Who?"

"The woman who caught fire during Chodo's birthday party."

"I don't know nothin' about her. I didn't look at her. But she was in a kitchen when it happened, wasn't she? What did you find?"

I'd found a little green egg in Big Boy's pocket. A dead ringer for the one on my curio shelf. Interesting. Some secret mutual identification charm for members of A-Laf's gang?

My partner could root that out.

"How many cases?"

"Seven that need a closer look on account of they all involved Chodo."

"Ah. Ah?"

"Chodo owned the places where the fires happened. Some of the other ones, too, but in these ones Chodo was there."

"You're shitting me."

"Not hardly. You're my favorite turd."

"Saucerhead. We're in mixed company here."

"As mixed as it gets, I'd say."

"Talk to me about Chodo's part."

"He was there. Every time. Hang on. I might be misspeaking. Somebody in a wheeled chair was there before the fires happened. But not when the bodies was found."

At this point Saucerhead's marvelous legwork petered out. Meaning there might yet be legwork reserved for me.

I went through the other Ymberian's pockets. He didn't have his own roc's egg. He did come equipped with a little teak box. Inside: "One of them metal dogs." Frost formed on it. Despair hit like a kick in the gilhoolies. Whispers of darkness filled my head. I just managed to shut the box. "Whoa! That was ugly."

Saucerhead and John Stretch were glassy-eyed, with

Tharpe smitten harder than the ratman. Cutlery hit the floor in the kitchen. A-Laf's boys didn't react. Because the Dead Man had frozen up. Those he controlled had followed his lead.

Old Bones had taken the psychic equivalent of a punch to the breadbasket. He huffed and puffed, on the mental side, getting his balance back.

"That was some bad shit," Saucerhead rumbled, shivering. "How about you don't open that friggin' box no more?"

"You got a deal, buddy."

55

The situation improved once those of us who weren't guests of the Crown surrounded a few beers. I told John Stretch, "You've been quiet."

"As a mouse." A joke? "My mouth has been full."

"You got a point. It's not full now, though. What's up?"

"We have located your lawyer."

"What?" I chomped down on Harvester Temisk's name in a moment of paranoia. "Why didn't you say so?"

"I just did. And your partner has known since my arrival." John Stretch no longer seemed intimidated. "There is no need for haste."

It was night out and winter out and the Dead Man wasn't excited about getting something done right away. Maybe it *could* wait.

Saucerhead reminded me, "Chodo don't move so fast and light no more, Garrett. I figure, wherever the mouthpiece has got him stashed, that's where he'll stay till he gets flushed out."

"That's the common wisdom now? That Temisk kidnapped him at Whitefield Hall?"

"Ain't no better theory ever come up. Some folks even wonder if the Green Pants guys wasn't just a diversion for to cover his getaway."

Interesting theory. "And, flushes him?" What? I felt an idea trying to be born. Kolda. Yeah. And my late bout with herbal poisoning. "Hey. Old Bones. What're the chances Belinda's been poisoning her old man? Temisk might be trying to get him straight."

If so, the woman is more clever than we credit. She has been here many times, betraying only her ongoing complicity in profiting from her father's misfortune. In the financial and emotional senses alike.

There may be substance to your speculation, however. If other parties had regular access.

"Didn't Merry say Rory has somebody inside?"

Interesting. Yes. Let me reflect on the possibilities.

"It would explain some stuff. You sure I shouldn't hit the bricks right now?"

You are not yet recovered.

John Stretch said, "My people will keep watch."

That wasn't reassuring. Ratfolk are notorious for cashing in on anything salable. The whereabouts of the kingpin might be the most marketable commodity in TunFaire today.

John Stretch tried to reassure me. "My watchers do not know who they have staked out. They believe we are watching a burglary ring whose plunder hoard we intend to convert to our own advantage. They know only that they are to inform me who goes in and out."

This ratguy was a natural. Dangerously bright. "Can you track somebody to their next hideout in this weather?"

"Singe can."

I was skeptical.

Your anxiety is understandable, Garrett. And not misplaced. But you must *regain strength. You are not yet capable of an extended journey, let alone physical excitement.*

"If John Stretch can find them, so can Rory or Teacher." Chodo had had friends on the Hill. No doubt Rory Sculdyte did, too. Those people and Syndicate bosses are sides of the same coin, down in their bloody, greedy black hearts.

And there are countless low-talent, self-taught storefront and street-corner magicians. Not all of them are charlatans.

"Good work, all," I said. "What do I owe you, Saucerhead? After deductions for food and beer?"

"What? You got no sense of hospitality. I wouldn't never try to charge you if you was a guest at my place."

"How do I know that? I don't even know where you live."

Saucerhead showed me one of his professional hardguy looks. It didn't take. After a pause, he said, "Singe paid me."

"If I go get in line now, a place might open up in the workhouse before I'm completely destitute."

"I wisht I was half as bad off as you're always poormouthing. I'd have to go live on the street."

I could see how. Saucerhead comes equipped with low expectations and a knack for showing up at suppertime.

John Stretch told me, "The stewed apples and Weider's Select are compensation enough for me." He had to work at "compensation."

I nodded but thought, "Not good." What insanity would the rat king drag me into if I stumbled into his favor-for-a-favor universe?

That kind of nightmare had me chasing Chodo now.

The Dead Man suggested, *You all should turn in for the night. Garrett, I will generate a distraction that will allow you to leave unnoticed in the morning. Mr. Tharpe. We have further need of your services.*

Evidently I was expected to improve dramatically during the night.

So I went upstairs and slept some more. I had to move Tinnie with a crowbar. If she'd been any more asleep, we would've needed an undertaker.

56

Singe woke me.

"Don't you ever sleep, girl? Where's Tinnie?" I was alone.

"She went home. Saucerhead took her. She was not feeling well. She was afraid she caught what you had. She wanted to be where she could get a real physician to visit."

"Crap!" Something to worry about on top of everything else.

"She said don't worry on her account. She will be with her family."

"Double crap. You know what that means."

"In my limited experience, I would say it means you had damned well better find room in your busy day to go hold Tinnie's quivering hand. You can rest after you are dead."

She'd read Tinnie pretty good. "Nothing I can do about that right now. So why wake me up?" There was no light from outside.

"The Dead Man says it will be time to get moving when Saucerhead gets back. Also, Mr. Dotes just returned. I thought that might be important."

I glanced at the window. It had better be real important. It was flat dark out there.

Singe told me, "Dean is grumbling like a volcano god, but he is cooking and fussing about going back to bed later. When you dress, remember that it is raining again. And looks likely to turn to ice or snow."

"Sounds exciting." I swung my feet onto the floor, stood. I didn't know how bad I'd felt before until I realized how good I felt now. "Wow! I think I'm cured."

"Yes. And your bed buddy left a little too soon." She nodded toward half-mast.

I glanced down. And flushed. "We're getting too casual and comfortable with each other around here."

Singe resisted further comment. "I should consult the poisoner. I'm due for a season. None of us need that distraction."

She was right. Ratgirls in heat distract everybody. They have no more control than a cat in heat.

"Where are our kittens? I haven't seen them for a while."

"Hiding from A-Laf's wicked men."

"I see." Interesting.

We all breakfasted while Morley explained his appearance at such an ugly hour.

"My place caught on fire."

"With you there? Your boys are more clever than I thought."

"Yes, with me there. And it wasn't their fault. To my surprise. Though, shall we say, not so much a surprise after all, considering. I hear you got your rock back from the guy who switched it out. May I see it?"

"Huh? On the curio thing. Top shelf." I looked at Old Bones. He wasn't inclined to explain.

"There are two here, Garrett. Which one?"

"The one with the scratches is the one that got flung at me."

"I don't see any scratches."

"You can feel them. And there's a chip out of the pointy end. Do you see that?"

"A little black spot?"

"Yeah. What's up?"

"The fire started in the dent where this hit my door. I don't know how. Or why. Or why now. It was like a charcoal fire. About this big when we found it."

He made a circle with his forefingers and thumbs. "It wouldn't go out. We ended up taking the door down. We piled ice and snow on, but it kept burning till the wood was all gone."

"I know a good door and hinge man."

"Well, you'd have to. Wouldn't you?"

"Ha! And ha again. Old Bones. What do you think?"

Consider the possibility that you were not the target of that stone. The intent may have been to burn Mr. Dotes' business.

"That's a long jump."

Not too long considering what I prized out of the Brittigarn person. And hints I find in these minds. Though one is a wasteland and the other remains mostly locked.

"What motive could these lunatics have?" Morley asked. "I hadn't heard of them then."

Possibly they wished to distract you from Garrett's situation. No. That is too great a stretch. We do not have sufficient information. You have eaten. Garrett, I suggest you get started. Mr. Tharpe is about to arrive.

"Am I up to this?"

Yes. Though you will not be alone.

"What's up?" Morley asked as Singe appeared, ready for the weather.

"Got a couple of things to check out. Buy Claxton first."

"Oh. I'll tag along on that."

I didn't argue with him or with Singe. The Dead Man told me, *Singe knows where you are going. Do you?*

Not unless he told me. Because John Stretch hadn't chosen to trouble me with that little detail.

57

First thing I noticed—after I stopped whining about the cold—was that Penny Dreadful was no longer across the street. "I hope she found someplace that's warm."

"She'll be all right," Saucerhead told me.

"You in this with Dean now?"

"Tinnie took her home. On account of she was half frozen. She was killing herself."

We went on over past The Palms, where Morley's troops lurked behind a down comforter hung in place of the door. He showed me the seared hardware. "Not much to see, is there?"

"There is a stench of all evil unleashed," Singe said. She breathed in little puffs, the way I would do around a badly blown carcass. When Puddle came out I told him how to get hold of Mr. Mulclar. "He'll cut you a discount if you tell him I referred you."

"That's exciting," Morley said. "Why am I suspicious of your generosity? Why do I think you're straining to keep a straight face?"

"I don't know. Why?"

If Mr. Mulclar hadn't changed his diet . . . heh, heh, heh.

Morley stayed with us. It was a short half mile on to the Bledsoe. It was getting light. The scaffolding outside the hospital was clotted with ice and snow. An incessant drizzle had no luck washing them away. The scaffolding seemed abandoned. The mortar boats were gone. Any bricks that hadn't been set had walked away. I was surprised the scaffolding hadn't disappeared.

"Armed guards," Saucerhead said. I didn't see any. He told me, "You want to, grab on to something that ain't yours."

"I take it you know who's on the job."

"They're Watch guys picking up a little extra on their own time. I would've done it myself if I wasn't already helping you."

"Who's paying them?"

Tharpe shrugged. He didn't know. And probably didn't care.

We entered the hospital unchallenged. Morley said, "I'll see what I can find out." One weak lamp burned ahead. Its light was enough to show us an unfamiliar woman at the reception desk. She was delighted to see Morley. His earlier conquest must've talked.

"I cannot come in here!" Singe told me suddenly, after not having spoken since we left home, except to whine about her tail dragging in the slush.

"Nobody will give you any crap."

"That is not the problem. The problem is the air. It is thick with madness. I cannot endure it."

"I'm sorry. I should've thought of that. Mr. Tharpe. Would you stay with Singe? In case some moron gets obnoxious?"

Tharpe grunted. He and Singe went back outside. Morley turned on the charm spigot. I headed for Buy Claxton's suite. And got there without seeing another human being.

I wasn't surprised. This was the Bledsoe, warehouse for the sickest of the poorest of the poor and craziest of the crazies. Their dying place.

Some crazies were venting madness right now.

Buy Claxton was awake. She was knitting by candlelight. A dead flower in a clay pot stood on a stand with the candle. She remembered me. She didn't seem surprised to see me. "See what the lady sent me?" She indicated the flower, uncommon for the season.

"The lady?"

"Miss Contague. She's quite thoughtful for a woman of her position."

"She has her moments."

"Did she send you to see how I'm doing?"

A small fib wouldn't be entirely misplaced. "And to see if we can't find out what happened, now that you're feeling better."

Mrs. Claxton put her knitting aside, teary-eyed. She controlled herself. "I'm no widow, you know. And I have two sons and three daughters. My Ethan died in the Cantard. He'd be your age. He's the only one with a good reason for not visiting."

"I'm sorry to hear that. Some people are thoughtless. Especially family."

"I'll bet you're good to your mother."

"My mother is gone. I did try when she was still with us." But I've been a louse since then. I haven't visited her grave in years. "But let's not be sadder than we need to be. Not here."

"That would be sound thinking, young man. How can I help?"

"It's the fire. I'm supposed to find out what happened."

"I don't know. It just happened. It hurt! Bad." She smiled weakly.

"I can tell you this, Mrs. Claxton. . . ."

"Call me Buy."

"Yes, ma'am. You might not have noticed because you weren't looking for it, but that didn't just happen. There must've been something leading up. So I want to go over the whole evening with you. Why were you there in the first place? You didn't work for the caterer."

"No. For Mr. Hartwell."

"Is that the Mr. Hartwell who manages the Contague estate?" A man I'd never trusted. A slimy type. But I couldn't imagine him stealing from the Contagues.

"His son. Armondy. He asked me to help set up, do kitchen work, and clean up afterward."

"So it wasn't odd that you were there?"

"No. I don't think."

"Interesting. When did you get there? Did anything unusual happen when you did?"

"A little after noon. There wasn't anything to do then. The unusual thing was that I caught on fire and almost burned to death." She ranted about her husband and children. I let her vent the anger.

"Who did you report to when you arrived?"

"When they finally showed up, them fancy boys. I just hung out till they got there."

"I met them. They were in charge?"

"They wanted to think. They were decorators. They were there to arrange the tables and chairs. I only paid attention if what they said made sense. No. I took my orders from Mr. Temisk. I knew him from years back."

"Harvester Temisk?"

"That's the one."

"So Mr. Temisk was there. Early. In the back." I hadn't known that. Nobody had mentioned seeing Temisk.

"Where I first run into him was in the pantries. I don't know why he was back there. Looking for lamp oil, he said. Since I seen some in the kitchen, brung by the fancy boys, I showed him where I seen it."

"What about Miss Contague? When did she show?"

Mrs. Claxton confirmed my suspicions. "She was already there when I got there. With her bodyguards. Checking for trouble, I guess."

"Mr. Temisk wanted lamp oil? Why?"

"Well, he took out this little wood box and shook this green, flaky stuff in the oil and shook the jars. He said it was incense. He had me fill the lamps to go on the tables."

This didn't look good for Harvester Temisk. "Then what?"

"I don't know. Then he went away. I didn't see him again. I worked around the kitchen. Oh. And Mr.

Temisk gave me this little jade pin. For being so help-
ful, he said."

Didn't look good for Temisk at all. "This flake stuff.
Did any get spilled? Or miss getting into the lamp
oil?" If it was what I suspected, it got tracked around
by an unwitting rat.

Mrs. Claxton considered. "Come to think, he did
fumble the lid of the box when he started to spice up
the first oil jar. He cussed something awful. Because
the spice was so expensive, he said."

Yes. No doubt. We talked a while, mainly about her
sad family. I didn't learn anything useful. "Did anyone
else see Mr. Temisk?"

"I don't know. I never seen no one else around."

"Did you see the lady's father? Chodo Contague?"

"Well, no. But he musta been there somewhere,
eh?"

Temisk's timing had been amazing if he'd been
missed by my pixies and rats. Although there hadn't
been any reason for them to watch for him and no
reason for them to recognize him if they did see him.
A guy named Garrett was the only one who needed
to miss him. Plus Chodo's beloved only child and a
few underbosses, the latter of whom had no reason to
visit the kitchens.

This was beginning to look like a huge, ugly Harvester Temisk murder scheme piggybacked onto whatever plot Belinda was running. Which meant that
Temisk used me from the start.

Everybody's schemes disintegrated in the chaos inside Whitefield Hall.

I'd have some hard questions for lawyer boy when
I caught him.

"Thank you, Mrs. Claxton. Do you want me to
check on your family?"

"Thank you, young man, but no. I'll handle them
myself. I *will* get out of here someday."

"I hope so. You keep that attitude, it won't be
long."

58

Morley was reluctant to leave. His new friend was loath to let him go. But other people were arriving for work. Being people, they were nosy, noisy, and demanding.

"You learn anything?" I asked as we slipped outside. And, "Where the hell did those two go?"

Singe and Saucerhead were nowhere to be seen.

"A trust fund pays for the guards. There's Tharpe."

Saucerhead beckoned from a gap between buildings where overhangs provided some protection from the drizzle.

"Is it worth chasing the money trail?"

"Why bother? Unless you've got something going that I don't know about. Block and Relway might give it a look, though."

"I've got a feeling they've lost interest in the Ugly Pants Gang. For now. What're you guys doing over here?"

"Trying not to be noticed by Plenty Hart and Bobo Negry," Saucerhead said.

"Who?"

"A couple of Rory's men," Morley told me. "Middle level. Dangerous. What would they be doing here?"

"Maybe Merry is inside," I speculated. "He was in ragged shape when the Dead Man was done with him."

"Maybe." Tharpe doubted it, though. "They was looking for somebody."

"Us? Did Big Boy not do a good job of getting us away?"

Tharpe shrugged.

"Singe?"

"Do not ask me. I am a tracker. I can help you find an answer only by tracking those men back. If they came here on our trail, that would be obvious in a short time. Do you wish to try that?"

"Would it take long to make sure?"

"Ten minutes," Singe promised.

"Saucerhead, stick with her. Soon as she makes up her mind, head for . . . where, Singe?"

"The Tersize Granary."

"Sniff Morley and me out, Singe."

"Or Garrett and I," Dotes said. Then, once they took off, "You planning on rushing into this?"

"You have a suggestion?"

"Same old, same old as always. Be ready for trouble."

He meant weaponry. Armaments, in fact. He'd lug a siege ballista if he could get one into a pocket. And use it at the least excuse. And feel no remorse afterward.

"I have my stick."

Morley was not overawed.

"If I need something nastier, I'll take it away from somebody."

"You're not as young and quick as you think you are."

"Is anybody? Ever?"

"So stipulated. Without excusing your silly refusal to look out for yourself."

"Oh-oh. I get the feeling my weapons habits are about to take second place to my dietary habits."

"Since you bring it up . . ."

And so it went. Thirty minutes later we sighted the Tersize Granary. Which, till recently, had been the

Royal Karentine Military Granary, whence vast ton-
nages of feed grains, flours, and finished baked goods
(read rock-hard hardtack in hundredweight barrels)
barged down a canal to the river and thence to the
war zone. The operating Tersize family acquired it
from the Ministry of War, cheap after the killing
stopped.

I said, "The Tersizes are related to the Contagues
somehow, aren't they?"

"Chodo's stepsister Cloris married Misias Tersize.
But they weren't in bed with the Outfit. That I've
heard. The place isn't what it used to be," Morley said
of the sprawl of redbrick milling and storage facilities.

Much of it appeared to have gone derelict. "You
know this area?" I didn't. "I don't see any sign of
squatters." TunFaire is inundated with refugees from
a war zone that no longer exists.

"No. The place used to be a fort. The millers and
bakers couldn't get in or out without a military pass.
You want to wait for Saucerhead and Singe?"

Recalling times when I'd just charged in, "I think
so."

"Developing a taste for caution? At this late date?"

"I have responsibilities now. Dean. The Dead Man.
Seven kittens. And a girlfriend who'll hunt me down
in Hell if I get myself killed before I can visit her in
her sickbed."

"Why don't we just slip into the lee of one of these
buildings while we wait, then? Because I've just figured out why there aren't any squatters."

I caught what his sharper elfish eyes had spied
already.

Three sizable men ambled along the street beside
the westernmost wall of the granary. One checked the
doors that existed at regular intervals, formerly for
loading and unloading. The street-side walls of the
granary were the outer faces of the various structures
included in the complex, connected by the outer faces
of single-story sheds. Tinnie's family lived in a similar
complex. It included family housing, worker housing,

warehousing, and manufacturing workshops. The Tate compound, though, had a smaller footprint and was less imposing vertically.

"You know, brunos look pretty much the same wherever you find them. But I have a definite feeling that these three wouldn't be embarrassed if their mothers dressed them in green plaid pants." Had Block cut them loose? Or were there more of them than suspected, now avoiding the Bledsoe project and public attention?

The door checker of the three performed his function again, using a stick much like the one I carried. The others were better armed. Or worse, if you have a tendency to acknowledge the law. One carried a set of swords, long and short. The other lugged a siege engine of a crossbow, drawn and loaded. They were looking for trouble.

"You have a nasty way of thinking, my friend. But you're right. Go talk to them. See if they have a country accent. If they are Green Pants people, we'll know why there's always more of them than we expect to see."

"You go. Beauty defers to age."

"Speaking of beauty and beast. Tharpe and Singe should have been here by now. I'm getting a chill."

"If we have to walk all the way around the place, you'll warm up. . . . Uh-oh!"

The stick man had found a door that swung inward. That it shouldn't have done was obvious instantly.

Blades came out. The crossbowman backed off a few steps. The stick man moved in, with no caution whatsoever.

Ratmen boiled past him. Preceded by a swarm of missiles that might have been tavern darts. That was so remarkable that stick man and sword man alike failed to do anything but duck. Crossbowman managed only to take the striped stocking cap off the head of an especially long, gaunt ratman. The pack was too chaotic for an accurate count. They disappeared before the security men pulled themselves together.

The three looked around, realized there was nothing they could do about the ratmen, went inside to see what the ratmen had been doing.

Ratmen materialized. I recognized John Stretch. They slammed the door shut and nailed it in place. Then the rat king headed our way while his minions congratulated one another.

"He knew we were here," I said.

"Yes." Morley examined our surroundings thoughtfully.

I checked for normal rats myself till John Stretch was close enough to hear me ask, "What was all that?"

"We wanted the patrol out of our fur. They will not be missed for a while. But we have no time to spare."

"You timed all that for our arrival?"

The ratman seemed concerned about my intelligence. "No."

"But you did know that we were lurking around out here."

"Yes. Where is Singe? I expected her to bring you here."

"She's coming." I explained the delay.

And here she came. Trudging through the snow, holding her cold tail, looking miserable. Saucerhead limped along behind.

A flurry of activity commenced at what would've been the next door checked by the trapped patrol. A flood of ratpeople went in. Then the stream became bidirectional. Those exiting were loaded down. Singe took one look, dropped her tail, and tied into her brother. "Are you mad?"

"Easy, girl," I told her.

"This is insane! The humans will forget the Other Races! The Watch will help the racialists persecute our folk."

"Easy, Singe. Did you think about that, John?" While he considered his reply, I asked Singe, "What's the word? Were we being followed?"

"No. They just took the same route for a long

time." Then, sort of vaguely, "But they might have been looking for us even if they did not know they were following us."

I shook my head. She was starting to think like the Dead Man. "What's your story?" I asked Saucerhead. He was hanging on to a wall, favoring his left hip.

"I fell. On some ice. It was under some fresh snow. It's snowing back there, just a couple blocks."

"Really?"

John Stretch said, "There will be no complaints to the Watch."

"Oh?"

"Thieves do not complain to the law when other thieves take what they have stolen."

He'd never swapped war stories with veterans of the Watch, I guess. But I got his point. "There's illegal stuff going on over there, eh?"

"All this part in back. Behind the smokestacks. It is all shut down and sealed off from the rest. Not used anymore. Except by criminals."

"I see. Saucerhead. How are you going to babysit me if you keep falling on your ass yourself?"

He muttered something about how dumb do you have to be to let Teacher White ambush you and make you eat noxious weeds?

I sneered, asked the ratman, "These bad boys look like the ones who caused a fuss in our neighborhood. Are they foreigners?"

"Out-of-towners. Yes."

"Definitely explains why there's always another one around after the Watch thinks they've got them all."

Morley observed, "We didn't come out here for a committee meeting."

"Good point. John Stretch. Where is my friend the mouthpiece?"

The ratman sighed. "Follow me."

Our path led past the door the ratmen had nailed shut. Tremendous impacts hit it from the other side. Dust and splinters flew.

I said, "That convinces me. They're just not wearing the pants. I've never seen anybody that stubborn."

John Stretch showed concern. "They will be in a bloody mind when they do get out."

"Likely. They're not used to not getting their own way. Your guys threw darts. Weren't they poisoned?"

"No. I did not know where to acquire that sort of drug."

Too bad. But I wasn't inclined to clue him in now. Singe offered no suggestions, either.

59

We used the doorway the plundering ratpeople were running in and out of. Who stole all that in the first place? The crew from Ymber wouldn't waste the time.

John Stretch led us up a dusty, rickety stair slick with bat droppings. The bat smell was potent. He led on through a maze of ups and downs. The granary had been built in stages, over generations. The army had wanted everything connected. The ratman said, "I am sorry. I have not yet seen this myself. There must be a more direct route. I believe we are close now. Be silent."

Silence it was. We're good at silence. All of our lives have depended on silence at some point. And we're all still here.

We got around by light that leaked through gaps in roofs and walls. There were plenty of those. Unfortunately, they also let in critters and the weather. Eventually, Singe smelled smoke. Flickering light appeared ahead and below. "Looks like firelight."

We entered the loft of what once had been a vast stable. Moldy hay still lay here and there, inhabited by Singe's unimproved cousins.

The flickering light came from an indoor campfire. We advanced carefully. Everybody wanted to see. And what we saw was half a dozen people trying to keep warm around a fire being fed wood torn from nearby horse stalls. There were tents around the fire, four of them, facing the warmth.

The camp had been there awhile. There wasn't
much lumber left. There was trash. Laundry hung on
lines. That included green plaid pants. Which I noted
only in passing. I concentrated on Harvester Temisk
and the old man in a wheelchair. Who looked more
lively than a man in a coma ought.

I got down on my belly, at the edge of the loft.
Morley dropped beside me. Chodo wasn't talking, nor
was he moving. Still, he was farther into our world
than when last I'd seen him.

John Stretch settled to my right. Ordinary brown
rats collected around him, worshipful.

Were Temisk and Chodo prisoners? Guests? Or in
charge?

The unrelated things were converging, suggesting
potential cause and effect relationships.

Chodo had an arrangement with the A-Laf cult. It
went back a long time. A-Laf's thugs came to town
to charge their nickel dogs with misery. Before Temisk
got in touch with me. Before Penny Dreadful turned
up with her spooky kittens.

The appearance of the Green Pants Gang must have
emboldened Harvester Temisk. He decided to rescue
his boss. Powerful old allies had arrived. And they
owed Chodo.

But that left plenty of questions. How had Temisk
meant to use me? Surely, Teacher White, Rory Sculdyte, and others hadn't been factored in fully. They
hadn't been expected to survive the Whitefield Hall
fire. Then there was Penny Dreadful. Her kittens had
been a jinx on everybody.

Was Penny the straight goods? Was she getting up
all our noses for a reason? Was most of what she'd
told Dean true?

Her presence certainly excited the Green Pants
Gang. My front door was proof.

And the human combustions? I had only hints.

And now a new question arose. How the Tersize
family fit. Warehousing stolen goods and housing out-
of-town religious gangsters wouldn't happen without

them noticing. Hell, they were using A-Laf's Ugly
Pants sextons for security.

And why had that stone been slung my way? I
couldn't make that fit. It had gem-plus value because
of its dark capabilities.

Had Colonel Block and Director Relway taken
stones off the Ymberians they'd arrested? Would they
guess what they had?

Something to think about.

60

A tall, thin old man with wild white hair and exaggerated facial features rushed into the camp. He moved fast for his age but had a major stiffness in his hips. He walked goofy. I couldn't hear what he said, but it had to be about ratman raiders. Everybody but Temisk and his buddy moved out fast, armed.

"Showtime," I whispered. Morley nodded.

I didn't sneak now. I went to a ladder and climbed down. Those two weren't going to run.

As I descended I noted a coach hidden in a shadowy corner. No doubt the vehicle used to spirit Chodo away from Whitefield Hall. There was no sign of a team.

My advent startled Temisk. He pulled himself together quickly, though. "How did you find us?"

"That's what I do." Chodo, I noted, seemed fully alert.

"The trouble outside is a diversion?"

"No. But I'm taking advantage."

"So you found us. Now what?"

"Now you tell me what's going on."

He thought about that. Then he leaned aside and stared, eyes widening in fright.

I'd been joined by several hefty rats. They perched on their haunches like squirrels, studying Temisk.

Temisk gaped. More rats arrived. He gasped, "You . . . you have the power to control rats?"

"We have a working arrangement."

Temisk shuddered. Squeaking, he took a swipe at a big bull clambering into Chodo's lap.

"Don't do that." How did John Stretch know Temisk had a problem with rodents? "There're more of them than there are of you."

"There were rats in the kitchen at Whitefield Hall. The rats told you how to find us."

"Rats go everywhere. They see everything. They hear everything."

Temisk had the full-blown heebie-jeebies now, but his brain hadn't shut down. "You got this connection because of the ratgirl, eh?"

"Talk about what you've up to, solicitor. Not about rats. I know all I need to know about rats." No horses for the coach. I wouldn't get Chodo and Temisk out the easy way. "I'm not happy with you."

"I just wanted to get Chodo away from those people. All right?"

"You tried to kill people. A lot of them. Deliberately. Including me. With fire. But none of us died."

He put on a show of confusion.

"You tried to set me up, Temisk. But it fell apart. Before it came together. Same for your friends from Ymber."

I kept an eye on Chodo. He was intensely interested.

I waved at the air. Morley and Saucerhead materialized. Singe took longer. She climbs ladders faster than she comes down them.

John Stretch remained unseen.

I said, "We need to move these two out before those thugs come back. Singe. You recall that evil stone?"

"Yes."

"Sniff around. See if you can find another one. Or anything else interesting. Morley. Peek out that street door. Check for witnesses."

"You aren't thinking about just rolling them out of here, are you?"

I had been. But I saw the problem before he pointed it out.

"You really think you can wheel Chodo around in public and no one will notice?"

"Let me think about that."

Morley reported, "We don't want to leave this way. There's a mob out there grabbing stuff the ratpeople didn't get before they took off."

"We'll go back the way we came. Me and Saucerhead will take turns lugging Chodo." Tharpe put on an expression of pained disbelief. "You and Temisk handle the chair. Singe. You find anything?"

"I just started. You should stop talking and start doing."

Temisk was terrified now. He had a notion what the future held. He didn't want to go there. Chodo wasn't thrilled, either.

Saucerhead hoisted Chodo as though he were weightless. And there wouldn't be as much of him as once there had been. I told Temisk, "Grab that chair and start climbing, solicitor." I heard voices approaching. "Singe, hurry up."

She beat me into the loft. "I will lead the way." There was no sign of John Stretch.

He would be watching, though.

61

Morley peeled off near The Palms. He needed to clean up for the evening trade.

I was squeezed up inside a borrowed covered goat cart with Chodo and his wheelchair. Saucerhead and Harvester Temisk pulled. Renewed weakness had overcome me soon after we escaped unnoticed from the Tersize Granary, with a battle between Green Pants guys and wannabe looters warming up around the corner.

So now another stolen cart would turn up outside my place.

Singe hurried ahead to alert the Dead Man. Complaining about her cold, wet tail as she faded into the distance.

Occasionally, I suspect Saucerhead of being less dim than he pretends.

My nap ended when he backed the cart up suddenly—bang—into the corner of a building. The cart's tongue rose slowly, putting me at increasing risk of getting dumped into an icy mess in the mouth of a dark and fetid alley.

A voice said, "How about you grab back onto that cart, Tharpe? Otherwise, you could get hurt." I didn't recognize the voice.

Saucerhead let me know. "You kidding, Fish? I'm on a job. I ain't gonna let you mess it up."

Fish? That would be Fish Bass, then. One of Rory

Sculdyte's less daunting associates. A manager, not a serious physical threat.

"Plenty, get Temisk. Bobo, Brett, spank Tharpe if he interferes. And see what's in the cart. Chodo Contague his own self, I'll bet. Because where would Chodo be if he wasn't with his lawyer pal? Rory wants to talk to you, Temisk. Damn it, Tharpe—" A meaty thump interrupted. "Shit!"

Harvester Temisk squealed. Suggesting Saucerhead had laid a good one on Plenty Hart.

Saucerhead said, "You try to run, lawyer, you wake up wishing you was dead."

Meanwhile, I dribbled out the back of the cart, counted arms and legs to make sure I hadn't left any behind, then unlimbered my head knocker and iron knuckles.

I heard grunts and thuds as Tharpe exchanged love taps with Rory Sculdyte's infantry. There was some chatter farther off as people gathered to be entertained. The cavalry didn't arrive.

I checked the situation from ground level. Saucerhead had gone into action on the side of the cart where it butted against a wall. So, although he was cornered, nobody could get behind him. And I had room to go to work.

I sucked in a bushel of air, bounced into the contest. I smacked a startled Fish Bass between the eyes, whacked Harvester one that put him down and discouraged him from taking a powder, then popped Fish again so he wouldn't interfere.

I approached Saucerhead's dancing partners from behind. "Can I cut in?" Bobo Negry was no problem. Saucerhead had hold of him with his left hand, using him as a crutch. Iron knuckles to the back of his head shut him down.

Which left Brett Batt. Brother Batt had a big mouse over one eye, a bloody nose, and several split lips. And was having the time of his life hammering on Saucerhead. Tharpe was going to lose this one. He was too exhausted to fight much longer.

My first mighty swing missed Brett. My second was a glancer that did little but get his attention. I didn't have much go left myself.

Brett flailed behind him, knocked me down, resumed demolishing Saucerhead.

I put everything into a whack at Batt's right knee.

Good enough. Brett yelped. His leg folded. Saucerhead launched a roundhouse kick he'd saved for the right time, connected with Batt's left temple.

Two more kicks and a few more love taps from my stick and the wide load went to sleep. Finally. He would enjoy aches, pains, bruises, a headache, and a bad limp for days to come.

I got my feet under me. "We've got to get out of here." I checked the others.

Fish Bass had him one thick skull. He was a hundred feet down the street and gaining speed, though unable to navigate a straight course. Harvester Temisk was inclined to make an exit of his own, but his world was spinning so briskly he couldn't keep his feet under him. I tossed him in with Chodo, then asked Tharpe, "You all right, man? You look like shit."

"Just shut up and get me to your place."

"But—"

"He got me in the goolies, all right? Go! We got to disappear."

Yeah. Word was spreading. I hadn't heard any whistles, but Watchmen would be closing in. Let them find nothing but broken Sculdyte henchmen. And better hope none of the gawkers were civic-minded enough to follow us.

We ran into Singe on Wizard's Reach, tail in paw, coming back to meet us, a block from where the Dead Man would be able to offer some protection. A swarm of shivering pixies accompanied her. Saucerhead and I had kept one another going while making sure Harvester didn't escape. And he did try.

"What happened?" Singe asked. Melondie Kadare hovered behind her, trying to keep warm.

"Ran into some bad guys. His Nibs ready to bring us in?"

"Yes. But—"

It hurt to talk. Still, "We got to hurry. Then this cart needs to go away. Fast. People will be looking for it."

"So move if you need to move. Mr. Tharpe should get somewhere. . . ."

"I think it's going to snow again." We resumed trudging.

"What? What the hell do you mean, Garrett?"

"I mean you ought to calm down and—"

"Look out!"

I was supposed to look out for Teacher White, leaping out of cover with wild eyes, wilder hair, and no obvious awareness of the misty drizzle. He looked like he had been living on the street. But he did come equipped with a fully loaded, cocked, safe-catch-off war surplus crossbow. It looked huge from my downhill end. A wild grin full of bad teeth shone behind the weapon and a seedling beard. "You ruined me, you son of a bitch! But I got your freakin' ass now!"

A man ought not to get so worked up he forgets what he wants to do. I know. I overthink all the time.

I never broke stride. Teacher swung his aim to track me. Melondie Kadare darted into his face, stabbed him in the tip of the nose. His eyes crossed. Melondie's companions buzzed his ears.

Teacher let go the crossbow with his left hand. I placed a long jab on the back of the hand he'd raised to his nose. He yelped. Tears blinded him.

He dropped the crossbow. It discharged. The bolt whizzed away, ricocheting off brick walls.

I said, "Go home, Teacher. Better still, go somewhere where Rory won't look for you. Lay low. The Sculdytes won't last out the week."

"You broke my nose!"

A good pop in the snot locker has a way of clearing the mind behind. "You're right. And if you don't want it getting uglier, disappear."

Anger and humiliation hadn't abandoned Teacher, but his nerve had. He limped away, holding his nose, glowering.

Saucerhead hadn't said a word or done a thing. He glowered back. He was not in a good mood. He'd have bloodied somebody if he'd had the strength to do anything but keep on putting one foot in front of the other.

Teacher kept moving. Melondie and her friends buzzed him, kept him going. Singe collected the crossbow. "Damn! This thing is heavy."

"Dump it in the cart. It's illegal. We don't want to attract any attention."

A sense of foreboding came over me as we approached the house. But I didn't see even one obvious watcher.

62

The Dead Man's glee was almost malicious. He couldn't believe I'd enjoyed such complete success. But, boy, was he eager to capitalize.

Singe and I got our captives, our cargo, and Tharpe inside as fast as we could. Dean even lent a hand. Then he grabbed the cart's tongue and took off downhill. I gawked.

I sent him. He was doing nothing useful. Come inside, please.

Uh-oh. He was being polite. That's never a good sign.

You will find yourself dealing with the Watch if you do not cease dallying immediately.

Now he was seriously impatient.

With cause. We were about to be visited by Captain Ramey List and his shadows. Both henchmen now wore complete new uniforms.

I got in and closed the door. Old Bones told me, *Something big is happening. Captain List is the only body the Watch can spare for a stakeout.*

"There'll be a big dance with the Outfit. Going on already, I think. Because of the material we provided." I had to get a copy to Belinda still. I'd been too sick or too busy to figure out how. "Did you pry anything useful out of our guests?"

Absolutely. I understand much of it now. It all ties together through the people involved. None of whom are pulling in the same traces. But I see that residual weakness is about to bring on a collapse. Take a nap.

"I can last awhile. With your help."

I do not have the attention to spare. Mr. Tharpe is injured. We will not be able to get a physician past the Watch anytime soon.

I let it drop. You can't win with Butterbutt. And fatigue was about to overwhelm me.

Captain List hammered on the front door. He bellowed nonsense that would amuse the neighbors. His best effort was embarrassingly feeble compared with those of the Green Pants guys.

"I'll just park it in my chair. You need to know what I got from Buy Claxton. Poke around when you get time."

Vaguely, as I drifted off, I heard Saucerhead groan.

The Dead Man couldn't read my mind and control Tharpe's pain, both. He must have been using all his mind power to control the Ymberians and deal with Captain List. List's essential nature would make him try to win himself a name.

I slept.

63

I wakened. There was something in the air. Cooking smells. And a girlie fragrance suggesting something tastier.

Something tastier arrived with a steaming tray.

Clearly, Captain List had gone away.

An agent from the Unpublished Committee came. Captain List was needed for a secret assignment that could be handled only by one of the top members of the Watch. Director Relway and Colonel Block were tangled up in obligations they could not shed. It was critical that this assignment be handled immediately.

I chuckled. "And he took the bait. Along with the hook, the line, and the pole."

He did.

"I love it." I felt good despite my fresh collection of bruises. "It's got to be something that will end up with Ramey List embarrassed in a big way."

The possibility bubbled in the back of Mr. Scithe's mind.

I gave Tinnie a peck on the cheek and a suggestive leer a foot to the south, then prepared to pile into an equally beautiful omelet. "I thought you had what I had, darling."

"I do some. But mostly I was just tired."

But I think it more likely that Captain List will die an heroic death.

"Really? Do they hate him that much?"

Mr. Scithe came on behalf of Director Relway, not

Colonel Block. Mr. Relway, you may have noted, has simple, direct ways of handling personnel problems. This time because he sees an opportunity to end a threat to the Watch.

"Morley and Relway ought to be pals. They think a lot alike."

One would murder the other within hours. That sort of personality does not tolerate itself well in others.

He was right, of course. "What do we know now that we didn't know yesterday?" I gave Harvester Temisk the fisheye. He remained terrified. Chodo appeared to be napping. Even guys in wheelchairs need to sleep.

We know the Bledsoe drew the Ymberians to Tun-Faire. The Bledsoe is the mother lode of despair. Their nickel idols accumulate despair. The idols they installed in the Bledsoe walls are connected by sorcery to smaller companion pieces in their headquarters. Which always has been that place where you found Mr. Temisk and Mr. Contague. They plan to scatter the charged idols in areas where they intend to proselytize. You found one of the smaller sort on our guest deacon. The intent is to broadcast oppressive despair—which the priests of A-Laf will dispel, inside their temples.

"I see. And those wouldn't be located where the prospects don't come equipped with plenty of money."

Truly, you are possessed of a deep, humming streak of cynicism.

"Am I right?"

Probably more so than you think. When the cult of A-Laf fell into the hands of fundamentalists—aided by Mr. Contague, remember—the brains in charge were not motivated entirely by spiritual fervor. Mr. Contague worked hard to install his allies. Nevertheless, they did not join forces with Mr. Contague—though, as we know now, they helped advance his career by eliminating human obstacles.

Eventually, the Ymberian end forgot its connection with the TunFaire underworld, except at the most shy level.

"Until they came to town, eh?" A baby cat bounced into my lap.

The kitten put its paws on the little table by my tray. He sniffed. And eased his nose ever closer to my plate. Never glancing back like he might actually need permission. Like, "I am the cat. The cat rules. All else exists to attend the cat."

The little tyrant hadn't gained an ounce since his arrival.

The kits have realized that the scary men are harmless. For the moment. They are incurable optimists. They cannot remain frightened long. The optimism of A-Lat is a major contributing cause of its conflict with A-Laf. Which might seem unusual, A-Lat being the Queen of the Night. But that does not make her a dark goddess in all her aspects.

Her principal aspect is the feminine.

Be that as it may, it is not our concern. We must concentrate on those problems that have caught us in their web.

"Go," I said. I pushed the cat aside. He paid no attention. He went right back to sticking his nose in my plate.

Some weeks ago Mr. Temisk became aware of the arrival of the A-Laf cultists. They, of course, were unaware of Mr. Contague's state. Knowing the balance of obligation tilted toward Mr. Contague, Mr. Temisk contacted Ymberians. He invoked their obligation, as he did yours. The cultists knew him as the interlocutor for Mr. Contague, so he continued in that role.

"How did he kill all those people? And why?"

Ah. Now it becomes convolute.

"Uh-oh. That's what you hear when somebody is fixing to make an excuse for somebody." I couldn't imagine him doing that for anybody but himself, though.

We are not amused.

"Leave that alone." I flicked the kitten's nose.

"Don't do that." Tinnie snapped. She'd come to

check my tea. Carrying a tray. I was buying breakfast
for my guests.

"We've got to figure a way to make money out of
this, Old Bones. I'm feeding half the city."

We will profit. Though perhaps not in cash money.

"No chickens. No moldy bread. No spoiled sausage.
No skunky beer. I don't take payment in kind any-
more." As I raised my teacup, I spied a glint in
Chodo's eye. He was awake. "Where were we?"

*I was about to inform you that circumstances sur-
rounding the deaths of those who burned are more
complicated than it would appear. Mr. Temisk is, indeed, responsible. But was not, at first, aware that he
was responsible. However, once he understood that
there was a connection between the fires and his visits
to Mr. Contague, he remained willing to send personalities like Mr. Billy Mul Tima to their ends.*

I'd had my suspicions about Temisk but hadn't had
information enough to work it all out. Maybe if I
hadn't been sick all that time.

*We would not have discovered the truth without
bringing Mr. Temisk here. There is no evidence outside
his mind. He has been clever about leaving no traces.
Miss Winger has been on Mr. Temisk's story for days
and has yet to find anything even circumstantial. Mrs.
Claxton was his sole loose end. Which he has had no
opportunity to tie up. He felt he did not dare leave Mr.
Contague alone with the Ymberians.*

"He's a lawyer. They're naturally crooks."

The Dead Man was not amused. Maybe he was a
lawyer in another time and place.

"So Brother Temisk was behind the burning
deaths? And he did it for his pal?"

*In essence. But it is a bigger story. Mr. Temisk, de-
spite protests to the contrary, has solid contacts inside
the Contague household. Which could be true for Mr.
Sculdyte as well. Mr. Temisk suspects that Mr. Rory
Sculdyte knew the truth but was abiding an opportunity
to make best use of the information.*

"I'm guessing Chodo's been drugged. Systematically and continuously. I'm thinking he would've recovered by now otherwise."

True. He has been drugged regularly. But he would not be in command now if he had not been fed those drugs.

I grunted. Tinnie had her back to me. She was bending over the subject of our conversation, spoon in hand. I couldn't concentrate.

Mental sneer. *Mr. Contague's interior is scrambled. He is mad in a deeply sinister way. Ultimately, he is more responsible for the combustion deaths.*

"Can you get to your point?"

No. More amusement.

I dragged my attention away from Miss Tate long enough to pull the kitten off my plate. There were several of those in the room now, all over everybody. Including the scary people. One perched on the Ymberian deacon's shoulder, washing a paw. The deacon knew. He was apoplectic.

The Dead Man noted my interest and was amused yet again. *That should crack the final barriers in his mind. If his heart does not explode first.*

"The combustion deaths, partner?"

Mr. Temisk's agents in the Contague household told him they thought Miss Contague might be poisoning him.

"Might?"

There is some ambiguity. Someone else might be guilty.

"Doesn't Chodo know?"

He was drugged.

"Gah!"

Wait! There is madness there, as noted. Extreme and dark. Worsened by the drug. Mr. Temisk's contacts identified the poison. Mr. Temisk searched for an antidote.

"Which he found. And which has something to do with people catching on fire." I was making intuitive leaps left and right. Maybe the fever left me psychic.

Yes. Be still. Mr. Temisk's contacts informed him that Miss Contague came to town once or twice a month, and more frequently in times of crisis. Her father accompanied her. Always. She would not trust his care to anyone at home.

"With good reason, obviously."

Obviously. When she did come to town Miss Contague secreted her father in a tenement her family owns on the north side, on the edge of Elf Town. Mr. Temisk knew the building because he handled its acquisition and management. Mr. Contague operated his early business out of there. Once he knew Miss Contague's routine, Mr. Temisk acted.

To conceal his role, he hired alcoholics to sneak in and medicate the man in the wheelchair with the antidote. These men received one-quarter payment beforehand and the balance afterward.

Sounded risky. The drunk would brag about his score. "But the drunk turned into a human torch. Right?"

Not the first few times. Not until Mr. Contague began to shake the influence of the poison. Once he was able to understand his situation, frustration at his helplessness drove him mad.

"Temisk turned Chodo into a mass murderer by trying to help him?"

Essentially.

"I'll bite. How?"

The antidote is a crushed form of the stone hurled at you at Mr. Dotes'—

"That causes fires!"

64

Harvester provided his cat's-paws with a flaked form of the stone, which resisted powdering. He acquired it from the A-Laf cult, at an extreme price. The cult obtained a hoard of the stones when it took over the temple of A-Lat. Numerous stones went astray before being inventoried. A-Laf's sextons were not as devout as their superiors desired.

Bittegurn Brittigarn wasn't wrong when he connected the stones with rocs. The Dead Man said they originated in rocs' gizzards. The phoenix legend came about because roc chicks, like kids, will swallow anything. Which sometimes makes the stones ignite. That chick goes up in flame while its nest mates bail out, possibly giving a distant observer the impression that he's watching a rebirth.

The stones were priceless because they could start fires. Anywhere, anytime, in most any material, from a distance, if you knew how to trigger them. Using sorcery. Or a mental nudge after the manner of the Dead Man.

Chodo discovered that he could spark residual firestone flakes on the hands and clothing of Harvester Temisk's alkies. Not being suicidally mad, he eliminated them only after they left him.

Harvester Temisk's crime was that he kept hiring disposable people after Chodo began killing them.

"He tried to burn Whitefield Hall down with everybody inside?"

He did. Doctoring the oil in the lamps. Mrs. Claxton was targeted specifically. She received a pin because she had seen Mr. Temisk at work. It ignited much earlier than Temisk planned. Mr. Contague was in a rage. It was chance that the doctored lamps were out of his range by then.

"So the mystery of the human combustions is solved."

More or less. There have been incidents that cannot be traced back to Mr. Contague and Mr. Temisk. But we are not interested in those.

"I've got a lot of questions, Smiley. Who slung a rock at me? Why? How come it took so long for Morley's door to catch fire? What about Rory Sculdyte? And Belinda? These damned cats and Penny Dreadful? And what do we do about Temisk and Chodo?"

I owed Chodo. I had to discharge that debt. Which clunked me right into a bubbling pot of moral quandary.

The Dead Man knocked the Ymberian deacon out so he could free up enough brainpower to show me the nightmare inhabiting Chodo's head. A nightmare as bad as that of a claustrophobe trapped in a coffin and unable, ever, to die. It was just a glimpse. Just a little teasy peek, secondhand, of a seething black hell haunted by genius. Supreme ugliness under only the most primitive, selfish control.

The madman was imprisoned in an herbal cage. Though the cage had created the madman, the madman now belonged there.

The kittens seemed fond of him, though.

"What do I do, Old Bones? We can't turn that loose."

Worry about something else. Concentrate on Mr. Temisk, whose own madness is gaining momentum. His conscience is withering. He is no longer troubled about what he might be unleashing. Though he is not blind to the possibility that he might be its immediate victim.

"He's like me, then. Obligated to good old Chodo.

Wanting to believe that this is the same old Chodo. He just can't walk or talk."

Worry about something else.

So I watched Tinnie feed the Ymberians. Beauty and the beasts.

Singe leaned through the doorway. "Do we have a plan for dealing with the people out front?"

"Who is it?" Pounding had occurred, off and on, for hours. The Dead Man seemed uninterested. I'd taken my cue from him.

"That List person."

"He's still alive?"

"He must be lucky."

"Is the door holding up?"

"Mr. Mulclar's pride is in no danger."

"Any idea what he wants?"

"Maybe somebody saw us bring those two in and recognized them."

I didn't think so. We would've drawn somebody more important than Captain Ramey List. "Hey! Smiley! We done with Big Bruno yet? How about I fling his ass out like I did Merry and his crew?"

The Dead Man did not respond. For one panicky instant I thought he'd fallen asleep. But he was just too busy to be bothered.

The racket up front stopped. Ramey List went away again.

I decided to indulge in another nap. I dragged my disease-ravaged carcass upstairs and dumped it into bed.

65

Tinnie was there when I woke up, but she wasn't feeling playful. I avoided irritating questions till after breakfast. Then I asked about the weather.

"Am I supposed to know? You were there. Did I suddenly pop outside?"

I sighed.

Singe cursed. Dean cursed. A drunken Melondie Kadare cursed like a platoon of Marine storm troopers. Incoherently. She'd been in the kitchen sucking it down when we'd brought Chodo and Harvester in. We needed to put her in a cage. Those cats couldn't ignore their own nature forever.

"So the weather hasn't gotten any better."

Tinnie growled and grumbled like it was all my fault she couldn't go home and get to work.

Being a rational, reasonable man, I noted, "If you can't get to work, neither can anybody else. So there wouldn't be any reason for you to try."

"You are so full of crap. . . ." And so forth.

The patient sort, I waited for the black tea to kick in.

Garrett.

I jumped and ran. Pure horror reeked off the Dead Man's summons.

"What the hell?"

Do not speak. Not one more word.

I'm a quick study. I sealed my yap. It had to be hugely important.

We are on the brink of a holocaust.

I'm so good I just stood there and said a whole lot of nothing.

Being careful not to let Mr. Contague or Mr. Temisk see you, pocket those firestones and get them out of the house. I believe you can fathom why. Several seconds later, he added, *We should have recognized that danger earlier. I should have seen it.*

Somebody should have. It was right there in front of us. The end of us all. Maybe the gods do love fools, drunks, and their favorite toy. Or they've got something uglier planned for later.

This once I was in such a hurry I forgot to look out the peephole first. I opened up and got smacked between the eyes with the wonder of snow gone wild. I told Singe, "I was six last time I saw it like this."

There was a fresh foot on top of the old mess. More pounded down in hunks so big each flake should've made the earth shake. I couldn't see the other side of the street. Meaning a watcher over there couldn't see me slide out.

I trudged over to Playmate's place. That took an hour. I wasn't in good shape when I got there. It was going to be a long time before I got my old vigor back. And I didn't like this feeble new me, even temporarily.

I needed to get into a conditioning routine. Right after . . . whatever I thought up as needed doing first.

I'd give procrastination a bad name—if I ever got around to it.

Playmate asked, "So what's this I hear about you trying to die on us?"

"It wasn't quite that bad." I gave him the full story.

"Your luck amazes me. The Dead Man was awake and Tinnie put aside her grudges."

There was no arguing that. I explained our current best theories. And added, "I need to know what to do with these firestones."

"You brought them with you?" That made him nervous.

"They don't blow up. They need a psychic nudge to set them off."

"Tell me about them."

I did. It didn't take long.

"I wish I could experiment. Since I can't, let's put them in a lead-lined iron casket and bury them under the stable floor. If they go off and melt through the box they'll just sink down into the earth."

"Ingenious." I got the stones out. I'd also brought the little box we'd taken off the deacon. "Put this in there, too. No! Don't open it." I explained about the nickel idols. "They turn into pure, concentrated despair when they're charged up. You're close to them when they cut loose, you hear ghosts telling you to kill yourself." Maybe you took sick, too.

What a weapon for someone into dirty politics.

Playmate considered, then asked, "You poked around inside the Bledsoe?"

"I visited the woman Temisk tried to kill. That's all."

"I'm wondering if there isn't an upside to this villainy. A chance that, with evil intentions, they might be managing something good."

Playmate might be the only guy in TunFaire able to worry about the pavements of the road *from* hell. I asked, "How so, Swami?"

"If the nickel idols suck despair out of the Bledsoe, then the inmates might be getting better."

"The statues might drive wack jobs sane?"

"Seems logical. Though despair isn't the only reason people go mad."

I began to see possibilities. I began to get excited. "The right arms get twisted, the Bledsoe could actually do some good."

"You'd need the Ymberians. They know how the system works. I doubt they're interested in curing anyone, though. But yes, think about it. Just suck the pain right out. Smash it into the idols and . . . uh-oh."

"Yeah. The charged idols would be dangerous. And men who'd use them for their own purposes outnumber you and me. This'll take some thinking. We've got to get it right."

"We?"

"What?" He never shirked a chance to do a good deed.

"I do see it, Garrett. But I'm only one man. Who'd have to fly into a frenzy of ambition. Which I don't have much of anymore."

"I see." I saw. "It wouldn't be a one-man mission, Play. If it's workable. We can worry about that later. I'll see what Max Weider thinks. I just had to get this stuff out of the house. We'd be in deep brown if Chodo had one of his psychic spasms."

"Is there anything else?" Playmate hadn't offered the customary hospitality. I could've used a drink. He must've had a woman stashed. Or wanted to get back to work. Or something less flattering to my ego.

I thought I'd stop by The Palms, take a break. After half an hour of slogging through snow up to my knees, into the wind. Uphill. Barefoot. . . . But the place was boarded up and showing no light.

66

The Dead Man heard my thinking about the Bledsoe and whispering nickel idols. *Creative. Consider deep-sea disposal. With the charged jackals sealed into slow-rusting containers. The idols would discharge their darkness very slowly, down in the darkest deep.*

That was supposed to be a joke.

We could call that part of the ocean the Depths of Despond.

"I got it. We'd have a lot of depressed fish. Not to mention the big uglies that live down there. Picture a school of really cranky krakens."

An interesting fabulation. But I have another concern. One we can discuss with Colonel Block once our present troubles clear.

"Yeah?"

Two things concern me.

"Is this an auction?"

Three things. But your attitude, like the disposal of the nickel jackals, can abide a less stressful moment.

I figured staying quiet would cause him to get to the point.

It worked. He felt impelled to fill the vacuum. *First, the child, Penny Dreadful, has not responded to the seeds I planted in her mind. Second, we have had no contact with Miss Winger for several days.*

"You gave her work?"

I did. As mentioned. I have her examining Mr. Temisk's back trail.

"You paid her up front?"

A percentage.

"Big mistake. She won't turn up till she thinks you're asleep. Then she'll try to con me about something you supposedly promised her."

You are too cynical. But we will table that, too. Singe's brother approaches. His thoughts are veiled, but he is troubled.

I opened the door. The snow hadn't let up. John Stretch looked as miserable as a ratman can get.

"In, brother," I told him. "That's incredible."

"It is like nothing my folk remember. Some wonder if stormwardens are not feuding."

Singe met us at the door to the Dead Man's room. She had hot cocoa for her brother.

"How about it, Old Bones? Is this weather natural? Is there any precedent?"

There is no obvious storm sorcery. Yes, there have been worse snowfalls. But Mr. Pound did not come here for small talk about snowfalls. Mr. Pound?

John Stretch shook like a dog drying off.

"Creepy, ain't he?"

"Some. But he is correct. I came to report that there is war in the streets."

I considered a crack about a chance to get rich selling snowshoes to the combatants. *Hush. This will be important.*

"Who's fighting?"

"The Syndicate. The part that belongs to Rory Sculdyte. And the Unpublished Committee for Royal Security. They hit the Sculdytes hard, everywhere, at the same time."

I was surprised Relway had started so soon. Though, surely, he'd had plans roughed in ahead. He thought that way.

"I expected something. But not so soon."

"They have killed most of the Sculdyte crew. Rory and Merry and a few others have escaped, so far."

The Palms was boarded up. Had Morley gone underground?

You are correct. We must be on guard. The Sculdytes could make a connection between us and their parlous circumstance. And you were seen entering with Mr. Temisk and Mr. Contague. If they were recognized, we will draw a great deal of interest.

"Count on Mr. Mulclar. Dean. How are we fixed for supplies? Honestly."

It seemed we were good as long as we could survive without stewed apples and beer.

We couldn't hold out forever, though. And forever wouldn't be long enough if Block and Relway wanted to root us out. Assuming they survived their current adventure.

Aloud, I wondered, "Do you suppose they went now because they'd have a better chance of getting away with it in this weather?"

Given the devotion of Mr. Relway's department, the weather should prove an advantage. News will be slower to reach those inclined to interfere. People who are loath to get their feet cold or wet. Colonel Block and Director Relway are bright enough to recognize a window of opportunity. But that is their crusade. Ours is . . . I am no longer certain what ours is. The adventure has been exciting but anticlimactic.

I was no longer sure, myself. I'd done my bit for Chodo but didn't feel I'd discharged my debt. I hadn't rescued him. Harvester Temisk had enjoyed more success, though not yet as much as he'd wanted.

I hadn't done well with the Green Pants Gang, either. Though any threat they'd posed had been negated. The Watch knew them now.

They came to TunFaire in quest of converts and wealth. They will not create a bigger Ymber now. Inadvertently, they may cause considerable good. All because Dean was a pushover for a girl with sad eyes and a sadder story.

"We still need to talk to that kid. She might be a villain herself."

An interview should prove instructive. Particularly if she approached Dean in hopes of provoking exactly what has happened. She could be using us to fight A-Lat's war with A-Laf.

That would mean Penny Dreadful carefully figuring us out before she conned Dean into taking care of a bucket of kittens. You hate to think a kid that young could be so calculating.

"Having any luck working the kinks out of Chodo's mind?" I knew he'd planned to try.

There has been little opportunity. The deacon is a multiple-mind project himself. He possesses secrets, still. For example, why a firestone would have been slung at you or The Palms. Neither of our guests sees the sense, but both believe the deed must have been done by one of their own. No one else had access to the stones. They are kept in the heart of A-Laf's temple.

"Yet our boy here had one in his pocket. And Temisk bought flake as a pharmaceutical and a murder weapon."

Even among true believers there is corruption.

"And the sky is blue on a sunny day."

More cynicism.

"Always. Rooted deeply in everyday observation." I chuckled. The Ymberian deacon had become a gathering point for kittens. He wasn't pleased. But the more furious he became, the more cats arrived.

He may suffer a stroke.

"Good old apoplexy. That would save some trouble."

You need something to occupy you.

Oh-oh. Smelled like a job assignment creeping up. "I was thinking about going over to check on Tinnie."

And I was thinking you might prepare a report on the Tersize Granary for Mr. Relway and Colonel Block.

"Redhead trumps. Have Singe do it." Those guys were busy, anyway.

He didn't like my idea. Singe was too slow.

Singe didn't like it, either. It would get in the way of her quest to get rid of the beer supply.

"Too bad pixies can't write."

Pshaw!

The wee folk were in semihibernation because of the weather. Even Melondie Kadare, now, despite her determination to support Singe in her mighty quest, had been put away at the insistence of her family.

67

I was exhausted—again—by the time I got to the Tate compound. The snowfall continued, light but persistent. A teenage cousin whose name I couldn't remember let me in. He pretended he was pleased to see me. I pretended I didn't know every male Tate and all their forebears nurtured an abiding desire to see me suffer some debilitating misfortune. Or that Tinnie would come to her senses.

The boy made chitchat. He seemed terribly young and inanely naive. I couldn't help reflecting that if these were the war years, he'd already be engaged in part-time basic training in anticipation of his call to the colors.

"It was a bad day," I told Tinnie. "Mostly a bad day. You weren't in it. How did yours go?"

She tried giving me the grand glower with rheumy eyes. I was on her list for barging in when she was at less than her ravishing best.

"Don't start that. You were there when I was dying. Now I'm here."

"I just have a bad cold."

Sounded like it, too.

"Tell me about it," she suggested. Once I had, she said, "We should've suspected the Tersize people. There had to be a reason they bought a business that has no market for its product."

"They still do some legitimate baking and milling. You know them?"

She shrugged. "I never liked them much."

There would be more to the story. Maybe some history.

She grabbed my hand. "Don't mind me. I'm glad you're here. You must be exhausted."

I nodded but didn't go on about it.

"My father wanted me to marry one of the Tersize boys when I was fifteen. He wanted the business alliance. He didn't have his heart set on it. I got around him."

I couldn't imagine her not manipulating any men before she was out of diapers.

She mumbled, "I know some of the answers to the questions you still have."

"Great! How about the meaning of life?"

"Life's a bitch. And then you die." A moment later, she started snoring.

So I held her hand and fell asleep myself.

A teenage niece popped in. Food and drink were her excuse. Tinnie's people are busybodies, too. Only there're more of them. This was a fifteen-year-old edition of the professional redhead. Sizzling. And knowing it. And stoked up with all the attitude I would've expected of Tinnie at that age. She was disappointed in us old folks. Antiques, just holding hands. And snoring. Not doing anything embarrassing.

Tinnie rips a mean log. Naturally, she'll never admit an accomplishment so unladylike.

We ate. I said, "You were going to give me the answers to all my questions. After which I'll launch the cult of Saint Tinnie the Delectable."

She said, "Kyra, invite yourself out. Please." "Please" as an afterthought, in the command form.

Showing a pout that guaranteed she'd lurk in the woodwork, eavesdropping, the apprentice redhead departed.

"Don't be such a chicken, Garrett. Grab hold of my hands again."

"But then you'll kick me."

"I might." She smiled. But she didn't mean it.

Time to be a little less me. "Sorry."

"You can't help it. Your mouth takes over when you're nervous."

"I'm not nervous."

"Of course you are. You're scared shitless that I've gotten up enough nerve to decide what I want from you and me."

Good point. I'm always afraid that will happen and I'll respond by shoving both feet a yard down my own throat. But I was afraid we'd never work it out, too. "Some," I confessed. "Because chances are, someday you'll have an attack of good sense and make me go away."

"That, probably, would be best. Half the time I just slow you down. But I'm spoiled. I grew up overindulged. I can't picture my life without you in it."

Gah! This was gonna get deep. "I know what you mean. I can't, either."

"But that isn't what I want to talk about. That just came out."

Sure. The woman has no self-control whatsoever.

"I wanted to talk about Penny."

"Oh?" I squeaked. She saw the relief flood me. She managed a credible scowl. The effect of which was lost when she had to blow her nose.

"All right. What about Penny?"

"She isn't really a priestess."

"No! The surprises never stop."

"Knock it off, smart-ass. She isn't a priestess because she wasn't ever invested. She was too young. She's still too young. She's only thirteen. Though you'd never believe it if you saw her undressed. Which damned well better never happen, even after she does turn fourteen."

"I'm missing a detail or three to pull all that together."

"She turns fourteen—she's officially an adult. In her cult, that means it's time to be a holy semipro. Putting it out to honor the goddess—and add a little cash to the temple pot—until she finds a husband."

"Ymber must have been interesting, back in the day."

"You would've loved it. You would've been in church every damned day instead of just for weddings and funerals."

Could be. If the religious catch wasn't too big. "I could surprise you."

"You could, but I doubt it. You'll never be anything but sixteen when it comes to that. You can't see beyond the moment."

She wasn't entirely incorrect. But we were getting personal again.

She said, "That's not what we need to talk about. I shouldn't fuss about that. She won't let you get near her, anyway. She's scared to death of you."

"Huh? But I'm just a big old huggy bear. Why be scared of me?"

"Because—"

"Tinnie." Theses words were scarcely louder than a whisper.

Penny Dreadful, pale as the weather outside, peeked round the frame of Tinnie's open bedroom door. She did look scared as hell.

"Are you sure?"

"I have to do it sometime."

68

I retreated toward the dormer window on my side of Tinnie's four-poster. That put the bed between me and the immigrant urchin priestess princess.

She oozed around the doorframe by degrees. Somebody had run her down, stolen her rags, scrubbed and rubbed her, washed, combed, trimmed, buffed, and polished her, then stuffed her into something old of Kyra's. Yep. She'd worked wonders disguising herself as a boy.

"I've seen you before," I said. As a girl Penny Dreadful looked familiar.

Tinnie slapped my hand. "Stop drooling, big boy. She's still a baby."

"You're wrong this time, sweetness." Then, "Where do I know you from?"

The girl shivered, turned pale again. Which made her look like the ghost of Belinda Contague's past.

That was it. She resembled Belinda, though her hair, clean, was auburn with a hint of natural curl.

My ancient talent for leaping to conclusions coalesced. "Chodo Contague was your father."

Tinnie gasped, choked on some phlegm. "You're insane, Garrett," she hacked.

"Probably. But—"

"You're right," Penny said in her tiny, frightened voice. "My mother said . . . how did you guess?"

"In this light, dressed like a girl, you look a lot like your sister."

"Belinda. . . . she wouldn't . . . she . . ."

"You talked to her?" Belinda hadn't ever mentioned Penny or a half sister. Or any visit from somebody running a lost-relative scam.

"She wouldn't see me." Penny grabbed the bedpost kitty-corner from me, her knuckles whitening. "When our temple was besieged my mother told me about my father. Which is against the rules. We're not supposed to know.

"I tried to see him, too. They wouldn't let me, though."

Prodding gently, I got Penny to tell her life story. "This man came to see my mother twice a year. And me. He always brought presents. I didn't know who he was till my mother told me. At the end. But he stopped coming after he got important here. I never saw him after I was ten. A-Laf's priests started going wild after he stopped coming. First they took over the city offices. After a while there wasn't any difference between the town elders and their council of deacons. Then they started on the other religions."

Unsubtly. Bullying adherents and committing arson. The weak of faith converted. The stronger fled or died. In time, only A-Lat remained, and her empire consisted entirely of the mother temple. "Then they came for us."

"And you got away."

"My mother sent me away. She made me bring the Luck to TunFaire. In disguise. She told me to find my father. So I came. And I can't get to him."

Penny didn't appear to have witnessed her mother's murder. I gave that no weight. Witnesses do have trouble keeping time straight. When she was told to run and when she took flight could've been weeks apart.

A skilled cynic keeps his mind open to all the darker possibilities, though.

Penny teared up. "I thought it would be easy. I'd just find my father and he'd make everything right again. He's an important man."

"You really want to see Chodo?"

Frightened little-girl nod.

"Does he know who you are? Would he recognize you?"

Another nod, but not entirely confident.

A scheme began to stir in the shadowed rat's nest of my mind.

"I can take you there."

She seemed honestly excited—till she realized that I must want to take her home. Her pallor returned. She looked ready to bolt.

How carefully had she studied us before she swooped down on Dean?

"When did you come to the city?" I asked.

"Uh . . . months and months ago. Right after the war was over."

She was a kid. Kids don't pay attention to anything that don't have them at its center. Which I say based on personal experience. I used to be a kid. "So A-Laf's people arrived after you did. They came looking for you?"

"No. They didn't know about me. They thought the Luck had been destroyed. They wouldn't have found out, either, if I didn't get caught spying on them."

"Is it me you're afraid of? Or my partner?" I asked after she began to relax, thinking she'd changed the subject.

Tinnie, I noted, was quite interested in the answer.

Her suspicions abide in a realm distinct from mine. She thinks any female within stone's throw will fall under my spell.

Yeah. Right.

I hear tell a rich fantasy life is a good thing.

Again, yeah, right. "Tinnie will always be right there, ready to jump in between us."

That earned me an evil glare from my honeycomb.

"It's not you. I learned how to handle men in the temple."

"That's good to hear." Tinnie didn't relax a bit. "So

why be worried about my associate? Did Dean hand you one of his tall tales? Old Bones is harmless. Like a big old stuffed bear."

Tinnie managed a straight face. But Penny wasn't buying. "I know what he is."

I considered telling her the Dead Man wouldn't get into her head uninvited. But he'd tried already. "What secrets can a girl your age have that would embarrass a four-hundred-fifty-year-old Loghyr? What do you have to lose? If it has to do with those weird cats, he already knows." If he did, though, he hadn't told me.

"Uh . . . no. It's just too personal. It'd be like rape."

I've never felt that way. Most people don't. Still, some might.

"Your father is at my house. It isn't likely he'll leave soon."

You could see her emotions warring. Cynical old Garrett wondered if she was acting. Cynical old Garrett suspected that Penny no longer needed to connect with Chodo. Her problems with A-Laf had been resolved, at least locally.

Block and Relway wouldn't let the cultists resume their wicked ways—particularly now they were known to be part of a criminal enterprise.

I told Tinnie, "Talk to her. She won't trust anything I say."

"About?"

"Having a chat with my sidekick. Colonel Block and Director Relway will need all the ammunition they can get when friends of the Tersizes intercede for them and their immigrant pals."

The Tersizes had high connections, forged during generations of war. As did the Tates. But the Tates found legal new ways to make money. Some of which float my boat a little higher.

Tinnie said, "Leave us alone. We'll talk."

"Don't tell her too many lies about me." I eased round the bed. I could raid the kitchen during my exile.

Tinnie read my mind, in her own special way. "You stay right there in the hall. I don't want you around Rose or Kyra."

Rose would be Tinnie's evil cousin. The black ewe of the family. I hadn't seen her for a while. I hadn't missed her, either.

I slid into the hallway, commenced to amuse myself working heavy math problems. Two times two is four. Four times four is . . . uh . . . sixteen! Sixteen times sixteen is . . . uh . . . well, enough of that stuff.

Later, hovering at the brink of some huge intellectual breakthrough, I got porlocked. Tinnie yelled, "Garrett! Get your homely tail back in here." I got. Too much thinking is scary. "We have a deal. Let me get dressed. Then we'll head for your place."

"You sure? You up to it?"

"Yes."

"Oh, boy. Let me get my fingers loosened up and I'll help."

"Back in the hall, daydreamer. Penny can help. We're still talking."

I went back out. I tried to remember what my great breakthrough would've been, worried about Tinnie's health some, then wondered how she'd gotten to the kid.

69

I went in first, delivered Tinnie's message. Which was that she wanted to come have a sit-down about the need to leave Penny's head alone if she came to see us.

The Dead Man agreed. He granted every wish. Even before Tinnie finished laying out the terms. Suspicious. I know my fairy tales.

Chodo had supplanted the deacon as favored loafing place for the cat population. He had about two dozen splashed all over him. And seemed pleased. Unlike the deacon, he smiled. Sort of. His eyes tracked. His mind was active. He managed enough expression to approve my choice in women when Tinnie stalked in. He didn't seem able to move anything else.

"Made any headway?" I asked the Dead Man.

Some. But a saber-tooth never stops being a tiger.

"The deacon seems subdued."

He is in an induced coma. He is strong and stubborn. He refuses to accept defeat. He fights on despite no longer having anything to protect.

"So what great secrets did you ferret out?"

Chodo watched me move around. He watched Tinnie, too. Hungrily. Creepily. She shuddered.

Little of direct use. His compatriots mean to conquer the world, purportedly for the greater glory of their god, but in reality because they like being rulers instead of the ruled. He was a dastard and a crook before he converted. He remains a dastard and a crook. He was,

*in fact, one of Mr. Contague's significant associates in-
side A-Laf's cult. Today, either would happily sell the
other's soul to get out of this house.*

"And you wonder why the Goddamn Parrot made
his getaway."

*I am fully cognizant of the facts in that matter, Gar-
rett. I note that Miss Tate accomplished what you considered impossible.*

Miss Tate had that look people get when the Dead
Man starts rooting around inside their heads. It's a
cross between pants-wetting terror and severe
constipation.

"Penny has issues with men. But she's desperate to
see Chodo."

Excellent. We can accommodate her. He is ready.

"Are you?" I checked Chodo. He seemed close to
human, buried in kittens. Almost the Chodo of old.

*I offer my most sincere bond. I will not enter the
girl's mind unless she asks me in.*

I asked Tinnie, "Can you make her believe that?"

"Is is true?"

"His word's always been good, far as I know."

"A ringing endorsement for sure."

Singe came in with a bunch of paper. "Do we have
any more paper? I don't have enough to finish this
report."

"Huh?"

"What we have for the Colonel. From our guests."

"Hmm." Interesting. "We?"

"That poisoner. Kolda. He is in the small front
room, recording what the Dead Man wants put into
writing." Facing the Dead Man, she added, "He needs
rest. His penmanship is becoming unreadable."

"Kolda's been here all the time?" I wasn't sure why
I thought he'd left while I was out. Maybe my frugal
side was hoping I'd shed a hungry mouth.

Tinnie interjected, "Don't we have something more
pressing to deal with?"

"So go get her, my treasure. Work your wiles on
somebody who don't wear pants." I turned to the

Dead Man. "You have Kolda jot down anything from
Mr. Temisk or his best pal?" I was thinking maybe
we now had us a record of where the other bodies
were buried. That could be handier than a wagonful
of spades.

Tinnie left. After giving me a poisonous look. Singe
let her out.

"You have something up your sleeve, Smiley. Be
careful. Tinnie is steamed already."

He seemed mildly amused.

Dean came in complaining about shortages.

"We aren't under siege right now. Jump on out
there. Get what you need. Keeping in mind that we
will end up besieged again if anybody finds out who
we've got here."

The Dead Man volunteered, *No one is watching at
the moment.*

Excepting Mrs. Cardonlos, of course. But she didn't
count for much, anymore. Even the other biddies
don't have much use for a known informant.

Funny how everybody favors law and order in the
abstract, but don't want to get into the kitchen and
help cook.

Dean was ready to go. Singe let him out. He was
gone before I realized that I'd just given him the
chance he'd been laying for. "Damn! I wanted to keep
him away from the girl."

Not to worry. He is focused on marketing.

I became distracted myself. How much of the true
tale had we gotten out of Chodo? Could we use that
to restrain the man?

Probably not. Chodo was clever enough to weasel
his way out of almost anything. Usually at somebody
else's expense.

70

Penny Dreadful came in shy as a mouse, ready to bolt at the least excuse. Nobody said a thing. Chodo was the last person she eyed, excepting for the deacon, whose presence disturbed her.

Her presence bothered him, too. Despite his supposed unconsciousness. His nose pointed her way. His nostrils flared, then squeezed shut against an offensive odor.

"Friend of yours?" I asked.

She spit on the deacon, then plopped into my empty chair. Cats came from everywhere, swarmed all over her.

"Somebody's glad to see you," Tinnie observed.

Penny scowled at Chodo.

He recognized her. Even I could feel the emotion.

There was a human bone in the kingpin's body. A paternal bone.

I'd seen it before, of course. He'd been uncommonly indulgent with Belinda. Who'd loathed him all the more for it.

Find a way to lure Miss Tate out of the room.

What was he up to? "Sweetums, let's see if Dean left the kettle on."

Lame. It earned me a dose of maximum-potency fisheye. She smelled something. She didn't catch on, though.

While we got the kettle on, my fat old weasel partner sold Penny the notion that the only way she could communicate with Chodo would be through him. Which, at the moment, was true. But the process didn't have to include unfettered access to the inside of her head.

It was that old chestnut about age and treachery trumping youth and talent. She let emotion override reason.

Which was why he wanted Tinnie out of the room. She might warn Penny.

He fed me a trickle of news so I'd know to keep Tinnie occupied while he facilitated the exchange between Penny and her pappy. That smidgen was interesting in the extreme. *The stone is explained.*

"Huh?"

Tinnie's gaze popped up from loading the tea ball. "You get more primitive by the minute, don't you?"

"Ungawa! See fire hair woman! Yum. Me grab'um."

"You want hot water down your pants leg, keep it up."

"Make up your mind, woman."

Meantime, Old Bones continued. *The girl slung that stone at you. That is the main secret she wants to protect. The presence of the sexton there was not accidental. He was looking for her. He had been following her.*

He anticipated my question. *She wanted you out of the way. You were making it too difficult for Dean to help her.*

"She's just a kid." But Chodo's kid. Of course.

Tinnie gave me the fisheye. Again.

The level of malice was not high. It did not occur to her that she might kill you. She wanted you injured so you would be out of her way while she got to her father and won him over.

She was sure he would help her turn the table on A-Laf. Being unaware that Mr. Contague helped midwife the modern cult.

She does not, by the by, appear to be aware that the phoenix stones start fires, nor even that the priestess of her temple considered them particularly valuable. Along with the kittens, her mother gave her sacred jew-

elry, holy books, and a sack full of rocks. Without
explaining the importance of the jewelry or rocks. Were
I as cynical as you I would suspect that most of the
stones confiscated by A-Laf's partisans were really
creek pebbles.

Tinnie caught on. She swatted my hands away,
snatched at the kettle. "You're a total swine, aren't
you? What's he doing to her?"

"She tried to kill me."

"Bull. She didn't, either. She just—"

"You knew?"

"We talked a lot. She's lonely without her kittens."

"And you didn't—?"

"It was private, Garrett. You didn't get hurt, did
you?"

I rolled my eyes in appeal to the sky. Even my best
girl now?

Before I could protest further, she said, "Somebody's at the door."

It couldn't be critical. Old Bones wasn't spouting
warnings. Dean couldn't be back already, could he?
The redhead wasn't *that* distracting.

Singe appeared. "Saucerhead is here. With that
woman."

"Which woman?"

"Winger." Her tone left no doubt about her esteem
for my friend.

Tinnie looked relieved.

"Saved by the cavalry, eh?"

She stuck out her tongue.

"You'll pay, woman. Mark my words, you'll pay."

She just sneered.

Winger was more wasted than Melondie Kadare
ever managed. "Garrett!" she burbled, blurry-eyed,
using both walls to stay upright. "Yer a sum um a
bitch, even if yer one a the good guys." She leaned
against one wall. "Jes need a minute. I'm fucked-up."

"What's this?" I asked Saucerhead.

"A very drunk woman."

"That part didn't get past me. I've got skills. I was thinking more along the lines of, why? And why here? She might make a mess."

"I think she's done all of that she can. Less'n she can get her socks up."

"Even so. Singe, stand by the door. We'll toss her out if—"

Tinnie interrupted, "It'll take all of you to do it."

Winger started snoring. She sank toward the floor.

Tharpe told me, "The Dead Man said bring her in. He wants to know what she found out."

"She found out there's a limit to how much she can drink."

"She's upset. She's misplaced Jon Salvation. She don't remember where. Or how. She's scared she might've killed him. Or something."

"Great! Well, let's see if we can't drag her—"

There is no need to bring her in. I have examined her memories. They support what we have learned from these other sources while including little of additional interest.

Winger's snores turned into what sounded like a desperate fight for air. Her eyes popped open. She climbed the wall. "I know what I done wit' 'im. I t'ink. Damn fool." She stumbled toward the front door.

"Winger, you ain't in no shape to go out there," Tharpe told her. "You'll freeze your ass. Tell me where he's at. I'll go scoop him up."

"Head, yer a sum um a bitch, even if yer a one a the good guys."

"So you keep telling me. Why don't you just relax? I'll find Jon."

"The Remora? You know where 'e's at?"

"You were going to tell me."

"You been holding out on me, Head. You never did like him." Winger began to sag. "That place that's like a ship. Grimes' Cove. I 'member he was wit' me there."

Tharpe turned toward the door. The Dead Man filled us in on what Winger knew without knowing she knew. I said, "You don't want to go back out without warming up, do you? Tinnie and I were making tea."

"A snack wouldn't hurt, neither." Tharpe shook his head, looking at Winger. "The things we do for folks just on account of they're friends."

I avoided any comment.

Saucerhead was working on a stale roll when Singe yelled. We burst out of the kitchen. Singe indicated Winger. Winger was making weird noises. She had her guts behind them.

"Come on!" I swore some. "Get that damned door open!"

Tharpe and I each grabbed an arm. Tinnie sort of nipped around the booted end, like a puppy trying to help without knowing how. Singe flung the door wide. Cold air blasted us. It woke Winger as we heaved her out against the rail on the stoop.

Her socks came up.

"Hey!"

Dean was back. With a cart. Which I hoped wasn't stolen. Winger's rude greeting missed him by inches.

Dean wasn't alone. Seemed he always found somebody to help with the cart. Whoa! Hell. That bundle of rags was the lone member of the Contague tribe not already installed in the Dead Man's room.

"You. Get inside before somebody recognizes you." Potential watchers should all still be gone to war, but why take chances?

Draped over the rail, Winger gasped, "Blindar, yer a bitch even if yer a one a the good gals." She cackled. "An' yer sure as hell ain't." She tried to laugh, but her stomach revolted.

I said, "Inside. Wait in the hall with Tinnie. I'll help Dean." Singe came out, too, while Tinnie took charge of Belinda. With little of her customary empathy. "Did you clean out the whole damned market?"

Saucerhead concentrated on Winger. Winger was trying to aspirate her own puke.

"You told me to get ready for a siege," Dean said.

"I did, didn't I? Where did Belinda come from?"

"I ran into her in the market. She was pretending to be a refugee. I told her to come get warm."

I grunted under the weight of a sack of apples.

"I thought that would be better than maybe having her go back into the Tenderloin."

"Yeah." Damn! Those apples were heavy. "But why is she here? She should be back home waiting out the storm. She has to know there's a war on."

"I think she's afraid there're traitors there."

"What does she know about the situation here?"

"She knows it's warm. And safe."

I started to growl. Exhaustion was closing in again. I was getting cranky.

"I told her nothing. Her problems come from her disaffection with her father. It might be useful if she confronts him."

"Good thinking." Maybe. I didn't like his deciding what was best for somebody else. He tried too much of that with me.

Singe went by. "Once again the ratgirl does the work while the human folk stand around jawing."

Belinda wasn't in the hallway when I went inside. "Uh-oh."

It is under control. Join us once you deliver your cargo.

Leave the rest for Dean? Fine with me.

71

Belinda took three steps into the Dead Man's room.
She froze, gaped at her father.

Chodo sensed the new presence but could not see
who it was.

*Take the deacon out when you go. Put him into the
cart. Get rid of him.*

Dean gave me a hand. For reasons probably having
to do with externally applied inhibitions, I didn't wonder what Colonel Block would think about us turning
his prisoner loose. Nor did I wonder why Old Bones
wanted him running free. With my experience I
should've been more suspicious.

After a long adventure through nasty streets, Dean
and I abandoned cart and deacon not far from the Al-
Khar. We trudged home exchanging lies about who
was more tired. I got there to find the seating arrangements in the Dead Man's room revised. There seemed
to be plenty enough kittens to provide several for
every Contague. The big boy from Ymber was snoring. Harvester Temisk looked like he was dead. But
he kept on breathing. Poor Harvester. His only role
now was to take up space.

I asked, "What happened to Saucerhead and
Winger?"

"Winger is in your office," Singe told me. "Saucerhead went looking for her friend and to find someone the Dead Man wants to consult."

"Who? Why?"

"I was not invited into the planning."

The way things usually work around here. "Winger is in my office? Gods! I hope she's empty."

"She is now."

Dean muttered something about the ever-expanding population of the house and disappeared. I thought he was off to whip up something to eat. Instead, he dragged his sorry ass off to bed.

I settled in the Dead Man's room, leaning against the wall. There were no seats available. Nor would be soon, I suspected. I was ready to collapse from exhaustion. Yet again. But I didn't want to miss anything.

The Dead Man was working some Loghyr mojo on our dysfunctional family guests. Assisted by a gaggle of cats.

Chodo was more alive than ever. I stared. I wasn't frightened. I felt creepiness instead. In times gone by there'd always been terror when I was near the kingpin.

"Am I over that?" Seemed like a good time to find out if my sidekick was paying attention.

Unlikely. Changes are going on inside Mr. Contague. The impact of the kittens is much greater in the company of their high priestess. Which the girl has become by default, as sole survivor of her temple. A-Lat herself is hidden inside the child. And inside the Luck. Too scattered to have much power. Which is our great good fortune. We would not stand up to her otherwise. Nevertheless, the effect here will not be one hundred percent. And there is little chance of permanence.

I made grunting sounds. Deities make me nervous. There are a zillion of them, all real, all at cross-purposes, all unpleasant. Ninety-nine out of a hundred have no interest whatsoever in the well-being of mortals. Particularly if the mortal is named Garrett. And there was little evidence that this encounter would turn out positive—despite A-Lat's salutary impact on Chodo's madness at the moment.

"Can I note that more than one heart is in agony here?"

Careful what you wish for. Some may not enjoy being cured.

Not till later did I realize he was painting *me* with that brush.

I told anybody who cared, "I'm going to bed. We can wrap this up tomorrow." I had some thinking to do, too. I do that best without distractions.

72

Singe wakened me. She'd brought tea. "Don't you ever let up?" I was accepting no peace offerings today.

Somebody kicked me in the back of the legs. "Shaddup!"

"So that's it, huh? Trying to catch us up to something again."

"No. The Dead Man wants you."

I got kicked again. "This don't seem like a hot sell, Miss Tate," I grumbled at the bushwhacker. "If this is what I've got to look forward to." Which got me kicked again. In my own bed. I suffered the slings and arrows, rewarded my long-suffering with a hot cup of tea.

Ten minutes later, biscuit and mug in my left hand, half a foot of sausage in my right, I trudged into the Dead Man's room. Dripping grease. I was groggy but no longer cross-eyed with exhaustion. I was looking forward to the day I had my old self back.

"Looks like I'm the first man on the job." Sleeping folks were strewed everywhere.

Excepting Singe, Dean, and I. And the Luck.

Yeah. Several dozen cats were on the bounce.

"Weather any better? Can we move these parasites out?"

Probably not. Not comfortably. Unless you move fast.

"Huh?"

An associate of Mr. Dotes brought a message while

you were loafing. There was an overwhelming implication of paybacks for all the times I'd complained about
him snoozing when I had a strong desire for a little
genius backup.

"What's on your mind?"

*I wish to propose that you have fulfilled your abiding
obligation to Mr. Contague.*

"What? He's just . . . he's still . . ."

*He remains confined to his wheelchair. It is unlikely
that he will ever leave it. Only a Loghyr mind surgeon
can repair damage done by a stroke. Loghyr mind sur-
geons were rare as roc eggs even when our tribe was
bountiful. But Mr. Contague is possessed of a powerful
will. I would not bet heavily against him accomplishing
anything—if he can stay out of the hands of those who
wish him ill.*

"Meaning family?" Family was snoring a yard from
my feet. Belinda and Singe had quaffed a few quarts
after I went upstairs.

*Family, yes. But Miss Contague was not the worst of
his tormentors. He possesses recollections of being
force-fed by persons other than his daughter. Persons
most likely associated with Merry Sculdyte. Who was
not always forthright with his brother.*

"Merry was working against Rory?"

*At cross-purposes, certainly. Mr. Contague recalls in-
cidents that distinctly suggest an enduring hatred by
Merry toward his brother. There are deep shadows in
Sculdyte's mind. He is twisted and torn because he
loves Rory, as well. You will find the details in the
written history. That is not important at the moment.
Decisions about what to do with Mr. Contague and
Mr. Temisk are.*

"Huh?"

Have you not been considering what to do next?

"Sure." Though not very hard. Chodo and his pal
couldn't hang out here forever. And I couldn't see
Chodo going back home. That would put him back
where he started. But my conscience wouldn't turn
him loose on the world again, either. Nor would it

allow me to tell Old Bones that I was satisfied that I no longer owed Chodo.

I anticipated as much.

Uh-oh. He was up to something. And was way ahead of me in whatever his scheme was.

"You say he's more or less sane now?"

As much as can be. To roughly the baseline that existed at the time of his stroke. More than that is beyond even the Luck of A-Lat. And that will persist only so long as he remains within the influence of the child and the kittens.

"So what do we do with him?"

Exactly.

"Well?"

Waiting on you, Garrett. I owe him nothing. I would hand him off to Colonel Block. Along with his memoirs. Then he issued one of his cryptic, one-hand-clapping pronouncements. *There is a workable answer implicit within the existing situation, though it is as complicated as the situation itself.*

All right. He's a little windy for a perfect master.

Passing everything and everyone off to the law was, no doubt, a rational final solution. And one I wish I was hard enough to invoke. But I'm me. Garrett. The old softy. "What about his family?"

Also as healed as can be. But wounds leave scars. And scars never go away.

"Hey! What about that message from Morley?"

Mr. Dotes says the Sculdytes and their associates are dead or in custody. He suggests we wrap up anything we don't want examined closely because we may find ourselves the focus of the Watch as soon as Colonel Block and Director Relway have rested.

"You should've told me that first."

The matters are related. Mr. Contague, Miss Contague, and most of these others need to be out of here when the law invites itself in. Make no mistake—if they make a hard decision to get us, they can.

"I have no interest in a game of macho with the Watch."

*We may not have many more unencumbered hours.
I have set certain processes in motion, but no good will
come of them in time.*

Of course. They'd start out just watching. But well-
rested men would rotate in behind the first wave, two
or three for one, and so forth, till they stood shoulder
to shoulder. If Block and Relway felt the need. They
were planners. They didn't move without being prepared. For all the speed they've shown trying to estab-
lish the rule of law.

Crushing the Sculdytes wouldn't mean an end to organized crime. Nobody is dim enough to think that's possible, or even entirely desirable. But the Outfit's power to
corrupt would be reduced dramatically. Its power to play
favor for a favor would be pruned way back. Meaning
those villains on the Hill wouldn't have so many dirty
hands on call. Let alone the occasional beakful of
found money.

"Singe. Get Tinnie down here. Dump a bucket of
slush on her if you need to."

"I will defer to the grand master on that."

"Huh?"

"Do your own dumping. Tinnie dislikes me
enough already."

73

Colonel Block came himself. He'd believed Constable Scithe, who'd believed me when I told him Chuckles was snoozing. Or, as seems more likely, he didn't care. He thought he didn't need to hide anymore.

He came in looking tired, ragged, and suspicious. His gaze darted around like he expected trouble. He must've been right out there on the sharp end of the spear.

"You seem awful twitchy."

"It was a close-run thing. Thank heaven I've got committed people. And had bad weather. That kept my friends off my good back. They couldn't help me with negative advice. But they'll catch up yet. I may be looking for work soon."

Dean showed up with refreshments. Then Singe brought Kolda's voluminous scribblings. I told Block, "You'd have time to read all this then."

He paid no attention. Just held the papers in his lap. "Where are they?"

"Where are what?"

"The people you were hiding here."

"Kolda is in the small front room, sleeping off a bad case of writer's cramp. The big bruno from Ymber is in with the Dead Man. His boss we dragged back over to your shop on account of he was too strong and stubborn for Chuckles to manage and keep up with everything else he wanted to get done before he drifted off."

"Same old Garrett. I don't give a rat's ass about those people."

"And Tinnie's upstairs, in bed. Sick."

"A higher power than I has decided the A-Laf cult is too dangerous to tolerate. I want to know where Harvester Temisk, Chodo Contague, and Belinda Contague went."

I put on my dumb look. Like all my sergeants during basic, he didn't buy it. Coldly, he reported chapter and verse of comings and goings at my place for the past several days. Every one. From a very specific point in time.

The Dead Man was more flabbergasted than me. He thought so much of himself. When he'd said nobody was watching he'd done so in absolute confidence.

"Captain Ramey List," I said. "He wasn't what he seemed."

Captain List was exactly what he seemed. He brought something in without knowing it. Almost certainly aboard one of his spear carriers, who would have been more than he seemed. Now that I am aware of its existence I will not be long locating it.

"Now that it's too late and doesn't matter."

Colonel Block allowed himself a thin smile.

He is not aware of details. Director Relway was behind the plant. Which appears only to have betrayed comings and goings, not anything that was done or said.

"Then we're in good shape."

"Where are they, Garrett? We could put paid to the whole underworld right now."

"You can't possibly believe that. It's part of the social fabric. All you've done is make life easier for Belinda. You got rid of the people most likely to have eliminated her. Made for a smoother transition of power."

"Stipulated. But the baddies won't be the old bunch. Well?"

"Well, what?"

"You refusing to tell me what I want to know?"

Colonel Block's recent activities left him more ex-hausted intellectually than he is aware. He is not think-ing clearly. Consequently, he is dramatically overconfident. It is not necessary to be stubborn. He will not remember anything he hears.

"Not at all. Not at all." Probably wouldn't hurt to tell him everything, even if he did remember. Old Bones wasn't clueing me in about much these days.

Several kittens chose that moment to set up housekeeping in the Colonel's lap. Block petted them but paid no attention otherwise.

Chuckles and the Luck made a dangerous team.

"Tell you the complete truth, I have no idea where they went or what happened to them. The way it was explained to me, what I don't know I can't blab to some nosy Watchman."

I wouldn't overdo the truth stuff in any case. The Dead Man isn't infallible. Block's confidence might be justified. He might've had a metal plate installed in his head to block out Loghyr thoughts.

I wasn't untruthful. I *didn't* know where the crowd had gone. I couldn't think of anywhere to stash them that the Watch wouldn't look right away.

I wasn't confident that Saucerhead, Winger, John Stretch, and Jon Salvation could manage that crowd, either. However much Penny Dreadful seemed in-clined to cooperate now.

Being a natural-born, ever-loving, blue-eyed cynic, I didn't buy that kid being satisfied with a father who wasn't the avenger with flaming sword she'd come to find.

Block kept trying to get steamed up. But another kitten arrived every time the red began to show in his cheeks.

I changed the subject. "You heard anything to ex-plain this strange weather? I don't like it. People can't get out and show off their three-wheels. The fad might go away before I get rich."

"You'll never be rich, Garrett. You don't have what it takes to hang on to wealth and make it grow."

"I'll buy that. I should get rid of these freeloaders. Thanks, Singe." She'd brought beer.

He was distracted. He'd begun to look confused. Like I do when I walk into a room, then stand around trying to remember why.

The Dead Man had Block, subtly enough that the Colonel didn't realize it. But then, we'd lied to him about Old Bones being asleep.

We had a few beers, relaxed, solved most of the problems of TunFaire. On Block's side, that reflected Deal Relway's conviction that to set the world right we need to kill the people who get in the way. Every little bit, he'd realize he was out of character and get upset. A cat or two would pile on long enough to distract him. After Tinnie joined us the cats were unnecessary.

The man would offer some competition if he could.

You can release him back into the wild, Garrett. The worst is past. He is not likely to be concerned about us for several days now.

74

I shook hands with Block. He frowned, unable to shake the suspicion that he'd missed something critical. He went down to the street hugging his bundle of papers, stopped, shook his head, went on. He had trouble steering a straight line.

I shook hands with a groggy and thoroughly confused Kolda, too. The poisoner winced. He couldn't close his fingers into a fist. It wasn't much, but it was some payback. He headed out, dispirited. He passed a bent old man coming uphill slowly, leaning heavily on an ugly, polished teak cane.

I just had time to notice him, then had to get out of the way as the Green Pants wide load shuffled out of the house. A-Laf's sexton had less grasp on the world than did Kolda. And smelled bad besides.

Watchmen moved in on him, grinning. The big guy went along docilely.

Penny Dreadful observed from her usual perch. How did she shake loose?

The little old man reached my steps. He stopped. He wore a huge brown overcoat, far too large for him. He pushed hard on his cane, forcing his body upright. He looked at me. He didn't seem impressed. "You Garrett?"

"Garrett! You going to hold that door open until we all freeze?" Tinnie was not in a good humor.

"Yes." Meant for the old man but heard by the redhead. And taken to heart.

Bring him to me.

"Who?"

Silverman.

"I am Silverman," the old man announced. As though that explained creation itself.

"How marvelous for you." What the hell was this? "Come on in."

"I'll need help. These steps look treacherous."

The air was warm. The snow was melting, making the footing dangerous. There'd be flooding in the low parts of town.

On cue, in a roar of tiny wings, pixies exploded from my wall. The swarm streaked out into the weather. Except Melondie Kadare. Mel tried to flit into the house. Tinnie slammed the door before she got there.

I went down to help Silverman, baffled. "I suppose you're expected."

He gave me an odd look. "Stay close. Catch me if I slip." After a three-step climb he paused to catch his wind.

"Wouldn't be a big cabbage eater, would you?"

"Eh?"

"Never mind. Who are you? What are you?"

Melondie perched on my right shoulder.

"Silverman. You don't know why you sent for me?"

I'd overlooked it when I became a dual personality. The one in charge now didn't have a clue. "I don't think so." If you were two people in one slab of meat, would you know it? Werewolves usually do.

"Your man came. He seduced me away from my work. He said you can get my daughter moved up the priority list. . . ."

"But— Stop that, Bug!" Melondie was messing with my ear.

I sent for him, Garrett. Will you cease dawdling? Bring the man here. I caught a hint of unease. Something wasn't going quite the way he wanted. I didn't think he was fussed about the pestiferous pixie, though.

Nothing for it but to ride the tiger now.

The door was locked.

"Lookit here, Mel. I got time to deal with you." I faked a swat. She buzzed and pouted. Her husband and family materialized. A typical pixie debate commenced. The subject, Melondie's drinking, got lost in the general uproar.

Tinnie opened up, sheepish and defiant. I grumbled, "I hope we aren't headed there." I jerked a thumb at the wee folk. "It isn't sport to me."

Shaking his head, Silverman eased past Tinnie. He didn't fail to note her fine points. As usual, she did fail to note his appreciation.

We met Dean and Singe in the hall. They carried an array of refreshments. Silverman's good opinion was important to my resident stiff.

Silverman wasn't intimidated by the Loghyr. Maybe, like the Dead Man, he had roots so deep in time nothing bothered him anymore. He settled into my chair. His eyes widened when Old Bones made contact. He didn't react otherwise. He built a complicated cup of tea, sipped, relaxed, asked, "Now, sir, why did you lure me away from my art?"

Old Bones meant to have fun with it. Whatever it was. He didn't include me in the conversation. I soothed my bruised feelings by easing over to Tinnie, where I got some exercise getting my hands slapped.

Chuckles stopped that. *Silverman is a jeweler, Garrett. A custom designer of uniquely powerful pieces. Shall I have him create something special for you two?*

Panic.

Amusement from the realm of the dead.

Sigh of relief from me once I understood that Tinnie hadn't caught any of that.

But I could include her.

"I'll be good."

More amusement.

I have to get over this, somehow.

Silverman didn't say much. The Dead Man answered his questions before he articulated them.

Singe got the expense ledger and cashbox. I caught

the twinkle of noble metal as she put money into Silverman's wrinkled pale hand. Under instruction, of course. Then, not under instruction, she sidled over to show me the inside of the cashbox.

It contained a handful of gritty green copper and two cracked, blackened silver pieces of indeterminate but exaggerated age. The kings could no longer be recognized.

"I knew it! What have I been telling you all? You people have finally done it!"

Quiet. You will recover your investment. In time. Ah. At long last. I had no trouble sensing his relief. Plainly, he'd been worried about something. *Stand by to answer the door.*

"And make sure Melondie doesn't get in. I can't afford to support her bad habit."

You go, Garrett. Take your stick.

"She gonna be that much problem?"

Do not be contrary. It does not become you. The stick is a precaution, unlikely to be needed.

That wasn't reassuring, even so.

I was going to be a whole lot contrary for a big long time. They really were spending me into the poorhouse.

I did as he suggested. The situation, of course, wasn't as bad as my instructions implied. Dean didn't show up trying to figure out how to work his crossbow.

75

I was speechless. A state apparently desirable, if some can be credited.

Tap-tap-tapping was the A-Laf deacon Old Bones had cut loose. Looking determined but bewildered. Like someone naturally slow on the uptake valiantly pressing forward in life. With him was a matched pair of bruisers, mortified by having to appear publicly in disguise. Twins, distraught because they couldn't wear their signature ugly pants.

There'd been guys like that in the Corps. The uniform helped them define who they were. Without it they became rudderless.

Will you cease dallying? Time is critical. Colonel Block's minions have noted their arrival. Someone may want to investigate.

"Wouldn't mind finding out what—"

Move it!

Whoa! Somebody was getting cranky.

I moved it, not without sulking.

The Ugly Pants crew entered without pleasantries. With a "My feelings are bruised just by being here" kind of attitude.

I grumbled, "I might be a little better motivated if I knew what the hell you were up to."

I am trying to wrap this neatly, with maximum benefit to all. Before the advent of the new millennium. Bring them here. Today.

Sometimes you've just got to go along and see
what happens.

I herded the daft deacon and his water buffalo into
the presence. "Anything else you need? Dancing girls?
Tinnie might come stumble around. Or can we get to
the point?"

*I wonder if that samsom weed might not be coming
back on you again.*

That was a thought. I did my best to ignore it. But
there could've been something to it.

The A-Laf deacon went straight to Silverman. One
of the big boys placed a box in the old man's lap.
Silverman produced a loupe. He opened the box.

I jumped.

The casket contained a nickel dog. A pup. All right!
A jackal.

This one wasn't charged, though. It was just a hunk
of metal.

Silverman studied the critter. Then he stared at the
Dead Man.

Then he studied the statue again. "It will be difficult. But I enjoy a challenge. Especially work in unusual metals. This won't be enough material, though."

Voice barely audible, the deacon said, "More is
available." He was cooperating only because he wasn't
strong enough to fight the Dead Man.

"I need ten more pounds," Silverman said. "Prefer-
ably in small pieces." Responding to a query from the
Dead Man, who hadn't included me. He was amusing
himself. Getting back. All that juvenile—

Garrett!

I responded with a scowl. But I paid attention.

*Accompany Deacon Osgood and his associates.
Make certain they move the necessary materials to Silverman's workshop. Stick with Deacon Osgood until
he has executed his commitment in full.*

"Hey, all right." I confess to a certain sarcasm.
"You gonna bother telling me how I'll know when he
has? There's always a chance—remote as the moon,

naturally, but statistically possible—that I won't figure
it out for myself."

Deacon Osgood is going to surrender A-Laf's de-
spair confiscation system. Mr. Silverman will make
modifications. Deacon Osgood and his henchmen are
not pleased, but have spent enough time in our
forward-looking city to appreciate the enthusiasm of
the Watch.

He was smug. Proud of himself. And likely twisting
everything to make a certain defunct Loghyr look like
an ingenious trouble tamer.

I have planted strong mindworms in all three ser-
vants of A-Laf. Deep fears and compulsions will carry
them through the wrap-up. Even so, arm yourself. The
deacon has a strong mind. The proximity of active jack-
als may attenuate the mindworm's efficacy.

"I see." I didn't comment on the fact that mindworms weren't imaginary anymore. Though I'd suspected hanky-panky with the facts when he'd sold the
goods to Teacher White.

Relax now. I have to fill the vacuum inside your skull
with what you need to carry this stage through to its
best conclusion.

76

A-Laf's minions hadn't done badly, making connections round TunFaire, building on foundations provided by Harvester Temisk and Chodo Contague. Their associations with the Bledsoe and the Tersize family had been useful. Best of all, from their viewpoint, was an alliance on the Hill, with the Spellsinger Dire Cabochon, birth name Dracott Radomira, cadet of the royal family, a comparative unknown whose name never came up in any review of the ruling class's crimes and misdemeanors. Cabochon was particularly useful because she was defunct, in fact though not yet legally. Unlike my resident cadaver, the old witch just sat in a corner mummifying. Her pals from out of town hadn't reported that the air had gone out of her.

The out-of-towners didn't note the unnatural post-demise good health of the remains, either.

The old witch must have sung spells around herself before she surrendered to the unavoidable. The right people might be able to bring her back. If they were of a mind.

Not my problem. I wasn't of a mind.

Tinnie made noises indicating repugnance. I comforted her not at all. She'd insisted on tagging along. Let her enjoy *all* of it.

I was still wasting mind time looking for an argument pointed enough to penetrate redheaded stubbornness and make Tinnie understand that there were parts of my life she shouldn't share.

I said, "It don't smell bad for somebody being a long time dead."

Deacon Osgood's crew wasted no time. They collected metal dogs, metal scraps, and metalworking tools from a sitting room converted into a workshop. If I was a cynic, I'd have thought they wanted to hustle me out of there.

They piled everything into old vegetable sacks. Osgood was as happy as a guy working with a migraine. He feared the Watch would find out about this shanty now. But he couldn't not help me.

This would have been the administrative headquarters for A-Laf's TunFaire mission. The base in the Tersize establishment had been living quarters.

I checked the dead woman. It wasn't immediately obvious whether her demise had been natural or assisted. Colonel Block could work that out.

There was a crackly sense about her that said, "Don't touch!" I didn't. That might be all it took to reanimate her.

Old Bones must have known. He hadn't informed the Watch. He didn't want his scheme hip deep in law and order.

"You. Garrett." Deacon Osgood seldom spoke. When he did he sounded worn-out. "Carry this sack. You. Trollop—"

Tinnie popped him between the eyes with a handy pewter doodad. Those eyes crossed. He staggered. His troops gawked. This was beyond their imagining. Still, I was glad Chuckles had taken time to stifle their natural tendencies to break people whenever something happened that they didn't understand.

"Ease off," I told Tinnie. She was winding up for the coup de grâce. "We need him."

She shed her weapon, but her look said hostilities would resume the instant the next chunk of sexual bigotry plopped out of Osgood's mouth. Sweetly, "You were about to ask me something, Deacon?"

Grunt. Headshake to clear cobwebs. "Sack. There. Carry." He couldn't get all the way to "please." But that was all right. He'd been disadvantaged in his up-bringing. By goats.

Shortly, I noted that everything in need of carrying was in the hands of someone who could do the lugging, but the good old deacon wasn't weighted down with anything heavier than his conscience. I asked Tinnie, "Worth making a scene?"

"Let's get what we want out of him first."

I'd seen that look before, mainly when I'd done something to offend. I'd enjoyed an opportunity for regrets every time.

Silverman examined every tool and every piece of metal before saying, "Satisfactory. I can work with this." He asked Osgood. "Are you one of the artisans?"

Osgood shuddered like a dog trying to pass a peach pit. The compulsion remained solid. "No. Those who survived are imprisoned now."

I asked Silverman, "Will that be a problem?"

"No. It will just take longer to fulfill your principal's needs."

Tinnie smirked, reading my mind. Deftly, I managed to disappoint her. "Not yet. Let's get what we want out of him first." Not that I knew what that was. The Dead Man had stuffed my mush with stuff without ever betraying his plan.

Silverman barked. Men and women, young and old, all obviously related, swarmed. They grabbed the stuff we'd brought. I muttered in language forms I hadn't used much since coming home from the war. I'd have my nose to the grinder for years to pay for this.

Silverman told me, "You. Out. I'll send word when it's ready." He told Tinnie, "You can stay."

Instead of popping him, à la Osgood, she kissed his cheek. He glowed.

The deal with Osgood was that he'd be cut loose now. We parted outside Silverman's workshop. I hoped he and his crew would hop a keelboat back to

Ymber, but told Tinnie, "Call me cynical. I'd bet we haven't seen the last of them."

Disgruntled, I headed toward home. Wondering how long the Watch would let Osgood run loose.

Those tailing us decided that keeping tabs on Ymberian rubes was more important than watching me. Which conformed to the Dead Man's prognostications.

I had instructions against the chance that I found myself running free.

77

"You know either one of those guys?" Tinnie and I were peeking around the corner of a decrepit redbrick tenement. The men in question had Harvester Temisk's dump staked. There was no foot traffic. They stood out. They weren't happy.

The weather was turning again. And wasn't going to be long getting nasty. The sky was filthy.

"No." Tinnie was shivering. She wanted to go somewhere warm. But she was made of stern enough stuff not to whine after having bullied me into letting her tag along. "I don't. Should I?"

"I hope not. They're the lowliest lowlifes. The tall one works for Deal Relway." I'd seen him with Relway occasionally. But I let her think I'd deduced it, employing special detective powers. "The other one is a gangland operator." Actually, more likely a stringer or wannabe on the pad now because Relway's fervent work ethic had drained the bad-boy manpower pool down to the muck on the bottom. I knew him by affected mannerisms and dress, paramount to him when it would be smarter to be invisible.

Relway's man recognized him, too.

He, however, hadn't made the lawman, despite his being right there in plain sight.

I explained. "So what you do is—"

"You're trying to get rid of me."

"I'm trying to utilize your talents since you're here.

Go tell the sloppy one you're lost. Bat your eyes. Get him to help you."

"Why not the tall, handsome one?"

"Because he's tall and handsome? And, probably, not likely to be distracted by a pretty face. Not to mention, if he leaves to help you, the other dimwit won't tag along. He doesn't know that Handsome is there."

She mulled that. "The tall one would follow?"

"I would. I'd figure that you were a messenger. I'd want to see what was up." Because I'd know that the Sculdytes had gotten hammered, so this fool would be working for someone else whose interests paralleled those of the departed faction.

In this neighborhood that meant good old Teacher White.

"Scoot," I told Tinnie. "Vamp the man. Get him out of here." I dug in my pocket. The key was there. Harvester Temisk had managed, somehow, to lose it while he was at my place. I didn't know what the Dead Man had gotten from him, just that he wanted me to toss Temisk's place. Something the Watch and the Outfit had done already, I suppose.

"If he touches me . . ."

"I'll die of envy."

She stuck out her tongue, headed out. Haughtily.

I couldn't have scripted it better. Her victim didn't have one ounce of brain above his beltline. Tinnie set her hook, pulled him in, and led him away in as much time as it takes to tell it. And Relway's man decided he needed to see what was going on.

78

It was gloomy inside Temisk's digs. Not much light crept in through the feeble excuses for windows. There wasn't a lot out there to spare. But I didn't fire up a lamp. Its light would slip out and alert the world that somebody was housebreaking.

The first thing I learned was that nobody had had a notion to toss the place. Though it did look like somebody had taken a polite look around.

I did little but walk around at first, getting a sense of the place. The Dead Man wanted me to find something. Unarmed with a single hint.

The building was three stories tall. Temisk had the ground floor, which wasn't all that big. Who lived upstairs? I couldn't recall having ever seen any other tenants.

I checked the street. It was a ghost town out there. Fat flakes had begun to swirl, anticipating the main event. I slipped out. It had gotten colder fast. A nasty wind snapped and snarled between buildings. I crossed, turned, immediately saw where the stair to the upper floors had been. It had had an outside entrance on the right side as I faced the building. The outside steps were gone. A bricklayer had done well matching colors but hadn't disguised the shape of the old entrance.

Upstairs windows had received the same treatment.

Not unusual in a city where everybody is paranoid about invasions and break-ins.

I caught movement from the corner of my eye. A long, lean, slumped figure shuffled toward me, obscured by the snowfall, hunched miserably.

I drifted back into Temisk's place.

Skelington hove to outside.

So. Teacher was still in the game. Without showing much imagination.

I resumed examining Temisk's place. Nothing jumped out. It wouldn't if it wasn't supposed to. But . . . there was a grand fireplace on the wall backing on the stairwell. A fireplace that didn't look like it saw much use. In a location that made no architectural sense.

I'd just discovered the iron rungs in the unnaturally ample chimney when somebody tried the street door. There were voices there. Querulous.

I quickly kicked the fireplace gewgaws back into place, hoisted myself. I'd just gotten the feet out of sight when the newcomers busted in.

"Where did he go?" Teacher demanded. "Quick. Check in back. Maybe there's another way out." Feet tramped around, fast and heavy.

"There ain't no back way," Skelington said. "I watched this place enough to know."

"Good for you. I'm really trusting your good sense and thinking these days."

There were four of them. I was in no shape to handle those odds. Not even Teacher and his clowns. It had been a long day. And the samsom weed still had some effect.

"Ain't no sign of him, Boss." I didn't know that voice.

"Allee allee in free, Garrett," Teacher called. "Come out, come out, wherever you are. Skelington, you sure he came in here?"

"I was right there in the damned street." Skelington didn't have much patience left for his chief. I couldn't imagine why he hadn't defected already.

"All right. All right. And you let the girl get away, Pike?"

"Wasn't no 'let' to it, Boss. I told you. That Tin Whistle was all over me soon as I made my move. She bugged on both of us. I wouldn't of come got you if she didn't. Hell, I'm lucky I got away from the damned Runner. I could be sharing a cell tonight in the Al-Khar."

Teacher grumbled something about maybe that would've learned him something.

None of those boys were happy. Nothing was going their way, they had no use for each other, and the guy in charge had gone totally whiny. They were sticking together out of habit and a slim hope that the worm would turn.

Teacher muttered, "That bastard is here somewheres. Temisk must of told him about his secret places."

"What secret places is that, Boss?"

"I don't know! Shit! Think, Vendy! He's a fuckin' lawyer. That means he steals stuff an' hides people from the Watch. An' shit like that."

Ah. Brother White had been loading up on the artificial courage.

"He never worked for nobody but Chodo, Boss."

"Don't you never believe that, Vendy. Don't you never. He mighta said that. He mighta had Chodo snowed. But he never really worked for nobody but Harvester Temisk. He's a fuckin' lawyer. He had something going on under the table. Where the fuck is that creep? I need to break some bones. Take a look up that damned chimbly."

That was it. I was caught. If I scrambled up, I'd give me away with the racket. But Vendy would spot me if I stayed where I was.

It was one of life's special moments.

A face appeared below. Vendy just looking so Teacher would shut the hell up. His eyes almost popped. I whacked on his bald spot.

He fell to his knees, mumbling. Conscious but incoherent. Teacher growled, "Ya fell outta the goddamn chimbly? You're one useless piece a pork snot."

I climbed while there was moaning and complaining to cover the noise. Only a few feet farther up I stepped out into the stairwell that had been bricked off at street level. Wan light dribbled down from a far skylight too small to admit the skinniest burglar. At high noon in clear summer weather it wouldn't have admitted much light. It served more as a beacon now.

I did not, however, go charging on up.

I explored the new territory foot by foot, looking for an ambush or booby trap.

Below, "You're shitting me. There ain't nobody in here."

Mumble whine mumble.

"Right. Skelington. Climb on up in there."

Graphically, and with a marked lack of respect, Skelington finally resigned his position with Team White. He had other options.

"All right. Pike, you go."

"Right behind you, Boss. I got your back."

The front door rattled and slammed. Teacher's whole crew electing to seek their fortunes elsewhere. A clever boy, rendered abidingly suspicious by experience, I didn't count on what I heard being what actually happened.

But it did seem to be.

Only Teacher stayed. He cussed and muttered and slammed things around. And slammed things around. And lightened a flask or two that he was lugging. He began to mumble in tongues.

Bottled courage, mixed liberally with stupid and anger, drove him into the chimbly. Muttering steadily, he climbed. He slipped twice before he got into the closed stairwell. "I knew that sumbitch had shit hid. Goddamn lawyers. They're all alike. Bunch a thieves." He climbed the stair one step at a time, a hand on each wall, forgetting that the danger ahead once looked fierce enough to send somebody else up first.

I heard my name mentioned. His opinion hadn't improved.

He was huffing and puffing and didn't put up much

of a struggle when I disarmed him. He just whimpered and gave up. I tied him up with whatever was handy. He started snoring.

I lit lamps and commenced a serious examination of Harvester's hideaway. And was amazed. Harvester Temisk definitely had an inflated notion of his own cleverness.

The first lamp came off a trestle table covered with the alchemist's gear Temisk had used to prepare his firestone surprises. Evidence to convict was there. A lot was on paper. Standouts were a map and notes about Whitefield Hall, that neighborhood, and the disposability of one Buy Claxton. The papers lay under a loaf of bread that had not yet sprouted a beard.

Harvester had visited since the birthday party. With the place being watched.

He had a secret way in.

No surprise there. In TunFaire, some neighborhoods have a problem with buildings collapsing because of all the tunneling underneath.

I'd look into that later.

So Temisk had hidden out here. Smirking. Without being as clever as he thought. It hadn't been that hard for me to get in.

Temisk was big on books. And not orderly. They were everywhere on the second floor. Dozens of books. Scores of books. A fortune in books. Only churches and princes can afford real books. I recalled my idea about ratfolk copyists. And wondered where Temisk had stolen those books. He'd never been flush enough to buy any.

The third floor was more orderly. It was furnished but hadn't been used. I concluded immediately that the mouthpiece had created a sanctuary for his friend. Long ago. And never got the chance to use it. When he did get hold of Chodo he hadn't been able to sneak the old boy in.

Back to the second floor, where I discovered that Harvester was a compulsive diarist. The Dead Man must've known. And hadn't bothered to tell me.

Almost every moment and every thought ever experienced by Harvester Temisk seemed to have been recorded, on a profusion of mostly loose papers.

The lamp was almost empty. I'd dozed off twice, though Temisk's memoirs were interesting. Each time I did, Teacher White stopped snoring. His trying to slip his bonds woke me up.

Then the yelling started downstairs.

I stayed quiet.

Teacher had a notion to fuss, then didn't because he recognized voices.

That was Winger bellowing. And Tinnie, slightly more ladylike. And Saucerhead, looking for me. Presumably in a snowstorm. In the middle of the night. All worried. And I didn't want to reveal my discoveries. Not to Winger.

I'd figured out the Dead Man's scheme. I thought.

If I didn't do something, though, they'd start looking for the body. And find everything else.

That damned Winger. Always in the wrong place at the wrong time.

I grabbed pen and ink. The devils in the sky smiled on me. For once. The nib was sharp. The ink was fresh. I wrote a quick note. Now to sneak it down where somebody could find it. I crept past Teacher and down the stairs. As I eased into the chimney I heard Winger cursing and banging things.

Tharpe said, "Control her, Jon Salvation." Laughing. "Garrett ain't under no wooden chair, dead or alive."

His suggestion that somebody could control her set Winger off all over again. She raved and slammed off to the back of the place.

"She drinks a bit," Tharpe explained. "Jon, we better watch her, just so things that don't belong to her don't accidentally fall into her pockets."

My luck stayed in. Sort of.

I fell out of the chimney as I tried to lean down for a peek. That was the bad news. The good news was,

nobody saw but Tinnie. Who kept her mouth shut
when I held my fingers to my lips. I passed the note.
And got back out of sight before Winger lumbered in
to investigate.

Tinnie said, "I knocked over these andiron things.
Trying to get this down off the shelf. It's a note from
Garrett. In case somebody comes looking for him."

"What's it say?" Winger smelled a rat.

Tinnie read it out loud.

"That say what she says, Jon Salvation?"

The little guy reported, "Word for word."

"You'd a thunk that asshole White woulda learned.
Whadda we do now?"

Tinnie said, "How about we go back to Garrett's
place?"

"Something's rotten here."

Saucerhead observed, "You don't have hardly no
flaws, darling Winger, but one teensy little problem
you do got is, you think everybody's head is just as
twisted as yours."

"What the hell is that supposed to mean?"

"It means most people don't have an angle when
they tell you what they think."

"Oh, bullshit! You ain't that naive, are you?"

That was the last I heard. The street door closed
behind them. A puff of cold hit me. Air did go up
that chimney.

I waited. Winger was the sort who might pop back
in, too.

I went down. They'd left lamps burning. I'd thought
Tinnie had better sense.

Ah. Of course she did. Including enough to realize
I'd need to see what I was doing.

79

Despite problems getting a schnockered Teacher down the chimney, I almost caught Tinnie and the others, heading home. And that despite the weather. Which hadn't turned as awful as I'd feared. Yet. Just cold and slick.

I brought White along. He needed some special Dead Man work to get his mind right.

I took Teacher straight to His Nibs.

Oh, my! We are in a mood, are we not?

"Yes, we are. It's time to quit fooling around. Hi, sweetie." I gave Tinnie a hug and a peck and ignored everybody else.

I stipulate that I was remiss where Mr. Temisk was concerned. However, I was preparing Deacon Osgood and had no attention to spare.

Half a minute later I knew the treasures at the lawyer's weren't part of his scheme. He hadn't been aware of them.

I expected more of you at Spellsinger Dire Cabochon's home. However, Osgood cleverly hustled you through and so did his own cause no harm.

I didn't get to pursue that. Somebody started hammering on the front door. With amazing enthusiasm.

That is Mr. Scithe. On behalf of Colonel Block, who became suspicious of the results of his earlier visit. Allow him to enter. But only him.

I went to the door. It was late. Dean was asleep. I didn't have him and his crossbow to back me. But

Saucerhead and Winger came to watch. They were enough to keep out the unwanted—except for a high-velocity pixie who surprised us all.

No matter. The kitchen door was closed.

I told Scithe, "You ought to demand a raise, the hours you're working."

"My wife agrees. But I do got a job. Plenty don't. You could mention it to the Colonel, though."

"I will. What's his problem now?"

"You visited the Hill today."

I didn't deny it. What was the point? "So?"

"So after you left, a gang of ratpeople stripped the place."

"After I left. Right. No doubt being watched every minute." I glared at the Dead Man. That inanimate hunk of dead flesh managed to radiate false innocence combined with smugness.

"Enough to know you didn't carry anything away personally."

A fib. Everybody but Osgood carried something out of Dire Cabochon's forty-room hovel. "I don't do that sort of thing."

"You hang out with ratfolk."

My resident ratperson had turned invisible during my trek to the door.

The Dead Man seemed more radiant than ever.

"That was the scheme, was it?"

"Excuse me?" Scithe didn't understand that I was snapping at my sidekick.

"His scheme. To try to blame me. He's always doing that. And he never gets me."

"I'm sure it's only a matter of time." Scithe wasn't quite focused. Tinnie Tate was in the room. And she'd smiled. At him. He mumbled, "There was a body in there."

"Sir?"

"Come on. An old woman. Dead. In a chair."

"I saw her," Tinnie volunteered. "I went there with Garrett."

That left Scithe with mixed emotions.

"He's like a four-year-old. Needs constant supervision."

That turned the situation around. Sort of. When the Tinnie weather let up momentarily, Scithe asked, "Where were you all afternoon and tonight?"

"I don't see where you got any need to know, but the fact is, I was trying to get a line on those guys your boss claims I'm hiding. Chodo and his tame lawyer."

He didn't believe me. Oh, wound me to the heart. But he had hopes Tinnie could tell him more about the dead Spellsinger, so he didn't press.

He didn't quite try to make a date. Probably because he remembered mentioning his wife.

Somehow, without getting many questions answered, Scithe became satisfied that he'd learned what he'd come to find out.

I let him out. Where his grumbling henchmen waited in the cold and the falling snow. Tinnie tagged along, smug as she could possibly get.

She'd begun to notice her power.

There was a crash in the kitchen.

"That damned Mel! How the hell did she get in there?"

With Singe, of course. That's where Singe had gone while I was letting Scithe in.

I opened up again. Snow was coming down in big, slow chunks. I told Melondie's tribe to come drag her home.

One of my less inspired ideas.

The brawl made so much racket Dean woke up and came down to restore order in the kitchen.

The mess was worse than after the thunder incident.

I threw up my hands and fled to the Dead Man's room. Singe tagged along, evidently summoned. She retrieved the cashbox and ledger, made entries, then paid Winger and Saucerhead for helping try to find me.

I didn't say a thing till after they left. Along with the pixie swarm, still squabbling, Melondie Kadare not alone in betraying signs of alcohol poisoning.

Sweetly, I asked, "Do we have a magic cashbox now? Always money inside when we open it, however much we spend on made-up jobs for our friends?" I spoke to Singe but eyeballed my sidekick. "Or did we pawn something?"

Chuckles ignored me. Of course. And Singe shrugged, indifferent to another incomprehensible moral outburst. "We had a windfall."

I started to get all righteous. His Nibs cut me off.

Would you feel more comfortable if the A-Laf cult's resources went to Director Relway? When their bad behavior depleted our resources? That is your alternate option.

It had been a cruelly long day. And the residual effect of the samsom weed really had kicked in. "I'm going to bed."

80

We had an easy ten days. More or less. Morley came by when the weather permitted, mostly to remind me that I faced a reckoning.

The repair and replacement of his front door had been a unique experience. The Palms had been forced to suspend business for days while the place aired out.

"My man Junker Mulclar is your proper modern vegetarian gentleman, ain't he?"

"Grumble rumble rabble bazzfazzle!"

"You muttered something under your breath, sir?"

"Browmschmuzzit!"

John Stretch was in and out. He seemed willing to make himself at home.

Equally frequently, Penny Dreadful, having conquered her terror of the Dead Man, visited the Luck. Without offering to take them away. She meant to open a temple—real soon now—as soon as she found the right place. I had my eye on Bittegurn Brittigarn's dump.

I hung around the Tate homestead plenty. Too much. Tinnie's male relatives made that obvious by their attitudes, though they never failed to be polite.

Business is business.

Deacon Osgood and the surviving lovers of A-Laf escaped custody. Bribery was suspected. They decided to end their mission to this fractious city.

I wished those boys devilspeed on their journey home, and foul weather all the way.

The unseasonable weather seldom let up. Before long it would be seasonal.

Colonel Block's people, and Relway's Runners, never ceased to be underfoot. Block was sure Tun-Faire would mend its evil ways if only he could catch good old ever-loving blue-eyed Garrett with his hand in the cookie jar.

My friend Linda Lee at the Royal Library knew the whereabouts and provenance of lots of special books. And she knew what books had gone missing from the King's Collection and private libraries over the past dozen years.

Using Winger and Saucerhead, because they couldn't read the messages they carried, I informed certain collectors that a cache of purloined tomes had surfaced during an unrelated investigation. It was possible some of their treasures were part of the hoard.

Harvester Temisk's memoirs, detailed though they were, recorded only the dates when he'd added to his collection. Neither sources nor the name of his specialist provider was mentioned. Nor did I get many opportunities to revisit Temisk's place. Good guys and bad alike kept right on watching it. Teacher and the Sculdytes were gone, but others still had designs on Chodo, his mouthpiece, and his designated heiress.

Finding people and things is what I do. Usually by being hired to, but finding is at the root of the Garrett reputation. After ten days, nineteen of twenty-four bibliophiles had made generous arrangements for recovering their treasures.

The others would come around.

Collectors are that way.

Teacher White stayed with us four days. He left with his mind washed clean and his heart set on a career as a knife sharpener. Playmate accepted him as a part-time apprentice. Play honestly believes there's good in everybody. Excepting maybe me. He'll make a great Godshouter someday. If I don't get him killed.

Old Bones didn't go back to sleep.

His uncharacteristic taste for the real world made me suspicious. Deeply, abidingly suspicious.

81

I'd just completed the successful reunion of several books with one Senishaw Cyondreh, the past-her-prime spouse of a grimly named habitué of the Hill. The woman had an eye so hungry I'd nearly run for it, shrieking. Once I'd gotten my hands on the ransom. Reward. Finder's fee. If I ever dealt with her again, I'd drag a squadron of eunuch bodyguards along.

I'd peeked inside before I turned the books over. They were what are called pillow books. Blistering. I blushed when we made the exchange.

There was something different about the old homestead. I sensed it when I spotted the odd coach among the abandoned goat carts. Having suffered a similar dyspepsia on occasion recently, I thought about heading on over to Tinnie's place. But I was carrying the take from the pillow book swap.

There are villains out there who can *smell* noble metals.

I took a glim at the weird coach before I went inside.

It had been fabricated of some silvery metal, then painted wood grain with paint I didn't recognize. "I have a bad feeling about this."

Distraction arose. Silverman, riding a donkey cart and surrounded by younger men afoot, all cast from the same mold, appeared. The youngsters carried cudgels. A Tin Whistle tagged along behind, curious.

"Ah. Garrett," Silverman said, reining in. "I've

completed the commission. Executed to a much finer standard than the original specifications. Tough to do even after I determined how the spells were written."

"Why aren't I surprised?"

Silverman straightened his bent back enough to meet my eye. He wasn't accustomed to sarcasm or back talk. He was an artist. And the old man of his clan.

"That forced us a little over on costs."

"Of course it did. So let's you and me just go inside and see what my partner thinks." Old Bones would sort the thief out.

I ended up carrying a heavy sack because two of the young guys were helping Silverman get to the door.

The Dead Man, of course, knew we were coming. Singe opened up as we arrived. "Who's here?" I whispered. In case it was somebody who didn't need to know about Silverman.

"Morley Dotes and a girlfriend."

A shiver hit me. I had no chance to pay attention. Silverman banged into me from behind. I moved on, to the Dead Man's room. Where a shadow of all night falling lay in ambush.

I squeaked in dismay.

A grinning dark elf occupied *my* chair, sipping *my* tea, while one of his sky-elf ladies occupied another and appeared to be in deep communion with the Dead Man. It wasn't the skinny, almost sexless woman that dismayed me, though.

My ancient nemesis, Mr. Big, best known as the Goddamn Parrot, was snoozing on her left shoulder.

Please pay Silverman another twelve gold florins.

Rattled, I managed only, "They don't make florins no more. Haven't done since the New Kingdom came in."

Morley saw my horror over the clown bird. He indulged in a grin of delicious enjoyment.

Then give him the current equivalent. Exasperation. *They did not change the weights, just the names. Correct?*

"Not exactly. They're called sovereigns. The closest."

Pay the man.

"But—"

The workman is worthy of his hire. Silverman is an artist. He took his commission well beyond what I asked of him. He is an intuitive genius. Pay him.

I didn't know if I could. Twelve florins translate to thirteen royal sovereigns.

Singe handled the payout. I couldn't bring myself to face my cashbox. Thirteen sovereigns is more than most people earn in a year. More than some of my acquaintances will come by during their entire ambition-challenged lives.

"Will you stop hyperventilating?" she whispered, smacking me between the eyes with the biggest word she'd ever spoken. "We are quite sound financially. Now."

Her assurances were no help. I glanced at the sleeping parrot. That thing might wake up any second. Which possibility drove me straight out to the kitchen. I tossed off two quick mugs of Weider's Select Dark. Less distressed, I went back to confront my terrors.

My best pal kept right on grinning like a shit-eating dog.

Silverman was just leaving. He told me, "I need a little head start. I'll meet you there."

His boys were lugging the same sacks I'd just helped haul in. He had no trouble getting around under the weight of all that gold.

I wanted to demand, "You're not even gonna keep what we paid for? After he robbed us?" But Old Bones leaped into my head before I could.

Please accompany Mr. Dotes. It is now within our capacity to place a satisfactory capstone on this affair.

Morley kept right on smirking. Enjoying watching me anticipate the hammer's fall.

I accompanied Mr. Dotes. Leaving the house last,

just to make sure the Goddamn Parrot didn't accidentally get left behind.

Garrett. You are forgetting the cats. Take the cats.

I wasn't forgetting anything. It hadn't occurred to me that there was any need to drag a herd of critters along. Why would it?

"Hang on," I told everybody. "I got to get something."

I found the Luck all piled into their traveling bucket, bright-eyed and ready to roll.

Creepy little things. They weren't kittens at all. That was just a disguise.

I took them outside. Their bucket went into Silverman's cart once I caught up. He wasn't wasting any time.

At some point Penny Dreadful attached herself to the parade. She was careful not to get inside my grabbing radius. I wondered if Tinnie or Belinda was to blame, or if she was still just that untrusting of the world.

Morley followed along behind, he and his friend in the strange metal coach drawn by the two-horse team that caused snickers all along the way.

No one out there seemed interested in us, otherwise. In particular, we were invisible to the city employees loafing around Macunado Street.

Half an hour later I knew where we were headed. Because we were there.

The scaffolding was gone. The bad boys from Ymber had finished their work, doing good despite themselves. The Bledsoe's masonry hadn't been in such good shape for ages.

I eyeballed the brickwork. Even work that hadn't been done last time was now complete. Had the Dead Man gone so far as to compel Deacon Osgood to finish his charity work before letting him go home?

Evidently.

Scary.

Morley dismounted. He announced, "I'm up."

"What?" Morley was . . . he knew what was going on when I didn't.

Me and my second banana needed to have us one long talk.

By the time I ambled inside, the little shit had his old friend Ellie Jacques, the volunteer, cooing and starry-eyed—right in front of, and without offending, his sky-elf friend.

Silverman knew what was going on, too. He and his boys followed Penny Dreadful into the deep gloom of the hospital, headed for the stairs. Penny, two-handed, bowlegged, hauled the bucket of cats hanging in front of her.

I hustled to catch up.

Chodo and Harvester Temisk occupied a suite. They shared it with Belinda. There were guards outside, Saucerhead's acquaintances Orion and June. I felt my purse being squeezed again. I whimpered softly.

They didn't know who they were protecting. Had they done, the temptation to sell that knowledge would've bitten them good by now. The door was locked from their side with three locks. I could've gotten through those, no problem, given a little time, but not in front of an audience.

Penny Dreadful had a key. So did Mr. June Nicolist. And, to my dismay, Silverman had the third, which he handed to me after he used it.

The system didn't make sense to me.

I was nonplussed about them being hidden practically in plain sight. How did Old Bones and the rest expect this to stay secret?

June Nicolist's key fit the middle lock. That one didn't secure the suite door—it let a small hatch swing open. Communications was possible that way. So how come the prisoners hadn't bribed their guards?

Number one sidekick had him a lot of explaining to do.

Once everyone with a key exercised his or her talent, I said, "June, this would be a good time for you guys to take a break. Mr. Dotes will handle the guard duties while you're away." Mr. Dotes and his harem had caught up. The Goddamn Parrot showed signs of fixing to commence to begin waking up.

Not good.

Comstock and Nicolist had been in their racket awhile. They didn't get miffed by any implied lack of trust. Nicolist said, "We was just changing shifts, anyways. I'll just head on home. Give Orion the key when you leave." Since it had done its job already, I handed it to Comstock now.

The door opened into a tiny foyer. Beyond that lay a sitting room as comfortably appointed as any in Chodo's own mansion. Without windows.

Chodo and Harvester were playing chess. Belinda was nowhere to be seen. The boys looked like they were staging. Like kids interrupted in the middle of mischief suddenly pretending exemplary behavior.

Penny released the Luck. Kittens streaked toward the men, excepting two who peeled off through a doorway to another room.

Silverman didn't seem impressed. Maybe he didn't recognize anybody. He spread out. Tools appeared. His boys started measuring and pounding. They ignored everybody.

Belinda came out. She was unkempt but looked less stressed than I'd ever seen. Penny darted over. They started whispering. Girl talk? Belinda suddenly being the teenager she'd never been, with her little sister?

Morley stuck his head in just long enough to satisfy his curiosity, then made like a sentry.

Chodo was in his wheelchair. He wasn't the breathing corpse Chodo of Whitefield Hall, though. He had strength enough to turn his chair. "Garrett." His voice had no timbre yet. It was a harsh rasp. But he was talking.

"Sir."

"I must thank you."

"Sir?"

"The favors I did you have paid their dividends. I'm

not really much less a prisoner now, but my mind has been set free. Thanks to you."

He didn't look at his daughters. They weren't interested in him. Under the current regime, family stress had to be managed through mutual indifference. Enforced company couldn't tear down those walls.

Harvester avoided my eye whenever I glanced his way. I expected a peck of lawyering weasel words. He didn't bother. Probably didn't want his good buddy to hear what I might say back.

Nobody mentioned the outer world.

Chodo husked, "Can I ask what they're doing?"

"Sure. But I can't tell you. I don't know. The Dead Man set it up." Silverman's guys were installing little tiny nickel dogs in niches they made in the walls.

My response didn't please Chodo. But his irritation faded even before the extra kitten arrived. The nickel critters were sucking up the dark emotion already.

Silverman beckoned Belinda. "You. Come here."

Her eyes narrowed. People didn't bark at Belinda Contague. But she did as she was told.

"Left hand."

She extended her hand. Silverman snapped a charm bracelet around her wrist. The charms were all tiny dogs in various doggy poses. All right! Damn it. Jackals. Every one enameled black. Presumably to prevent cold burns.

"Hold still."

Belinda frowned but did as she was told.

Silverman snapped a black choker around her throat. It boasted a half dozen squares of what looked like obsidian, each with a nickel critter inside.

Done, Silverman turned to Chodo.

Chodo would have indulged in a good old-fashioned shit fit if he could have. But Silverman was stronger than he was.

He didn't get a choker. He got bands on both wrists and a neck chain on which an enameled dog pendant hung under his shirt.

Harvester Temisk got one around his right ankle

and one on his left wrist. And a pendant to match his best buddy's.

"And that takes care of that," Silverman said. "I have a few extra pendants, any of you others suffer from mood swings."

I volunteered to pass. As did Penny. I did think it could be useful to make tons of this kind of jewelry, though—if it really sucked the crazy out of people.

"As you wish. I wouldn't do that, miss."

Belinda was trying to unfasten her bracelet.

There was a flash and a harsh pop. She yelped.

Silverman said, "You can't take it off. It won't let you."

I saw why the Dead Man thought so well of Silverman.

The old man told me, "Give them a few days to get used to their jewelry. Then you can release them to their regular lives."

I told him, "Thank you, sir. I'll move your daughter as far up the list as I can." A board meeting was coming up. I had some ideas to present, involving both Silverman and the employment of ratpeople to copy books. They'd let me talk as long as I didn't go trying to waken their consciences. I'd just need to talk business first.

"You're a good businessman," Silverman told me, with a smile I didn't figure out till later. "Thanks for everything."

I said, "I think we're done here, then. Belinda, Mr. Contague, I'll be back in a few days."

Penny stayed behind. With her cats.

Morley was patient while I visited Buy Claxton. Who was riding her stay for all it was worth, now that her health was not endangered. Human nature, I suppose. When I came back, I decided, I'd take her upstairs and see if she couldn't get back on with the family. While the shyster panicked.

Silverman's attitude soon explained itself.

My deceased associate had been bitten by the entre-

preneurial serpent. Possibly because he was tired of
having to wake up and earn his keep a couple times
a year.

He'd robbed the A-Laf cultists of everything there
was to know about the nickel dogs—all right! Jackals!
Then he'd rung in Silverman, who owned the skills
needed to exploit that knowledge.

They partnered up to drain the pain from the
Bledsoe. With Silverman somehow bleeding off the
accumulations and earthing them where they would
do the world no harm.

It wasn't many months before the improvements became noticeable.

Morley played the parrot hand for all it was worth,
heading back to the house. I suppose that wasn't un-
justified, after the yeoman blow delivered by Mr.
Mulclar.

He did say, "The underworld should calm down for
a while, just to sort itself out."

"Good news, good news. Maybe I can talk Tinnie
into going off to Imperial New City for a couple
weeks. We could tour the historic breweries. What the
hell is this?"

The street was blocked. Mummers, jugglers, people
in period costume, guys on stilts, whatnot, were cross-
ing in front of us.

"One of the playhouses trying to pump up atten-
dance, probably. Like everything else does, the playhouse fad has gone into overkill."

That's my hometown. When one man strikes gold
everyone else tries to cash in by imitating his success.
Instead of panning new gold.

This looked like a sizable show. It held us up for
ten minutes. I concluded, "I saw so much here. Why
should I go to their playhouse?"

"Because there you get a story?"

"I don't need a story. My whole life is a story."

Thinking no more about it, I trudged on toward my
showdown with a partner who insisted on toying with

his associate. And a date with the new keg of Weider Select that Dean was supposed to get in today.

Maybe I'd go see the redhead later, see if she was interested in a brewery tour.